Praise for
Katee Robert and the O'Malley Series

"Unspeakably hot." —*Entertainment Weekly*

"Brilliantly imaginative and blisteringly hot." —*Booklist*

"Katee Robert never misses."
—Hannah Whitten, *New York Times* bestselling author

"[This] might be the best book in this outstanding series."
—Fresh Fiction

"Robert combines strong chemistry, snappy plotting, and imperfect yet appealing characters." —*Publishers Weekly*

ruthless redemption

Also by Katee Robert

The O'Malleys

Dark Succession
(previously published as *The Marriage Contract*)

Heated Rivals
(previously published as *The Wedding Pact*)

Twisted Secrets
(previously published as *An Indecent Proposal*)

Beautiful Vengeance
(previously published as *Forbidden Promises*)

Lovely Corruption
(previously published as *Undercover Attraction*)

The Kings

The Last King
The Fearless King

ruthless redemption

KATEE ROBERT

FOREVER

NEW YORK   BOSTON

Forever
Hachette Book Group
1290 Avenue of the Americas, New York, NY 10104
read-forever.com

Originally published as *The Bastard's Bargain* in ebook in February 2018 and mass market in October 2018 by Grand Central Publishing

First trade paperback edition: August 2024

Forever is an imprint of Grand Central Publishing. The Forever name and logo are trademarks of Hachette Book Group, Inc.

The publisher is not responsible for websites (or their content) that are not owned by the publisher.

The Hachette Speakers Bureau provides a wide range of authors for speaking events. To find out more, go to hachettespeakersbureau.com or email HachetteSpeakers@hbgusa.com.

Forever books may be purchased in bulk for business, educational, or promotional use. For information, please contact your local bookseller or the Hachette Book Group Special Markets Department at special.markets@hbgusa.com.

Library of Congress Control Number: 2024938098

ISBNs: 978-1-5387-6686-6 (trade paperback), 978-1-4555-2804-8 (ebook)

Printed in the United States of America

CW

10 9 8 7 6 5 4 3 2 1

To every single person who asked me if Dmitri Romanov will get his own book. He does. Right here. Right now. Because you loved him as much as I do.

ACKNOWLEDGMENTS

Writing a book isn't done in a vacuum, and writing and publishing a series takes a small army of people to do so successfully. I've been very, very fortunate in working with an amazing team who has loved and supported and cheered on the O'Malleys from the very first moment that Callie appeared on the first page of *The Marriage Contract*.

None of it would have mattered without the support of my readers. It was your love and excitement that made this book, specifically, possible, and I cannot thank you enough. I never planned on Dmitri Romanov turning into such a force to be reckoned with, and I certainly never saw him and Keira coming. Thank you for your trust that I would bring our bad guy full circle and ensure that he actually deserved a happily ever after.

This series wouldn't be half as good without my amazing editor Leah Hultenschmidt cheering me on and pushing me to make these books even better than I could have dreamed. Thank you for getting my vision, even when I had trouble executing it. This series will always be so incredibly special to me because you trusted me to run with it, and reeled me back in when I ran a wee bit too far.

Thank you to the team at Forever. Your support from amazing covers all the way to getting these books into readers' hands has been wonderful. I appreciate you! Big thanks to Danielle Barclay at Barclay Publicity for helping push this series from day one. You are a rock star!

Hugs and many thanks to Piper J. Drake for always being there to help me keep my eye on the prize when reality threatened to kick me in the teeth. You are an amazing friend, and I am so thankful we found each other at RWA nationals that year for breakfast.

Special thanks to my reader group, the Rabble. I hope Dmitri was worth the wait! Being able to share bits of him and Keira with you early made all the difference in the world for me. Thank you for loving him just as much as I did long before you were able to read his story in full.

As always, I don't know if I'd survive the process of getting a book out into the world without the love and support of my husband and family. Tim, Terri, Hilary, Kristen, John, and all the various kids. We might not be a family by blood, but you are the family I choose and I love you more than anything.

ruthless redemption

CHAPTER ONE

Keira O'Malley stared at the empty bottle of vodka next to her bed. She had a second one stashed in her closet, but the effort to climb off her mattress and retrieve it was beyond her. Lethargy sapped what little strength she had, though she couldn't blame that on the alcohol any more than she could blame it on the weed. No, it was all her. She glanced at the digital clock painting red patterns across the clear bottle. Almost four in the morning—there would be no sleep tonight. Again.

She didn't sleep much these days—and not at all without some kind of liquid help—but this was worse than normal. Tonight, while she lay here with alcohol buzzing through her system and watching the smoke curl above her face with each exhale, she waited for news.

She hated that when shit hit the fan, her older siblings sent her to her room while they dealt with the crisis. She was twenty-one, and they treated her like a child.

Or a bomb about to go off.

She inhaled again, smoking her joint slowly, wishing the burning in her lungs could ease her racing thoughts. No one had come to update her since the whole house was put on lockdown. Right now, one of her brothers could be dead, bleeding out in the street, and Keira would be the last to know.

Like Devlin.

Pain slashed through her despite the barrier of numbness she'd carefully cultivated with weed and alcohol. One brother dead because of their family's "business" dealings, another in immediate danger, and nothing she could do but lie here and feel sorry for herself.

A buzzing vibrated against her hip, and her heartbeat picked up even as her stomach dropped when she realized it wasn't her normal cell. Not news, then. It was the burner phone Dmitri Romanov had given her, the one he used to contact her directly without leaving a trace for her family to find.

Her thumb hovered over the call reject button. She needed to be here for when news came in...but Dmitri often surprised her by knowing more than he should. Maybe *he* had news for her.

And maybe pigs will fly. You want to answer the call because you want to talk to him. It has nothing to do with noble motivations.

The phone buzzed again, and she answered before she could talk herself out of it. "Do you even know what time it is?"

"Are you still wearing my ring?" Dmitri's voice rasped through the line, his Russian accent making her stomach do a slow somersault.

She looked down at the giant diamond winking in the low light. Two weeks ago, he'd cornered her in a bathroom and slipped it on her finger. It wasn't the proposal she'd dreamed of when she was a little girl, but six-year-old Keira O'Malley never would have imagined a man like Dmitri. There was nothing innocent about him, nothing noble or even a little bit good. He was the villain of this story. The man who would take down her family—unless she became his bride.

And yet, Keira hadn't taken the ring off, though she couldn't begin to explain the impulse that had kept the jewelry in place. *Liar. That ring is nothing more than you deserve, and not because it's worth a small fortune. It's a promise that you'll do what it takes when the time comes... and the time is now.*

There was only one reason Dmitri was calling her at four in the morning, while her oldest brother was headed to a dangerous meeting in New York and the rest of the family was otherwise occupied, facing down a threat coming from a different direction. *Clever Russian. He's making his play.*

She swallowed hard. "Yes."

A pause, as if she'd surprised him with her honesty. Keira sat up and took another hit of her joint. She needed all the bolstering she could get for what would come next.

When Dmitri spoke again, his tone was cool and distant. "Your brother intends to break his word to me and cancel our engagement."

She froze. "*What?*" Surely she'd just heard him wrong. Aiden was too smart to risk the safety of their family and the people who depended on them for *her.* She was expendable. The youngest of seven—*six,* now—siblings, it only made sense to sell her to Dmitri. They'd fought too hard to prevent a war to start one now. Her family had dealt him three political blows in as many years. If the O'Malleys reneged on this, Dmitri would see every single one of them taken out. She had no doubt about it.

"You can stop it, Keira. Come with me now and I'll forget that he was going to break his word." If the devil existed, he had a Russian accent and used *that* coaxing tone when offering his bargains. *Come into my parlor, said the spider to the fly. I'll eat you whole, but you'll like it.*

She suspected it was even the truth.

She was safe in her room. He wouldn't bash in, shoot everyone, and take her. It wasn't Dmitri's style, no matter what anyone thought of him. But if she didn't go with him now, the O'Malleys and Romanovs would go to war. Nothing would be able to prevent it.

Nothing but her.

Have to play this right. "If I come with you now"—her voice hitched, but she pushed on—"promise me there will be peace. Give me your word."

He barely hesitated. "I give my word that I will do nothing further to antagonize your brother and the situation."

She'd been around too many power plays in her life not to know hedging when she heard it. "But if he comes after me, you'll finish what he started. No. I'm not signing Aiden's death warrant."

He cursed in Russian. "I will do everything in my power to broker peace *if* you come with me right this moment. The clock is ticking, Keira."

He'd keep his word. Dmitri might be borderline evil with a dose of psychopath, but he had his own code of honor. That promise was as good as she was going to get. If she said no now, she might very well be sentencing her family to war. Maybe they could win, but not without casualties. *I can't bury another sibling.* "Give me two minutes."

"Be quick."

Keira hung up and grabbed a bag. She kept an overnight one packed for emergencies. She paused and looked around her room. There wasn't a single damn thing that she couldn't live without. The jewelry her mother gave her hadn't been touched in well over two years. Her books lay unread. She finally snatched a picture of her and her siblings from the dresser and shoved it into the pack, followed by her bag of perfectly rolled joints and two bottles of vodka. Dmitri was Russian—he no doubt owned stock in vodka—but she'd rather have her own stash close at hand.

And then there was nothing else holding her to this place. She shoved the window open and climbed out. It was a route she'd taken more times than she could count, no matter how often her brother threatened to install bars to hold her in. She swung out of the window and climbed down the tree to the ground.

A bitter wind kicked her hair into her face and made her wish she'd thought to bring a sweatshirt, but it was too late to worry about it now. Keira shrugged her bag over her shoulder and started down the street toward the black town car and the man who stood next to it as if he didn't have a care in the world.

As if he wasn't in the very heart of enemy territory, stealing her out from under her family's nose.

Dmitri Romanov was striking in the way of fallen angels, his face a little too rough for perfection, his mouth a little too calculating and made for spilling lies, his gray eyes a little too icy to be anything other than exactly what he was—a cold-blooded killer who manipulated people to suit his purposes.

Against her better judgment, she picked up her pace, drawn to him despite everything that had happened between them—and everything that hadn't.

"Stop."

Dmitri moved. One second he was several feet away, and the next he pulled Keira to him—behind him. She blinked and peered around his shoulder to find her middle brother standing on the sidewalk, a gun in his hand.

A gun pointed at *Dmitri*.

"Put the gun down, Cillian." Dmitri spoke softly, his hands out to his sides.

Shielding me.

More like protecting his investment.

"I don't care if you helped Aiden and Charlie, you are *not* taking my sister anywhere."

Keira bit down angry words. Right now, the only thing that mattered was defusing the situation. Her brother wanted to protect her—she got that—but he was putting everyone they cared about in danger with this bullshit. She opened her mouth, but Dmitri spoke before she had a chance.

"You owe me a favor, Cillian O'Malley."

"The fuck I do."

"Break your word and our deal is null and void."

Oh God. If Cillian did that, it would be even worse than shooting Dmitri right then and there. Keira stepped around Dmitri and put her hand on his chest. "Cillian, please. Just let me go. I'm choosing this. I'll be okay. I promise." *Soft and easy. Lie with your words and tone and body.*

Cillian relaxed. The gun inched lower, finally aiming safely at the concrete at her brother's feet. "Aiden is going to come after you, Keira. You know that."

He couldn't come after her, because if he did, Dmitri would have the ammunition he needed to attack. She leaned forward, her voice low and fierce. "He promised to respect my choice." She had to get her message across or this would all be for nothing.

She turned and walked away, now gripping Dmitri's shirt to tow him after her. If she didn't, the boys were liable to whip out their cocks just to see whose was biggest. Better to remove Dmitri from the temptation of poking at her brother—something he had a long history of doing, given that Cillian was living with Dmitri's half sister. Keira held her breath the entire time, waiting for Cillian to push the subject, waiting for Dmitri to make a snide comment. But, miracle of miracles, both men stayed silent.

It wasn't until they were in the backseat that Keira relaxed enough to slouch against the leather and close her eyes. *We made it. I fulfilled my end of the bargain and no one got killed...yet.* "How long until we get to your place?" The sooner they got out of Boston—and O'Malley territory—the better it would be for everyone. Even Aiden would think twice about coming to New York where Dmitri had home-court advantage.

"We're not going to my place."

Goddamn it, she would strangle him herself if this was yet another game. *What am I talking about? Of course it's all a game. Game playing is what Dmitri does best.* She took a breath, and then another, striving to keep her reaction under control. Finally, when she was sure she could pull off the belligerent tone without the slightest hint of fear, she opened one eye. "Then where are we going?"

"A chapel."

* * *

Dmitri Romanov didn't permit himself to breathe a sigh of relief. This was only the first step in a path that could potentially span years. It didn't matter. Keira was here—was *his*. He had time.

He watched her look around the inside of the town car, cataloging everything with those witchy hazel eyes of hers. The faint scent of pot filled the car, giving evidence to what she'd been up to when he called. The woman was a mess, but he'd known that from the moment he met her. Dmitri didn't do projects. He preferred to be the one holding all the cards—it allowed him to anticipate how the people around him would act in any given situation.

He'd never been able to anticipate Keira. Not from the moment she picked his pocket and walked away from him as if she didn't give a fuck about the danger he posed to her. *Likely because she has a goddamn death wish.*

He'd deal with that, just like he'd deal with the rest of Keira's issues. In time.

Right that moment, time was the one thing they didn't have. Keira's oldest brother would be returning to Boston within hours, and Dmitri fully intended to marry her before Aiden realized she was gone. It was significantly more difficult to oust a wife than it was a fiancée.

He had Keira now. He wasn't going to let anyone take her.

She kicked her feet out, propping her chunky black boots on the seat. The long line of her bare legs drew his gaze up to her tiny sleep shorts. They were barely more than underwear, hugging her hips and ass. Her shirt wasn't much better, for all that it was long-sleeved. It revealed a slice of pale stomach and was fitted enough that he had absolutely no doubts about the fact that Keira wore no bra. Her small breasts pressed against the fabric, and she shivered beneath the weight of his gaze.

Get control of yourself. He leaned forward and nudged her boots back to the floorboard. Taking Keira was part of the plan—fucking her in the backseat was *not*. "There's no need for an adolescent tantrum."

She laughed, the sound rough and pain filled. "God, would you listen to yourself? You just showed up at my window to lure me into the night—to a *chapel*—and now you're bitching about my shoes on the seats? Russian, you have your priorities seriously out of order." She flicked her long hair off her shoulder. She'd dyed it a harsh blond that seemed designed to highlight how unhealthily skinny she'd become in the last year.

She's spiraling.

Not anymore.

"Our current situation is no reason to throw propriety out the window." He sounded stuffy, and he hated it, but with her sitting so close, wearing clothing she'd just been sleeping in... Dmitri dragged in a breath. "Keep your shoes on the floor."

"Or what?" She turned to face him. The move pulled her shirt even tighter against her chest, revealing the faintest outline of her nipples. Keira saw where his gaze went, and gave a bitter smile. "All the games, all the bullshit, and *that* hasn't changed." She leaned forward and hooked his collar with her finger, drawing him closer despite himself. "Tell me something, Romanov."

"Hmm?" He dragged his gaze up to her mouth. The wicked curve of her lips was matched only by the words she threw into the space between them with such abandon. The woman wouldn't know caution if it slapped her in the face.

"You're dragging me to your cave to be your Bride of Frankenstein." She shifted closer, her bare leg sliding over his slacks until her thigh came into contact with his cock.

He should move her. Set her back and explain that no matter what she thought of the situation, *she* wasn't in control. But the ring he'd put on her finger winked at him, a reminder that Keira wasn't the sister of his enemy anymore. She was *his*.

Or she would be in a few short hours.

He bracketed her thigh with a hand, keeping her in place, but didn't touch her anywhere else. There was no masking his reaction to her, not in their position. Dmitri didn't bother trying. "Calling me Frankenstein is more than a bit dramatic."

She looked up at him, her eyes holding a question he didn't have a satisfying answer to. "I think it's time to stop being in denial, don't you?"

He recognized the direction she was headed. "You know I want you. I wouldn't be doing this if I didn't."

Just like that, the shutters slammed down on her expression. She sat back and he let her go, watching her pull herself together. Her spine went ramrod straight, and she stared at the back of the driver's head rather than at Dmitri. She crossed her arms over her chest. "No lies between us. That's what you said. You want me, sure, but don't pretend any of this bullshit has to do with sex. You need to prove what an international badass you are by marrying the sister of your enemy. An eye for an eye—a wife and a sister. Remember?"

He knew exactly what she was quoting. The note he'd had delivered to Aiden O'Malley just over a year ago. *By my count, you owe me both a wife and a sister. I'll be content with one of yours.* He hadn't realized Keira had seen it.

Twin possibilities spun out between them. She was scared and vulnerable, and if he told her that it was *her* he wanted and not what she represented, she would believe him. It would even be the truth, at least in part. He hadn't been able to get Keira out of his head from the moment he met her, and he'd manipulated events to ensure they reached this exact moment.

Telling her that wasn't telling her the full truth, though. This wasn't some great love story where he'd been pining for her while her family kept them apart. Dmitri wanted her, yes. He craved the feeling of her body beneath his hands, her taste on his tongue, and her smart mouth around his cock.

But his craving her had no real relevance in the grand scheme of things. He needed one of the O'Malley daughters to regain his status after the blows the family had dealt him over the last two years. Keira was the only option left.

Liar.

It didn't matter what the truth was, full or otherwise. What mattered was ensuring Keira toed the line. He sat back, trying to ignore the throbbing of his cock, and studied her. "You knew what this was when you climbed out your window and stepped between me and your brother."

She finally met his gaze, her hazel eyes fiery in their defiance. "Yes, I did." Keira turned back to the window. "I'm tired. Wake me when we get to New York." She slumped against the seat and, for all appearances, passed out cold.

Dmitri watched her for a long time. He waited for her breathing to even out in actual sleep and for the last of the tension to bleed from her body. It was the first of many battles to come. He had no illusions about *that*. Keira wouldn't submit. She'd make him work for every single goddamn win, and she'd begin fighting again the second she recovered.

If he had any sense, he'd order Mikhail to turn the car around and dump her back on the O'Malleys' front doorstep. There were other women who would be suitable wives. Docile, biddable women who would trip over themselves to give him whatever he desired.

None of them were *this* woman, though.

He shrugged out of his jacket and draped it over her. It would have been simpler to turn up the heat in the backseat, but Dmitri liked the look of Keira wrapped in something of his. He might cultivate the gentleman-murderer mask, as she liked to call it, but he wasn't above the baser things in life.

Keira O'Malley. My wife.

But not yet.

He glanced at his watch. They had several hours left until they reached the courthouse. He'd set up a private appointment with a judge who owed him a favor. They would be married with the paperwork filed before Aiden returned to Boston, and then there was nothing the O'Malleys could do. Everything was going according to plan.

It didn't combat the uneasiness that rose in him with each minute that passed. He'd gotten what he wanted, but the battle was far from over. The very thing that attracted

him to Keira in the first place—her unpredictability—
might very well be his downfall.

Another glance at his watch. A grand total of a minute
had passed. Dmitri leaned forward and tapped the glass
separating them from Mikhail. His man lowered it. "Yes,
boss?"

"Drive faster."

CHAPTER TWO

Keira thought she'd hit rock bottom ages ago. She was pretty damn sure of it, in fact. She'd spent the last two years bouncing from one high to another, doing whatever it took to keep her numbness firmly in place. From that, there was nowhere to go but up, right?

So fucking wrong.

Rock bottom was signing her name on that marriage certificate.

When Keira was a little girl, she'd spent hours upon hours planning her wedding. The flowers would be purple and white hyacinths. They'd have cupcakes instead of one massive cake—more purple and white. She'd design her own dress and it'd be the most beautiful thing anyone had ever seen.

Instead, she was married in a dirty courthouse room with one flickering light, the faint smell of piss, and an official who couldn't be bothered to have the vows memorized. This wasn't a marriage. It was a goddamn business transaction, and not one that she'd come out on top of.

Dmitri jerked his chin at the two men he'd had act as witnesses, and then led the way out of the room. The courthouse passed in a blur, and she shivered as they stepped out into the September night. Keira clutched Dmitri's suit jacket closer around her. She should have thrown it in his face the second she woke up wearing it, but it was too cold for pride to have a foothold. *And it smells like him.* Considering it was his fault she was here in this situation, she shouldn't find his scent comforting, but her body didn't give a fuck about circumstances. It hadn't gotten the memo that wanting Dmitri Romanov was bad for both her health and what little sanity she had left.

"It's done." She hadn't meant to say it out loud, but the words were there and the sky didn't fall. She'd married Dmitri Romanov and the world hadn't ended. *Go figure.* "I suppose you have a victory parade planned to shout your superiority from the rooftops."

His lips twitched in something that was almost a smile. "The parade will have to wait. We have work to do."

"Oh man, is there a tiny slice of New York that you don't already own? Tragic." She shivered, her teeth clicking together, ruining a perfectly good snarky comment.

"Expanding my territory will have to wait, too." He touched the small of her back, guiding her down the steps toward where the car waited. "Having my wife freeze to death on our wedding day might put a damper on things."

Wife.

I am Dmitri Romanov's wife.

It didn't feel real. No, that was a lie. It felt *entirely* too real. As if her darkest fantasies had come to life and were playing out in front of her eyes. That was the problem with fantasies, though, they *weren't* real. Dmitri hadn't married her so he could orgasm her into submission and they could spend their days figuring out new ways to fuck.

He'd married her because he needed an O'Malley wife to prove to his enemies that he was the baddest mother-fucker in town. He didn't want a partner. He wanted a trophy.

He might have a healthy dose of lust for her, but he didn't want *her*.

She stopped short. "Romanov?"

His sigh spoke of the very end of his patience. "Yes, Keira?"

"You were with Aiden, right? Is Charlie okay?" *Is Aiden?* The question she hadn't dared ask. The reason she was essentially locked in her room. She pressed her lips together, trying to keep hidden how much the answer mattered to her.

Dmitri looked at her a long moment, his gray eyes giving nothing away. "Last I saw Charlie, she was being carried safely in your brother's arms."

Knowing that her brother and his fiancée were safe should have stopped the panic welling in her chest. It didn't. Too much had happened in the last couple weeks. Keira had spent years in a fog brought on by alcohol and drugs, and she'd finally weaned off enough of it to . . . care. Charlie was her friend. Keira should have known better than to let herself get attached to anyone in her life—even family. They all left, whether it was to walk away or leave in a body bag. Caring was an invitation to get her heart ripped out of her chest.

She stepped away from Dmitri's touch. She couldn't think when he put his hands on her, and what few survival instincts she had left went haywire in her need to get as much of him pressed against as much of her as possible. Until he did something to ruin it. Every. Single. Time.

To remind her who was in control.

Hint: it wasn't Keira.

She slid into the backseat and inched as far away from the door as she could before Dmitri joined her. *I can do this. I just have to last until we get to the house, and then I can crack open that giant bottle of vodka and not think for a little while.*

Dmitri apparently had enough of poking at her, because he sat silently as they cut through the streets in the direction of Manhattan. The ride passed quickly enough, though her hands were shaking by the time they pulled to a stop in front of an apartment building.

Keira laughed out loud at the sight. There weren't bars on the window, but there might as well have been a sign proclaiming it to be home of the resident evil overlord. It was in the overlarge front door—even bigger than the one in the O'Malley residence—and the massive iron-framed windows, each with dark curtains on the other side, blocking out any view of the interior. It was beautiful, but there was a definite modern gothic flair that she wouldn't have expected from Dmitri. "You called me dramatic. Those living in glass houses shouldn't throw stones."

"Hmm?" He climbed out of the car, her bag firmly in one hand, and held the door open for her.

"This." She stepped onto the sidewalk and frowned at the building. "You have private parking somewhere, I'm assuming." He didn't answer, but she wasn't about to let that stop her. "Would have been smarter to go in there, but you couldn't resist making an impression, could you?" Keira strode up the stairs to the massive wooden door. It looked like something that should be at a dark and stormy castle, complete with gargoyles. There was even an over-sized knocker right in the center of it. "It'd be better if this was a face, preferably screaming in agony."

"I'll keep that in mind."

She ignored the amusement in his tone and tried the handle. Unlocked. Keira pushed through the door and stepped into the massive entranceway. If the building looked like renovated apartments on the outside, the interior had been completely gutted and changed. She looked around, trying to feel something other than the itch to pop open a bottle, but she couldn't focus. "Where's my room? I want to be alone."

"Keira."

She could charge up the stairs, but her pointed exit would be ruined by not knowing where her bedroom was. She sighed and turned to face him. "Yes?"

"When is the last time you spent twenty-four hours sober?"

She was *not* touching that question with a ten-foot pole. "I don't remember reading anything requiring sobriety in the contract..." Keira snapped her fingers. "Oh, that's right. There wasn't a contract. There was just you being shady and expecting everyone else to play along." She had to get out of there. She was holding it together by a hair. Even though it went against everything she was, she let a little vulnerability creep into her voice. "Romanov, please. I'm tired and I'm worried about my friend and brother, and you just threw a surprise marriage at me. Cut me a break and give me some time to find my feet." She held her breath, watching him watch her.

Finally, he nodded. "Your room is on the second floor. Third door on the right."

That was it. No offering to walk her up there. No pointed comments about her wifely duties. She wasn't sure if she was relieved or disappointed. Keira pointed at the bag he still held. "My things."

Dmitri passed it over, though he didn't look impressed. "Whatever you need will be provided for you. Just let me or one of my men know."

Don't look at the bars of the cage. Look at all the pretty things you can have.

She clamped her mouth shut to keep from saying the words aloud, as if that would somehow make this whole shit show real. Keira nodded and headed up the stairs, feeling his gaze on her the entire way.

* * *

Alethea Eldridge studied her only daughter. She'd had such high hopes for Mae when she was a little girl, dreams of her daughter following in her footsteps and carving out a little territory of her own—*expanding* the territory they currently occupied. It was what Alethea herself had done when she'd reached the point where *her* mother trusted her with operations.

Those dreams were dust now. First when Andrei Romanov forced them to become part of his operation, and again when Dmitri Romanov tried to extinguish their existence completely.

Alethea knew her strengths. She never wanted to rule

all of New York—it was more trouble than it was worth—but being stripped of what little power the Eldridges had and treated as little more than a henchman?

It couldn't go unanswered.

The situation was even more dire now that Mae had lost control yet again. Alethea crossed her arms over her chest and looked down her nose at her daughter. "I had Romanov and O'Malley right where I wanted them, but you managed to get them to stop bickering and unite against us. *Twice.*"

"They insulted us. Maybe you could let it stand, but *I* wasn't going to." Mae lifted her chin. She'd never be a beauty, but she was strong and vicious, and Alethea had spent her life teaching Mae the ins and outs of their world. Not that the girl had listened. She liked blood too much, liked others' pain. That tendency could be valuable in an enforcer, but in an heir?

"Some insults are worth bearing if it will get you closer to the end goal." She wouldn't get through to her this time any more than she had the last few.

The temptation rose to just...walk away. To take what little money they had left after getting Mae out of jail and leave. Go west, or maybe take a flight to Europe and lose themselves there.

As soon as the thought crossed her mind, Alethea set it aside. Her mother hadn't raised her to be a coward any more than Alethea had raised Mae to be one. Several generations of Eldridges had spent money and blood carving out a place for themselves in New York, and she'd be damned before she let that upstart Russian drive them out.

There was no way out of this as long as Romanov and O'Malley were alive. O'Malley, they could avoid if they stayed in New York. He was new to his power and, with an upcoming wedding and a healing fiancée, he would be focused on Boston.

Nothing would distract Romanov. He had more at stake, and it was *his* territory they currently stood on.

No, the only way out was through him. He was the last of his family in the city. His extended family might not like it if she took him out, but anyone they sent to deal with her would be an outsider, and that would work against them.

Alethea opened her eyes, a plan already forming. "You *will* obey, Mae. Our very survival depends on it."

Mae stared at her with those cold, cold eyes, and Alethea caught herself wondering if she could draw the gun in her purse faster than Mae could get to whatever weapon she had secreted on her person. Then her daughter smiled. "Of course, Mother. I wouldn't dream of disobeying."

* * *

Dmitri stared at his phone. They'd been back in New York for hours, and he'd expected a call from Aiden O'Malley. The man wouldn't be able to let Dmitri taking his little sister go without at least an attempt at a fight. The fact that he *hadn't* called wasn't a good sign.

He drummed his fingers on the desk, irritated at himself. He'd told Keira that her brother was safe.

Fuck. Dmitri didn't lie. He didn't have to, because most of the time he held all the cards. It was a simple matter of playing the right ones to ensure the people around him acted accordingly. He'd told Keira that her brother was fine because he'd assumed it was the truth. If he was wrong, she'd accuse him of lying to her.

He grabbed the phone and dialed from memory. *Come on, you Irish bastard. Pick up.* The phone clicked over, and then Aiden was on the line. "You two-faced piece of shit. You must have bolted the second you left that warehouse to collect Keira."

Dmitri exhaled slowly. Aiden was alive. He hadn't lied to Keira, unwittingly or not. He hated that he'd doubted himself, even for a moment, and that irritation had him sniping at the other man. "You did promise that she and I would be married. Were you going to break your word, Aiden?"

He ignored that. "And *you* promised her a choice."

"She had a choice. She chose me." Under duress and with a healthy dose of manipulation, but Dmitri had never promised to play fair. He wanted Keira, and so he ensured that he acquired her. End of story. It was done, and Aiden damn well knew it.

"I want to talk to her."

"That's not an option. She's resting." More likely, she was drinking herself into oblivion. He'd recognized that wild look in her eyes when she walked away from him. It was the same one he'd seen the few times they'd interacted at the raves she always seemed to be at.

But if he didn't throw Aiden a bone, the man would undoubtedly do something ill advised. "She'll call you tomorrow. I'm sure Charlie needs time to recover, and you'll be wanting to focus on that."

"Don't tell me what I should or should not be focusing on. Charlie wouldn't have been hurt in the first place if you took care of your own territory. Don't think I'll forget *that.*"

This was getting them nowhere. He shouldn't have called

in the first place, should have waited for Aiden to contact him, but Dmitri at least had the answer he'd needed. "Your opinion is noted. Have a nice day, O'Malley."

"Romanov."

He sighed. "*Da?*"

"You do a single damn thing to damage my sister, and you won't like what happens next."

The threat wasn't unexpected, but it was wearisome all the same. Dmitri tsked. "She's mine now. I think, of the two of us, I'll be taking better care of her." He hung up before Aiden could say something truly regrettable.

He's promised to do what he could to keep the peace, after all.

Dmitri sat back and checked the time. Too soon to try to talk to Keira. She'd retreated after their interaction in the car, and he needed space to figure out how best to approach her going forward. They had to find a way to work with each other, and that wasn't going to happen if she shut him out every time he said something she didn't like. It was obvious that he'd injured her pride over the course of their interactions to date, but Dmitri didn't possess a time machine to go back and change that. Even if he could, he wouldn't. He'd made the only move available in the moment. Losing his head over Keira O'Malley when she was a complete wild card and beyond his control was *not* an option.

Losing his head at all wasn't an option.

I won't. I might want her, but that changes nothing. I'm still completely in control of the situation.

CHAPTER THREE

Dmitri's wife was drunk. Again.

He stood in the doorway watching Keira sway around the kitchen island, a bottle in her hand. *This is a problem.* He'd known she liked to drink, but he'd foolishly assumed she had it under control. There was nothing controlled about the woman in front of him.

She went up on her tiptoes and opened the alcohol cabinet. She set her bottle on the counter with a *thunk* and grabbed two more, humming under her breath. He couldn't even enjoy the sight of her here, in his home, because of everything wrong with this picture. Not only was his wife drunk in his kitchen, sourcing more alcohol, but she still wore the same pajamas she'd come into his home with two days ago, and had her hair pulled back into a messy bun that was more bird's nest than chic.

He'd given her space to settle in, thinking it would be enough.

Dmitri had underestimated Keira once again.

He cleared his throat and she spun unsteadily to face him. Twin red spots appeared on her pale cheeks, but he couldn't tell if it was embarrassment or the alcohol. Dmitri crossed his arms over his chest. "What, exactly, are you doing?"

"You have eyes, Russian. You tell me." She swiped the open bottle and took a long pull, her gaze never leaving his face. Daring him to do something.

Goddamn it.

"You're sober, starting now."

She laughed. "Go fuck yourself. If you think I can survive a marriage to you sober, you're insane."

"You'll have to survive. You don't have another option." He stalked toward her. "Put the bottle down."

"Fat chance of that." She backed away from him, the fucking bottle firmly in her grasp. He tossed the other two into the trash and made a mental note to have Pavel empty every drop of alcohol in the house. The men wouldn't like it, but Keira obviously couldn't be trusted.

"The bottle, Keira. Don't make me chase you."

"You'd like that too much." She sneered, but there was no heat in it. Instead, fear lurked in the depths of her eyes. Apparently the thought of being sober terrified her.

He could make several guesses as to why, but the why didn't matter. Alcohol was a crutch. It might prop her up at the moment, but it was a weapon that could be used against her—against both of them—just as easily. That was the only reason he needed her sober. She was a goddamn liability in her current state.

Dmitri darted forward, fully intending to grab the vodka out of her hands, but his sudden move startled her and she stumbled over her own feet in her attempt to get away from him. Keira toppled, and he only barely managed to grab her before she bashed her head on the floor. "What the fuck is wrong with you?"

"Oh, I don't know." She was completely limp in his arms, her head lolling against his bicep as she tried to look at him. "Maybe because you're the enemy and you basically only mostly kidnapped me and have locked me in your house-slash-tower and if I think about it too hard, the walls start closing in."

She was totally and completely wasted. "Keira—"

"Shh." She pressed her hand to his mouth, covering the lower half of his face. "I know I came with you. I don't need you driving home that point every single time we talk. I get it. That doesn't mean I like it." She closed her eyes and, for all intents and purposes, passed out cold.

Fuck.

Dmitri adjusted his grip and scooped her up. He couldn't leave her alone like this because she was just as likely to drown in her own vomit as she was to wake up, trip over something, and hurt herself. He strode out of the kitchen and nearly ran into Mikhail.

His man raised eyebrows but didn't comment on the fact that Dmitri's wife was snoring softly in his arms. Dmitri gritted his teeth. "All the alcohol is cleared out of the house—now. You and Pavel are responsible for seeing it done. The men bitch, you tell them they can bitch to me directly."

Mikhail opened his mouth but seemed to think better of whatever he'd been about to say. "We'll take care of it."

"Good." He headed upstairs.

As tempting as it was to take Keira to his bedroom, he

walked to the second floor, where he'd set her up in one of the guest rooms. She hadn't had much time there, but there was evidence of her in the smell of smoke lingering and the sheets kicked onto the floor. He laid her on the bed on her side and then sat next to her, using his body to ensure she didn't flop onto her back.

She might be out, but there was nothing relaxed about her. Her brows pinched together as she shifted, restless despite the alcohol in her system. She murmured words that sounded like her dead brother's name, and shuddered.

Dmitri reached out before he could stop himself and smoothed a hand over her forehead. "Shh, *moya koroleva*. You're safe now."

It was the first lie he'd told her.

* * *

Keira woke up in her bed with no memory of how she'd gotten there. The last thing she could place was arguing with Dmitri in his kitchen and then...blessed blankness. Her head pounded and she desperately needed some water, so she rolled over, reaching for the cup she'd left on her nightstand the day before.

"You're awake."

She froze, blinking against the light from the bathroom door that had just opened. "Dmitri? What the hell are you doing in my bedroom?" A quick mental check found her clothes firmly in place. He wouldn't touch her without permission, but she had no illusions about herself—for better or worse, she wanted him. It would be just like her to get blackout drunk and throw herself at him. Again. Maybe she even had, but he'd turned her down. Again.

He leaned against the door frame and crossed his arms over his chest. "You never answered my question."

"What question?" She might be hungover, but he definitely hadn't asked her anything in the last thirty seconds.

His gray eyes held no emotion. "When is the last time you spent twenty-four hours sober?"

They were *not* having this conversation while she lay prone on the bed and he stood over her. She didn't want to have the conversation at all. She pushed to her knees, waited for the sudden rush of dizziness to pass, and climbed to her feet. "That's none of your goddamn business."

"A week? A month? A year? Come now, Keira. Try to remember."

Why was he demanding this of her? She squared her shoulders, refusing to let shame take root. "What does it matter? I'm here. I married you like you wanted. You win, Romanov. Congratu-fucking-lations." She slow clapped. "Now, get out of my room and I'll stay the hell out of your hair until you need a convenient wife to prop up and display." *There's another purpose for a wife...* Keira shut that thought down *real* fast.

Damn him to hell, but he laughed at her. "Do you think that I can *display* you like you are now? You've been in my home three days and I already had to save you from falling down drunk and giving yourself a concussion." He shook his head. "You're a mess."

"Go fuck yourself."

"A mess with a limited vocabulary." He stepped forward, but stopped when she flinched away from him, his dark brows dropping. "When I met you, you dazzled me with your bravery, ill-advised as it was. You've never feared me until now, when I threaten to take away alcohol and drugs." He touched her chin, the contact so brief, she was half-sure she imagined it. "No, this cringing thing before me is not the woman I chose as my wife."

The barbs in his words hit true and dug deep. Keira had been so many things in her short life, but all of those were gone, leaving only ashes. There was nothing left of the girl she'd been—the closest she could come to recovering that fearlessness was when she drank.

And he'd just taken that option away from her.

She tried to keep her chin up and failed. "Then let me go home and be done with this. We can get the marriage annulled and move on with our lives."

"*Nyet.*" A sharp shake of his head. "You are mine now."

And round and round they went. She swallowed past a burning in her throat that was most definitely *not* tears. "What do you want from me?"

"A number of things." This time he did make contact, feathering his fingers over her cheekbone and down to her jaw. Dmitri stepped back before she could decide if she wanted to slap his hand away or lean into his touch. "But, for the moment, I will be satisfied with removing any trace of drugs from your system."

Keira snorted even as her stomach lurched. "Good luck. Unless you're planning on sending me to rehab, that's not going to happen." Aiden had tried to sober her up a number of times, but she always found a way to get what she needed, and eventually he stopped trying. Keira was something of a functioning addict—if one could call her life functioning—and so her brother settled with restricting her drug choices to pot and alcohol.

"You're right. I'm not sending you to rehab." He pushed gently on her shoulder, and she was unsteady enough that it toppled her onto her back. Keira shoved her hair out of her eyes as she sat up, but froze when she saw Dmitri now stood in the doorway to her room. "I'm bringing rehab to you." He shut the door and she heard the unmistakable sound of a key turning in a lock.

Keira stared. He hadn't... he *had*. He locked her in her room. She jumped to her feet and grabbed her bag off the floor. It was significantly lighter than it should have been. Even knowing what she'd find, Keira upended it on the bed. Her backup bottle of vodka was gone, along with her bag of joints. Dmitri really was forcing her to get clean.

Goddamn bastard.

* * *

Time ceased to hold meaning for Keira. It started with the sweating and only got worse from there. Distantly, she knew she was going through withdrawal, but the thought couldn't take root. She lay on the bed in her underwear and a tank top, and stared at the ceiling. *An addict. I am an addict.* The word felt as dirty as she did these days.

What would Devlin think if he could see her now?

There was no sheen of delirium to hold the memories of her late brother at bay. They assaulted her, one after another, an endless cascade of grief that she hadn't allowed herself to feel since the day she came home to realize she had lost the sibling she loved most in the world.

Ten-year-old Devlin, so much smarter and more mature than her eight-year-old self, taking her into the woods surrounding their Connecticut house and showing her a litter of baby rabbits, and then telling her every single detail he knew about the animal. Being Devlin, he knew everything.

Devlin at fifteen, using a huge chunk of the money he'd earned working at one of their family's legit businesses to buy her the fancy set of paints their father said was a waste of time and money. Her brother had been so damn proud of her art, so proud that she had something of *hers*. Something she loved.

Rushing into his room when he was nineteen to tell him that she'd gotten into RISD. Keira hadn't told anyone else that she was even applying, and it was Devlin who insisted she submit her work for the scholarship competition. Four years in art school, paid for because *she* earned it— a step she never would have thought to take without his urging.

Devlin at twenty, pale and still in his casket, shot in the street like a fucking dog because he was an O'Malley and their father had pissed off the Hallorans. A casualty in a war he'd never wanted any part of. A life snuffed out far too early. He'd had ambitions that actually meant something, and after he graduated college, he'd had every intention of putting his considerable knowledge and skill to use. For *good*.

What was her silly art when compared with that?

She blinked, her eyes gritty. Keira hadn't cried at his funeral. She hadn't allowed herself to. Instead, she'd done everything she could do to numb the pain.

There was nothing numbing it now.

She swallowed past her dry throat. "I miss you, Devlin. I miss you so fucking much. The world went to hell without you in it, and I don't know how to do any of this without you." Her chest burned, each breath a physical fight she didn't know if she would win. "You left and the rest of us fell like dominoes. One right after the other." She reached a shaking hand to mime tipping over the first domino. "What a fucking waste."

Keira closed her eyes in an effort to keep the burning inside, and when she opened them again, the light had changed. Darkness reigned, which was fitting, because *he* was there, sitting on the edge of the bed, his expression unguarded for the first time since she'd seen him. She couldn't work up the energy to do more than turn her head to get a better look at him. "Come to gloat?"

Dmitri didn't move, but she felt his attention sharpen all the same. "You think so little of me."

"Why should I think better?" She dragged in a breath, oxygen flooding her lungs. "You would have let my sister die. You would have let them all die." A different shootout, a different enemy. Endless. The tide against her was endless.

"My priorities are not your priorities, *moya koroleva*."

As if that made it better. As if she should be thankful that he apparently didn't want her dead. Keira turned her face away, preferring to look at the strange wallpaper instead of his treacherous gray eyes. Was the curving print moving? She closed her eyes and opened them again. This time, there was no time jump. It was still dark. He was still here, taking up too much room. She shivered. "I'm cold."

"You're burning up." A cool hand against her forehead. "The good doctor assured me this is normal, but..." He smoothed her hair back, the touch gentle. If she closed her eyes, she could almost pretend this was another time, another place. That she was just a woman and he was just a man, and nothing stood between them and the fabled happily ever after.

Hers wasn't that kind of story.

If Dmitri had a role in her life, it was as the villain who

locked the princess in the tower. But Keira wasn't a princess, and the Russian was hardly a beast looking for a magic kiss to turn him into something less monstrous.

She had to remember that, but it was so hard to keep her eyes open. "You promised peace."

"I promised to do everything in my power to ensure peace, short of sacrificing myself on the O'Malley altar."

He had such an infuriating way of twisting her words to make them unrecognizable. Keira wet her dry lips. "Peace."

"It takes more than one to broker peace."

"Then do it." Unconsciousness threatened to pull her under despite her best efforts. She twisted around to find him watching her with a strange expression on his face. "I'm coming out the other side of this..." She had to pause and wait for her dizziness to pass. How could she be dizzy when she was flat on her back? "When I do, if you haven't kept your word, I will make you pay, Dmitri. Every single day for the rest of my life."

"I have no doubt about that." It wasn't a reassurance, but she didn't expect that from him.

Keira nodded, and then grimaced when the top of her head felt like it might just explode and end her misery. "Why are you doing this to me?" The cry of a lost child with no safety in sight and a wolf breathing down her neck.

He didn't answer, and unconsciousness won the battle, sucking her down into the deep dark. But as she closed her eyes, she could have sworn he answered her. "For you, *moya koroleva*. I do this to you so you have a fighting fucking chance."

* * *

"It's been a week. We can't wait any longer."

Dmitri closed the door to Keira's room and gave Mikhail a long look. "It can wait."

"With respect, boss, it can't." He fell into step as they headed down the hall toward the stairs. "Mae was released on bail."

Dmitri stopped cold and swung around to face his second. "How is that possible? We did everything but gift wrap her for the feds. Even they shouldn't be able to fuck that up."

"And yet they managed." Mikhail passed over a manila folder, his expression severe.

Dmitri flipped through it and resumed walking. "My office. Now." This wasn't business that should be discussed where anyone could hear it. The fewer people who knew he'd been caught off guard with this news, the better.

Once they were safely shut into his office, he spread the handful of papers onto his desk. And cursed. "I should have known." Since Mae had been found torturing an FBI agent's daughter—also Aiden O'Malley's fiancée, Alethea was claiming entrapment and a whole host of other things. It shouldn't have mattered—tricking someone into a petty crime and kidnapping a woman to torture with the intent to murder were two *very* different things. Except apparently not according to the judge.

The charges against Mae hadn't been dismissed, but the judge granted her bail—and it had been promptly paid despite being an astronomical amount. There was no possibility of Mae suddenly becoming an upstanding citizen, which meant she and her mother were gunning directly for the one they'd blame for this whole situation—Dmitri. "*Blyad.* If I didn't have bad luck, I'd have no luck at all."

"What are you going to do?"

That was the question. Dmitri prided himself on staying ahead of the game, but he hadn't expected this. He'd been confident that the FBI would ensure Mae was put behind bars to await her trial—and that she'd be found guilty. The daughter of an FBI agent was a superb witness, and Charlie's reputation would be cleared by the time they went to trial. *Another fucking surprise.* Perhaps if he'd stayed instead of rushing to Boston to collect Keira...

It wouldn't have changed anything. His reach within the local government was long, but no judge on his payroll would have granted Mae Eldridge bail. Ultimately, his being there or not wouldn't make a damn bit of difference.

Alethea wasn't the problem. She was a crafty woman, but she could be reasoned with. She wouldn't do anything that would directly endanger herself or her family. If he pushed the stakes high enough, she'd take the hint and disappear.

Mae, on the other hand, was a wild card.

"Does Aiden know?"

"Hard to say. It went down in New York, and Finch doesn't seem the type to give him a courtesy heads-up."

No, agent John Finch was more likely to hang his daughter out as bait to see if Mae would bite again. Dmitri could have told him it was a lost cause—Mae didn't seem to have the same self-preservation that her mother possessed. She was the type who is more than happy to cut off her nose to spite her face—perhaps even literally—but she wasn't a fool. Being arrested would infuriate her and, if she couldn't get to Aiden and Charlie, she'd move onto the next best thing—Dmitri. Worse, Mae wasn't governed by the unspoken rules that most of the people who moved in their world were. She didn't give a damn about taking out innocents if it meant she was able to hurt her target.

She wouldn't strike directly at Dmitri. Even she was smart enough to know that was suicide. No, she'd hit him where she suspected it would hurt most.

She'd target Keira and the families of his men.

They had to find her.

"Pull our men's families into the available safe houses in the city. Ensure there are men there on a rotating schedule." They couldn't keep his people locked down indefinitely, but if there was one thing Mae lacked, it was patience. Alethea's leash on her daughter had snapped, and he saw no evidence that it would be reclaimed.

He picked up the phone and dialed Aiden's cell. Dmitri hadn't had any intention of reaching out so soon after the last less-than-civil conversation, but the situation had changed.

"You have a lot of fucking nerve calling me now."

"I'm afraid you're going to have to put your vengeance on hold for the time being."

"Fuck that. We're coming for you, Romanov."

He clenched his fist and then forced himself to release it. Losing his cool right now might be satisfying in the short term, but he had bigger problems than his and Aiden's pissing match. "Mae Eldridge is free."

That seemed to bring Aiden up short. "The fuck she is."

"She was released on bail this morning. Her attorney claimed she was entrapped by the FBI, and the judge bought it." He had to take a few seconds to fight down the curses that threatened to escape. "She and Alethea have dropped off the radar."

Aiden was quiet for several long moments. Probably living through those long hours in between when Mae took his woman and he was able to rescue her. Hours when they couldn't be sure Charlie was still alive. "She needs to be stopped."

"I concur." In addition to doubling the manpower he had on the search, Aiden's help would ensure the O'Malleys didn't move against him for marrying Keira. Two birds with one well-placed stone, though he would have rather traded barbs with the man if it meant Mae was safely locked up.

"I'll be in touch."

"See that you are." Dmitri hung up and turned to Mikhail. The dark-haired man waited patiently as he always did, the ultimate hunter. "Find them. Alethea's too smart to have gone back to the family home, but we can't take for granted that she didn't." Bailing Mae out was a calculated risk. Alethea had to know that both O'Malley and Romanov wouldn't rest until the threat to their respective women was eliminated, so she wouldn't have made that decision lightly. Mae was brutal enough to last in prison for some time unscathed, which meant there was a deeper game being played.

Now it was just a matter of finding out *what*.

A pounding on the door had him fighting a sigh. Only one person dared make an entrance like that. Sure enough, when Mikhail opened it, a tall redheaded woman stood there scowling. Always scowling. Between her coloring and size, she could easily pass for a lumberjack—and she had the shitty attitude to match. Dr. Jones.

Her thick brows lowered at the sight of him. "She's through the worst of it."

He didn't let himself sigh, because any outward sign of emotion was handing ammunition to the enemy. Dmitri had no illusions—the second the doctor left here, she'd

call Aiden O'Malley and report everything. The only reason she'd taken his call to begin with was because she'd
been on the O'Malley payroll for years. Keira might be
married to Dmitri, but she was still an O'Malley in the
woman's eyes. He'd called, and she'd come to New York to
help see Keira through her withdrawal.

Dmitri crossed to his desk and wrote out a check for the
agreed-upon amount. Dr. Jones wasn't a fool—she'd ensured herself a nice bonus for being inconvenienced. He'd
readily agreed to it because, even out of her mind, Keira
was more likely to trust a doctor she had experience with
than anyone on his staff. "Anything I should know?"

"She's going to be out of sorts for another week, at least.
Depressed, anxious, something else along those lines. No
telling how it'll present, because everyone is different, but
she won't be back to anything resembling normal even
though she'll think she is."

Fragile. For all her fire and spikes, his Keira was so
goddamn fragile.

"I'll take it into account."

She gave him a long look. "I'd also remove or lock up
all the alcohol in the place, and whatever other drugs you
might have lying around. She didn't choose this, so chances
of relapse are high."

He'd already accounted for it. Keira would find no easy
pickings in the household, and the men were under severe
threat if they supplied her with something Dmitri had forbidden. All of that wouldn't matter a damn bit if he couldn't
convince her that she had a good reason to stay sober.

Dmitri didn't lose.

He sure as fuck wasn't going to lose when it came to
Keira.

CHAPTER FOUR

Keira woke up restless. She tried to go back to sleep, but unfamiliar energy coursed through her, demanding she get out of bed and do something. She started by peeling off her clothes. They weren't the ones she'd worn to Romanov's—or ones that she'd packed—and she had no memory getting dressed in the first place. *Did that goddamn Russian do it?*

She wasn't sure what bothered her more—that he'd seen her naked or that he had seen her when she was defenseless.

Needing some armor back in place, she wandered into the bathroom. It was as big as some people's bedrooms, with a tiled walk-in shower and double sinks with a counter large enough to sleep on. The dark gray coloring was accented with deep red, and brought the word *decadent* to mind.

A second doorway led to a large walk-in closet filled

with clothing. She rifled through it, her eyebrows inching up. All in her size, down to the shoes lined up like little soldiers in their cubbies. *High-handed Russian.* That was his MO, though, so she wasn't exactly surprised. Dmitri Romanov was god of the world he moved in, and he didn't hesitate to bend people to his will to suit his purposes.

He wouldn't find her nearly as bendable as the others in his life.

Keira considered dolling herself up, but he'd see right through the ploy. Dmitri had home-court advantage, and he would use it without mercy. Her only chance to get one up on him was to act against expectations and use his surprise for her gain. She didn't know *what* she wanted yet, but she wasn't going to roll over and play Stepford wife just because she'd said yes at the altar.

If Dmitri had given her half a chance, she would have given *him* a chance.

Instead, he pulled high-handed shit that was right in line with her brother, and then locked her in a room for . . . God, she didn't even know how long it had been. Long enough for her to lose her damn mind and sweat out every single drop of alcohol and whiff of weed in her system. Another choice she might have considered making on her own but that he'd taken from her hands.

He'd pay for that, the same way he'd pay for the threat he'd leveled to draw her out of her home and into that goddamn chapel.

She took what was supposed to be a quick shower . . . right up until she realized how gross she felt. Both the shampoo and soap were expensive and smelled faintly of roses, and the water pressure eased tension from her shoulders. Giving up all pretense of rushing through it, she soaped herself up several times and then stood under the water, her racing thoughts slowing for the first time since she'd walked out of the O'Malley house and climbed into Dmitri's car.

Romanov wouldn't allow open rebellion. He'd expect it, but he wouldn't be able to let her run rampant unless he wanted to undermine his position—the whole reason he'd married her in the first place. Because of that, he would have guarded against it the same way someone child-proofed a house.

The last thing he'd expect was obedience—or at least the appearance of it.

Keira could play the game. She was out of practice, but it wouldn't take much to slide back into the rhythm of things. The Romanov operations were just another flavor of O'Malley. Dmitri would want kids at some point, but she'd cross that bridge when she came to it. There wasn't a chance in hell he'd push for that before he secured his power.

In the meantime, Keira would undermine him in every way possible. She wouldn't step into outright rebellion, but she wasn't going to make it easy, either. The terms Romanov had laid out were clear enough—as long as Keira was in his home as his wife, he would not pursue war with her family. She might like the idea of everything he loved going down in flames, but she couldn't risk trying to make it happen without fear that it would blow back on Aiden and the others.

And then her choice would be for nothing.

But that didn't mean that she had to play nice. She could make Dmitri's life a living hell. Subtly. She'd be the rock in his shoe, the sliver in his palm, the itch he couldn't quite scratch. As long as she didn't cross the line, the worst he could do was punish *her*. Not Aiden. Not the O'Malleys.

Keira could take anything he doled out, and she'd come back swinging the second she hit the ground. He thought he could buy a wife and that would be the end of it, but she'd been property for too damn long. If he wasn't going to give her the freedom she desperately needed, then she'd make him suffer until he relented.

If she enjoyed it in the meantime... well, she never pretended she was a nice girl.

She dried her hair and put on enough makeup that she didn't look like she'd spent the last week on the verge of death, and then got dressed. A pair of jeans and a slouchy tank top that showed a bright red bra with every move completed the look—put together without appearing to try too hard. *Chew on that, Romanov.*

One last look in the mirror made her pause. Even with the makeup, she looked like shit. Too thin, her cheeks hollowed out, her long hair lackluster, dark roots showing. That was priority number one—get into fighting shape. Charlie had introduced her to Krav Maga, and Keira had every intention of pursuing it going forward. She'd spent too much of her life helpless, and she wasn't about to go back to feeling like that.

The rest? It would fall into place as time went on.

But first, she had to go face the dragon and lay some ground rules.

* * *

Dmitri heard someone enter his office, but he didn't look up from the tally of numbers before him. Whoever it was wasn't a threat—Mikhail wouldn't have allowed them in if they were—and it wasn't good form to drop everything to address interruptions. He wrote down the total and capped the pen. Only then did he look up.

Keira.

She padded across the thick gray carpet and slouched into one of the chairs across the desk from him, every inch a queen despite being dressed casually. Her bare foot swung, drawing his attention. The image of a barefoot Keira wandering his home filled him with a possessive feeling that he didn't know what to do with. "You're awake."

"I want to renegotiate the terms."

Surprise flared, though he fought to keep it off his face. "We didn't negotiate to begin with."

"Yes, we did. Peace in exchange for me." She straightened in the chair, bringing both feet to the floor. "I want an addendum."

What could she possibly want that she didn't already have? Granted, he hadn't taken the time to walk her through her new life, but judging from the clothing she wore, she'd found the closet he'd had outfitted for her. Dmitri leaned back. "There's an account already set up in your name. I have access to the information, but it's yours alone. There will be money deposited on the first of every month to do with as you will." He found himself curious as to what she'd buy when her every other need was taken care of. It would tell him a lot about the woman, and he craved the knowledge.

Her expression didn't give an inch. "I expect nothing less."

Brazen. So damn brazen. He shouldn't like her arrogance, but he was drawn to it all the same. "Outline your addendum."

"I want access to a local Krav Maga gym."

"Consider it done—though one of my men will accompany you to and from, and I'll choose a gym that is trustworthy."

She rolled her eyes. "Fine."

That had been easy enough. He'd even expected it, though not so quickly. She'd spent time at a gym in Boston with Charlie Finch, and from all the information he had gathered, she'd enjoyed it immensely. It would keep her busy and content, which was his intent. He picked up his pen. "If that's all—"

"It's not." Keira crossed her legs and leaned forward, the move making her shirt slide down and revealing a lacy red bra that exposed as much as it covered. Dmitri got one breathtaking glimpse of her nipple through the lace before she sat back, shielded once more. A long look at her face revealed no manipulative intent, but she'd shown herself to be just as good as he was at masking her emotions.

He waited.

She stroked a finger along the seam of the chair arm. "You'll want heirs."

Dmitri froze. He hadn't outlined the need for children specifically during their previous conversations, but it was something that would be required of her...eventually. Never in a million years had he thought she'd broach the conversation herself. "Yes."

"You'll have them." She lifted her gaze, her hazel eyes cold. "But you'll have them when *I* say so. We aren't having sex until I choose it."

"I am not going to force you to have sex with me, Keira." The fact that she seemed to think he would...

She waved that away. "No shit. You're a monster, but

you're not a total piece of shit." She met his gaze again. "But let's not fuck around—it's going to happen one way or another. You know it. I know it. You set your mind on seducing me, and I might not topple like a domino, but I'd be fighting both myself and you to hold out."

He bit back his first response and considered her. It was no secret that she wanted him. They'd had several near misses over the last year, though he had been the one putting on the brakes at the time. With Dr. Jones's warning about her emotions ringing through his head, he hadn't planned on broaching that subject for at least another week or so. To have Keira state it so baldly intrigued him. He leaned forward. "You want me."

"I'm not going to say it twice." She shook her head. "My point—my *addendum*—is that you will not try to sway me to sex. When I decide it's time, I'll let you know in no uncertain terms."

That surprised a laugh out of him. "No."

"What the hell do you mean, no?"

He leaned forward and laced his hands on the desk. "No. *Nyet.* Whatever language you prefer. As you said, I want you, you want me. I will not force you, but we both know I won't have to."

"Arrogant prick."

Dmitri nodded. "Without a doubt." It wasn't arrogance if it was the truth. And it *was* the truth.

But it was also the truth that Keira craved some kind of control. He could respect that, even if he refused to budge on certain things. They would be consummating the marriage sooner rather than later, but he said he wasn't going to force her, and he wouldn't. "You may choose when we have sex, but I plan to seduce at will."

She blinked. "Seduce at will. You seriously just said that."

"*Da*. Because it's the truth." He took in her appearance again. She was a long way from healthy, but he *would* have her by the time of the wedding reception in a few weeks. "We will have dinner tonight."

"No."

"We will have dinner tonight," he repeated. "There are things in play that you need to be aware of, and I will not chase you around the house to inform you as they develop." He liked the thought of chasing her entirely too much, so Dmitri set it aside. "Seven."

"I'm not a dog you can just call when it suits you." She seemed to struggle with something, and her chin dipped. "But I'll think about it."

Curiosity grew, digging its claws in deep. She relented, but not because he'd won. Keira wasn't shaking in fear anymore, but she hadn't bounced back to the fierce woman she'd been before. There was something different about her, as if she'd reached a point where, forced to either bend or break, she'd bent. It changed the shape of things, but he was at a loss as to what to expect from her. "If you attempt something violent, it won't go well for you."

"Aww, Russian, I'd almost think you were scared." She popped to her feet and gave him a mock curtsy.

He watched her walk away. Too many skipped meals, her curves whittled down to barely nothing, her body showing the wear of the abuse she'd forced on it. And yet...

And yet.

Keira was beautiful. There was no two ways around that truth. Aiden might not have been taking proper care of her, but if Keira were allowed to grow and flower, Dmitri couldn't begin to guess what she'd become. A force to be reckoned with, that much was sure.

Mikhail stepped into the room, but didn't shut the door. "Better to put her in her place now than to indulge this." He spoke in Russian, as was their custom. To Dmitri's knowledge, Keira didn't know the language, but he'd need to ensure that was the truth before speaking it in her presence.

"If I wanted your opinion, I'd ask for it."

Mikhail hesitated, but continued. His position as second gave him certain liberties other enforcers didn't enjoy. One of those included questioning Dmitri—within reason. He cleared his throat. "You might have her cowed, or she might be playing the part to undermine everything you've been working for."

It was possible. Dmitri would be a fool to ignore it as an option, no matter how unlikely. Aiden was a more formidable opponent than Dmitri had expected, so it was possible that he'd orchestrated this...

He shook his head. "*Nyet*. Aiden O'Malley would never sacrifice his sister like this. Not Keira. Carrigan? Possibly. But not Keira." The man would do anything for his family. His siblings might not be able to see it because of his methods, but to the outside observer, it was pathetically apparent. It might as well have been a big shiny red button inviting enemies to push it. It was that loyalty that predicted Aiden would come around once again to ally against the Eldridge women. The man was as predictable as he was honorable. No, he wouldn't try something like this.

But Keira?

Dmitri found he couldn't conclusively say one way or another what Keira was thinking—or what she would do.

CHAPTER FIVE

Keira skipped dinner. She mostly did it to see what Dmitri would do, but other than a gruff Pavel conveying that they'd reschedule at a later date, nothing had happened. She laid low for two full days to give Dmitri a false sense of security before she started losing it. Her rooms were big enough to live in and never leave, but she was bored out of her goddamn mind and she could only sleep so much. Best she could tell, this building took up the greater part of a city block. *Plenty of places to hide bodies.*

Not that Romanov would ever be crass enough to commit murder in his own home. He was too savvy for that. He wasn't the type to get his hands dirty unnecessarily, though he must have at one point or he wouldn't be head of the family.

She layered up in a tank top and cardigan thing and a different pair of jeans and went exploring. There wasn't anyone stationed outside her room, but she didn't think for a second that she could walk out of here without some kind of tail attached. *If* they even let her leave at all.

No, Romanov wasn't that different from her brothers after all.

The hallway twisted strangely, and she wondered again who had decided that converting old apartments was a good way to go about building a freaking mansion in New York. *Someone with something to prove.*

The second floor was consigned to guest rooms. After the third door opened into one decorated similarly to hers, she gave up and went to the stairs. Dmitri's study was on the first floor, and she wasn't ready to face him again. Keira wasn't sure who gained the point for the win in their last conversation. He'd agreed to let her train and not to force her, but... she hadn't really thought he'd force her to begin with. If he was the kind of man to do that shit, it would have already happened. She'd sure as hell put herself in vulnerable positions with him over and over again.

They *would* have sex. It was a given—had been a given since the moment she set eyes on him.

Keira stopped at the top of the stairs and tried to picture how the hell *that* would go. She wasn't a virgin. Far from it. But Dmitri wasn't some blitzed guy in the back of a club. He was... a different animal altogether. He'd touched her once in the backseat of his town car, and the look on his face hadn't been controlled or locked down. He'd seemed half a second from taking her right then and there.

And then he'd shut it all down.

Would holding out drive him into a frenzy?

She shivered, her skin prickling at the thought. It didn't matter what Dmitri wanted. He wouldn't force her, and she'd be damned before she traded away her only advantage before she was good and ready to.

No matter how sexy the Russian was.

Determined to put it out of her mind, she moved down the hallway. It was shorter than the one on the second floor, broken up only by two closed doors and ending in a third. Keira poked her head into the first. Her stomach did a slow flip at the sight of the crib positioned in the corner. She stepped into the dim room, taking in the rocking chair sitting at an angle to the crib, the changing table on the other side of that. The other half of the wide room was devoted to the next age group up. There was a teepee with pillows scattered inside it, a low bookshelf with kid-appropriate board books, and even an easel with tiny paints and colored pencils. All of it untouched as if just waiting for a child.

Her child.

She pressed her hand to her stomach. She wasn't even sure she wanted kids. Fuck, she was only twenty-one. If she *did* want them, she didn't want them *now*. She'd been sober all of a few days. *Hot mess* did not begin to cover the shit show that was her life.

This nursery wasn't something Dmitri had set up—of that, she was sure. It had the feeling of love, even tenderness. The sheets in the crib and the pillows were new, but the books had creases in their spines where they'd been read repeatedly, and there was a person-sized dent in the seat of the rocking chair.

Was this...Dmitri's nursery? As in the one he'd grown up in?

She spun on her heel and marched out of the room. The concept of Dmitri as a child freaked her the fuck out, and she didn't like how strange she felt when she pictured him there. Maybe it had been set up for his niece? The fact that Dmitri's half sister Olivia and her daughter were now living with Cillian O'Malley was just one more thorn in Romanov's side. Hadley had the look of her uncle. It wasn't any particular feature, but sometimes she got a calculating expression on her face that screamed Dmitri. *I bet he was a little shit when he was a kid.*

She stepped into the hallway and shut the door behind her. It was only then that she realized she wasn't alone. "Don't you have something better to do than skulk around here?"

Dmitri raised his brows. "I'm not skulking."

"You are the very definition of skulking." She jerked a thumb over her shoulder. "Didn't anyone tell you that nurseries are creepy as fuck? I bet it's haunted."

If anything, his amusement deepened. "I have it on the best of authority that there are no resident spirits in the nursery—or elsewhere."

She tried to picture Dmitri hiring a supernatural expert and failed. "What did you do? Bring in a ghost hunter to exorcise this place? Because it's actually a really good idea. Think I could hire one to take care of the O'Malley house? There are definitely some bad vibes there." She realized that it wouldn't matter if those bad vibes were gone, because she'd never be going back, and wilted. *Damn it, no. I am not some princess who was tricked into captivity. I chose this. And* no one *can keep me against my will.*

Dmitri turned and moved to the door just down the hall from the nursery. "Give me some credit. If I were going to exorcise anything, I'd hire a priest."

"How very orthodox of you." She followed him, drawn closer as if he'd attached a magnet around her middle. Or lower.

He looked more relaxed today than she'd ever seen him. His dark hair was slightly rumpled, as if he'd run his hands through it, his dark gray shirt unbuttoned two more than normal. Not that she noticed how far up he buttoned his shirts. That would be the height of insanity. His lips quirked in something of a mocking smile. "You like what you see."

"You're not ugly. Stop pretending you don't know it. No one likes a pretty person who fishes for compliments."

"Ah, but it's different when it's my wife complimenting me." He practically purred the words.

Keira opened her mouth to tell him to shove right off, but reconsidered. What was that saying? Catch more flies with honey or some shit? She smiled sweetly. "I'm going to begin Krav Maga lessons next week. Find me a suitable gym by then." She hesitated and forced out, "Please."

"Of course. I have one already in the process of being prepared."

In the process of being prepared. She wasn't going to touch *that* with a ten-foot pole. She hesitated when Dmitri walked into the second room, but curiosity got the better of her, and she followed.

The master suite.

She walked straight to the bed and peered up. It was massive. The bed itself was bigger than a king size, but what caught her attention was the canopy that was a good ten feet off the mattress. It looked like a place where giants slept, rather than a mere man. "Tell me the truth— you wait until all your good little Russian men have gone to bed and then you jump on this thing, don't you?"

"Guilty."

She shot him a look, but his expression was serious. Keira shook her head. "Everyone's a comedian." She poked the white down comforter and then ran her fingers down the sheer fabric of the canopy. It looked like something out of some fallen angel's daydream...until she pictured Dmitri in the middle of it, naked and looking at her like the very devil.

Heat crept up her chest to her cheeks. She turned away and practically ran to the bathroom. It wasn't any better. She couldn't look at that shower with its clear tiles without picturing the water sluicing down Dmitri's body, or examine the claw-foot tub without thinking about him there, his head back and eyes closed. The closet didn't grant her a damn bit of a reprieve. Suits lined half of the space, each more expensive than the next, and it *smelled* of him. Dark and spicy and tempting.

The other half of the closet was empty.

Waiting for her things.

She couldn't deal with *that* any more than she could deal with the fact that Dmitri's presence was imprinted on this very space. "I'm keeping my room."

"For now." He said it the same way he'd said that he wouldn't force her—as if it was already decided.

As if she'd be there one way or another—sooner, rather than later.

As if he was so fucking sure he'd get his way.

That knowledge, more than anything else, drove her to step closer to him. She didn't touch him, but she closed the distance until she had to lean back to look into his face. "Dmitri."

"Da?"

Was it her imagination, or had his voice gotten a little hoarse? She reached up and ran her fingers up the fabric above the top button. Her knuckles brushed the tanned skin just below the dip at the bottom of his throat. *Oh yes, he* definitely *is holding his breath.* Keira inhaled deeply as if breathing for both of them, taking his dark, spicy scent into her lungs. She had to be careful, or she'd have traded in one addiction for another. Getting close to this man was dangerous.

It didn't change the fact that she wanted him.

If anything, his being dangerous made her want him more.

She went up onto her tiptoes, so close that if he moved his head a fraction of an inch, he would have kissed her. "I'm keeping my room." Keira dropped back down to her feet and turned on her heel. She made it a grand total of three steps before his arm snaked around her waist and pulled her back against a chiseled chest. "You're teasing me, *moya koroleva.*"

She tried not to notice how he dwarfed her. Dmitri didn't look particularly huge, but this close, he felt like a fucking giant. It was everything she could do not to press back against him, to submit to the command in every line of his body. Keira gritted her teeth. "You had something on your shirt."

His chuckle went straight through her. "You may keep your room, but as of tonight, your belongings will be moved into mine."

"*What?*" All the delicious feeling in her body disappeared, replaced by sheer rage. "You can't do that, you high-handed son of a bitch."

"I think you'll learn that I can do whatever I damn well please." He didn't move, didn't abuse the position he had her in, but she felt the promise of his words all the same.

She elbowed him, slammed her boot into his instep, and ducked under his arm. Keira spun to face him, hands up. She might be able to throw a punch, but she wasn't a martial arts expert. Dmitri really could do whatever he damn well pleased to her and she would be helpless to stop him.

He straightened his shirt, looking at her as if he'd spooked a wild animal. "Dinner. Tonight. You seem to have forgotten our plans the other day. Don't forget again." This time, there was no mistaking the threat. Apparently her grace period was at an end.

She lifted her chin. "Game on, Russian."

* * *

Dmitri studied the box on his desk. Generic in every way except its size. It sat in the middle of the desk, a rough three-by-three square. Mikhail stood on the other side of it, his hand on his gun. A gun wouldn't do anything against whatever was enclosed, but it was good for his man to be alert. "Who sent it?"

"I don't know. I came into the office and it was here."

He cut the nondescript tape on the top and opened it. Styrofoam peanuts sat in a perfect layer, but the smell told him everything he needed to know—*death*. "I need gloves."

Mikhail went to the cabinet in the corner and returned with leather gloves. Dmitri pulled them on, never taking his gaze from the box. He delved into the peanuts, coming up with a sealed envelope. It contained a plain card with a note scrawled in it.

A preview of what's to come.
—M

"Where is Keira?" He set the note aside. He'd expected Mae to make a move—she wasn't the patient type, and it had to be infuriating in the extreme to know he bested her. It was entirely in character for whatever the box contained to be dramatic—and bloody. Alethea's leash had slipped before, and it had obviously slipped again. There was no controlling Mae.

Mikhail shifted from foot to foot, the only sign of his unease. "She found the library. She's been in there for hours."

At least something had caught her interest. Krav Maga would help as well, but he was going to have to give her something else to keep her occupied—and out of trouble—soon. Dmitri focused on the box. "Let's see it." He carefully swept the peanuts to the side and delved deeper than he'd gone to find the note.

A head. That bitch put a head in a box.

He lifted the head, dark hair swirling through the peanuts and then a face emerging. Dmitri froze. *Keira.*

But no, it wasn't Keira, because his Keira was safely ensconced in the library. "Send one of the men to her, now."

Mikhail didn't ask for clarification. He dug his phone out and called Pavel. A quick conversation, and then a short wait for the confirmation text. He looked up from his phone. "She's safe."

Dmitri didn't release his breath in a sigh of relief. He couldn't afford to. But with Keira's location confirmed, he could step back enough to study the dead woman's face. *Not Keira.* They had the same straight nose and sharp features, but this woman's lips were thinner, and her eyes were the wrong color—two things he should have picked up on immediately. He carefully replaced it into the box and removed the gloves. "Find out who she was—and who put the box here. Any packages should have been vetted by you first. I want to know why this one wasn't." It didn't sit any better than the dead girl's similarity to Keira. Mae had made a statement, and she would follow it with something worse. He might find anticipating Alethea's moves challenging, but Mae was a rabid dog. All she knew how to do was attack. She might be crafty in the way she went about it, but she would attack all the same.

"Yes, sir." Mikhail lifted the box and strode from the room.

Only then did Dmitri sink into his chair. He'd known the game when he crossed Alethea Eldridge. It was a calculated risk, but ultimately she had had every intention of killing him and wiping the Romanov name from the earth, so Dmitri had acted first. He hadn't expected the FBI to botch things so intensely, but he should have known better.

Keira's presence in the house had him distracted even when he wasn't sharing space with her. The wedding had been too rushed, and she hadn't officially been announced as his wife, so it wasn't perceived as real yet.

That changed now.

He dialed the extension to the library. A few rings later, Keira's voice eased over the line. "You know, it's creepy how you have a phone in every room of this house."

"It simplifies things."

"If you say so. It's better than finding a phone in my panty drawer."

He almost smiled, but there were more important things to deal with right now than enjoying verbally sparring with her as they took a walk down memory lane. "Circumstances require a change in plans. I'll be working late tonight."

"I'll be sure to cry myself to sleep about it." Dramatic to the very end.

Irritation flared. "Stop being such a child." It wasn't a

valuable trait, and her tendency to say whatever popped into her head made her a liability. He'd thought he'd have more time to bring her around before he announced her as his wife, but it wasn't to be. That required her to grow up—quickly. "There's a dinner tomorrow evening here. You'll be required to dress for it. I can arrange—"

"As creepy-sweet as it was of you to stock an entire wardrobe for me, I'm more than capable of finding a suitable dress. I need to get the hell out of this place for a while."

"That's not an option." It was far too easy to transpose her features over the dead woman's. He knew damn well that was Mae's point in sending it to him in the first place, but that didn't negate the reaction. Or the threat. Keira had been in danger before, but it had grown exponentially with Mae being bailed out and Alethea going into hiding. He wasn't letting Keira out of the house without a goddamn army.

She was silent for so long, he thought she might have hung up. Finally, Keira spoke. "Sure. No problem. I suppose you have someone on retainer who can bring in stuff?"

"I do." *That was too easy.* This was the same woman who had all but scaled brick walls to escape her brother's household night after night. Her nighttime wanderings hadn't ceased in all the time his people had been watching her. *So why now?*

Keira didn't sound bubbly, but it was close. "Have your goon give me the contact info and I'll arrange it." She must have known he was going to argue, because she cut in. "Look, Romanov, throw me a fucking bone here. You have me locked up like a less-than-virginal princess in a tower. The least I can do is pick my own damn clothes."

It was a small freedom in the grand scheme of things.

What was more, positive reinforcement would encourage her to obey him. It was only clothes, after all. "Pavel will pass on the information shortly."

"*Spasibo*." She hung up.

He set the phone down. The whole exchange defied expectations. Admittedly, he'd only interacted with Keira a handful of times up until marrying her, but Dmitri was a firm believer in research. He *knew* her, even if it was all secondhand information. Nothing in those reports gave any evidence that she'd suddenly become an obedient wife within the first week of marriage. He was tempted to chalk it up to her being sober for the first time since he'd interacted with the O'Malley family, but that didn't feel right.

Or perhaps you're looking for complications because you're disappointed.

It was true that he'd enjoyed the way Keira didn't seem to care who he was or fear him beyond all reason. Dmitri had anticipated a vigorous fight from the second she walked over the threshold of his home.

He should have known better than to pin his expectations on being continuously surprised by a single person. Keira *had* surprised him, but since she'd come through her withdrawal, she'd been subdued—almost submissive.

It was for the best.

The last thing Dmitri needed was a home front battle on his hands when he had the threat of the Eldridges circling. Keira's actions might be puzzling, but it was one less thing he had to deal with in the meantime.

Truly, it was for the best.

He ignored the twinge of disappointment and picked up the phone again. It was time to get things moving.

CHAPTER SIX

Mr. Romanov had very specific criteria of what he wanted. This...does not fit that criteria."

Keira had been going back and forth for an hour with the dressmaker Dmitri had hired. Cathy looked like she should be in a kitchen somewhere, baking cookies for her grandkids. Her long hair was unashamedly silver, and she had the plump body of a life well lived. The one time she'd smiled, it had made Keira want to do something to make that expression reappear.

But Cathy wasn't going to win this particular argument.

She put a sweet smile on her face. "Cathy, I'd actually like three of the dresses. I'm recently married, you know, and I want to surprise my husband."

The woman narrowed her eyes. "Then buy some lingerie."

The two dresses Keira had her eye on were more revealing than most lingerie she'd seen, but she knew better than to say that aloud. "I plan to seduce him over a long dinner. Doing that in lingerie is trashy."

Cathy nodded to concede the point—just like Keira expected she would. The woman chewed her bottom lip. "The black and the nude, then. Wear the green tonight. It does good things for your skin, though your hair is a mess."

It was an effort not to roll her eyes. *Yes, Mother.* Getting her hair back to something resembling her natural color was high on her list, so she'd already taken steps to do that before the dinner later. "That sounds great. If you don't mind sending Dmitri the bill..." She made a show of looking at the clock. "I have to work on my horrible hair."

Cathy turned red, but she didn't stammer or try to apologize. It made Keira like her, just a little bit. The woman pulled the three dresses off the racks she'd brought in and transferred them to Keira's closet. "It's not my place to say it, but I hope you aren't planning on doing anything reckless."

She smoothed out her expression. "You're right. It's not your place."

Cathy stammered and blushed a deeper red. "Sorry. I didn't mean anything by it. Give me five minutes and I'll be out of here."

Keira nodded and walked into the bathroom. She had two hours until dinner, and she needed a full hour to fix her messy hair. Going blond had seemed like a good idea at the time, but it was a decision made more to relieve her boredom than for any legit reason. She'd hated it as soon as she saw the results, but Aiden caught her on her way to the store to grab different dye and he'd made such a fuss about it, she'd felt honor bound to keep it out of spite. *Reckless and stubborn to the bitter end.*

She dug the box of dye out from where she'd stashed it

beneath the sink. Pavel seemed to be her designated guard dog, and he'd only balked a little when she'd explained she needed to go to the store. Once she started throwing around the word *tampons* and describing the various sizes and specifics, he'd decided maybe it was best if she go with an escort rather than send one of the men.

Keira stripped down to her bra and went through the motions of applying the dye. It would supposedly be a rich brown when all was said and done, but she'd learned the hard way that grocery store hair dye lied. If she had a little less pride, she would have asked Dmitri to send her a stylist, but she already felt like a kept creature. No need to make it worse.

By the time she was done, Cathy was gone and Keira was alone. She set the timer and snagged the coat she'd worn to the store. Setting it down, she sank onto the floor and extracted the three travel-sized bottles of vodka she'd slipped into her pockets when no one was looking. They felt both too small and too large in her hands. She rolled them across her palm, her entire body clenching with the need to uncap them and drain what little liquor there was down her throat. It wouldn't be enough to get her even slightly buzzed, but it would feel good while she was doing it.

Addict.

She hated that voice. She hated it even more because it sounded a little like Dmitri. *Yeah, maybe I am. So what?*

Impossible to gain the upper hand if you're focused on stealing alcohol and drinking yourself comatose.

She didn't know if there *was* an upper hand to be gained. For all her talk of making Dmitri pay, the only thing she'd managed to do was avoid falling into bed with him. So far.

Maybe she was fooling herself if she thought she could actually...

No. Stop that. You are not this weak, sniveling defeatist. You are a motherfucking O'Malley, and you are not going to give up until the bitter end.

She carefully set the bottles in the back of the bathroom cabinet, behind some cleaning supplies. Keira released a long breath and pushed to her feet, shutting the cabinet door a little harder than necessary. She could *feel* the presence of alcohol in the room as if it was a shining beacon, and that alone had her turning to the shower. She checked the timer and decided it was close enough.

She rinsed her hair and then washed it, watching the dark rivulets of water run down her body. Impossible to see that visual as anything other than representation of the poison leaving her system. It didn't matter that it had actually happened days ago. What mattered was that *she* had made the choice today. No one had made it for her.

And that put a tiny bit of power back into her hands.

Keira took extra time getting ready. It had been forever since she'd worked the glam look, and she was out of practice, but the final result was pretty fucking good. Her now-dark hair was pinned up in a way designed to bring on bedroom thoughts, as if one sharp move would send it tumbling down her back. Subtle smoky makeup brought out the green in her hazel eyes, and she'd painted her lips a bright fuck-me red.

But it was the dress that really brought the whole look home.

The green dress that Cathy recommended was high-end and screamed money and class. That wasn't the one Keira chose. Instead, she put on the black one. She pulled on a pair of heels and walked to the door to her room, the heavy dress shifting against her skin with every step. It felt decadent and sinful—and looked even more so than the lingerie Cathy had suggested. *The Russian won't know what hit him.*

There would be others here for this event, but Keira couldn't give two fucks. Her body wasn't her own, just like her life wasn't her own. It never had been. She'd bargained both away, and even if she hadn't pulled the trigger on sex, she *would* at some point. There was no doubt about it. Dmitri *owned* her.

Well, if he wanted a pet, she'd look like a fucking pet—and she'd make him choke on the truth. She might have technically chosen this, but it wasn't what she wanted.

Keira lifted her chin and headed downstairs.

* * *

She's late.

Dmitri didn't let his impatience show as he greeted his cousin. "Ivan, welcome."

Ivan was a big bear of a man who had a laugh that could roll through an entire room, and was more than capable of smashing skulls with his bare hands. He covered up a clever intellect with meandering words and had been constantly underestimated when they were teenagers. He was *still* being underestimated, despite being in charge of Romanov operations in the South. "Hello, Dima!" He smacked Dmitri on the back hard enough that he would have stumbled forward if he hadn't braced for it. "Where's this wife of yours? I have to bring back a report to my Natasha and she's going to demand details. O'Malley, was it?

She's, what, the third choice? Fourth? Not like you at all to settle for scraps."

Dmitri kept his smile tight and unwavering. "Keira was the only *suitable* choice." It was the truth, even if reality was slightly more complicated. He'd originally intended to marry her older sister Carrigan, but that deal had gone sideways almost as soon as it was made—she was in love with another man, after all. The other sister, Sloan, had never really been an option for various reasons.

None of it mattered. The moment he'd met Keira and she picked his pocket, he knew that he had to have her. No one else would do.

Ivan looked past him into the obviously empty room. "Where is she? Don't tell me she took advantage of your distraction and climbed out a window."

Since that was *exactly* the sort of thing Dmitri expected of her, he'd stationed a man at both the front and back of the residence to ensure she didn't do something foolish. But Keira had been closeted in her room all afternoon. He'd been assured that she picked several suitable dresses, but Dmitri couldn't help thinking it was too easy. She hadn't fought him, hadn't done anything to exact revenge for his having moved her belongings into his rooms. It made him cagey.

He moved to the small bar set up against the wall and poured himself a second glass of vodka. "She'll be down shortly. You know how these women are."

"My Natasha takes hours." Ivan chuckled. "The woman is as beautiful as they come, but she needs half a day to pretty herself up for company. The logic astounds me." He stretched long arms and legs and cracked his neck with a loud pop.

His cousin was dangling the conversational thread in front of him, obviously wanting to keep to safer topics, but Dmitri wasn't interested. He met Ivan's gaze directly. "Where are the others?" The invitation for tonight had gone out to three men, and it appeared Ivan was the only one who'd bothered to show up. That didn't bode well. That didn't bode well at all.

Ivan huffed a sigh and poured himself a drink. "You know how it is, Dima. Things have not been stable for the last few years. Kirill and Sasha blame your missteps. The family back home is considering sending someone to monitor the situation." He downed the vodka in a single gulp and poured more. "It is a good thing you have married this O'Malley woman and put some of that to rest. A very good thing."

Dmitri had to work to keep any expression off his face. He'd known the extended family had lost confidence in him, but he hadn't realized how far it'd gone. If he read the situation right, the only reason Ivan had shown up was to honor their friendship. If Dmitri was anyone else, Ivan would have passed on the invitation as well. *Fuck.*

It wasn't the end. He still had time to fix things. The wedding reception would go a long way toward repairing the hits his reputation had taken—especially if the O'Malleys showed up. Even if they were furious, their presence would demonstrate that he had the upper hand.

The Eldridges were a different story altogether. He had to take decisive action there, and he had to do it as soon as possible. *Damage control.* Mikhail hadn't gotten any satisfying answers about the package in Dmitri's office. For all intents and purposes, it had appeared there magically without assistance.

Which meant he had a traitor.

The door leading deep into the house opened. Dmitri's relief died a terrible death as Keira stepped into the room. She wore... It took every single ounce of control he had to keep his expression neutral. He didn't have a damn bit left for words, and wouldn't have been able to find them in any case. Her lips were the same color red that they'd been the first night he met her—the same night she'd rolled that decadent body against his and offered to fuck him... and then lifted his wallet and his watch. Her newly dark hair had been pinned back in some artful just-fucked look.

And the dress.

It covered her from neck to wrists to floor, except a diamond-shaped cutout that stretched from the bottom of the collar—and the thick neckline bracketing her throat couldn't be termed anything but a collar—to just above her belly button. That cutout alone wouldn't be enough to stop him in his tracks. The fact that the dress was completely transparent *did*. The smaller diamond pattern carved out of the fabric did nothing to hide her rosy nipples or the fact that she was wearing black panties.

She looked like a caged wild thing—proud and furious and determined to punish him if given half a chance.

They stared at each other for the space of a single breath. Then her red, red lips curved into a small smile. "Hello, husband."

Ivan shifted, and reality slammed into Dmitri. This man might be as close to a friend as Dmitri allowed himself—might be family—but he still couldn't guarantee that Ivan wouldn't do something to damage his power base. If Dmitri fell, it would open up a space for an ambitious man, and Ivan and the others were nothing if not ambitious.

He crossed to his treacherous wife and took her hand. This close, he could hear the dress slither as she moved, the beading in the pattern making it cling to her body. "You're playing with fire."

"Maybe I like the burn." Her smile never wavered, even as her attention shifted over his shoulder to where Ivan watched them avidly.

"Mmm." He leaned closer to press a kiss to the corner of her mouth. "And maybe *I* am going to cut that fucking dress off you tonight."

"Ah-ah, Russian. You're showing your beast. Rein it in." Her grin brightened, and she lifted her voice. "Who is this delightful creature? Sir, you look like the proverbial Russian bear that I hear wanders Siberia."

It was official. He was going to kill her. The little *rebenok* had known if she showed up late, she'd tie his hands. He couldn't drag her out of the room to change without broadcasting the fact that he didn't control his wife. This man might be a friend, but he'd take that information back to the men *he* answered to, and it would be nothing good for Dmitri. And even if Ivan didn't stab him in the back, he *would* tell Kirill and Sasha, and they'd made their alliances clear.

The only course of action was to move through the meeting while acting as if he wasn't torn between wanting to turn her over his knee and wanting to fuck her against the wall. *Both. I want both.* And, damn her, Keira knew it.

Ivan walked over, his bushy eyebrows raised. "Charming creature, aren't you?" He took her hand and pressed a kiss to her knuckle for a full three seconds too long. "I am desperately in love with my Natasha, but if I were a younger man and single, I would steal you away, married to my cousin or no."

"It seems I'm not the only one who's charming." Her laugh boomed out, sounding happy. Keira cast a glance over him that was just shy of an invitation, but then shook her head in mock sadness. "But I'm afraid it wouldn't happen. My Dmitri keeps me more than satisfied."

My Dmitri.

It was an act, but the words still rang through him. If he had his way, his wife would have already been *satisfied* several times over today, but the only person who knew it hadn't happened—wouldn't happen—was Keira.

"My Natasha would like you, I think." Ivan gave Dmitri a lingering look.

"I'm going to take that as a compliment."

He transferred that look to Keira. "You should. Excuse me." He headed back to the bar and poured himself a double.

The night was going nowhere fast. Dmitri had expected some rebellious act, but this was...something else altogether. Keira allowed him to take her hand, her dress shifting around her. Her pale skin shone beneath the black beading, and his attention was drawn back to her nipples again and again.

"See something you like?" she murmured.

Yes. He hated it, but he also fucking loved that dress. He wanted her to wear it for him at a private dinner, where he could touch her, could drink in the sight of her, without eyes on them. The fact that there *were* eyes on them—on her—had him speaking without intending to. "You look like a high-class sex worker."

"Isn't that exactly what I am?" Her smile never wavered, and she didn't look at him. "You might not have paid in cash, but you bought me all the same." With that, she expertly detached her hand from his and moved to perch on the single chair next to the fireplace. "Ivan, you must tell me how you met my darling husband." Her hazel eyes twinkled, and he almost believed the lie in every line of her body. "I'm sure you have some hair-raising stories to share from his formative years."

CHAPTER SEVEN

Keira had been under the impression that this was a meeting with several men, so she'd been surprised when it quickly became apparent that Ivan was the only one who showed. *That had to sting, Russian.* Apparently, Dmitri wasn't as all-powerful as he would have liked if he couldn't compel family members to come to something that should have guaranteed attendance.

Layers within layers there. The O'Malleys didn't have much interaction beyond their immediate family, but Keira's father had only ever wanted Boston. He wasn't interested in spreading his empire beyond the city, though he would have liked to take the city entirely. The Romanovs were different. From what she gleaned of Dmitri and Ivan's—blessedly English—conversation, the Romanovs were the big players back in Russia, and they had representatives of the family in several of the big port cities in the US. Dmitri in New York, Ivan in Texas, Kirill in LA, and Sasha in Seattle.

Finally, Ivan checked his watch and rose. "I must be going. My Natasha gets irritated when I'm late." He waggled thick brows at Keira, making her laugh. "She's far too good with a knife to risk displeasing, no matter how enchanting the company." He took her hand and pressed his lips to it, releasing her almost instantly, and then turned to Dmitri. "I wish you and your bride the best of luck, and a long and healthy marriage."

Dmitri didn't appear amused. "You'll convey that to Kirill and Sasha, of course."

Ivan's eyebrows lowered further, almost covering his eyes. "Of course. No need to be so crass as to point it out. The marriage mended some of the issue, but if you don't control your territory, it won't make a difference. Fix things, Dima. Fix them fast."

She half expected Dmitri to threaten him or do something to slap him down for his attitude, but he just nodded. There was no reason to take it personally. This man didn't care about her, no matter how charming he was, any more than Dmitri ultimately cared about her. She was a pawn in a deeper game they played, and she was slowly coming to realize that the rules she'd grown up with—the O'Malley rules—didn't apply here.

She had to learn the lay of the land—and fast.

Dmitri's hand on her arm urged her to stand, and they walked Ivan out. She tried to pay attention to what they were saying, but they'd switched to Russian, and Keira didn't know more than a handful of words. Whatever it was, it didn't seem particularly serious, because their body language was relaxed and open. *Or they're better liars than most people you know.*

It wasn't until the front door closed behind Ivan that the

reality of her situation sank in. Dmitri was *furious*. He might have faked it for his friend, but he stood next to her, a pillar of stone with anger coming off him in waves. His grip on her elbow didn't hurt, but if she'd tried to leave, he would have restrained her.

She should be afraid. She should be *terrified*.

Keira's heartbeat picked up, adrenaline kicking in. She swung to face him with a fierce smile on her face. "You didn't compliment me on my dress." It was a work of fucking art. She smoothed her free hand over her hip and up her side. "Actually, you called me a high-class sex worker. Is that any way to speak to your *beloved* wife?"

His gray eyes followed the movement, a muscle ticking in his jaw when she cupped her breast. "I meant it when I said you're playing with fire."

That wasn't just anger on his face now. No, it was rapidly being overtaken by sheer lust. An answering feeling sent a bolt straight to her core. She stepped back, and he released her instantly. A strange feeling coursed through her, straightening her spine and making her want to laugh out loud. *Power. This is what power feels like.*

He wanted her. He wanted her so badly, he had his hands clenched at his sides to keep from touching her again. But he wouldn't until she gave the green light. Keira took another step back. "I have a hypothetical question."

"Ask." His voice was rough. The way he watched her made her feel like prey, and she liked it far more than she should—because she *wasn't* prey. Keira had her own teeth and claws, and Dmitri would learn that as time went on.

"Hypothetically, if I said yes tonight...how do you imagine that would go?"

He stared at her a long moment. "*Nyet.* I'm not playing

this game with you." She blinked and he was on her, one hand snaking around to press against the exposed small of her back, the other tangling in her hair. "We are not children, *moya koroleva*. These games don't become us."

He kissed her. There was no cautious exploration or easing into it. Dmitri kissed her like a conquering warlord who was sure of his welcome because he owned everything in the room—including her. There was no fighting this. She didn't even want to try. Keira slid her arms around his neck and pressed herself more firmly against him. His cock was a hard length with too many layers between them. She rolled her hips, an invitation she wasn't sure she was ready to follow through on.

Dmitri slid his hand down to cup her ass, guiding her movements. Long slides up the length of his cock and back down again. The tight goddamn dress kept her from spreading her legs wider, from getting him exactly where she needed him. Her nipples rubbed against his shirt, the silk incredibly decadent across her sensitized skin.

"Keira. *Moya koroleva*." He kissed down her jawline, tilting her head back until she had to arch her spine to accommodate the position. "Did you enjoy his eyes on you? Ivan's. The man who owes allegiance to me. Anyone who cared to look."

It took her desire-drugged brain a beat to catch up, but by then he was already growling out more words against her skin. "Did it make you feel powerful to know he was imagining stroking the nipples you flashed with such impunity?" He moved his hand from her ass to do exactly that, dragging a finger over her puckered nipple. "He wanted the body you so proudly put on display." His voice roughened. "He wanted what's *mine*."

Say something. If you don't say something right now, you're going to give in tonight and then it will all be over.

He moved his hand to her back and bent her until she relied solely on his strength to keep her off the ground. And then Dmitri's wicked, wicked mouth closed around her nipple. The weight of the beaded design seemed heavier with his tongue flicking the engorged bud, making his touch that much hotter. She couldn't hold back a moan as he moved to her other breast.

Dmitri dragged his mouth up the center of her chest, the only part of her not caged in the dress, stopping at the thick collar. He flicked the hollow of her throat with his tongue. "This is my favorite part of the dress." He ran his thumb over it. "This, more than anything else, marks you as mine."

A collar for a kept pet.

It was as if he'd doused her in icy water. Keira went rigid and shoved Dmitri away. She almost fell when he released her, but she regained her balance at the last second. They stood mere feet apart, breathing hard and staring at each other. *I am no one's pet.* She slashed her hand through the air. "I might be your wife, Russian, but I'm not *yours*. I'll never be yours."

She could actually see him replacing his aloof mask, piece by piece. It took the space of a heartbeat to hide the desire and rough edges, to cage the beast. Then there was only the icy gentleman-murderer looking out at her. He smoothed his shirt down. "You may fight it all you want, but you were right before—you sold yourself to me the second you walked down the aisle. You *are* mine. You will always be mine. There's no escaping it."

Once upon a time, he'd told her that he couldn't offer her love. She'd accepted that—love was a pipe dream in her world—but a loveless marriage and an...ownership... were two different things. Keira drew herself up straight. "Good night, Russian."

Nothing flickered in his expression. "I've changed my mind."

Keira froze. "What the fuck are you talking about?"

"You have a week. After that, you'll be in my bed."

The blood rushed out of her head, leaving her swaying despite her best efforts to keep it under control. "I disagree."

He didn't give an inch. "I'm not fucking you, Keira. I gave my word and I'll keep it. But you are my wife, and the current arrangement no longer holds, so you'll sleep next to me as if you were my wife in truth."

Another choice, taken from her.

Another man, thinking he knew best.

Another head of a family, expecting her to follow his orders like a good little solider.

Well, fuck that.

She'd forgotten, for a few seconds. Forgotten that he was the enemy, forgotten that she couldn't let her guard down—not even physically.

Keira had been playing at rebellion before now. A part of her had still believed that she'd get her happily ever after despite all signs pointing to the contrary, and she'd been hesitant to do anything she couldn't take back. But, as Dmitri had told her time and time again, he wasn't Prince Charming in the guise of a beast. He *was* the beast.

No one was coming to save her. There was no ending where the princess got out of the tower and exchanged vows with her one true love. It was time to put those childish dreams behind her, once and for all.

It was time for Keira to save herself.

* * *

Dmitri waited for confirmation that Keira was safely in her bedroom before he went to his office. *Tonight didn't go as expected.* A vast understatement. Kirill and Sasha's absence didn't bode well, though he was happy Ivan made an appearance. Things would fall out with the family back in Mother Russia as they would, but he couldn't count on any assistance with the Eldridges. That was to be expected. He hadn't intended to ask for help in the first place.

A threat against his wife was a threat against him and everything he stood for. He'd been careful with his handling of Alethea before now, but he couldn't afford to do so any longer.

He also couldn't afford to wait for Aiden O'Malley to pull his head out of his ass.

"Mikhail." He didn't raise his voice, but he didn't have to.

The man in question stepped into the room and closed the door behind him at a nod from Dmitri. He frowned. "Yes, sir?"

"I need the name of the man who delivered the package here." Either he'd done it because Mae paid him or because she had blackmailed him. The why didn't matter as much as the threat this mystery man posed. Dmitri prided himself in the loyalty of his men, and Mae had pulled that assurance out from beneath him. There were only two men he was reasonably sure weren't guilty—Mikhail and Pavel. Everyone else was suspect.

Since he couldn't clear out the house and leave them fully vulnerable, Dmitri had to play the odds. He'd assigned Pavel to Keira, but he had another job for Mikhail.

"I'll get on it—"

"No, I'll do it myself. What I need from you is to find where Alethea and Mae are hidden. I want you on this personally, Mikhail. Take whoever you need, but I require answers by the end of the week." It gave him another few days before the wedding reception. The official announcement of his and Keira's marriage. He had to put this last remnant from the past to bed before he could focus fully on the future.

"I'll start tonight."

He paused. "The girl. Do you have a name yet?"

Mikhail shook his head. "No one reported missing in the last few days matches her description."

Which could mean anything from her being taken from a different city to being someone who *wouldn't* be reported missing in the first place. Dmitri sighed. "That information will have to wait. Alethea and Mae's location takes first priority."

"I'll take care of it."

"Go." He waited for the door to shut before he let himself slump back into the chair. There was so much at stake, and the only thing he could focus on was that fucking dress. Temptation personified. Keira knew what she was doing when she chose it, the same way she knew what she was doing earlier today when she'd teased him. He should remove that inkling of power before she got a taste for it, but Dmitri found himself curious of what her next step would be.

He'd pissed her off tonight. Keira wasn't fond of the thought of being owned, which was a pity because she didn't have a choice in the matter. The world worked in a certain way, and that way involved his ring on her finger and her under his protection. Ownership was just a less delicate way of labeling marriage. If he'd been thinking clearly, he wouldn't have said it—at least not until he and she were on solid ground.

But then, he made a lot of missteps when it came to that woman.

He ran a hand over his face. Here, alone in his office, it was too easy to picture her sliding out of that dress. Unpinning her dark hair to let it fall around her shoulders. Slipping off the panties that were the final thing shielding her from his gaze. His mind conjured a few extra curves that would fill out once she put a bit of time and distance between her and her poisons of choice.

Keira was beautiful now, even without being fully recovered from her shitty lifestyle choices. In full health and trusting him...magnificent didn't begin to cover it.

Getting ahead of yourself. She can't stand you.

She would come around. She had demonstrated herself to be a smart woman, and a smart woman knew when to fight and when to fold. Dmitri wouldn't let her go—he'd been clear about that. As his wife, she would eventually step forward as his partner in full. He simply had to wait her out.

Unfortunately, they didn't have the luxury of getting used to each other in a more leisurely manner. Enemies had a habit of multiplying the moment they sensed weakness or distraction, and the last few years hadn't been kind to Dmitri. He'd had his plans foiled again and again by the O'Malleys, and every low-life crew in the vicinity of New York now looked at his territory with greed instead of fear. He had a significant amount of lost ground to recover.

Between marrying Keira and making an example of the

Eldridges, he'd go a long way toward reclaiming the reputation his father had handed down to him. Honoring the family legacy.

His phone rang, which had him double-checking the time. *Late, but not so late as to be unusual.* He checked the number and had to restrain a surge of triumph. *Right on time.* "Hello, Aiden."

"I'll help you, but seeing as how you can't even provide the promised phone call from my sister, first I want to see her and hear for myself that she's where she wants to be."

"Always business with you. How's the weather in Boston? It's been far too cold down here for my liking, but then winter is my least favorite time of year." He shouldn't poke at Aiden, but Dmitri was hardly a saint, and the O'Malley made it so damn easy to get under his skin.

But, for once, Aiden didn't rise to the bait. "You're due for a visit with Hadley."

Dmitri went still, no longer amused. *Crossing the line, Aiden.* "My arrangement regarding Hadley is between my sister and me."

"Your sister is married to my brother and living under my roof. Her business is my business, which means her daughter falls under my protection." It wasn't quite a threat, but Aiden wasn't crude enough to lay it all out there the way some would.

He gritted his teeth. "What are you proposing?" Giving up the visits to his niece was not an option. Olivia might not particularly like him, but she was blood, and her daughter was as well. Cillian O'Malley had all the makings of a good father and husband, but Hadley was also Dmitri's late second in command's daughter in addition to being Dmitri's niece. Responsibility for her care fell to him, even if his half sister wouldn't thank him for pointing it out. Allowing Hadley to grow up surrounded by the Irish with no connection to her family—to him—was out of the question.

"Tomorrow. Bring Keira when you come for your visit. If I'm satisfied with her answers, she'll return to New York with you." His tone said how unlikely he found that possibility.

"If you try to take her from me, you'll be facing war."

"Romanov, if you've hurt my sister, you won't have a chance to start a war, because I'll kill you myself."

CHAPTER EIGHT

Keira slept late, but eventually her curtains couldn't block out the sun enough to keep hiding. Humiliation almost kept her in bed despite that, but she wasn't ready to throw in the towel. Last night she'd almost said to hell with it and taken Dmitri up on the promise his body had been making. *Almost.* But she hadn't. She'd managed to hang on to her tiny edge, and she would damn well keep doing it until she had a better plan.

In the meantime, her stomach was growling, and boredom made her twitchy. She spent a solid five minutes staring at the bathroom cabinet where she'd stashed her vodka, before forcing herself to grab a quick shower instead. Drinking now had no purpose, and she had been weak enough last night without adding to the shit show. Get some alcohol in her, and she didn't trust herself not to track Dmitri down and do something *really* reckless, like sit on his face. Keira threw on the first things she found—black jeans, a long-sleeved gray knitted sweater, and thick wool socks.

She peeked out her door, but there wasn't anyone in the halls. Even though she knew Dmitri must have men stationed around, she'd yet to see any of them, and it was... strange. Back home, the house was filled with people. Two of her brothers and their women lived there, along with Olivia's kid, Hadley. *Dmitri's niece.* Not to mention the half dozen men who were there at any given time for protection and to run whatever schemes Aiden had going.

Compared to that, the Romanov home was a ghost house. It felt like she and Dmitri were the last two people on earth, and she was pretty sure she hated him, so that didn't bode well for the future.

Does it get lonely for him here?

She'd always considered Dmitri to be some stone-cold angel who existed without the needs of a normal human, but last night there had been desire in his eyes. He felt things, no matter how well he covered them up. He was a mostly only child and his parents were both dead, his half sister and her kid were gone, and there was only the man and this ridiculously large house...

Stop it. Stop humanizing him. He's a big boy and he can take care of himself. The only reason he brought you here is because he needed you to secure his power. Do not forget that.

She headed for the kitchen and threw together a quick breakfast with two eggs—her usual. Normally in the mornings, she was so hungover that she had to force herself to eat, but Keira found her fork scraping the empty plate and her stomach still demanding more, so she dug through the refrigerator and came up with the makings for a smoothie, too. No one showed up by the time she was done, so she cleaned the dishes and set them in the small drying rack beside the sink.

She was just considering her options when the phone hanging on the wall trilled. Keira looked around, but there wasn't anyone else to answer it. While she was considering it, the ringing stopped...and promptly started up again. *Oh yeah, that's definitely for me.*

With a sigh, she walked over and picked it up. "Romanov kitchen, Keira speaking."

A pause. "Cheeky."

She rolled her eyes. "Hello, Dmitri, lovely morning we're having. Is there something you need, or were you just enjoying interrupting my breakfast?" He had to either have people around here that she couldn't see, or there was some kind of security equipment that she'd missed. She turned around to lean against the wall and narrowed her eyes. There didn't *appear* to be a camera around, but the tech was fancy enough these days that she might not be able to pick it out. "You have cameras in this house."

"If I did, telling you would just make it easier for you to evade them."

Which was as good as admitting they were there. She shrugged her sweater off one shoulder. "Are you watching me right now?"

"We don't have time for games. Come to my office immediately."

Oh, Dmitri, there is always time for games. Especially when she needed a little boost after the way things had fallen out last night. Keira tugged her sweater down a little further, exposing her breast. She hoped like hell that the house was as empty as it seemed, or she was in danger of making a fool of herself. *Too late. The train has already left the station.*

A strangled sound came down the line. "My. Office."

"Mmm. I'm enjoying myself." She let her head rest against the wall and used her free hand to roll her nipple between her thumb and forefinger. Pleasure sparked through her, the feeling only heightened by the knowledge that he was most *definitely* watching.

She left her breast exposed and inched her sweater up until she could undo the button of her jeans. "I'll be up in a few." She dragged the zipper down.

Dmitri cursed, sounding so fucking feral that she paused. He spoke slowly, his accent thick, clipping his words as if through gritted teeth. "If you're going to touch your pussy, *moya koroleva*, I'm going to have to insist you come to my office, take off those pants, and spread yourself over my desk so I can appreciate it properly."

The image slammed into her, stealing her breath. Of him sitting in that chair between her thighs, not touching her, not until she gave him permission, and her naked and arched back, stroking herself while he watched avidly. She tried to catch her breath, feeling like all the air had been sucked out of the room. "Sounds like a party."

The silence stretched out, timed to the beat of her erratic heart. If she followed through on it... *Playing with fire doesn't begin to cover it.* "Dmitri—"

"We have a situation." He sounded more in control, though his tone was still ragged around the edges. "Come to my office immediately... please."

It was still an order, *please* or no *please*, but he was

obviously trying to make an effort. That didn't mean jack shit to her...or it shouldn't. *I'm bored enough, I might as well see what he wants.*

Whatever you have to tell yourself to sleep at night.

She buttoned her jeans slowly and let her sweater drop back into place. "I'll be right there." Keira hung up before he could say anything else. She did her best not to think too hard about what she'd almost just done—what she still wanted to do. She filed away the information that Dmitri had cameras everywhere for later use. That had to be why he allowed her to wander without a muscly shadow at all times—and it also meant he was most likely watching her. She wanted to see his setup to be sure, but in the meantime, she wanted to know what he needed in his office.

Somehow, she imagined it wasn't going to be as fun as what he'd threatened her with.

Dmitri wasn't behind the desk when she walked through the door. He stood next to a man she vaguely recognized, speaking in low Russian. *Note to self: learn Russian so they can't talk about you when you're standing here like a fool.*

Yeah, going to get right on that.

The conversation ended, and the man walked out. Keira glanced around the office, but there was no convenient set of monitors to display where the cameras were in the house. *Another thing to add to the list.* She squared her shoulders. "You rang?"

"*Da.*" He looked her over and gave a short nod. "Come with me."

She dogged his heels as he headed out and wove through the hallways to a part of the house she hadn't made it to yet. "Where are we going?"

"Boston."

She missed a step. "What? Are you taking me home?"

Dmitri spun around so fast, she almost ran right into him. He caught her shoulders, steadying her. Anchoring her. "Make no mistake, Keira, you *are* home. We are visiting your family for a short period of time and then driving back to New York."

Ah, so it wasn't a generous gift, then. This was business. She really needed to work on *not* seeing the best in Dmitri. It was glaringly obvious the longer she spent in this house that there was no best in the Russian. There was just cold calculation and a willingness to move pawns about his personal chessboard without concern for their feelings. They were only pawns, after all.

She waited to speak again until they were safely in the back of yet another town car and pulling out of his garage. "I'm assuming I have some party line you want me to toe."

Dmitri crossed his ankle over his knee. "I expect you to tell the truth. You chose this. Your brother doesn't believe it, and he'll keep fighting to retrieve you until he does."

Oh, Aiden. She'd hoped his new fiancée would keep him busy, but she should have known better. The only thing Aiden loved as much as Charlie was his duty to his family. Keira might be the black sheep of the group, but he'd never stopped trying to look out for her.

She leaned her head back against the seat. "I'll talk to him." He'd listened to Sloan, but Sloan was in a love match with a baby involved. Keira barely liked Dmitri on the best days. He hadn't forced her to marry him but...She shot straight up. "Did you tell him we're married?"

Dmitri didn't look over. "That's one task to accomplish with this trip."

She couldn't help it. She started laughing. "Oh. My. God. He's going to kill you. You should have delivered the news over the phone. Or, better yet, by letter. Hell, smoke signals would have been preferable to putting yourself close enough from him to throttle you."

"Your brother will do no such thing." He even sounded like he believed it.

She just laughed harder. "You don't know Aiden half as well as you think you do." A thought stopped her cold. "Hey, if you get murdered, does that mean I inherit it all?"

At that, he finally looked at her, incredulous. "You're joking."

"I'm your wife. That means I get it all." She enjoyed his expression so much, she gave a little bounce. "Maybe this marriage thing isn't half-bad." She didn't relish the thought of Dmitri's death, but the idea of a truly outstanding amount of money at her disposal and no ties to anything was an intoxicating one.

His hand closed over her knee, the touch shocking her back to the present. The heat of his hand soaked through the denim, branding her. It should have been innocent—it was her *knee* for fuck's sake—but that heat shot straight to her core. Keira tried and failed not to shift to accommodate her body's clench.

She dragged her gaze to his face, finding him watching her in that predatory way again, gray eyes hooded. He stroked his thumb along the curve of the back of her knee. "Tell me, *moya koroleva*. What would you spend all that money on?"

"Travel."

He raised his eyebrows, his hand inching higher. "To where?"

Even though she knew the smart thing would be to slap his touch away, Keira uncrossed her legs and spread them, just a little. She held her breath as he seemed to consider her before sliding his hand slowly up her thigh, inch by torturous inch...stopping just south of where she ached. "You didn't answer my question."

She blinked at him, trying to focus. "I'd go anywhere. Everywhere. Fly to California and start driving south until I ran out of road, and then fly to Africa and do the same thing heading north." She expected him to tell her all the reasons such a fanciful trip wasn't an option, but he just studied her.

His hand tightened, just a little, and she had to bite back a whimper. Dmitri shifted closer on the seat next to her and dragged his thumb over the zipper of her jeans. Over her clit. "Control and freedom—those are the things you crave."

I crave you. She didn't say the damning words. She couldn't. Instead she lolled her head to look up at him. "Do you have cameras in every room in the house?"

"*Nyet.*" His grin made her breasts tighten in anticipation. "Not the bathrooms."

But every other room.

Keira's breath picked up in time with her heartbeat, little gasps that were almost pants. She had to fight not to arch into his touch as he kept up that torturous stroking. "If I finger myself on my bed, will you be watching—or one of your men?"

He palmed her through her jeans, branding her there the same way he had her knee. "I'm the only one who has access to the feed from your room."

As if that made it better. *I'm going to fuck with you*

so hard over this, Russian. She licked her lips. "And the library?"

His brows slanted down. "You're going to finger yourself in the library?" Dmitri shook his head. "I forbid it."

Keira's laugh was more gasping than mocking, but she got it out all the same. "Didn't stop me in the kitchen. Won't stop me in any other room I choose."

"Then let's make one thing clear." He released her, but didn't move back. "Undo your jeans."

Her hands shook as she obeyed, and she didn't let herself think about how damn eager she was for this. It was all a game, and just because she wanted his hand down her pants didn't mean she was going to jump on his cock in the back of this car. *Liar, liar, pants on fire.*

He stroked his hand down her stomach and into her jeans, delving beneath her panties. The shock of the contact drew a sharp exhale from her, but it turned into a moan as he pushed two fingers into her. *Dmitri Romanov is finger fucking me in the backseat of his town car. I'm his wife. The world has gone mad.*

He let loose a string of Russian that sounded like a curse. When he switched back to English, his accent was thicker than she'd ever heard it. "Tell me, *moya koroleva*, were you wet because I was watching you in the kitchen, or because you wanted what I threatened to do to you in my office?"

"Both." She gripped the edge of the seat to keep from reaching for him, her breasts heaving with each breath. "Both turned me on."

He pumped slowly, leisurely. Her jeans kept him from withdrawing all the way, but that only made it hotter. He cupped her pussy like he owned it, and even though she knew she shouldn't get off on that feeling, her body hadn't gotten the memo. "Tell me something else." He slid his fingers up to spread her wetness over her clit before pushing them into her again.

"Hmm?" She was concentrating so hard on not rocking to meet his strokes, she could barely focus on his words.

"Knowing that I *will* do exactly what I promised if you stroke yourself in one of the public rooms..." Dmitri pressed his face against her neck and inhaled deeply. "Are you going to do it again?"

Not only was it hotter than hell to imagine him watching her masturbate, but being dragged to his office, stripped down, and doing it on his desk while he was close enough to touch... Keira bit her lip. "Oh, yeah."

He pulled her into his lap without ever taking his hand from its position, her back to his front. She tensed, but when he kept fucking her with his fingers, she relaxed to lay her head back on his shoulder. "What am I going to do with you, *moya koroleva*?"

She arched back into him, feeling his hard cock press against the cleft of her ass. "Take my pants off."

Dmitri uttered a hoarse laugh. "That's a start." He withdrew his hand long enough to skim her pants and underwear off, leaving her naked from the waist down. The sweater was slouchy enough to hit the top of her thighs, but he drew it up with his free hand as his other went back to her pussy. "You are so wet and tight and *mne nuzhno chuvstvovat' tebya.*"

She had no idea what that meant, but it sounded like the promise of something good. Keira shrugged her sweater off one shoulder. Dmitri's curse was music to her ears, and it only made it hotter when he tugged the fabric down to expose the same breast she'd flashed him in the kitchen.

Her gaze landed on the closed glass separating them from the driver. "Can he see us?"

Dmitri rolled her nipple between thumb and forefinger—the exact same way she had touched herself earlier. "Does it matter?"

Her entire body clenched. "No."

"It does to me." He pressed the heel of his hand against her clit, the pressure increasing in time with the tempo of his strokes. Dmitri palmed her breast, the move screaming *ownership*. "You will keep your peep shows for me and me alone, Keira. Obey me and you will be rewarded." He flicked his fingers against a spot inside her that had her eyes threatening to roll back in her head.

Still, she managed to draw out words. "And if I don't?"

"Then you will be punished." And, with that, he took away his touch, leaving her teetering on the edge of orgasm with nothing to push her over.

CHAPTER NINE

This woman made Dmitri wild. He still couldn't believe that she'd been so brazen as to expose herself in the *fucking kitchen*, let alone to all but promise to do it again at the earliest available opportunity. He kept his hands on her hips, holding her against him even as she cursed him. "Obey, Keira."

"If you don't make me come, I'm going to do it myself."

And deprive him of her orgasm? Out of the question. He caged her wrists, drawing them behind her to nestle at the small of her back. The position arched her spine, and he could see the fury and desire written over her face in the reflection of the partition glass. "Your orgasms are mine now." He slipped his hand between her thighs again, craving the tight clamp of her pussy around his fingers, her wetness coating them as he drew her closer and closer to coming. It was all too easy to imagine his cock in the place of his fingers, and he thrust against her ass.

"Romanov."

Always Romanov and Russian with her. Never his name. *"Da?"*

"Please let me come." She sounded almost contrite—the exact opposite of the promise of retribution her expression conveyed.

"If you were in my bed, it would be like this every fucking day. You would have to but tell me you need me, and I'd meet your every need." He picked up the pace of his strokes, responding to the cues of her body. "You would never go without."

Not physically, at least.

He could promise her orgasms. Protection. Anything money could buy.

But nothing more.

"My own personal Russian orgasm machine," she gasped out.

He kissed her neck and flicked his tongue in time with her pulse thundering there. "Come for me, *moya koroleva.* The first of many." As he spoke, he pushed both fingers against that spot inside her at the same time that he rubbed little circles against her clit with the heel of his hand.

Keira cried out, her back bowing, the force of her coming nearly tearing her wrists from his grip. He kept up the strokes, gentling them until she slumped against him, completely spent. "The first of many," he repeated.

"You're awfully sure of yourself, Russian."

She was damn near comatose and still managed to throw verbal barbs. He'd be impressed if she wasn't so fucking vexing. Something welled up inside him, a wildness he had kept locked down since as long as he could remember. Control was essential in his world, and there was nothing controlled about the thing that took hold of him. He let go of Keira's wrists and dragged her sweater over her head, leaving her naked.

She roused enough to twist to look at him. "What are you doing?"

There was no space for words, but words rose all the same. "I am not a fucking toy for you to pick up and discard at will." He dumped her onto the seat next to him and was already moving before she'd stopped sputtering, kneeling on the floorboard between her thighs. "You make me fucking *psikh*."

Her pussy was pink and swollen from her orgasm, the wetness there gleaming in invitation. She shook, her hands going to the seat cushion. "Russian, you're scaring me."

Scaring her.

That wasn't the goal. That had never been the goal, no matter how aggravating he found her disobedience. He reined himself in enough to grit out, "I'm going to taste you now."

"Ummm." Keira shifted, as if she wasn't sure what her play should be. Damn her for always thinking when she stole that ability from him.

Dmitri captured her chin, forcing her to meet his gaze. "I am going to taste you now, Keira. I'm going to lick your aching clit, and I'm going to fuck you with my tongue until you come. And then I'm going to do it again, and again, until I'm satisfied."

"Until *you're* satisfied." She shot a look down at his cock before tipping her chin back up.

"*Da*." *Rein it in, Romanov.* He forced himself to take a breath, and then another, trying to think past the scent of her arousal. "Unless you do not want me to."

Keira blinked. "Is that a trick question?"

"Nyet."

She hesitated. "I don't want to have sex."

"Yes, you do." He continued before she could protest. "But you have not given permission, and so we will not." He would keep control enough to hold back from that. He wouldn't risk breaching that trust. If he did, there would be no going back, and any chance they had of a future would die a terrible death.

Keira gave him a single heart-stopping grin. "In that case, tongue fuck away." She leaned forward until her lips brushed his with each word. "This pussy is yours for the duration of the trip."

Dmitri guided her back to the seat and slid down until he was exactly where he needed to be. This woman was infuriating and beautiful and broken and so damn calculating. He wanted her as wild as he felt.

He wanted her wilder than he was.

But there was no room in his head for calculation in the current situation. There was only Keira and him and the lust that drugged the air between them. He descended to kiss her just below her belly button, and then lower on the top of her shaved mons. He used his thumbs to part her folds and licked her up her center, her cry assuaging some of his fury. Whether he was furious at her or himself was up for debate, but he wasn't regaining any semblance of control until he was satisfied with her pleasure.

Until she had no thought but of him and what he could give her.

Her taste. Fucking hell, her taste. He sucked her clit into his mouth, rolling the sensitive bud between his lips and tongue, gauging her response. She went so taut, he had to hold her hips down to keep her from dislodging him.

Keira blinked wild hazel eyes at him. "Romanov, that thing you just did..."

He barely lifted his mouth enough to say, "You liked it."

"I loved it. Don't stop." She reached her arms up to wrap around the headrest, baring her body to him completely. He doubted she recognized the significance of the movement—the implied trust—but *he* did.

Dmitri didn't stop.

He gave himself over to the feel of her against his mouth and the taste of her on his tongue in a way he hadn't given himself over to anything in living memory. She was hot and wet and shaking and it was because of *him*.

His wife.

His Keira.

His and yet not his at all.

He hitched her legs higher and wider, opening her to him so he could do exactly as he'd promised. He thrust his tongue into her, relishing her cries even as he relished the act itself. *His.*

And yet not his.

Keira released the seat to lace her fingers through his hair, holding his face against her pussy as she ground against his mouth. "I'm so close, Dmitri. Don't stop."

His name on her lips only spurred him on. He increased his tempo, growling against her heated flesh. And just like that, she was coming, her cries filling the car, her body so tense it was a wonder it didn't shatter.

Dmitri rested his forehead on her stomach, breathing hard. He wanted to keep going, to drive her to orgasm again and again until all she knew was the feel of his mouth and the sensation of his touch. Until he became her world.

It wouldn't solve anything.

When she managed to recover, she'd still hate him. She'd still do everything in her power to undermine him and work against his goals. Keira was furious at him, and it may be time to admit she had reason to be.

The issue was that, for the first time in his life, he wasn't sure how to fix a problem. He didn't know how to fix *this*. He couldn't outmaneuver her into being less difficult. Every time he thought he had her locked down, she turned around and managed to surprise him. She wasn't going to quit. She absolutely wasn't going to roll over and obey his commands. She didn't even seem to fear him most of the time.

He finally lifted his head to find her watching him. She cleared her throat. "If you throw that into the bargain on a regular basis, I might reconsider sharing your bed."

A small concession, but a concession all the same. He didn't grin, but the impulse was there. *Maybe there is a way to convince Keira to cleave to my commands.* He dragged his mouth from one of her hips to the other. "Every night, *moya koroleva*."

"You keep calling me that." She shifted to let him nip at her inner thigh. "What does it mean?"

"Would you have all my secrets in the space of an hour? *Nyet*, I will tell you another time." He licked over the dip where thigh led to pussy. "Stay in my bed tonight, Keira." He wasn't self-delusional enough to pretend his insistence was for his own purposes. He wanted to know this woman, and part of that was seeing her when all those glorious defenses were down. He wanted to observe her in the small moments upon waking and before sleep.

He wanted her available for his every whim, to reach for in the night when he woke desiring her. He wanted to sink his cock into her pussy and discover her desires and needs when sex was on the table.

But, for now, he'd be content with her in his bed at all.

She shuddered out a breath. "Tonight. One time only."

Still with the stipulations. He growled against her skin. "Tonight, and we'll discuss tomorrow tomorrow." It would give him plenty of time to find a way around her protestations and convince her that it was really *her* idea to be in his bed—permanently. "In the meantime, I'm nowhere near satisfied yet." He slid his hands under her ass and lifted her to meet his mouth.

* * *

Keira woke up to find the car still and quiet. She rubbed her eyes and looked around, totally disoriented. She'd passed out sometime after the sixth or seventh orgasm, tucked against Dmitri's body with his hand idly stroking her thighs. Now there was no one in the backseat except her.

She dressed as quickly as possible with her legs still feeling like Jell-O. No lie, she'd known it would be good with Dmitri Romanov, but she hadn't anticipated *how* good. They hadn't even had sex yet and he'd made her body sing...though he hadn't let her touch *him*. She stopped in the middle of slipping on her shoes and frowned. That was weird, right? Every guy she'd been with up to this point had seen sex as a transaction—each side paid in orgasms. It wasn't always equal, but both parties came at least once. Usually.

What game is he playing at now?

There had to be some reason behind it, even if he hadn't seemed particularly cool and collected when he'd gone after her pussy like it owed him money. She shook her head. It didn't matter what his motivation was. She'd gotten hers, and she hadn't given anything in the process. Best to put it out of her mind because if the car was stopped, that meant they were back in Boston and she had to face her family.

What was left of it.

Her good mood evaporated. She couldn't be in the O'Malley house without looking for the missing piece. Every time Keira walked into the library, she half expected to find Devlin holed up with a book, and every time the door to her room opened, she'd held out hope that it would be him coming in to tell her what new brilliance he'd gotten up to with his tech stuff.

She hadn't realized how much of that pressure had disappeared in New York until she stepped out of the town car and found herself in front of her old home. *God, I miss him so much.*

Shut it down.

But there was no convenient haze of alcohol or drugs to keep the grief from sinking deep and taking hold. It had been three years since Devlin died, but all that meant was that he should have graduated college by now and be in the middle of his great European adventure. He wasn't supposed to be *dead*, rotting six feet underground while the rest of them went on as if nothing had changed.

Nothing, and yet everything.

"Keira."

She was pathetically grateful for Dmitri's presence intruding on her thoughts. She turned to find him leaning against the trunk of the car. He caught sight of her expression and pushed to his feet. "Come here."

"I'm not a dog you can summon whenever you want." But she took his hand and let him pull her against him. His thighs bracketed her in, but for once she didn't feel trapped. The contact grounded her the same way his spicy scent did. She inhaled and exhaled slowly, trying to calm her racing heart. "I'm fine."

"I know." He slipped one hand along her jaw to guide her face up, and then he kissed her as if he'd done it a thousand times before. This wasn't the claim of ownership their last had been. He brushed his lips across hers once, twice, a third time, and then traced the seam of her mouth with his tongue. Asking.

She gave herself over to the kiss, to him, parting her lips even as she tucked her arms into his jacket to wrap around his waist. *What are we doing?* The reason—because there was a reason for every single goddamn thing Dmitri did—didn't matter as much as the distraction he offered. With his tongue stroking hers, she wasn't thinking about the town house looming behind them, or the coming confrontation, or even the memories that had plagued her for years while she lived in this place.

No, there was room only for this man.

A throat cleared, and she jumped and spun, nearly clocking Dmitri on the chin. He kept her held between his legs, his hands on her hips as she turned to face . . . "Aiden."

Her oldest brother and leader of their family. He looked so much like their father with his dark hair and the line of his jaw, but she couldn't fault him for the similarities because she shared more than a few herself. However, she *could* fault him for the murderous expression he was aiming over her shoulder at Dmitri.

If he attacks Romanov, all this will be for nothing.

The only option was to play to her strength—being a pain in her brother's ass. "Get that look off your face, Aiden. You were going to marry me off to him, so you don't get to throw a bitchfit because it didn't happen on *your* timeline."

His attention fell to the massive ring on her left hand. "Come inside, Keira. We have things to talk about."

Dmitri's grip tightened ever so slightly on her hips, and his murmur reached her ears alone. "Remember what I said, Keira."

She elbowed him and slipped out of his grasp without responding. She'd made her choice, and she didn't need him threatening her to remind her of that fact. Her brother and her husband stared at each other like junkyard dogs about to attack, so she stalked past Aiden. "Let's get this over with so I can check in on Charlie." The last she'd heard, her brother's fiancée had been taken by the enemy and might not survive. Obviously, Charlie was okay, but Keira wouldn't quite believe it until she saw it for herself.

Aiden fell into step behind her as she marched through the front door and headed down the hallway to his office. In the ten seconds she was in the house, it already stood in stark contrast to the Romanov home. Voices came from the kitchen, accompanied by the clink of dishes, and somewhere upstairs it sounded like elephants were stampeding. Elephants, or Dmitri's niece.

Aiden touched Keira's shoulder and turned back to where Dmitri stood in the front doorway. "I'll have Olivia bring Hadley down." He jerked his chin to the library. "They'll meet you in there."

For once, Dmitri didn't have anything to say to that.

He held Keira's gaze for a long moment and then turned and walked obediently into the library. *That's a first.* She knew what he was doing—keeping his promise to her. He wouldn't antagonize Aiden beyond smart-ass remarks because peace was the condition to Keira agreeing to be his wife. He might be sneaky as fuck, but he'd keep his word. *Good.*

The office had been their father's before it became Aiden's, and although he hadn't done anything overt to it, it *felt* different. Not welcoming, exactly, but more comfortable. Keira took her customary chair, but to her surprise, Aiden didn't sit behind the desk. He leaned against it in front of her and crossed his arms over his chest. He seemed to be debating how to handle her, and she was so goddamn tired of being handled. In reality, her role hadn't changed all that much—from possession to possession, even if one label was a sister and the other was a wife.

Keira cut to the chase. "I chose this."

"Really? Because it sounds like Dmitri forced your hand the same way he forced Cillian to let you walk out of here. He waited until he knew I wasn't going to be here, and then he coerced you to leave with him."

It was more or less the truth, but Aiden was missing one very important fact—they couldn't afford a war. Three years ago, the conflict with the Hallorans hadn't reached more than a few skirmishes and Devlin had *died*. If they went to a full-out war with Romanov and his people, there was no way her remaining siblings were all going to walk away unscathed. And their alliances would pull in the other two families in Boston, and maybe even Sloan and her husband from wherever they had settled down, and endanger her new nieces and nephews, too.

What was a marriage to Dmitri Romanov when weighed against all that?

She couldn't say that to Aiden. He wouldn't understand, for all that he put their family first over and over again. It was okay for *him* to make sacrifices, but for his baby sister? No, he wouldn't see things her way at all.

Keira leaned forward, trying to make him understand. "I want him."

"Bullshit. You're just spitting out the rhetoric he rehearsed with you. I know what you're doing, Keira, but you don't have to. We're stronger than we've ever been, and he's weaker than he lets on. I'm not going to sacrifice you at the altar of Romanov's pride and power."

He wasn't exactly wrong—the dinner last night had more than proven that truth—but even without being at 100 percent, Dmitri was more than a formidable opponent. It was only sheer stubbornness preventing her brother from admitting that. Frustration took hold. "You let Sloan leave with Jude."

"Sloan is head over heels in love with that asshole, and he'd die for her and their baby. It's a different situation, and you damn well know it." Aiden clenched his fists and then made a visible effort to relax. "Nothing's been done that can't be undone. Just let me fix this, Keira."

Fix this. Bring her back into the fold so she could keep living her half life holed up in her room, because every time she left it, she had to face down the missing piece evident in every board of this goddamn house. She *hated* this house.

She knew her brother, and she knew the stubborn expression on his face. She'd worn the same expression more times than she could count when she looked in the mirror.

If she didn't force him to accept her decision, he *would* bring her back, whether she wanted to come or not. "It's too late. We're married. Signed, sealed, and delivered."

He froze, his green eyes going icy just like their father's did before heads rolled. "Have you slept with him yet?"

It was such a Catholic thing to ask. "Yes," she lied. "We've fucked on every surface of his house. If I'm not already pregnant, it'll be a goddamn miracle." *Liar, liar.* Her brother flinched with every word as if she'd reached out and struck him. She hated hurting him, but it was for his own good. "In fact, we fucked on the ride up here. It's no use, Aiden. There's no annulment option, and neither of us wants a divorce. You *can't* do anything about it, so you might as well let me live my life like I've been asking you to since I turned eighteen. I know what I'm doing."

If anything, his expression went subzero. "If I kill him, it wouldn't come to divorce."

She shot to her feet. "What the hell is wrong with you? I didn't like Charlie when she first came around, but I wasn't threatening to *kill* her. Jesus, Aiden, you sound like our father."

He flinched again, but his eyes thawed. Just a little. "That's different."

"No, it's not." It was totally different. "I don't know how many ways you're going to make me say this—*I choose him.*" *I choose peace. I choose to keep the family safe. I choose the only option I ever really had.*

Aiden hissed out a breath. "Fine, Keira. Just...fine. I'm not going to strong-arm you over this, but if you change your mind at *any* point, you just have to say the word, and I'll get you out and to hell with the consequences."

Her brother was a good man. She might throw the barb

about him being like their father when it suited her, but it couldn't have been further from the truth. Maybe one of these days he'd actually believe it. She went up onto her tiptoes and kissed his cheek. "Thank you."

"You're in over your head."

Without a doubt. "I love you." She turned on her heel and went in search of her husband.

CHAPTER TEN

"What did you bring me, Uncle Dima?"

Dmitri held out a hand and smiled. "You'll have to come over here to see."

Hadley raced at him and threw herself into his arms. She was so tiny to contain so much energy, but then her mother had been the same at that age. He lifted her and spun in a quick circle before settling her on his hip and producing a book from his jacket.

Her cherub face fell almost comically. "A *book*?"

"*Da.*" He waited for her to take it and ruffled her hair. "Do you know that your grandpapa used to read these same stories to me when I was your age? You've never met him, but this is a piece of your history all the same." He looked over her dark head as he said the words, meeting his half sister's gaze.

At first glance, Olivia didn't look much like a Romanov. She was his sister by way of his father's mistress, and they shared the man's jawline and straight nose. Olivia leaned against the wall and watched him with her daughter. In the year or so since they'd made their deal, she'd relaxed enough that he knew she trusted him not to harm his niece, but that didn't mean she *trusted* him.

Nor should she.

He pointed to the overstuffed armchair next to the fireplace. "Shall I read you one?"

"Yes, please." Hadley said it primly, the very picture of a pretty princess deigning to let her subject have his way.

He settled in with Hadley on his lap and read her the first story in the book of Russian fairy tales—"Vasilisa the Beautiful." Through it all, though he was focused on her, he kept one eye on the door for Keira's return. Dmitri didn't believe for a second that Aiden would steamroll his younger sister's protests, but he didn't allow himself to relax until she slipped into the room and took a position on the couch across from them.

Hadley waited until Dmitri closed the book to leap to the floor and rush over to her. "Keira!"

"Hey, Hadley." She plopped her onto the same couch cushion as if they'd done it a thousand times before. "How's it hanging?"

"I have to have a *tutor.*" His niece said it like it was a dirty word.

Dmitri raised his eyebrows at Olivia, who took it as her cue to move to the couch on the other side of Hadley. "We talked about preschool, but decided that bringing someone in would be the better choice—at least for now." She set her shoulders. "She *is* going to a normal kindergarten, even if it's a Catholic one."

Ah. Her words had the flavor of an old argument

between her and Cillian, which was interesting. Dmitri wouldn't use it as leverage to get what he wanted...for now. Olivia was happy here. More importantly, *Hadley* was happy here. Cillian looked at her as his own daughter, and he'd die for her if it came to that. Dmitri couldn't have placed his sister and niece in a better location if he'd tried.

Keira twisted to face Olivia, a frown on her face. "She needs to be around other kids."

"I agree."

She narrowed her eyes. "He's harping about safety again, isn't he? Just compromise and have extra security set up around the preschool." Keira cocked her head to the side, and he swore he could actually see the wheels turning behind those beautiful hazel eyes. "In fact, we will supply the extra men if Aiden can't spare them. Hadley is family, after all."

Olivia froze. "Keira, that's sweet, but—"

He saw it in the hesitance in his sister's stance and the way Keira's shoulders twitched as if about to droop. Whatever she was about to say wouldn't be positive. Keira had offered a solution, and Olivia was going to shoot her down. Everyone in the room knew it.

So he stepped in. "I think that's a wonderful idea," Dmitri cut in smoothly. He spared a smile for his niece. "Hadley needs to be socialized with other children. You want that. You said as much yourself."

Olivia's chin set in a stubborn line he knew all too well. "I didn't say that."

"Not in so many words, but you *do* agree with it." He pretended to consider, and switched to Russian. "*Unless it's* me *that you're trying to protect my niece from.*"

She jumped like he'd reached over and struck her.

"*Nyet, of course not. If I wanted to protect her from you, I wouldn't allow these visits.*"

"*I've given you no reason to call them off.*" Agreeing to her terms had been easy enough. He had no reason to manipulate Hadley into doing anything but caring for him. She wasn't a pawn in his game. The girl may be illegitimate, but she *was* family—the only family Dmitri had left of this particular Romanov line. If the visits had the double benefit of getting the O'Malleys used to his presence, well, that was a different play in a different game.

"*Yet.*"

"Hey, guys, still sitting right here." Keira waved a hand in front of Olivia's face, breaking their staring contest. "Speaking Russian in front of someone who doesn't speak the language is a dick move."

"You should learn," Dmitri said.

"Yeah, yeah, it's on my list." Keira sat back against the arm of the couch. "Take the help, Olivia. It gets you what you want, and it will be good for Hadley. There aren't any drawbacks."

From the look on his sister's face, accepting any help that came with a Romanov label was too much, but she was smart enough to know when she was backed into a corner. "I'll talk to Cillian about it."

"Do that." Keira pointed an imperial finger at him. "You. I'm pretty sure my brother needs to talk to you. Don't get any blood on the carpet—or anywhere else."

The mantle of power looked good on her. She held herself like a queen, watching him with those witch eyes as he stood and crossed the room. Dmitri paused in the doorway. "I won't be long."

"If you're about to tell me not to get into any trouble, don't waste your breath. I was born for trouble."

He gave her a sharp grin. "I know."

* * *

Keira didn't release a breath when Dmitri left the room, but Olivia did. Her sister-in-law slumped back against the couch cushion. "Hadley, why don't you play for a few minutes before we hunt down some dinner?"

"Okay." Hadley hopped off the couch and scooped up the book Dmitri had brought her. Now that her beloved uncle was out of the room, she climbed into the chair he'd vacated and paged through the book in utter seriousness. *Smart little cookie, playing hard to get.*

Olivia closed her eyes. "It never gets any easier dealing with him. He's scarier when he's being civil."

Scary.

Scary didn't begin to cover Dmitri Romanov, but he had been on his best behavior since they walked through the front door. Keira didn't imagine for a second that he'd keep that up once behind the closed door of Aiden's office, but his actions and words were above reproach up to this point. "He would never hurt you."

Olivia opened one dark eye and gave her an incredulous look. "What are you smoking? Of course he would. Not without a reason, but our being half-related wouldn't stop him."

Keira knew that was true—she did—but a part of her rebelled at it all the same. *Still determined to think the best of him. You never learn, you fool.* "All the same, the offer for extra muscle is a legitimate one. There's no way Hadley's identity will fly under the radar indefinitely, and having the showing from both families will make anyone assuming she's an easy target think twice. It will keep her safe, which is what everyone wants." She might not be able to divine the motivation for a good portion of the shit Dmitri pulled, but she was confident he didn't want his niece hurt.

"You're right. I know you're right." Olivia sighed and sat up. "I'll think about it, talk to Cillian, and let you know."

That was as good as it'd get, so she said, "Okay."

Olivia narrowed her eyes. "Did Aiden take care of things?"

Things meaning her running off with Dmitri. Keira wasn't in the mood to keep defending him when it ultimately didn't matter what anyone thought. Aiden wouldn't move on Dmitri until he thought he had a good chance of succeeding. He didn't believe that she was in love with the Russian, and for good reason—she wasn't. She could bring her brother around eventually, but if she suddenly declared herself head over heels, he'd know it for the lie it was. "I'm sure he will." She stood and headed for the door. There was one person she wanted to see while she was here, and with her time ticking down, she had to do it now. "I'll talk to you later."

"Keira—"

But then she was through the door and into the hallway. Keira made it to the entranceway when a female voice called from the top of the stairway. "I *know* you're not leaving without saying hello to me, because I will kick your ass from here to New York and back."

"Charlie!" Keira took the steps two at a time.

Charlie Moreaux stood at the top of the stairs, her white-blond hair pulled back in a ponytail, dressed in faded jeans and a tank top. She grinned. "Hey there, trouble."

"Me trouble? *You* trouble." She grabbed Charlie's hands and lifted her arms to get a better look at the cuts scabbing over her pale skin. They formed a neat little line up one arm and down the other. "Fuck, that bitch did a number on you." *Tortured.* She wouldn't say the word aloud. It made it all too real, and she didn't think her friend would like the reminder.

"I survived." She said it simply—a fact—but her blue eyes were concerned. "I know you don't want to be handled with kid gloves, so I'm just going to put it out there. Are you okay? Last anyone heard from you was Cillian frantically calling Aiden to say Romanov had taken you."

"He didn't take me. I left." It wasn't quite the truth, but it was the only one that mattered. Keira took a deep breath. It was easier to play the pissed-off sister with Aiden. His protective instincts made him act like a fool sometimes. Charlie wasn't like that. She was Keira's friend—or at least they'd been headed in that direction. "Look, not too long ago, you asked me if I was falling for him."

"Pretty sure you told me to fuck right off with that nonsense."

"Yeah, well." Keira looked away and then back. "Maybe it was a case of the lady protesting too much."

"Keira…" Charlie pressed her lips together. "You're a smart girl. He might be dangerous and kind of sexy in a murderous sort of way, but you have to know that you're just a pawn for him."

"It's not as simple as you think—or anyone thinks." Keira shrugged, going for somewhere between nonchalant and angsty. If they thought Dmitri was manipulating her into giving them the answers he wanted, nothing would stop Aiden from going after Romanov with everything he had. "We meet each other's needs. It's a mutually beneficial agreement." She could see the disbelief simmering in her friend so she held up a hand. "I'm sober, Charlie. Actually honest-to-God sober. I haven't had a drink or a smoke since I left."

"Seriously?" Charlie frowned. "Doc Jones told Aiden you were through withdrawal, but it was hard to believe."

She very carefully didn't think of the vodka she'd stashed in her bathroom cabinet. Keira was nowhere near out of the woods, but she'd only weaken her argument if she admitted it. "It was a bitch. I don't want to go through that shit again as long as I live."

She still didn't look convinced, but she sighed. "If you wanted out, you'd tell me, wouldn't you?"

Not a chance. "Yeah, of course. I might be the purveyor of bad life choices, but I don't have a death wish." Not anymore. Dmitri had effectively shocked her out of the numbness that had already started melting away with Charlie's addition into her life, and she didn't want to check out like that again. But that didn't mean she had a clear view of where she wanted to go. She was Dmitri's wife, but he only saw her as his possession.

Keira was damn tired of being moved around like an inconvenient table lamp.

Charlie nodded. "In that case, I'm sure there's some shit you want from your room." She made a face. "We threw out your drugs and did your laundry—gross, by the way— but everything else is untouched."

"Thanks." There were a few things she'd left behind

that she'd wanted, and Keira grinned. "While I pack, tell me what you've been up to since I left. And write down your number for me again. This whole not talking to you thing has been a bitch."

"You're telling me." Charlie followed her down the hallway toward her room. "We're working on the Eldridge threat, but Aiden's insisting on setting a June date for the wedding, so I'm having to deal with your mother for that."

Keira winced. "My sympathies."

"You're telling me."

CHAPTER ELEVEN

G ive me one goddamn reason why I shouldn't shoot you in the face and be done with this mess."

Dmitri sighed. "Again with this? You won't kill me, because not only would it upset your sister, it would destabilize the power structure in New York and allow the Eldridges to capitalize on it—and become more of a threat than they already are. Then you really *would* have a war on your hands." He pinned Aiden with a disdainful look. "But you already know that, don't you? Don't take your frustration out on me, O'Malley."

"It's not *frustration* I want to take out on you." Aiden's entire body was tensed as if he fought to hold himself back from attacking. For a man who had renowned self-control, he wasn't exhibiting much of it lately. He leaned forward. "You married Keira."

"I told you I was going to."

A muscle in Aiden's jaw jumped. "You also told me that you'd give her a choice, or was that a goddamn lie, too? You had to have broken every single fucking speed limit to get to Boston ahead of me, and then you took her like a thief in the night."

"I did not *take* your sister. I offered her a choice. She chose me." He waved a hand through the air, feigning nonchalance. "It's a moot point now. She's my wife. I will not relinquish her, and she has no desire to be relinquished. There are more important matters to discuss."

"There's nothing more important than my family."

He and Dmitri could agree on that, though who they termed family varied significantly. "In that case, you're about to renew our alliance against the Eldridges. Officially." He paused. "Have you received any gifts from Mae?"

Aiden hissed out a breath and sat back. "She sent me a set of women's hands with a ring almost identical to the family heirloom Charlie has on her finger." His gaze sharpened. "Why? What did you get?"

"The head from the body I assume the hands were once attached to." He waited a beat. "The dead woman bears a startling resemblance to your sister."

"Fuck."

"My thoughts exactly." Just remembering the feeling that had coursed through him at the sight of that head— something akin to fear—pissed him the hell off. "She's changing the game and isn't playing by the rules. No one is safe, Aiden. Not Charlie, not your sisters, not your nieces and nephews. The only way to remove the threat is to *remove* it. Immediately."

For the first time since he'd walked through the door,

Aiden looked at him like he was a person rather than shit on the bottom of his shoe. *Progress.* "I suppose you have a brilliant plan."

"You give me a lot of credit." Credit where credit was due. He permitted himself a small smile. "I have my best man working to find them. Someone is running their business in their absence—either that, or they haven't gone far."

"If they were close, you would have already found them." No credit there, just a statement of fact.

"Da."

"What do you need from me?"

Now we're getting somewhere. "Your man Mark is highly motivated to see Eldridge blood run."

"If you already know it for a fact, there's no reason to say it out loud. I'm not going to pat you on the back for having spies in my house."

Dmitri snorted. "Please. There's no need for spies when human nature is so predictable. Mae Eldridge shot Mark's cousin, so he's uniquely situated to want vengeance, and he's got a skill set that makes him useful. Send him to New York to eliminate the person holding the power in the Eldridges' absence, and I'll have my men accomplish the rest after the first domino falls. If my man hasn't found Alethea by then, the resulting events will draw her and Mae out."

Aiden drummed his fingers on the desk. "I'll think about it."

"Think fast." He rose. "We want the same thing, Aiden."

"No, Romanov, we don't." He didn't move, just kept up the damn drumming. "My sister tells me that you're fucking on every available surface."

Did she, now? He lifted one shoulder in a shrug. "She's

a beautiful woman. We're married. I would think it'd be stranger if we *weren't* fucking."

Aiden's expression didn't shift. "You'll be having a wedding reception." Not a question, but not quite a command, either.

You're learning, O'Malley. "Invitations went out today. It's set for next Saturday."

"We'll be there." He waited for Dmitri to take a step to continue. "All of us. O'Malley. Sheridan. Halloran. Every single one of us have a vested interested in Keira's health and happiness."

Smarter to keep his mouth shut and allow Aiden to hold the high ground, but Dmitri couldn't let that comment stand. It was all well and good to crow about family loyalty and their beloved youngest sister, but not a single fucking O'Malley had stepped in to stop her free fall after Devlin O'Malley's death. Not *one.*

Oh, Aiden tried after he'd taken control of the family, but by then it was too late, and his attempts weren't nearly strong enough to breach Keira's walls. Understandable, perhaps, but unforgivable when taken hand in hand with his holier-than-thou attitude. Dmitri smoothed down the lapels of his suit. "Really, Aiden, if her *health and happiness* were so important to you, I would think you'd have acted much sooner to try to get through to her. You forgot about her while in pursuit of your own goals—every single one of you."

He didn't flinch. "We've all made some mistakes when it comes to Keira—even you, Romanov."

"Without a doubt, but if there's a villain in this piece, it's not me." This conversation had just confirmed what he already knew—Aiden would never stoop to using Keira against him. The man still saw her as the baby sister she'd been while they were growing up, making no allowances for the formidable player she could become in her own right. "I'll be waiting for your answer." He walked out of the room before his temper could push him to say something he didn't intend.

All these Irish, so fucking superior in their moral high ground. They were no different than he was, save that he was better at the game. That was the problem, though. They were so busy blundering around, thinking with their hearts instead of their heads, that they were sometimes tricky to predict. It changed nothing—they had blood on their hands, same as he did.

He stopped into the library to say good-bye to Hadley, all too aware of the man at his back, shadowing his every move. Aiden was too smart to let Dmitri wander his house unwatched, but the muscle had stayed further back before their meeting.

He stepped out of the library. "You have something to say."

Mark Neale shifted out of the shadows. "Aiden will work with you. I'll be in contact."

That didn't take long. The damn man knew what his decision would be before Dmitri arrived here. It wasn't much of a delay, but it irked all the same. He itched to be back in New York again, away from these goddamn Irishmen.

But he let none of that show on his face. "I look forward to hearing from you."

"Keira is upstairs." He made no move to back away, so Dmitri walked past him to the main stairway curving up the inner wall. It was ostentatious in the extreme, but he was hardly one to throw stones. His home wasn't humble in the least. Both were designed to make an impression, and he climbed the stairs with a strange feeling taking up residence in his chest.

This was the home Keira had grown up in.

He'd known that, of course—the whole O'Malley brood was raised between here and a secondary country residence in Connecticut—but somehow walking these halls brought that truth home.

He knew which room was hers, and walked past the other closed doors without so much as a sideways glance. If Mark hoped to catch him snooping, he was in for a disappointment.

Keira's door stood ajar, and he took it for an invitation, using a single finger to send it opening the rest of the way. His wife sat on her bed across from Charlie Moreaux—formerly Charlotte Finch, daughter of the fed who had let Mae slip his cage. The blond woman looked up and froze at the sight of him. "Romanov."

"Charlie." He had no interest in digging at her further. Aiden was more entertaining to bait, and the actions of Charlie's father a few short weeks ago had proven exactly where she was on the totem pole. The woman's only political value now lay in her pending marriage to Aiden O'Malley. It was just as well—nothing good came from meddling with cops.

Keira closed the suitcase before he had a chance to examine what she'd packed. "I'm ready."

"No need to rush on my account."

She sent him a censuring look. "I'm relieving my family of your presence. It upsets them." Charlie snorted and Keira rolled her eyes. "What? You know I'm right."

"That was almost political. I'm proud of you." Charlie

pushed to her feet and crossed to stand before Dmitri. He knew what the move must have cost her, and something akin to admiration pulsed when she lifted her chin. "I'm sure Aiden has already said it, but if you fuck with Keira, we'll bring everything in our arsenal at you. You'll end up behind bars for good or..." She trailed off and shrugged one shoulder. "Or."

"I see that your fiancé's bloodthirstiness is rubbing off on you." It made him like her more, which was damn inconvenient. His life would be a whole hell of a lot simpler if he could mark the entire O'Malley clan as enemies and remove them from the earth.

Her grin wasn't happy in the least. "Or maybe I'm rubbing off on him."

Keira lugged the suitcase over. "Stop threatening my husband, Charlie. It'll make for awkward holiday meals."

Charlie's blue eyes went a little wide. "Holiday meals."

"Yep." Keira shoved the suitcase at him. "Thanksgiving here and Christmas in New York. It'll be a real treat. Totally enjoyable for everyone."

She shook her head. "Honey, you're out of your damn mind."

"It's one of my many charms." She pushed him toward the door, and he allowed himself to be herded down the hallway and stairs to the front door. Aiden was nowhere to be seen, which was just as well. Mark and Charlie were more than enough of a good-bye party. He stood back while Charlie hugged Keira tightly.

Dmitri waited for the blonde to release her and nodded at the door. "Let's go."

He scanned the street as he paused on the front step. Pavel leaned against the town car and nodded—nothing was amiss. Knowing Mae's fondness for drive-by shootings, that didn't mean much in the grand scheme of things, but at least no one had tampered with the car in the meantime. Dmitri handed over the suitcase to be stowed in the trunk and then held the door open for Keira.

She didn't look back as she strode down the steps and climbed into the car, and he wasn't fanciful enough to see it as a sign. Keira was his. She might not have made her peace with that—yet—but it was the truth. The sooner she accepted it, the better for both of them.

He joined her in the backseat and waited tensely for Pavel to drive them away from the town house. It wasn't until they left the Boston city limits behind that he relaxed against the seat.

"You thought he'd do something."

"No." He hesitated and then relented. "Your brother has a long history of doing the logical thing as long as one remembers that he puts his family above all else. But there are never any guarantees."

Keira watched him closely, her hazel eyes narrow. "You must have been desperately lonely as a kid, huh?"

He had to fight not to react. "What makes you say that?"

"No one becomes that good at observing other people unless they spent a whole hell of a lot of time shoved in a back corner by themselves. The other reason is if they're victims of abuse—their life can depend on reading people right." She didn't move. "Andrei never laid a hand on Olivia. I'd bet good money on that, though he had other ways of terrorizing her—both of you did. Did he hit you?"

She'd been closer to the mark with the first assumption. "*Nyet.* My father wasn't a good man, but he wasn't abusive."

"Lucky you."

There it was again. There'd been a few times where he'd wondered at the extent of Seamus O'Malley's crimes against his children. Andrei Romanov was hardly father of the year, but he never raised his hand to either of his children. "Did your father hurt you, Keira?"

She shut her eyes, closing him out. "It doesn't really matter what my father did or didn't do. I'm more out of his reach now than I've ever been. The past is the past."

"The past shapes us." A person was an accumulation of all that happened to them. Knowing the past meant Dmitri had a better than decent chance at predicting the future— or at least future actions. People could change, elements could change, but the core of a person remained the same.

"If you say so." Keira didn't look at him.

She looked younger than her twenty-one years with her face relaxed and the knowledge she kept in her hazel eyes hidden from view. Even knowing she was far from innocent, he found himself wanting to... *What? Protect her? The very idea is laughable.*

And yet it dug down deep and refused to budge. Dmitri slid closer to her and picked her up to tuck her into his lap.

Keira shot straight up, and it was only some creative maneuvering that kept her from slamming her head into the roof of the car. "What the hell are you doing, Russian?"

"Hush and let me hold you for a little while."

She stared at him like he'd grown a second head. "Did my brother slip you some drugs while you were in his office?"

"*Nyet.*" It stung more than it should have that she thought he had to be drugged to want to hold her. Dmitri forced himself to relax his grip on her. "Let me hold you, *moya koroleva.*"

"Tell me what that means."

He permitted himself a small smile. "Another time."

She glared, but didn't move away. "Why?"

There was no misunderstanding her question, and he didn't bother trying to pretend. "You are my wife." Something so simple and yet infinitely complicated.

Keira sighed and it was as if the strength left her body. She melted into him, nestling her face into his chest. "It's criminal how good you smell. What cologne is that?"

"No cologne. I dislike them."

She lifted her head enough to frown. "That's just wrong. No one should smell this good naturally."

"Lucky you for marrying a man who does, then." He shouldn't keep pushing her on that fact, but her insistence on thinking the worst of him irked. He wanted her as his wife in truth.

Patience. You've waited this long. You can wait a bit longer.

He just hoped like hell that Keira didn't make him wait forever.

CHAPTER TWELVE

Keira did the one thing she'd thought impossible—she fell asleep in Dmitri's arms. She didn't mean to. She had every intention of holding still for the allotted time and moving away, but his warmth soaked into her body, and the strength of his arms felt more like he was protecting her than caging her in. Even though she *knew* it was a lie, she let her eyes slide shut.

And woke up to him laying her on a bed.

Keira reacted without thinking. She flailed out of his arms, managing to punch him in the face in the process, and then drew both legs up and kicked him directly in the chest. Dmitri shot back several steps and hit the big dark wood dresser, making it rattle.

She scrambled back until the headboard stopped her motion, her mind frantically flailing around to catch up with the change in location and circumstance. Dmitri started to take a step forward and seemed to change his mind. "You're safe, Keira."

That spawned an ugly laugh. "Not that, Russian. Never that."

He inclined his head, a king surveying his domain. "Let me rephrase—you're safe right now, with me. You were tired. I thought it more effective to put you in bed and not interrupt your rest."

"*Your* bed."

"*Da.* You agreed to it earlier."

Damn it, she had, hadn't she? Keira rubbed the back of her hand across her eyes. "Sorry. You're right—this time."

He still didn't move from his position against the dresser. A bright red spot had bloomed under his right cheekbone where she'd hit him. "I won't move you while you're sleeping again." He said it with utter seriousness, not a single mocking word in sight.

"Thank you." She felt dramatic reacting so strongly. Of course Dmitri would carry her to bed when she passed out on him in the car. She probably drooled on his chest and he just took it, and the way she paid him back was by punching him in the face. Exhaustion pulled at her, and the bed was like sitting on a tempting cloud, but she couldn't let things stand as they were now. *She* had fucked up. Not him.

She scooted to the edge of the bed and climbed to the floor. "We'd better get some ice on that cheekbone. My brother Teague taught me that right hook, and even without all my weight behind it, you've got a good chance of bruising."

"That's not necessary." There he was, her cold Russian.

Keira almost missed a step. Cold, yes. Not hers. Never hers. She had to remember that. To cover her reaction, she pivoted and headed for the bathroom. If there wasn't ice, a cold washcloth would work in a pinch. Better to get this taken care of now and move on. The less time she spent staring into Dmitri's striking gray eyes, the better.

He was *still* in the same spot when she returned. Keira frowned. "You should sit." At five seven, she wasn't exactly short, but he was at least an inch or two over six feet, and it would be easier to get to the bruise if he sat on the bed.

Do not think about Dmitri on the bed. Definitely don't think about Dmitri on the bed.

He moved to the bed and sat slowly. "I can do it myself."

"I reacted poorly and attacked you. Just... sit there and shut up and let me take care of you, okay?"

He stared at her long enough that she had to fight not to fidget. Finally, he nodded. "Do your worst."

"I think I already did that." She stepped closer, but the length of his legs made it awkward to reach his face.

"Keira." He said her name almost as a sigh. "Come here." Dmitri nudged her closer until she stood between his thighs. His fingertips barely touched her hips, but she felt them through her entire body. Or maybe it was his presence overwhelming her by being this close. With him sitting and her standing, it should have put her in the dominant position, but there was no mistaking the fact that Dmitri was perfectly in control of this situation the same way he always seemed to be in control.

She pressed the cold washcloth against his face. "Do you ever just... relax?"

"I was relaxed. And then my wife woke up and reacted poorly to my having moved her."

"Oh, for fuck's sake." She glared. "You were *not* relaxed then, so stop with the bullshit. I bet you're plotting in your dreams when you sleep, aren't you? Carrying me to bed wasn't enough to put you off something you do as second nature."

"If you already think you know the answer to the question, why ask it?"

Which wasn't an agreement...but it wasn't a disagreement, either.

She lifted the washcloth and winced. "This will bruise."

"It's an impressive right hook."

Now was the time to press him about Krav Maga, or to ask one of the half a million questions she had brimming inside her. But Keira found herself hesitant to break the moment. She pressed the cloth back to his face.

"Why did you stop painting?"

The question set her back on her heels. "That's none of your damn business." She was *not* going to think about painting or the whys or what she'd lost.

His big hand covered hers where she held the washcloth. "It's just a question, Keira."

"It's not just a question. You're probing for information. It doesn't matter whether it's part of some intricate plan or to satisfy your curiosity—I am not going to trot out my pain for your amusement."

His grip tightened slightly. "You don't have to keep running."

The audacity of him almost left her speechless. "Why?"

He frowned. "Why?"

"Yes, Dmitri, *why*? Why don't I have to keep running? Is it because I'm safe here?" She motioned with her free hand. "We both know that's a fucking lie. I'm no safer here than I was in Boston—less so, because anyone targeting you will target your wife as well. Am I safe because *you're* here? Please. You're the most dangerous to me of all. You were honest when you said that you couldn't offer me what I needed—don't try to change your tone now."

His frown deepened and then cleared. "Love. You're talking about love."

Five little words to cut right to the heart of her. She let go of the washcloth and stepped back, all too aware that he allowed her to do it. "I know better now."

"Keira—"

"Can we just be done for tonight? It's been a long day, and I'm tired." Her exhaustion surged again, threatening to buckle her knees. As much as she didn't want to share a bed with him, the thought of walking down the stairs to hers was too much. She pulled her sweater off and slid out of her jeans. When she turned around, he was staring. "What now?"

Dmitri gave a sharp shake of his head and stood. "You are safe tonight."

The implication being that she wasn't safe other nights. It would be worrying, but it was a truth she'd known since she was a child. The type of danger might change in any given situation, but it never went away completely.

She waited for him to walk into the bathroom before she climbed into the massive bed. It really was like wrapping up in a cloud. By all rights, she should have passed out the second her head hit the pillow, but her mind unfurled like some dark-winged thing chased it.

Going home had been a mistake. She knew it was necessary, but the world seemed so far away when she was closed up in the Romanov residence. Being back in Boston, even for a limited time, had memories banging against the walls of her mind that she had no interest in dealing with.

It had been far too many years since her siblings were happy. Since they were close. Not since Aiden left for college, though things had started fracturing before then, but she'd just been too young to realize it. *Too selfish.* What did she care if her oldest brother was straining under the pressure their father put on him as heir? *She* was living as close to the dream as she was allowed. While her siblings slowly drifted away, one after the other, she'd lost herself in her art and her goals. She'd once had Devlin, after all, and *that* relationship was just as close as it'd ever been.

Until it wasn't.

Until he died and she realized how alone she really was.

Until the illusion fell from the bars of her cage, revealing just how trapped she'd been from the very beginning.

The world was an ugly place, and the art she was so goddamn proud of didn't do a damn thing to change that. All it did was remind her of the silly girl she'd been—so willfully stubborn, doing anything she had to in order to ignore the truth of her situation.

Trapped. Helpless. A pawn in a game she never wanted to play to begin with.

Nothing had changed, even if the city she lived in had. She was still a character in someone else's play, required to dance to the tune not of her making.

God, I need a drink.

"Keira."

Dmitri's voice reached out to her in the darkness of the room. When had he come to bed? *I really am a mess if I'm checking out so thoroughly that I didn't notice him.* She swallowed past her burning throat, trying to convince herself that she wasn't about to cry. "I don't want to talk to you anymore." It sounded childish, but she couldn't help it.

"We don't have to talk." He shifted, turning onto his side to face her. "Let me hold you, *moya koroleva*. I'll keep the demons at bay tonight."

She should say no. Doing anything to damage the reality—that Dmitri was no knight in shining armor—was dangerous in the extreme.

But if she didn't do something, she was in danger of climbing out of bed and charging down to the vodka she'd hidden in order to drown out her racing thoughts. She teetered on an edge far more dangerous than the man next to her. She was clean. Actually clean. It was one thing to comfort herself with the lie-not-lie that she only wanted an escape from her shitty life. It was another to not be able to get through a tiny bump in the road without a substance as a crutch.

It was unforgivably weak to need alcohol. She didn't want to be that girl again. Knowing that didn't make it any easier to resist the driving force inside her that was creeping higher with every exhale. A sleeping monster that her grief had woken. Her fingers itched for a bottle, her throat craving the familiar burn. Just a little drink. Just to take the edge off.

"Keira?"

She turned to him in desperation. "Kiss me, Russian."

He hesitated in the darkness, as if he wanted to dig deeper, but he finally drew her into his arms. "We will talk eventually."

Not fucking likely. "Sure."

Dmitri sifted his fingers through her hair and then ran one hand down her back to press her hips against his. "We're not fucking tonight."

She blinked into the darkness. "I didn't put it on the table."

"Not yet." He kissed her jaw and then her neck. "You're hurting, *moya koroleva*. You would regret it if we took that step now."

She relaxed against him, tilting her head back to give him better access. "What do you care?" Giving him everything sounded like a goddamn dream right now. With his body sliding against hers, maybe her mind would actually deliver blessed *silence*. Maybe she could actually reclaim the distance her drugs had given her—at least for a little while. Dmitri's presence drowned out everything else.

He should be jumping at the chance to get her further under his control, and yet he was holding back. She didn't know how to deal with that. The man defied the nice little boundaries she drew up for him, and kept surprising her. Keira didn't like surprises. She needed him to act like the monster she knew him to be. Any softening would fuck with her head, and her head had been fucked with enough.

The only answer her gave her was his mouth brushing hers. A request rather than a command. Another surprise. His kissed her bottom lip and then her top lip, a slow exploration that made her head spin. Before she could relax into the feeling, his tongue was there, requesting entrance. She opened for him immediately. His touch drove away the bad thoughts, and she'd take whatever he'd give her.

Last time he'd kissed her, he'd kissed her like he owned her. This time, he kissed her like he wanted to memorize her. Slow. Agonizingly, deliciously slow.

Fuck that.

Keira shoved his shoulders, toppling him onto his back. There wasn't a doubt in her mind that he'd allowed the move—if Dmitri wanted to pin her in place, he could do it easily enough. She ended up straddling him and, holy fuck, what a place to be.

The darkness of the room licked at him, only furthering the impression of a fallen angel. No, not an angel. This man was subservient to no one. He was at home here in the shadows, sprawled on this sinfully massive bed like some dark god.

It was right about then that she realized he was naked. Keira went still, trying to tamp down the urge to rush for a light switch. *He's my husband, right? That means I'll see this again...and again...and again.* The faint light coming in from the window didn't give her nearly enough to work with, so she ran her hands down his chest. He was cut in the way boxers were, though she hadn't noticed it before because his clothes fit him so damn well. But there was some serious muscle here.

She traced his pecs and then lightly raked her nails over his abs. "Fuck, Russian, how many sit-ups do you do a week?"

His dark chuckle went straight through her. "Perhaps one of these days, I'll show you."

She took half a second to picture him working out in only a pair of shorts, sweat slicking these same muscles as he pushed his body...Keira shivered. "Not until we're fucking." She wouldn't be able to resist that. She knew herself well enough to know that. The fact that she'd resisted at all was a goddamn miracle.

Here. Now. They were both naked and in his bed.

And he'd taken sex off the table.

She didn't know how to tempt or tease or seduce. Keira had never bothered with that bullshit. If she wanted to fuck someone, she fucked them. The only person who'd ever turned her down was the one she currently had naked between her thighs. She leaned forward and braced herself on one hand so she could use the other to stroke his cock. It was the first time she'd touched him like that, and she took her time exploring him. Long and wide and fucking perfect. *Because of course.* It would be too much to ask the universe to give this man a single physical imperfection.

His body went tense as she stroked him again, and she enjoyed the moment of total control. It didn't matter that Dmitri could flip her and do whatever he damn well pleased and she'd likely love every second of it. What mattered was that *she* was on top, if only for a limited time. "I want to ride you, Romanov."

He spit out something in Russian, which was enough to make her vow to learn the language if it was the last thing she did. She wanted to know what he was saying to her when his control slipped.

"Keira. *Moya koroleva.*" He grabbed her wrist, but he didn't remove her hand from his cock. "Sex is not on the table."

"Who said anything about sex?" She ran the heel of her hand up his cock. "Now, lie back and think of Mother Russia."

CHAPTER THIRTEEN

Dmitri should stop Keira before this thing got out of control. He knew that. She was hurting and wounded, and he was a right bastard for allowing her to use him as another kind of drug. When they had sex, it had to be her choice while she was completely in her right mind, or she'd accuse him of coercing her. Taking advantage.

But he didn't stop her.

Instead, he let her have control. There wasn't enough damn light in the room to see more than the line of her body, the curve of her breasts and hips, the way her hair shifted around her shoulders. She pressed his cock down against his stomach and lined up her pussy over the top of him.

And then she began to move.

She was so fucking wet, and she spread her arousal over him with each sliding stroke, dragging herself over his cock but never granting him entrance. Seeking her own pleasure.

He ran his hands up her sides and cupped her breasts, pinching her nipples lightly. "Take what you need."

"I plan on it." She rolled her hips, pressing down harder. "The angle is wrong."

Dmitri leaned up enough to hook the back of her neck and pull her down to him. He kissed her even as he urged her hips to start moving again. Judging by her moan, she'd found her angle. She kissed him with a need identical to the feeling building in his chest.

He didn't lose control. Ever. Dmitri didn't go into a situation unless he knew he'd come out on top, and he had yet to manage that with Keira. Oh, he'd won a few skirmishes, but she undermined his control with every breath she took, and he liked it far more than he should.

She went still, and he realized her intent. He tore his mouth from hers. "Don't you dare."

"Or what?" She shifted her hips, and his cock was at her entrance. Keira writhed against him, each move sinful and desperate. As if she couldn't get enough. "What will you do to me, Dmitri?"

He'd destroy worlds to hear his name on her lips in exactly that tone of voice. Lustful. Needy. Teasing. *Not like this*. He grabbed her hips, holding her in place when she would have thrust down onto him. "This isn't what you need tonight."

"Funny." She licked his jaw and then bit his chin. "I think I know what I need more than you do. And right now, I need your cock filling me." She gave his throat an open-mouthed kiss. "I want you to fuck me so hard, I feel it in the back of my throat."

Fuck.

Keira shifted again, dragging her breasts over his chest.

"God, you make me so fucking hot, I can't think of anything else." And then she went in for the kill. "Your wife needs you, Dmitri. She aches for you. She's so fucking empty without you. Will you really deny her?"

He growled. "There is no going back from this. You want this, you will take it in full. There will be no waking up in the morning and claiming you didn't really choose it. No regrets, *moya koroleva*. You want my cock?" He released her hips. "Then take it."

Part of him thought he was calling her bluff.

He should have known better.

Keira slammed down, taking him to the hilt. She froze, her breath leaving her in a rush. "Damn, Dmitri."

"Are you hurt?" He held perfectly still, cursing himself for not seeing where this was going, even as the beast he never let off the leash raged to flip her and thrust hard and deep. He touched her hips. "Talk to me."

"I'm fine." She rocked her hips ever so slightly. "It's been a while and you're bigger than your average bear."

He blinked, trying to pick that sentence apart, but she didn't give him the opportunity. Keira pressed her hands to his chest and slid almost all the way off his cock before slamming down again. "God, that's good."

She was so fucking wet and tight and . . . *Fuck.* "Condom."

"Seriously?" She cocked her head to the side, sending her hair spilling over her shoulder. "You want little Russian Irish babies, but it's a moot point because I'm on birth control. I'm clean as of my last doctor appointment, which I would be highly surprised to find that you didn't know."

He *did* know—he'd pulled her medical history the moment they met, and he'd done it again before carrying out his plan to marry her. "That's beside the point."

"It's really not. Unless you're about to tell me that you, Dmitri Romanov, are anything less than diligent when it comes to protecting yourself during sex."

"*Nyet.*" That was the point. He never lost his mind enough to forget himself like he just had. There was too much at risk, and he never forgot that.

Until now.

"Want to know a secret?" She straightened and twined her arms over her head, leaving the long length of her body open to his view. Keira rolled her hips again, circling his cock. "Well?"

"Tell me." He had no idea what would come out of her mouth next, and even her pussy clamping around his cock wasn't enough to distract him from whatever secret she was about to impart.

Her white teeth flashed as she grinned in the darkness. "I haven't been with anyone else since that first night we met."

Rushing sounded through his ears, a possessive feeling surging in him that he had no goddamn right to. *Mine.* "No one."

"Mm-hmm." She tilted her head back and drew another circle with her hips. "I knew you were bad for me, but it didn't matter because I wanted you. I still want you. I thought it would go away with time, but it only got worse. Stronger."

She might as well have been describing his experience. He hadn't taken her up on her offer that first night—or the second—but he'd wanted to. Something about the broken, beautiful woman drew him despite his best efforts.

He looped an arm around her waist and rolled them, pinning her hands over her head in the same move. "A secret for a secret, then, *da*?" He thrust deep, the possessive need to mark her as his growing with each stroke.

"*Da*." Her accent was nearly flawless. He liked to imagine a time when they'd speak his mother tongue to each other, but it wouldn't be now.

He ground his pelvis against her clit, their breath sharing the scarce distance between their faces. "I haven't touched another woman since that night. After you, no one else would do."

Keira arched up and took his mouth, her tongue mirroring what his cock was doing between her thighs. She raked her nails down his back, the biting pain in direct contrast with the pleasure drawing his balls up. He ground against her again, growling in Russian, "*Come on my cock, moya koroleva. Take what's yours.*"

"Can't understand you when you speak Russian." She bit his shoulder. "Harder."

He couldn't have resisted her if he wanted to. The night had more than proven that truth. Dmitri hitched her legs higher and obeyed her command. *Harder.* The feeling of her clenching around him drew words he had no intention of speaking. "*You feel so good, wife. Wet and tight and gripping my cock like you never want to let me go.*"

* * *

Keira had no idea what Dmitri was growling in her ear, but it made her so hot, she was on the verge of exploding. *I am fucking Dmitri Romanov.* As many times as she'd imagined it, it didn't come close to reality. His body overwhelmed hers, his solid thighs forcing hers out and up, his shoulders blocking out what little light there was, his hands everywhere at once. What made it even hotter was how intensely focused his attention was on her. She could *feel* it, even in the limited light.

He dragged his thumb over her nipple. "Stay with me, *moya koroleva.*"

"I'm here." And she was. She laced her fingers through his hair and kissed him even as his rhythm picked up, driving her closer to the edge with each thrust.

He barely let her get a taste before he kissed down her jaw and set his teeth to her neck hard enough to make her jump and moan. "Mine."

She tried to focus past the pleasure beating in time with her heart. "What did you just say?"

"Mine, Keira." He drew back even as his hips never missed a beat. "You are mine. Your body, your pussy, your conniving mind." He tapped her temple. "All mine."

Of course he had to ruin a perfectly good fucking by opening up his goddamn mouth. "Go fuck yourself."

"Why would I, when I can fuck you instead?" He kissed her.

She bit his tongue hard enough that he drew back with a curse. "Go. Fuck. Yourself. Get off me. Now."

Dmitri shoved off her, still muttering in Russian. He raked a hand through his hair. "I do not understand you."

"Why would you bother?" She drew her legs up and turned onto her side, watching him warily. Her body shook from the denied orgasm, but she'd be damned before she let that bullshit go down without a fight. She chose this, yes, but not like *this*. "I'm just a possession, after all."

He cursed, long and hard. "You are deliberately misunderstanding me."

"No, I don't think I am." It felt too representative of

their relationship for her to stay prone while he towered over her, so she shoved onto her knees, getting in his face. "You bought me. I'm your real life blow-up doll, and you want to own every part of me. Guess what, Romanov, *I'm a fucking person.* You talk to me like that again and I'm gone, and to hell with the consequences."

"Over my dead body."

Just like that, it was all too much. He'd never let her leave him. She knew enough about how he operated to know that. He might not like locking her up, but he couldn't afford to be made a fool of for the third time by an O'Malley.

And where would she run?

Not back to Boston. She'd never bring down his fury on her family, and Dmitri was too smart to push Aiden into a war he wasn't sure he could win if she was gone. She couldn't go home. She didn't even want to.

No, the truth was that Keira had nowhere to go.

She wouldn't let that stop her, though.

She shot out of the bed, dodging his hand when he reached for her. "Don't touch me."

"Keira, stop."

She snatched a robe off a nearby chair and spun to point at him. "I'm naked, Romanov. I'm not going to go sprinting into the darkness of the night. I just need some fucking space."

"*Nyet.* You will not run from me again."

That was exactly what she'd do. "Space. Respect it." Keira fled the room before he could say anything else unforgivable. Her body ached as if it resented the distance she put between them.

She'd done this.

She chose this, every step of the way, and now she was in over her head and she had no one else to blame but herself. That didn't make it any easier to bear. She might not have signed on to this situation hoping for a great love, but she *had* dared hope that she'd be something to Dmitri. Maybe not a partner, but more than a goddamn pet. If they kept this up, she wouldn't be surprised if he bought her a fucking collar to make it official.

Caged. Always caged, no matter which way I turn.

Desperation beat in her blood and she picked up her pace. She couldn't breathe, couldn't think. Keira just needed to...disconnect.

The stairs loomed before her, and she had to check her pace before she fell. She paused to shrug on the robe, finding it long enough to drag on the ground and draping several inches past her fingertips. But it was warm and comfortable, and even if she despised him currently, she couldn't deny that Dmitri smelled good.

She lifted the hem like it was some bastardized version of a ball gown and hurried down the stairs. No footsteps sounded behind her, but she didn't doubt for a second that Dmitri would send someone to fetch her. Even this small rebellion would be crushed.

It took precious minutes to reach her bedroom, lock the door, and head for the bathroom. She sank onto the floor and opened the cabinet, moving fast enough that she knocked over the vodka bottles, but not caring. She picked them up with shaking hands and lined them up in a little row on the floor in front of her crossed legs. Not enough. But it would have to do.

She unscrewed the first cap and inhaled slow and deep. The rubbing alcohol smell should have repelled her, but it smelled like a different sort of home. Like penance. Keira lifted the bottle to her lips.

It never made contact.

It was ripped from her grasp, leaving her gaping at Dmitri as he flung it into the sink hard enough that it bounced like a pinball. She gasped. "What the hell are you doing?"

"One could ask you the same thing." He pointed at the sink where the little bottle lay in a pool of liquid that she could smell from where she sat. "What. The. Fuck. Are. You. Doing?"

She crossed her arms over her chest. "I would think that's obvious."

"Oh, *da*, it's obvious enough. One bump in the road, one hint of a fight, and you almost fling yourself down the stairs in your haste to get to the bottle."

He'd been following more closely than she realized if he'd seen that misstep. She held perfectly still, even though every fiber of her being screamed at her to grab another bottle before he did something unforgivable. "If I want to drink—"

"Finish that sentence."

She'd never seen him so threatening, not even when he was actually threatening her or someone she cared about. Dmitri's gray eyes blazed at her, daring her to do exactly as he commanded. She lifted her chin. "It's my business."

"Wrong. So fucking wrong. You do not get to drink yourself to death, using me and everyone around you as an excuse while you do. That is where this road ends, Keira. It doesn't stop at the bottom of this bottle, or the next, or the next. It ends with you in a coffin and every single fucking person who cares about you standing around as they lower it into the ground. Your brothers. Your sisters. Charlie. Me."

She stared, trying to process. "It's one fucking drink."

"Lie to yourself if you must, but you will *not* lie to me."

His gaze flicked down to the cabinet she'd been hoping he would forget about, and he moved forward with purpose. "I thought withdrawal would be enough to deter you. I was wrong. If I have to assign you a babysitter to ensure you don't backslide, I will do it. Do *not* think I won't."

It wasn't a bluff. If he thought for a second that she was a danger, he'd ensure that she wouldn't have access to anything resembling alcohol. Keira leaned back against the wall with a thud as Dmitri grabbed the remaining pair of bottles and set them on the counter next to the sink. She snarled. "God forbid your *possession* be in less than perfect working order."

He muttered in Russian and poured the first bottle down the drain. Keira watched the clear liquid disappear and had the uncomfortable urge to drag her hands over the surface of the counter to drink whatever she could manage. *Fuck me, I'm a mess.*

It took less than two minutes to empty the two remaining bottles and wipe down the spilled vodka from the counter. Only then did he turn to her. "What do you want, Keira?"

Shock stole her breath for several long seconds. Had anyone since Devlin ever actually asked her that? It took two tries to find her voice. "I don't know."

His expression softened for a split second before he set his jaw. "You don't want to be a possession? Fine. Figure out what you *do* want to do and go for it. Stop being a victim and *fight*."

"I have no power!"

His eyebrows rose. "No power." Dmitri huffed a laugh. "For fuck's sake, Keira, you have more than you know and I'm a damn fool for telling you as much."

Surely he didn't mean...

She didn't have power over him. That was absurd. *He* owned *her* as he was so fond of telling her. It wasn't the other way around.

Except...

She'd seen Dmitri with nearly every member of her family, and he'd never acted around them the way he acted around her. Even as early as their second meeting, he'd indulged her, just a little. She dropped her arms to her side, letting the robe gape open. It was hardly indecent, but his gaze followed that slight bit of skin all the same. "You want me."

"You're stating the obvious. Again. Why? You know how to play the game, Keira. You've proven you have brain in that beautiful head of yours. It's only that poison that dulls it." He slashed a hand through the air toward the sink. "Choose now—perpetual victim or the role you were always meant to play."

What game was he at now? She tried for a belligerent tone. "And what role is that."

"My motherfucking queen."

CHAPTER FOURTEEN

Dmitri didn't sleep. Instead, he went to his office and cued up the monitors surveying the rest of the house. The whole night had been one giant mistake, from climbing into bed with Keira to letting her convince him that it wasn't too soon for sex to laying one of his most valued cards on the table.

He'd misplayed things badly.

He *knew* she wasn't ready, but he'd let his own desires override his plans. Just like he had time and again when it came to Keira O'Malley. Following her into her room and finding that bottle at her lips had stopped his fucking heart. It didn't matter that she would hardly drink herself to death tonight—if she took that sip, eventually she would. He might have threatened to put someone on her night and day, but the truth was that if she wanted alcohol or drugs, she'd find a way to get them no matter how tight the security.

The only thing that would stop her was if *she* made the choice herself.

He couldn't make it for her. She was right—she wasn't a possession that he could put in a glass box and only take out when it suited him. His life would be simpler if that was what he wanted from her, but he'd told her the truth. He didn't want a toy. He wanted a queen to his king.

The problem was that he didn't know if it was bait enough.

She wanted power. She'd as much as said it herself, but wanting something and being willing to take it were two very different things.

His phone rang, and he was pathetically grateful for the break. "Romanov."

"Answering your own phone at this hour? Tsk-tsk."

He went still. He knew that voice, but he wouldn't have guessed that the bitch had the audacity to phone his direct line. "Alethea Eldridge. What a pleasant surprise."

"I think it's hardly that. Did you get my present, Romanov? I picked it out just for you."

Now it was his turn to tsk. "We both know who sent that gift, and it wasn't you. Though it begs the question—did you command your daughter to do it, or have you lost even a modicum of control over her?"

"It's a moot point. The gift got its point across." Alethea paused. "How is your darling wife, by the way?"

He expected the dodge, and allowed it. Alethea was too smart to admit she'd lost control of her daughter, even if they both knew it was true. Dmitri considered her words. "I have no doubt that you love your daughter, but if she so much as touches my wife, I'll skin her alive while I force you to watch. You be sure to let her know that."

"So quick with the threats. You must really care about the girl." Alethea laughed. "Though I don't know that I'd be making threats I can't follow through on, Romanov. You don't have ready access to Mae, but I *do* have access to something you lost. Or should I say some*one*?"

He went still. *Fuck.* "I have no idea what you're going on about."

"Don't you? He was remarkably difficult to break, but my Mae is gifted. Mikhail Sokolov. He didn't give us much more than that, but I laid down boundaries to what my daughter could do. Make one wrong move on your part, and she's under orders to kill him in whatever creative way her twisted little mind can come up with—and we both know Mae is an artist when it comes to such things."

An artist was one way to put it.

He wanted to call her bluff, but Alethea wouldn't have contacted him over anything less than a sure thing. Which meant Mikhail was under their tender care—and had been long enough for them to force his name out of him. Knowing the man, it took more than simple torture to get even that much.

Dmitri had failed him. He'd sent him off and immediately become so enthralled with Keira that he hadn't checked in or sent anyone else to do the same. Another misstep. He tried to think fast and find an angle to exploit, but ultimately Alethea had him painted into a corner, and she had to know it. She wouldn't have waited until now to make contact if there was a way for him to regain the upper hand. "I'll take that under consideration."

"You do that."

He gritted his teeth and then forced his face to relax so that tension wouldn't bleed into his voice. "In the meantime, any damage done to my man from here forward will be repaid in kind, so think carefully about what you want to accomplish, Alethea."

She laughed, a harsh, grating sound. "We both know that the second you get your hands on me, you'll *repay in kind* regardless of whether he's further injured. Don't toy with me, Romanov."

"You will bring him to me. I'll consider sparing you if he's not irreparably harmed." Mikhail might very well die despite everything Dmitri had to throw at Alethea. The thought made his hands shake, and he had to press his free one to his desk to keep from throwing something. Dmitri didn't make mistakes, but he'd made a massive one when it came to Alethea—two now, if he was keeping track.

"I'll take that under consideration," she parroted back to him, and hung up.

Dmitri roared and swept the shit off his desk. "That fucking *bitch*." She'd outplayed him. He could blame his distraction on Keira, but the only one responsible was Dmitri. He'd incorrectly assumed that because the Eldridges were in hiding, they were weak and focusing on surviving.

He should have known better.

* * *

Alethea hung up the phone and turned to the man handcuffed in the dingy tub. "You know, I think Romanov might actually care whether you live or die. Fascinating."

Mikhail stared at her with hateful eyes. She'd gagged him before making the call—no one liked interruptions—but now she reached over and unbuckled the strap holding it in place. He coughed and turned his head to the side to spit. "He won't deal with you. Not for me."

"Perhaps." It would bother Romanov if this man died, but he was too smart to risk himself or his wife for a mere second in command. That wasn't what this was about. She needed Romanov off-center and expecting an attack from any quarter while her mole inside his operation did what was required. Expecting an attack from the outside would keep him busy in the meantime.

Mikhail studied her. "You can't win. You have to know that."

"Do you have any children, Mikhail?"

His expression instantly shuttered. "*Nyet.*"

It was a lie, but she chose to let it stand. Mikhail was only a means to an end. Hunting down his family was a waste of time and resources—but it wouldn't hurt for him to think otherwise. "It wouldn't matter. Fathers are wonderful, but ultimately replaceable. There's nothing in this world as pure as a mother's love." She picked up the scalpel Mae had left behind and cleaned it in the bathroom sink. "My mother created a safe space for her children to grow up in. I merely expanded it for mine. All I wanted was the freedom to operate as I saw fit. I'd bend a knee to Romanov, but being his lapdog was too much to ask."

"You are not special. Everyone who swears allegiance to him is treated the same."

"And if they're not, he plots their deaths." She set the scalpel down on the sink with exaggerated care. "He would have killed Mae and me simply for being too good at running our territory within his territory. I won't stand for it."

"Mae is *psikh*. She will kill you in the end."

She shook her head and forced the ball gag back into his mouth. "That's enough out of you. I know my daughter's faults better than anyone. It changes nothing." She would move forward with her plan through sheer self-defense. Alethea took no pleasure in the thought of killing every man and woman inside the Romanov household, but she'd do what it took to survive.

To do anything else went against her nature.

* * *

After Dmitri had walked out and left her sitting there on the floor, a few things had become clear to Keira—the main being that Dmitri was right. He'd thrown her a life raft, but he couldn't force her to climb in. He hadn't been playing a game or a part when he'd stormed into her bedroom. With the exception of the two times they'd hooked up since she arrived in New York, it was the first time she'd seen him without his carefully mocking mask firmly in place.

If she didn't know better, she would have thought he cared whether she was sober or not—and not only because he needed her not to embarrass him.

He'd offered to make her his queen.

She didn't know what to do with that. He didn't have to make her his partner, even if it was the illusion of being a partner. Queen to his king. All the power she'd craved, but no more freedom.

There was no freedom for Keira. It was time she made her peace with that.

She pulled herself from the floor. Nothing good came from poking at their last interaction, to go over it again and again, peeling the layers away to try to get to the good stuff beneath. He'd offered her what was essentially a business transaction, but if she didn't set the terms now, he'd try to steamroll her just like he had in the past. He wouldn't be able to help himself. Dmitri was a force of nature, and her being his wife wouldn't save her from his machinations.

If anything, she was more at risk than anyone else.

She padded downstairs on bare feet, praying she wouldn't run into anyone on her way to Dmitri's office. The door was closed, but no one was around to tell her to stay out, so she opened it and slipped into the room.

And stopped cold.

Papers and pens and the phone lay on the floor, scattered as if Dmitri had swept everything off his desk in a rage. Considering how clean said desk was, that had to be exactly what he'd done. He bent over it, his hands braced on the shiny surface, his shoulders heaving as he dragged in a breath. *Oh my God, I've broken the Russian.*

"Romanov?"

He didn't look at her. "Now is not a good time."

She skirted the junk on the floor and sank into the chair across from him. Last time she'd seen Dmitri, he was furious, but this was something else altogether. Her gaze fell to the phone. "Something happened."

"Keira..." He dropped into his chair and scrubbed his hands over his face. She could almost see the wheels turning, see him considering if he should tell her or order her out of the room. Holding her breath wouldn't do a damn thing to push him one way or another, but she did it all the same. Finally, Dmitri sighed. "You know the feds arrested Mae Eldridge after what she did to Charlie."

"Yes. They all but caught her red-handed. Even if the Eldridges have people in the FBI, if they hadn't arrested her, it would have been suspicious." She had a feeling Aiden was behind the suspicious timing of the police showing up just as he was rescuing Charlie, but there was no point in confirming. He'd gotten Charlie out safely. Mae was arrested.

He nodded. "They most definitely have someone on the payroll, or managed to use some sort of leverage against the judge, because Mae made bail."

"*What?*" That didn't make any sense. There was a reason people who were exceedingly violent or posed a flight risk weren't granted bail—and Mae fit both categories.

Dmitri cast a look at the empty cabinet set against the wall perpendicular to the door. She'd bet her last dollar it used to have alcohol in it. With his current level of frustration, it made sense that he was craving something that would burn down his throat and warm his stomach.

Stop that. You're sober. You didn't just have this revolutionary moment so you could stumble now.

"I sent one of my men, Mikhail, and a small team to attempt to flush her out. It went bad."

"They have him." She stated it as a fact, instantly connecting the dots. If she wasn't the reason Dmitri was pissed right now, it meant something bad happened to his man. "Is he alive?"

"*Da,* though I don't know if he'll stay that way." The icy gentleman-murderer was nowhere to be seen. The fury lacing his tone was white hot and ready to strike out at his enemies.

"Do you know where they are?" Keira leaned forward, thinking fast. "A rescue isn't a good bet, but maybe you could tip off the cops. It obviously won't keep the Eldridges locked away, but it might save your man."

He shook his head, though his gaze sharpened on her as if seeing her for the first time since she walked into the office. "I'll look into it. Thank you."

She nodded and then hesitated. She'd had a purpose for coming down here, but it seemed bad timing to throw her personal revelations at Dmitri. Her shit could wait until they had Mikhail back safely. She moved to stand, but his voice stopped her.

"You have something to say."

Keira hesitated, but if he was asking, she might as well get it out. "I'm not ready to drink myself to death. That was never the goal."

"It never is."

Keira sighed, and let her legs slide to the ground. "I don't know how to do any of this, Dmitri. I don't know how to be in anything resembling a relationship, even if it's for show. I don't know how to lead. I don't know how to be a partner. I've only ever been a pawn."

"Never a pawn. A queen in waiting." He spoke softly, the intensity of his gaze on her making her shift. As if he saw something more than that woman sitting there in a borrowed bathrobe. As if he saw the queen he'd called her.

"You keep saying that." She cocked her head to the side. "I might be a little misguided, but I'm not a fool. It's in your best interest to keep me happy and occupied so I play good little wife to you. I get that. But I'm taking you up on your offer, and you *will* deliver."

He held himself perfectly still as she stood and crossed to stand in front of the desk. "And what, exactly, will I be delivering?"

"Everything."

He didn't speak, didn't move, didn't seem to so much as breathe. She leaned forward. She had to get this all out there now. "I want full partnership. I won't contradict you or challenge you in front of your men, but all bets are off behind closed doors. You give me equal weight in important decisions, and I'll return the favor. And you remove the order for house arrest. I need to get out of this damn house, and I will not ask again." Through it all, she kept her tone even and professional. She'd already thrown enough fits tonight, and it didn't matter how justified her reaction was—she'd screwed up. She brushed her hair back. "And you won't call me yours. Not like that. Not again. I might be your wife, but you don't own me."

His lips thinned. "You're insisting on misinterpreting what I meant when I called you mine."

"I'm doing nothing of the sort. That macho bullshit might work with other women, but I've been owned, and I have no desire to continue to be so. I might never be free, but fuck if I'm going to keep letting everyone around me make decisions that impact *my* life." There was no thrill at being owned by him. She didn't have a submissive bone in her body, and she might like the way the Russian fucked, but that didn't mean she'd kneel for him.

You called me your queen, and I'm going to make you choke on it.

CHAPTER FIFTEEN

Keira made an effort to keep her shoulders back and her spine straight as Dmitri stared at her. She could practically see him mulling over her words and considering the best way to guide her into the actions he wanted her to take. She didn't give him the chance. "Alethea Eldridge is going to use Mikhail to leverage her way into our reception next week." The writing was on the wall. She'd called to feel Dmitri out and give him enough information to drive himself to distraction trying to find his man and the Eldridges. In a day or two, when she figured he was really desperate, Alethea would call and give him an ultimatum.

It's what Keira would do in her situation.

"That's what I suspect."

"She'll kill him anyway." The Eldridges were still new players in the game as far as Keira was concerned, but Alethea had proven to be both brutal and merciless. Her daughter and heir, Mae, was even more so. "She'll do it for spite."

"That's my thought as well." He nodded. "Tracking his cell is the first step. A moment." He picked up his phone, and it was like watching him cloak himself in a mask. Gone was the man who watched her with that indefinable emotion in his gray eyes. The easy posture, the lack of tension in his shoulders, gone as well. In their place was the cold bastard who could order deaths without losing sleep at night, the one who didn't see people as people but as objects on a scale that needed to tip in his favor.

He dialed, his long fingers moving over the keys. Whoever was on the other end of the line answered almost immediately. Dmitri's voice sounded even colder, as if he'd breathe ice instead of air. "Alexei, I have a task for you. Track the last known location of Mikhail's phone." He listened for a moment, and then his voice went hard. "Then find someone who can. Immediately." He hung up.

She whistled. "Do you practice that voice when you're alone? It's not as douchey as Batman's, but it's something else."

"Keira." He shot her a look, and a flicker of amusement lit those gray eyes before he doused it. "It's entirely possible that Alexei won't be able to find a tech expert who's trustworthy to carry this out. Mikhail took the only one we have with him."

Which meant he was likely already dead if Alethea wasn't using him as leverage as well. It wasn't a good sign that she apparently knew exactly which pressure point to use to trigger Dmitri to do what she wanted, but they'd deal with that after they had his man back safely.

Then she realized what he was very carefully not asking her. "You want me to bring in Cillian."

"That's your decision."

She rolled her eyes. "That's very nice of you to give me a choice, but you just said Alethea has your man, which means he's at Mae's mercy, and I saw Charlie's cuts from that bitch." Mae only had Charlie for an hour or two, but it was more than enough. She'd had Mikhail for longer. "You know that whatever Cillian knows, Aiden will know."

"It's a risk I'm willing to take."

That decides it. Dmitri wouldn't ask for outside help unless he absolutely had to. That he was so willing meant he was desperate. Her asking was barely one spot removed from him, and he had to know that. She held out her hand. "Give me the phone, please."

He grabbed his cell from where it'd fallen on the floor and passed it over. She considered for a second and then dialed the landline to the O'Malley home. If Aiden was still keeping his normal hours, he'd be up. Her brother didn't sleep much, especially when there was a crisis in progress—which felt like more often than not these days.

Sure enough, he answered with a brisk, "I don't have time for your shit, Romanov."

"It's Keira." She put the phone on speaker.

Instantly, his tone changed. "I can have men there in a few short hours."

She sighed. Always the same song and dance with her brother. Keira didn't hold it against him, though. He wanted to protect her, and his heavy-handed tactics might be annoying as hell, but he genuinely loved her. It didn't mean she was going to let him steamroll her, but she still had to steel herself against the soft feelings that rose when she thought of it. Soft wasn't what she needed right now. Dmitri called her a queen, but she wasn't a queen to the O'Malleys. "My decision hasn't changed. I'm actually calling to talk to Cillian."

A hesitation and then her brother disappeared, replaced by the leader of the O'Malleys. It was a tone she was familiar with—he wore it every time she fucked up and had to be hauled before him in his office to explain herself. Aiden's words were clipped. "It's business, then. Otherwise you would have called him directly."

"It is." She'd considered going around Aiden, but there wasn't a chance in hell of Cillian keeping this request a secret, so it was better to do it officially. Neither of them would like it, but she wanted to be taken seriously, and time was of the essence if the Eldridges had Dmitri's man.

"Give me a minute to get him."

"Of course." She could feel Dmitri's gaze on her, but she kept her attention on the painting on the wall behind his desk. It was a winter landscape, a dark forest under a blanket of new fallen snow. Breathtaking in its stark beauty, but something about it gave the impression that, just behind one of the trees, blood marked the virgin snow. An unwary soul would face certain death in that forest, be it from the weather or the predators that she was certain she could feel out of sight.

She loved it.

Rustling on the line brought her back to the present and then Cillian was there, faintly breathless. "Keira. I was sorry to miss you earlier."

"Me too." She didn't ask what he'd been doing. He wouldn't tell her the truth even if she had. She cleared her throat. "I need a favor."

"I'm listening." Once upon a time, Cillian was the impulsive party boy brother. He'd grown up a lot in the last three years, and his business voice was almost as good as Aiden's these days.

She took a careful breath. "I'm assuming that I'm on speakerphone."

"You're assuming right."

There was nothing of the brother she adored in his words, but she'd expected as much. By calling, she was putting herself firmly in Romanov's camp in a way that her marriage hadn't. They could comfort themselves that she hadn't had a choice in saying her vows, but that justification wore thin when she was calling and asking for an official favor.

No point in pussyfooting around. "One of our men was taken by Alethea Eldridge. He was tracking her and apparently got too close, and we need the last location on his cell phone in order to narrow things down and retrieve him."

"What makes you think we won't take that information and track her down ourselves?" This from Aiden.

She still didn't look at Dmitri. It was hard enough to focus with him in the room, his presence soaking into the very air. "Because you're going to give me your word that you won't move until our men are in position. You have reason to hate the Eldridges just as much as we do—more after what happened to Charlie. I'm not interested in a pissing contest over who gets to carve the bitches up. My main priority is retrieving our man and ensuring they're removed as threats."

"You keep saying 'we.'" Cillian cursed. "Are you one of them now, Keira? That didn't take long."

Her heart lodged in her throat, but none of her sorrow showed in her voice. "I married Dmitri. I would think that goes without saying. Will you help us or not?"

"What I—"

"Yes," Aiden cut in. "Text Cillian the information he needs and he'll track the phone. We won't move unless it's a coordinated effort, but we expect you to be transparent with your information."

"Of course," she lied smoothly. That call wasn't hers to make, and Aiden should damn well know that. If he didn't, it wasn't her problem.

She finally shot a look at Dmitri and found him wearing a satisfied smile. *He did this on purpose.* He knew that nothing she promised would be binding, as long as he had some degree of reasonable doubt. *Sneaky, sneaky Russian.*

"In return, you will owe us a favor to be repaid at my choosing."

"Deal, with the exception of demanding I come home. It won't happen, and if you try to fuck with my marriage or my people, the fact that you're my brothers won't save you."

Aiden cursed long and hard. "Damn it, Keira, if you'd just—"

"Thank you for the favor. I look forward to hearing from you."

Keira ended the call. "What's Mikhail's cell number?" She typed out a text to her brother as Dmitri rattled off the information, but her mind was a million miles away—or two hundred, to be more accurate. She hadn't missed the reservation in Aiden's tone—or the fact that Cillian hadn't spoken much after initially answering the phone. She'd made her choice, for better or worse. Dmitri over her family. She could comfort herself saying it was a choice she'd made to protect them—and it was the truth—but if she wanted to step into the role of partner, she needed to do it in full.

Which meant she had to let them go.

Something must have shown in her expression, because he studied her. "That was more difficult than you expected."

"I don't know what you're talking about. It went swimmingly." She might be willing to work with him while they figured this out, but that didn't mean she was going to lay herself bare for his perusal. *Fuck that.*

The look on his face said he wasn't about to let it go, so she acted before she could think too hard about what she was doing. Keira stood and shrugged off the robe—*his* robe—letting it fall to the floor to pool around her feet.

Dmitri inhaled sharply, and his gray eyes seemed to swallow up the light in the room. "You can't dodge hard questions forever, *moya koroleva.*"

"I know. But I'm dodging them tonight." It was easier to rattle off the words with a confidence she didn't feel when he was looking at her like *that.* She took a step toward him, and then another.

His lips quirked even as he raked a look over her from the top of her head to her toes. "We tried this already, and it went poorly."

"My fault." She could offer him that truth. They'd already talked about it, after all. Keira skirted the desk and moved into the small space between his chair and the polished wood. Dmitri didn't retreat, which left his face in line with her breasts. Feeling almost shy, she cautiously reached out and stroked her fingers through his dark hair. "It won't happen again."

He closed his eyes, not quite leaning into her touch. "It's challenging to argue with you while you're naked and I can scent our sex on your skin."

She kind of loved how his accent got thicker when he was turned on. Keira kept stroking his hair. He wasn't going to turn her down, and they both knew it, but she was willing to let him take his time coming to that conclusion. "I'll remember that."

"That's exactly what I'm afraid of." He opened his eyes and tilted his face up to meet her gaze. The move had his breath ghosting across her nipples, and she shivered. Dmitri noted the move the same way he seemed to note everything in his vicinity. "You chose earlier."

"I did." She might not have liked what he'd said while they were fucking—or been proud of her reaction to it—but she'd made the choice to get them there despite his cautioning her otherwise. Keira traced a finger along the shell of his ear. "I'm choosing now, too."

Still, he didn't touch her. "Make no mistake, Keira. You're mine. You may not like hearing it, but it's the truth. You see it as my wanting to put a collar around your neck. That's not what being mine means." He shifted to take her left hand and lifted it between them. Her giant ring gleamed unnaturally bright in the low light. Dmitri stroked his thumb over the backs of her fingers. "You took my ring. You'll take my name. You are *my wife*."

"All that means—"

"Let me finish."

He twisted his hold until his hand was on top. It was only then that she realized he wore a ring, too. *Should have noticed that before now*. It was thick silver with a darker silver band in the middle of it. Nothing close to as flashy as hers, but she'd bet it was damn near unbreakable—it didn't look like normal silver. So typically Dmitri.

He lifted his ring finger and let it drop. "I wear a ring,

too. We are meant to play different roles in this and my men will always answer to me first, but that doesn't mean your role is the lesser of the two. You are mine, yes, but I am yours as well."

Yours.

"Mine." She tried the word out, liking how it fit. But she wasn't about to let him take full control of this the same way he had on everything else—no matter how attractive she found the idea. "I'm hyphenating my name."

Dmitri barked out a laugh, the sound shocking in its authenticity. He lifted her onto the desk and slid his chair closer, forcing her to spread her legs to accommodate him. "O'Malley-Romanov."

She didn't actually care one way or another, but she liked pushing his buttons. "I don't know. Romanov-O'Malley kind of has a nice ring to it."

Dmitri guided her feet up to the armrests of his chair and then pushed her knees out, leaving her totally exposed. "I'll make you a bargain." There was nothing in his tone to show he was affected by having her in this position, but his eyes burned hot, and his touch was almost reverent as he coasted his hands from her ankles up the outside of her legs, and then around to her inner thighs.

Yes, yes, yes. She had to work to keep her anticipation in check and forced her voice to sound as polite and distant as his. "I'm all ears."

"If you can keep from coming until two, you can have the order your way." His lips curved in a wicked smile. "But if you cannot hold out, you will be Keira O'Malley-Romanov."

She kind of liked the ring to that, but she refused to give in on principle. She checked the clock. "I don't know,

Romanov. You only gave yourself five minutes. I can last that long."

"We shall see, won't we?" He kissed the side of her knee. It was a chaste touch as such things went—there wasn't even a hint of tongue—but she felt it like a bolt to her core.

Keira clamped her lips together to keep a moan inside as he dragged his mouth up her inner thigh. Dmitri took his time as if he wasn't the least bit worried about the seconds ticking down to her victory. He licked the dip at the top of her thigh and then pressed his face to her pussy and inhaled deeply. He growled in Russian against the most private part of her as if telling her all the things he planned on doing to her.

It shouldn't be so hot to hear him speak his native language against the most private part of her...except, she couldn't think of a single thing hotter. Keira gripped the edge of the desk and fought to hold perfectly still.

He ran his tongue reverently over her, exploring her folds. Tasting her. Savoring her. Dmitri used his thumbs to part her. "You are beautiful everywhere, *moya koroleva*. But a man could become addicted to seeing this little bud swell for him." He breathed on her clit. "So responsive. So fucking sexy. I could spend a lifetime fucking this pretty pussy with my tongue, my fingers, my cock. I'll never get enough of you."

"Dmitri." His name came as a whimper instead of the command she'd been aiming for. She cast a wild glance at the clock. *Two minutes to go. I am so fucking screwed.*

As if sensing her thoughts, Dmitri spread her folds and circled her clit with his tongue. Once, twice, and then flicks that had her crying out. It was too much and not enough, and the seconds ticking down only made the whole thing immeasurably hotter. He pushed two fingers into her, pumping slowly as if he had all the time in the world while he worked her with his tongue.

She looked down her body and found those gray eyes on her, hot and possessive. It was too much. She'd never stood a chance to begin with. Keira dug her fingers into his hair and came with his name on her tongue.

CHAPTER SIXTEEN

Dmitri licked his lips and cursed when someone knocked on the door. "Hold," he barked. It was one thing to have Keira spread for him on his desk. It was entirely another to have any of his men witness the show. It was for Dmitri and Dmitri alone. He kissed first one thigh and then the other. "I have a task for you."

She blinked those hazel eyes at him. "I'm going to need a minute before I regain the use of my legs."

Sheer satisfaction flared. The sated look written over her face was *his* doing. She'd be feeling the aftereffects of pleasure for a while now, and every time she did, she'd think of him.

Tomorrow, he'd give her more to think about.

"Dmitri," she prodded. "The task."

He dragged himself back to what had to be the priority. "I need you to take charge of the reception."

"What? No."

He spoke quickly and firmly. "This is important, Keira. I'm not giving you busy work. This will be our first event as a married couple, and as such, we'll have half a dozen families there who want to kill each other. Your family will be there, which means both the Sheridans and Hallorans will be represented as well. Ivan and his wife will be there, watching to report back any weakness they see. It is vital that it proceeds without any issues."

She thinned her lips, but finally nodded. "I don't know how to throw a party."

"I find that hard to believe. You might have never been a host, but you've seen countless ones put together." He saw the flicker of doubt and relented. "I have a woman who I usually hire to take care of these types of things. I'll set up a meeting for the two of you in the morning."

"Okay." She hesitated. "Are you coming to bed?"

A loaded question if he'd ever heard one. "Not tonight." It was more complicated than he wanted to go into, but it had become increasingly clear that Keira truly could be his if they could get out of each other's way long enough to make it happen. Dmitri didn't think he knew how to do that any more than she did, and they didn't have the luxury of time to figure it out.

Sink or swim.

Those were their only options.

He caught her around the waist, holding her in place, and waited until she met his gaze. "I want to. I would give damn near anything to spend the rest of the night with you. But if I come upstairs now, we will fuck, and you need time."

"I think I know what I need more than you do."

He tightened his grip. "You need sleep more than you

need my cock. Part of what it means to be a leader is making personal sacrifices. Not being with you tonight is a sacrifice that has to be made."

Keira finally nodded. "I get it." He released her, and she immediately slid off the desk and went to grab his robe. She shrugged into it, and a part of him mourned the loss of the view.

"Have dinner with me tonight—tomorrow night, I mean."

"We already tried that—several times."

"No politicking. No guests. Just you and me."

Keira tied the cloth belt and hesitated. "Fancy shit?"

As much as he wanted to have her the way she was now, her hair tangled from their earlier fucking, her skin flushed from her orgasm, naked but for his robe, he wanted to capture that glamorous version of her, too. He permitted himself a smile. "Fancy shit."

"Then hold on to your ass, Romanov. I'll show up ready to wow." She strode out of the office, and he watched her go. It was a gamble putting her in charge of anything, but one he had to take.

More, one he wanted to take.

What would Keira become if given the freedom and power to do so?

Only one way to find out.

Alexei appeared in the doorway after Keira had left. "There's new information on the Eldridges. I sent it to your computer."

"Spasibo."

He spent the next hour wading through the new intel. He needed to know how Alethea had secured Mae's bail. Obviously the woman had dirt on someone higher up, and knowing who would be vital in continuing on this path. If she was doing something as mundane as blackmail, her victim would likely thank him for removing the issue. If it was a partner or some sort, that changed things.

The problem was that Keira's scent had permeated the office. With every inhale, he was transported back to the vision of her spread out on his desk, her hazel eyes hooded with pleasure, her body primed for him. All he wanted was to leave the office and climb the stairs to the master suite so he could finish what they'd started here.

The phone rang, and Dmitri took a few precious seconds to get his head on straight and check the time—five a.m.—before he answered. "Romanov."

"I have the location for you." Cillian O'Malley's voice was perfectly businesslike, just like it was every time he was forced to deal with Dmitri.

He didn't even blame the man for it. If their situations were reversed, he imagined he'd feel the same. The only difference was that Dmitri wouldn't show his dislike every time they interacted and give his enemy ammunition to further get under his skin.

There wasn't time for any of that at the moment. "I'm listening."

"I've e-mailed it all over, though you'll have to click through a few links to unscramble it."

Dmitri blew out a silent sigh of relief. He'd been sure Cillian had the skill set, but it was one thing to be sure in theory and another to have the man following through on his promise. "If I find them, I'll relay the information."

"No, you won't, and we both know it. Which is why Mark will be arriving shortly."

Fuck. The last thing he wanted to deal with was an

O'Malley man underfoot. They had enough going on without adding to the dynamic, and he didn't know how Keira would react. Would she be pleased to see Mark? The thought didn't sit well with Dmitri. Mark lived in the O'Malley house. He would have had unlimited access to her over the years. Dmitri wasn't aware of their relationship being anything other than platonic, but he'd also missed the fact that Seamus had hurt Keira.

Going home had done a number on her. He hadn't had a chance to address it yet, but that was the event where everything pivoted. She might not have been settling in here, exactly, but she'd withdrawn after going back to Boston. Dmitri initially thought it was because of homesickness, but she walked out of that house with ghosts in her eyes.

"Romanov."

He shook his head. He shouldn't be mentally wandering while on the phone with an O'Malley. Even Cillian. *Especially* Cillian. "I'll discuss it with Keira, and we'll make arrangements for him to stay where she's most comfortable." *Somewhere not in this fucking house.*

"You're really married to this fantasy that she wants to be there, aren't you?"

"I'm really married to her."

Cillian cursed. "She's barely more than a child."

"She's twenty-one and more than capable of making her own decisions. But that's the problem, isn't it? Not that you think I forced her, but that she chose me."

"I know how you operate. You wouldn't have to force her if you leaned hard enough on the right pressure points."

It was a valid argument, and it *was* how Dmitri pushed Keira into coming with him in the first place. That changed nothing. "She made her choice. Respect it."

"I'll respect it when I believe it was actually her choice," Cillian fired back.

Her family would never believe it. Even if her feelings for him turned into something real, they'd still doubt and question and chip away at the fragile balance Dmitri had fought so hard for. There was too much history between him and the O'Malleys for them to do anything else.

For the first time, he regretted the plays he'd made—just a little.

"Thank you for the information, Cillian." He hung up before either of them could say anything further. They would never be friends, but he respected Cillian for the way he treated Olivia and Hadley.

That didn't mean he'd let the man do whatever he damn well pleased, though.

Dmitri pulled up his information on the Eldridges and plugged the range of coordinates into his system. He doubted they'd stay in one of their publically owned properties, but he knew a number of their safe houses—the very ones Mikhail had been searching.

It was almost impossible to pin down an exact location on a phone that had been turned off or destroyed, but Cillian had noted the towers it had pinged last and created a circle that Mikhail must have been inside at the time. The Eldridges could have snatched him off the street and transported him elsewhere, but there hadn't been so much as a single sighting since Mae posted bail. He didn't doubt that Alethea had her people working on her behalf, but the Eldridge territory was on the opposite side of the city from where Mikhail had been.

No, Dmitri's instincts said that his man had gotten too close to their hiding location. Normally, he'd have the other man who went missing with Mikhail—Yuri—working on any electronic searches required, but he couldn't for obvious reasons. Dmitri had the ability to do this; it would just take him longer.

He pulled up the file he had with the addresses of known Eldridge safe houses and checked them against the map Cillian had provided, but none of them were within the range of the coordinates. They weren't even close enough to warrant Mikhail stumbling on the Eldridges. Dmitri stilled. *Stumbling on them.* That had to have been what happened. Mikhail was the best there was—he wouldn't have allowed himself to get caught while confirming a property. They must have caught him unawares, which meant they saw him before he saw them.

If none of their safe houses were in that area, it meant they were staying with someone else. The first thing he'd done when Mae took Charlie was to reach out directly to every single person who might owe allegiance to Alethea and let them know in no uncertain terms that he'd eliminate any and all hints of betrayal. To a man, they'd gotten out of his way. Alethea should have no one to turn to among that group.

He'd still check, but it didn't feel right. She had to know Dmitri would hunt her down without mercy. She wouldn't risk herself and Mae by staying with someone who would betray them. The only people she could be *sure* were loyal was her family, and right now that consisted of Mae, who had no resources of her own.

No, there had to be someone else.

He picked up his phone and dialed from memory. Ivan picked up almost immediately. "I didn't expect to hear from you so soon. Why aren't you still fucking that girl into submission?"

Ivan was the oldest of the Romanov cousins, which gave him some freedom the others didn't have. Namely, that he talked to everyone exactly the same fucking way—as if he had better things to be doing. "I need some information."

"That wasn't even an artful dodge." Ivan tsked. "All work and no play, and it's no wonder that your new wife has to act out to get your attention. It's a dangerous game you're playing, Dima."

You have no idea. It was achingly clear that Ivan wouldn't get around to business until he'd satisfied his curiosity, so Dmitri sighed. "It's nearly ten, Ivan. I have to let her out of the bedroom at some point. We have a reception to plan, after all."

He snorted. "Last time I saw the girl, you hadn't consummated your marriage. A fucking waste, if you ask me."

"I didn't ask you." His life would be a lot simpler if Ivan wasn't able to infer so damn much.

"You should have. We're family. What's more, we've been *friends* for how many years, Dima? And the first I'm hearing about this girl is when you summon me to your residence like some kind of servant. Then *she* shows up, this tiny furious package in a gown that couldn't have said 'fuck you' louder if it was written across those pert little tits of hers."

"Enough." He didn't want anyone talking about Keira's breasts. Fuck, he wanted to go back in time and haul her ass out of that room before the other man got an eyeful. It would have showed weakness, but at least she would have been shielded from Ivan. But no, he'd been too proud, too intent on playing his game, and she'd accomplished exactly what she'd set out to do—chaos.

Ivan chortled. "Got under your skin, didn't she? Never

thought I'd see the day where the proud Dima is brought low."

Enough was enough. He injected ice into his tone. "The marriage started off with some bumps, but they've been resolved."

If anything, Ivan laughed harder. "You're too smart to believe that. You don't give that girl a purpose, and she'll bring your house down in flames."

As if Dmitri didn't know that. He pinched the bridge of his nose. "I'm working on it."

"Be sure to keep me updated on how well that goes over." Another laugh and then, between one breath and the next, all amusement was gone from his voice. "You needed a favor."

"Less a favor than help recalling a bit of old gossip. Alethea Eldridge is rumored to have killed her husband around the time you were still living in New York. Does he still have family in the city?" It had been before Dmitri's time, and his father's files were woefully lacking in information about Clayton Norris and what remained of his people.

"Oh, that." Ivan grunted as if settling deeper into a chair. "She didn't kill her old man, though it served her purposes to have everyone think she did. You were too young at the time, and I don't know that I would have registered it at all, but Clayton Norris owed money to my mother's oldest brother. The fool liked to gamble and didn't know when to stop. I think Alethea tried to curtail it, but he just went behind her back to our territory."

"I have a list of Clayton's brothers—Jermaine, Dane, and Earl—but no other information. My father usually kept better files, but those three seem to have disappeared into the ether. There is no record of them anywhere in New York."

"That's because they're dead. Your father tangled with the Norris clan a few times back in the seventies, but they were dwindling fast by the time you were born. Clayton was the only remaining living child of his parents, and allying with Eldridges through marriage was their last-ditch effort to remain relevant—and it failed."

Damn it. If the brothers were dead, so was his lead. "You said she didn't kill him. Who did?"

"She was supposed to—her mother wasn't a fan—but ended up backing out at the last moment. Instead, she bought off his debts with my uncle and Clayton disappeared. We thought she'd sent him away, but there was a rumor a few years ago that he was back—if not *back*. You understand?"

He's alive. Adrenaline surged, and Dmitri had to pause a moment to get control of himself. *Got you, Alethea.* "One last question."

"Naturally."

He ignored that. "Does he have any known pseudonyms?" If anyone would know that, it would be the people he gambled with. Ivan's uncle had a reputation for being incredibly thorough when it came to people who owed him money.

"Just the one—John Cash."

"You're joking."

"I wish I was. I only remember because it was so absurd."

The whole point of a pseudonym was to fly under the radar—something impossible to do if one insisted on using the name of a famous musician. "Thank you for the information."

"Easily given. I look forward to your party, Dima. Something tells me that it'll be one for the record books."

It certainly was shaping up to be. "Good-bye, Ivan." He hung up before his friend could say anything more absurd.

Several minutes later, he had the confirmation he needed. Neither Clayton Norris nor John Cash brought up anything worthwhile, but a Clayton Cash owned a small apartment in Brooklyn—which happened to be almost directly in the middle of the area Cillian O'Malley had given him.

Dmitri called Alexei. He barely waited for the other man to answer to speak. "Gather the men. I believe I've found our Mikhail." He hung up. Calling Keira was tempting, but she deserved an update in person, and it wouldn't take but a minute to deliver the information.

And maybe he wanted to see what she'd gotten up to in the last few hours.

It would take his men a good ten minutes to be ready to leave, which gave him plenty of time to hunt her down in the grand ballroom in the center of the house. He'd always found the room ostentatious—much easier to plan things at a neutral location than to invite friends and enemies alike into his home—but it was the best option for the reception. The O'Malleys needed to be reassured. His allies had all been here before. The Eldridges were a wild card, but he fully intended to remove them from the playing field before they had a chance to do further damage.

Keira glanced up as he walked through the door. She looked like herself for the first time since she'd arrived in New York, wearing a pleated skirt that was several inches too short for his peace of mind, and a cropped muscle tank top with some band he'd never heard of written across the front. The black shirt showed off her pale skin, and he frowned when he realized he could count her ribs. "Have you eaten?"

"Yes, O benevolent overlord. I had two eggs twenty minutes ago to keep my energy up for this appointment you set up for me, and Pavel basically threatens me with snacks every hour or two." She stopped and frowned. "You're leaving."

"I found him." He didn't feel relief—not yet—but he hoped they wouldn't arrive too late. It was in Alethea's best interest to keep his man alive, and she was too smart to kill him and lose her pawn. But Mae was unpredictable, and he didn't have the utmost faith in her mother's ability to control her.

Keira set her notepad down on the table and crossed to him. "Be careful."

With her looking at him like that, he could almost believe she was worried about him. *Too much to ask.* He took her hands and pressed a kiss to each one of her knuckles. "Stay in the house until we return." He belatedly added, "Please."

He half expected her to throw a fit, but she just raised her eyebrows. "You think this could be a bait and switch."

"I think that there is little Mae Eldridge would like more than to see you dead." It was all too easy to remember the head she'd had delivered to him and superimpose Keira's features on it. *No. I will not allow it to happen.* He squeezed her hands, knowing damn well that if he tried to order her to stay, it would be as effective as waving a red flag in front of a bull. "I respectfully request that you stay put." He hadn't forgotten that someone had infiltrated the house, but Pavel could be trusted. *That,* Dmitri was sure of. "I'll send Pavel in when I leave. He'll hover, but allow it as a favor to me. Please."

She smirked, even as her hazel eyes were concerned. "You're being polite, which means you're worried. I'll be good and stay in my cage while you're gone—this time."

It was the best he was going to get. "Thank you."

"Come back safely, Romanov. No one gets to torture you but me."

CHAPTER SEVENTEEN

Keira lasted an hour. Sixty minutes before she went a little mad wondering what Dmitri had found. Or if it was a trap. If Keira were in Alethea's situation, she would have guessed that Dmitri wouldn't sit idly by. He might not be as superhuman as she used to believe, but he was still very, very good at what he did.

She just hadn't expected . . . loyalty.

She flung herself down onto the couch in the library and picked up the book she'd left there a few days ago, before setting it down again. She wasn't settled enough to read right now. She kept playing the look on Dmitri's face when he spoke about Mikhail. They weren't friends exactly—she got the impression that Dmitri didn't have much in the way of friends—but it genuinely grieved him to think of his man at Mae's mercy.

The temptation rose to call him, but whatever he was

doing, he didn't need the distraction. So she called Charlie instead.

She answered on the second ring. "Hey, stranger."

"Hey." Now that she had her on the phone, she didn't know what to say. They'd only had two weeks together after Aiden brought Charlie home, and it wasn't like there was a ton of history to pull from. *Maybe I should have called Carrigan.* But she didn't trust her sister's anger at Dmitri. If Carrigan thought for a second that she'd get away with it, she wouldn't hesitate to send Halloran men down here to snatch Keira and bring her home, and to hell with the consequences.

"Keira?"

She snapped back to the present. What was she doing? She didn't normally mentally wander in spirals. "Hey." Shit, she'd already said that.

"Is everything okay?" Charlie took a deep breath but seemed to reconsider before she offered an escape plan. Again.

Get your head on straight. Everyone is freaking the fuck out and you're not helping with this space case shit. "Yeah, things are fine. I'm just bored and I was wondering what you were up to."

"Ah. *That*, I know all too well." Someone spoke in the background and Charlie must have moved away from them, because the sounds got quieter and then disappeared altogether. "Is he letting you keep going with Krav Maga?"

"He doesn't have a choice." She rolled onto her side and stared at the doorway to the library as if she could will Dmitri back safely. "We've talked about it, and he said he'd found a gym, but shit keeps hitting the fan, and my actually going keeps getting pushed back." And rightfully so. Her restlessness was less important than the safety of Dmitri's people, but that didn't mean she was handling it any better. "I guess there's stuff I could be doing in the meantime, but I don't even know where to start."

"That, I can help with. Hit me with your e-mail address, and I'll send you over a few options for training plans to get your endurance and strength up. You'll still feel like you were hit with a truck for the first couple weeks, but it'll help."

"Thank you. You're a lifesaver." She rattled off her e-mail address.

"I try." There was a rustling in the background as if Charlie had settled into a couch. "I know I'm not supposed to ask, but how are you—really?"

The genuine worry in her friend's tone had something clenching in her chest. Keira knew she was loved. She had never really doubted it, even if she was often swept aside in favor of whatever crisis the family was dealing with at that given moment. It made it easier to leave with Dmitri, because at least this time, she could be helpful in averting said crisis.

Call her a fool, but she hadn't anticipated their reactions. She started to brush off Charlie's concern, but stopped. Charlie had been there for her—had *seen* her—when the rest of her family was off in their own little world. She was Keira's friend. If she couldn't be at least a little bit honest with her friend, who could she be honest with? "I'm... okay. Going through withdrawal was fucking hell and I never want to go through that again." If she concentrated, she could imagine the taste of vodka on her lips, and the craving never seemed to go away—especially after the near miss last night. Maybe it would fade in the coming days, weeks, months, but Dmitri's earlier words kept her rooted in place. *I don't want to drink myself to death. I want to live.*

"I'll admit to having mixed feelings about that. I'm glad you're sober, but Romanov's methods leave something to be desired."

She couldn't argue that, but Keira knew without a shadow of a doubt that if he hadn't kick-started that process for her, she might never have taken the first step. Numbness was too tempting—too comforting. She hadn't wanted to give it up. She still craved it more than she rightfully should.

She flopped onto her back. "It's weird being here. Not bad-weird, exactly, but the house is saturated with Dmitri's presence. It's like he's imprinted on the entire thing, and there isn't a room that's exempt."

She closed her eyes and, for the first time in years, tried to picture how she'd put that feeling into paint. *Black and white and every shade of gray I can manage. Bold slashes. A speckle of . . . blue? No, a deep royal purple. Because he's not a king—he's a motherfucking emperor.* Keira grinned and opened her eyes, her fingers itching for something that wasn't a bottle. "I think I want to start painting again."

Charlie was silent for a beat, another, a third. "Fuck, Keira, that's wonderful. I won't pretend I get what you see in him, but if you're happy, that's all that matters. It might take Aiden ten years to come around, but it *will* happen."

The words stilled some of her budding excitement for painting. Ten years with Dmitri Romanov. Ten years would mean there were children. Ten years . . . She tried to picture what that life would be like and couldn't wrap her head around it.

Things were too new, too unsettled. She and Dmitri

might be trying to find common ground, but they hadn't exactly managed it yet. Sex, they could do and do well—once she got out of her own way, at least. The rest of it? That remained to be seen. She couldn't think about it too closely. She refused to. "Thanks."

"I can't wait to see you—even if it's at your reception."

Her fucking reception. She didn't know what to think of Dmitri putting her in charge of it, but it was more complicated than she'd anticipated. There were so many moving parts. She had no idea how Carrigan did this shit on the regular. "Well, I'm the one organizing it and putting it together, so if there *is* a reception at this point, it'll be a goddamn miracle."

"I can't pretend I know a single thing about that." Charlie laughed. "I am not the party person. It's all politics and making sure the right people sit next to the other right people so you don't start an incident. It's too subtle for my skill set."

She could argue that Charlie was more than capable of being subtle when it suited her, but she and Keira got along so well because neither had that kind of personality. "You and me both."

"You could always call Carrigan."

She tried to picture how that conversation would go and sighed. "Only if I get desperate. I'm sure I can pull this thing out of my ass. It's just a matter of getting it done." She should be working on it right now, but after a meeting with the event planner where she snapped at the woman four separate times over things that shouldn't have been a big deal, Keira rescheduled the rest of the meeting for another day. She couldn't focus with worry over Dmitri nibbling away at the back of her mind.

She lifted the phone off her ear and checked the time. He'd been gone for three hours. No matter what kind of traffic he'd hit, he should have been there by now. Hell, he should have been there and dealt with it and called her to...

To report? Keira almost laughed, but not like anything was funny. Dmitri didn't report to her. He didn't have any obligation to check in with her like he was her husband. Even if that's exactly what he was.

She sat up. "Hey, Charlie, I'm going to call you later."

"Sounds good. Hang in there." She didn't offer to extract Keira, which she appreciated. The sooner her family made their peace with her choosing to be here, the better.

She checked her phone again—nothing. *Fuck this.* She couldn't just sit here and stew. She had to *do* something. Since she'd promised Dmitri she wouldn't leave the house, she stalked to their bedroom and rifled through the closet until she came up with some workout clothes. A quick stop to check her e-mail and print out the first plan Charlie had sent her, and she was off to the small gym on the first floor. She just had to keep moving and stay focused on something besides the minutes ticking by without a word from Dmitri.

If he finds out I was worried about him, I'll never hear the end of it.

* * *

Dmitri watched his men tear apart the little apartment they'd tracked down. It was grungy, and the appearance of a film over every surface wasn't entirely imagined. The kitchen had mismatched plates stacked in the sink, and the living room held a single couch that should have been burned years ago. The TV on the absurdly tiny entertainment center was huge and was the only new thing in the whole place. One of the bedrooms held a scattering of both men's and women's clothing—the difference between them as staggering as that between the couch and the television.

The bathroom was what turned his stomach. A bar had been mounted at the front of the tub, just above the faucet. From the way the metal was worn, there had been metal cuffs dragged over it again and again. It didn't take much connecting of the dots to know the kind of torture they'd set up here for Mikhail.

But the Eldridges were gone and Mikhail with them. From the look of the place, they'd left shortly after Alethea called him—possibly as recently as this morning. They *had* been there, though.

"Nothing, boss."

Nothing except the piece of paper he held in his hand. A taunt Alethea hadn't been able to resist.

Have to be faster next time, Romanov.

She thought this was a game she could win. He read the paper for the twelfth time. It didn't make sense. Even if she had a mole in his household, he and Aiden had her backed into a corner. They had ensured her daughter was arrested, even if Mae had posted bail. Alethea should be desperate and reckless right now in her attempts to find a way around Mae's charges—she shouldn't be taunting him as if she knew something he didn't.

Dmitri snapped his fingers. "Burner phone."

Alexei passed one over, and Dmitri wasted no time calling the one fed he believed to be beyond reproach. John

Finch was incorruptible—and had been since he was a beat cop in New York back in the seventies. He'd eventually made the jump to the FBI's organized crime division after his daughter was born, and he'd worked his way up the ranks. He had a sterling reputation—at least professionally.

"John Finch."

It took precious seconds for him to get a hold of his temper. Like most people in his world, Dmitri loathed the man, but he'd always had a distant sort of respect for him. No longer. Not after seeing the unforgivable skew of his priorities. Family should matter more than a job. For John Finch, it didn't.

But he kept all that out of his voice when he spoke. "Someone's been making questionable decisions."

"Dmitri Romanov." Finch's voice was flat. "To what do I owe the dubious pleasure of a direct call from you?"

"You didn't do your job. You had Mae gift wrapped for you—by your daughter, no less—and she's slipped through your fingers. Explain that."

"I don't have to explain shit to you."

He strove for patience. Surrounded by evidence of his man being tortured by those bitches, there was none to be had. "Wrong. You may think you're on the side of good in this little spat, but you're no different than I am. The only difference between us is that *I* don't let my enemies escape."

"I had nothing to do with that choice." Finally, some emotion bled into the man's voice. *Frustration.* "The judge ultimately made that decision. There isn't a damn thing I can do about it. It's out of my hands."

"You don't believe that any more than I do." Even if Mae

was technically beyond his jurisdiction, Alethea wasn't. Nothing had happened to deter them from continuing to investigate her. "Surely you have surveillance at the very least."

"I've been ordered to stand down." Finch's voice was so low, Dmitri thought he'd misheard him. But then he continued, "You're on your own, Romanov." He hung up.

Fuck.

He'd consider the implications of *that* later. "We're leaving. Now." There was nothing to find here, and if Finch wasn't authorized to keep tabs on the Eldridges, it meant they had leverage higher up the chain than he was. Which meant Dmitri and his men were likely under surveillance themselves—if they hadn't been already. *A mole and we're being watched. Enemies on all sides.*

He'd left Keira mostly unattended at home.

They didn't run out of the apartment, but they moved at a good clip. Dmitri dialed as he slid into the backseat of the car they'd stashed close by.

Keira answered, panting slightly. "You're alive."

"And you as well." He breathed a small sigh of relief. He hadn't really thought someone would attack the house, but at this point he couldn't take anything for granted. Alethea had outmaneuvered him multiple times in the last few weeks. He couldn't let his mistakes create an opportunity for her to hurt Keira.

She sucked in a breath. "Why wouldn't I be?"

"Are you okay?" Dmitri frowned. "You're breathing awfully hard."

"Shut up, Russian. I'm pathetically out of shape and weaker than I want to be, but I will still kick your ass from here to Boston and back."

The pieces clicked together. "You're working out."

"Ding, ding, ding. We have a winner." Another gasp. "God, I know this gets easier, but it sucks right now."

He didn't know what to say to that. Dmitri utilized the gym regularly because being in fighting shape was vital. One never knew when it'd make the difference between life and death—winning and losing. He couldn't remember the last time he took more than a day or two off, so there was no getting back in shape.

Something beeped in the background and Keira coughed. "Okay, you have my full attention. Did you find him?"

"*Nyet*. They knew we were coming and cleared out."

"Fuck. I'm sorry, Dmitri. It was a good lead."

They'd moved on it as quickly as they feasibly could. Those extra fifteen minutes he'd taken to find and talk to Keira hadn't made a difference...but he felt something akin to guilt all the same. "We'll find him." Somehow. If Alethea continued to dodge him, he'd have to dangle bait enticing enough to get *her* to come to *him*. "It's just a matter of reexamining the problem and coming up with a new solution." He realized he'd never told another person how his thought process worked. He was so used to functioning alone, but it felt like second nature to include Keira.

"We won't let the bitch win." She sounded almost normal now, if furious. "Come home, Dmitri. We'll figure this out."

Come home.

For the first time, he *felt* like it was actually coming home—as if that house might be termed a home instead of a residence. Keira's presence filled it with life, and she'd barely gotten started.

He settled back against the seat, reluctant to end the call. "How did the reception planning go?"

"Well, I'm in the gym for the first time in God knows how long—that brief stint with Charlie notwithstanding. That should tell you something. I rescheduled the rest of the meeting for tomorrow. She—shit, I forgot her name."

"Claudia."

"*Claudia.*" Keira snorted. "That woman is *scary.* And I know scary women. Her smile gets all tight and freaky when I do something she thinks I shouldn't be doing. I hope dental work is covered by her insurance, because she's going to bust a tooth or two by the time we get to the party."

He chuckled, the sound loosening something in his chest that had been claustrophobically tight since he realized the apartment was empty. "I'll see that she gets a bonus for her trouble."

"Do that. It can't be easy holding my hand through this process, but she's managed not to do anything totally fucking rude or patronizing yet, so she's earned it."

He usually didn't work closely with Claudia. She was a holdover from his father, and she'd planned enough events that he spent a single meeting going over what he needed and then trusted her to take care of the rest. "What time are you meeting her again tomorrow?"

"Ten. Unless there's something else you need me to do?"

She sounded so hopeful, he laughed again. "I know it's getting late, but perhaps we could still have our dinner."

"The fancy one?" He could almost see her perk up. "Wait, how long until you're home?"

There was that word again. *Home.* "An hour or so, depending on traffic."

"I can make that work. But I have to go right now. Bye."
She hung up on him.

He chuckled for the third fucking time in five minutes. What the hell was this woman doing to him? Dmitri
should be furious and scheming and tearing the city apart
to find Mikhail, but here he was, looking forward to a late
dinner with his wife.

He closed his eyes for a long moment, and then opened
them again. He had an hour to get the ball rolling on the
search. His leads would need until tomorrow morning to
begin to pan out, but at least he could start now. Foolish to
think he was getting soft simply because Keira was in his
life now, but it didn't change the fact that he'd missed more
steps in the last few months than he had in his entire life
leading up to the point where he encountered her at that
rave.

For the first time since his father died, Dmitri had something to prove—both to himself and to whatever enemies
might be watching.

CHAPTER EIGHTEEN

It took two minutes to put a call out to Blackbird for a carryout order and dispatch one of the Romanov men to retrieve it at the allotted time. Blackbird didn't normally do carryout, but Keira had no problem dropping Dmitri's name to ensure they complied. They were within his territory, and he'd made a passing comment the other day about how he looked forward to getting back to his regular meals there—with her at his side, of course.

Since Keira had no intention of going out in public with the dress she'd picked out, she'd just have to bring his favorite restaurant to him.

She took a quick shower to scrub the sweat off her body. Her stamina sucked, she was too goddamn skinny, and she'd gotten dizzy doing even the shortest workout on Charlie's list. Keira had never spent much time worrying about diets and exercise—other than the activities Devlin dragged her along on when he got a wild idea—but it was probably time to start thinking about that. Right now, she was a liability. If there was a situation where she had to run or fight, she was dead in the water.

Not a victim. Not to myself and not to anyone else.

She didn't know where to start with either—other than the Krav Maga gym she was *determined* to check out the day after the reception. Keira would make time, regardless of what else was going on. She had to.

She left her hair down but threw some product in it to accent its waves, and went classic with her makeup—smoky eyes and red, red lips. Then she stepped back and took in the full picture.

If we get through dinner without Dmitri fucking me on the table, it's going to be a goddamn miracle.

Keira grinned. She picked up the hem of her dress so she didn't trip over it and headed downstairs. Dmitri might need to change or shower or something, and she didn't want him to see her before it was time for dinner.

She met Pavel at the door to the family dining room—smaller and more intimate than the massive formal dining room off the ballroom. He had to be capable and trustworthy, because Dmitri had put him on her detail, but his cherub cheeks made it hard to guess his age, and his body was a little too lanky, as if he hadn't quite grown into his frame yet. He must be older than the eighteen she'd estimated his age to be.

His blue eyes went wide, and then he hastily averted them. "Mrs. Romanov, I've set up the food as you asked."

Mrs. Romanov. Or, rather, O'Malley-Romanov.

It had a nice ring to it, though she'd never admit it aloud. She'd technically lost that bet, though she wasn't sure coming against Dmitri's mouth counted as losing in any sense of the word.

"Thanks." She waited for him to step out of the way and strode into the room. The food was under covered plates, and there were two settings situated on either side of the small table. *Good.* Satisfied everything was as it should be, she walked to the window and glanced out onto the street before closing the thick gray curtains. There didn't need to be any witnesses for what would happen next.

Since there was nothing else to do but wait, she poured herself a glass of sparkling water and took a cautious sip. *Water with bubbles is fucking weird.* She'd stick with ginger ale next time. Grape juice felt too juvenile, even if it was as close to wine as she was going to get. Sparkling water was supposed to be fancy shit, but it was just plain unnatural.

Glass in hand, Keira moved to the painting dominating the wall across from the door. It had to be five feet tall, and easily twice as wide, taking up the entire surface. Something that size should have overwhelmed the space and made it claustrophobic—especially with the curtains shut—but it felt like a window into another world. The scene was framed as if looking out a window and into a small courtyard garden. Rough brown stone contrasted with flowers hanging from window boxes, the blooms creating rainbow waterfalls designed to lead the eye to the main attraction—the woman sitting on the edge of the bathing pool with her back to the painter. Her long dark hair was pinned up on top of her head, leaving her neck and shoulders bare, and she was half-turned as if she'd heard someone calling her name and was caught in the midst of responding.

It was utterly captivating.

"You like what you see."

She'd heard the door open, but wasn't ready to abandon the painting yet. "Very much." She could have stopped there, but with her heart too full and her mind still wrapped up with what the artist had accomplished, she kept going. "I wish I could do this kind of thing." Keira waved her hand at the woman, the flowers, the stone. "It's phenomenal."

Dmitri stopped next to her, his shoulder brushing hers. "Tell me about your paintings."

If he had asked her—demanded, really—in any other situation, she would have changed the subject, but Keira was helpless in the presence of the damn painting. "It's been years since I've bothered."

"Grief presents itself in strange ways." Just that. No demands for an explanation. No trying to convince her that she'd made the wrong choice when she put down her brushes and never picked them back up again.

"It might have started that way, but it wasn't what kept me from going back to it." Why was she telling him this? She didn't tell *anyone* this.

Dmitri didn't seem to move, but she felt his presence intensify all the same. "The alcohol and drugs."

It wasn't a question, but she answered. "There's a cost that comes with being numb." Finally, finally, she turned to face him. "I don't feel numb anymore."

His gaze never left her face. He had a guarded expression, but beneath that was something almost like hope. "Do you want supplies and a designed room to paint in?"

Yes. She tried to temper her response, but he saw it despite her not giving it voice. He nodded. "I'll see it done."

She exhaled slowly. "Thank you." *God, what is this? It's almost a civil conversation.*

"If there's anything specific you need, give me a list, and I'll send Pavel to retrieve it."

At the mention of her babysitter, she laughed softly. "Poor Pavel. He'll have a heart attack before the month is out if you keep him on my detail. He's very..." When Dmitri raised his eyebrows, she rushed on. "He's not exactly the picture of a hardened criminal who's seen everything."

"What makes you say that?"

Her cheeks heated, and the painting drew her gaze again. "I made him blush and stammer."

Dmitri barked out a laugh. "*Moya koroleva*, have you *seen* yourself? I stood in the doorway for a full five minutes before I regained control of myself. Poor Pavel didn't stand a chance."

She knew she looked good, but he was overstating things. She nudged him with her elbow, a part of her secretly thrilled at the easy contact. "Flatterer."

"Truth speaker." He turned and took her hands, shifting her to face him fully. Dmitri lifted her hands up and out, leaving her on display for him. "Where in all that's holy did you find this dress? I'm not sure if I should gift a fortune to the designer—or kill them."

* * *

Dmitri tried to dial back his words, but the sight of Keira robbed him of his calm and icy demeanor. She smiled at him with fuck-me-red lips, her makeup doing something to create the illusion that her hazel eyes were even larger than normal, and her hair had an artful tumble to it that brought to mind fucking.

Or perhaps the dress was to blame.

If her wardrobe at the last dinner had been a taunt, this one was a tease—an invitation. The ropes of silver rhinestones circled her neck and shoulders before turning into a netted pattern that clung to her breasts and hugged her ribs, narrowing down to the V of her legs. A second set of roping rhinestones circled her hips. On its own, the pattern would have been captivating, but combined with the sheer nude fabric beneath it, Keira's body was on full display.

For him.

He let go of one of her hands and traced his thumb along the top string circling her hip. The fabric might as well not have been there. As he watched, her dusky nipples pebbled and her lips parted. "Tell me something."

"Sure." Her voice was breathy and more than a little needy.

"How many of these dresses do you have tucked away? A man can only survive so many heart attacks." When he'd walked in and saw the line of her body covered with shimmering stones beneath the low light, he'd almost gone to his knees right then and there. He craved the taste of her, craved the feeling of her body beneath his hands, craved the way he was totally and completely present whenever they were together physically.

The outside world ceased to exist.

He couldn't live like that indefinitely, but the little pockets of time they carved out could be invaluable—if they found a good balance between them.

Keira winked at him, looking downright playful. "I guess you'll have to wait and see."

"If you'd worn this..." He squeezed her hips and then ran his hands up her sides to cup her breasts. Dmitri cursed. "*Moya koroleva*, if you'd worn this to the dinner with my cousin, I would have—"

"Don't you dare say you'd kill Ivan." Her smile dropped away. "I like him, and no one needs that toxic masculinity bullshit."

She was so fucking prickly. He shouldn't like it nearly as much as he did. Dmitri circled her nipples with his thumbs. "He is my cousin, Keira. He's just as much a monster as I am, but that changes nothing. There had to be loyalty to one degree or another. I wouldn't hurt him because you pulled a stunt like this." He pinched her nipples, earning a sweet gasp from her lips. "What I *would* have done was drag your disobedient ass into the hallway and fuck you against the door."

Her jaw dropped. "You wouldn't."

"I would have." He released her breasts and stroked up her arms and over her shoulders to cup her neck between his big hands. She didn't flinch, didn't look the least bit worried by the position, and he loved her a little bit right then for it. "Each thrust would have rattled that door, each cry from your mouth would have echoed through the room. Ivan would have known *exactly* what I was doing to you."

Keira lifted her chin, pushing her throat more firmly against his palms. "Maybe I *should* have worn this then."

"*Nyet.*" He gave a sharp shake of his head and leaned down. "I like having this view all to myself. I fully intend to savor it through our meal and then have you for dessert."

"Dmitri." She placed her hand on his chest, directly over his heart. "I want your cock tonight. I want you every way you'll give it to me. No freaking out. No bullshit. Just you and me."

"In every way I'll give it to you," Dmitri repeated. His body went hot at the possibilities she laid before him. Last night was hotter than it had any right to be considering they hadn't finished what they started. To have Keira with no holds barred for the entirety of the night... *For the entirety of our lives.*

He rocked back on his heels. "Let's eat. And then I'll feast."

She licked her lips. "It's a deal, then."

Dmitri followed her to the table, hanging back a few steps to enjoy the way her ass looked beneath the dress. She was still too skinny for her frame, so as soon as she removed the coverings from the food, he motioned to one of the chairs. "Sit. I'll serve."

"The gentleman-murderer Dmitri Romanov, serving me dinner? Lucky me." She grinned and put an extra bit of sway into her step as she moved past him to the chair he'd indicated.

Keira was stunning in nearly every situation, but a playful Keira was something to behold. He hesitated to say anything that could potentially damage her mood and went to work loading up two plates. It was only when he got to the roasted spaghetti that he stopped short. "This is from Blackbird."

"It is."

She sounded so pleased with herself, he had to smile in response. "I wasn't aware they allowed carryout."

"They don't." Her grin widened and she leaned forward and lowered her voice. "But I'll tell you a secret—all I had to do was drop your name and they bent over backward to give me whatever I asked for."

"Ah."

"Indeed. I tipped them absurdly, of course."

He chuckled. "Of course." It was so very like her to have put the fear of God in them and then turned around and paid a large tip to reward them for meeting her demands. *A good way to earn loyalty. I would wager they won't hesitate to give her whatever she asks for next time she deals with them.*

Dmitri set her plate in front of her and then took his seat. It was only when he settled in that he realized she was staring at him again. "Is something wrong?"

"No...just wondering who this plate is for because there's no way you think I can eat this much."

He frowned at the portions. They were large, but it wasn't as if she had food piled a foot high on the plate. "You lost weight you couldn't afford to lose while you were going through withdrawal, and you were already too thin to begin with."

Her eyebrows almost disappeared beneath her side-swept hair. "Are you going to throw me in an oven and eat me after you fatten me up?"

"That's ridiculous." He picked up his fork and set it down again, hating that he felt flustered. "You're putting words in my mouth. Your body is beautiful as it is, and you damn well know it. But if you're going to be expending calories you need by working out, you need to take more in to make up for the lack."

"Uh-huh."

He couldn't divine anything from her tone except surprise, and it drove him mad. Dmitri picked up his fork again. "I can walk you through certain dietary regimes that help build muscle if that's something you're interested in. If it's not, that's fine, but you can't afford to skip meals either way."

"Would that be why poor Pavel was trying to stuff two sandwiches onto my plate all casually this afternoon?"

He refused to look away. "Possibly."

Keira managed to hold on to her shocked expression for a full five seconds before she burst out laughing. She had to set down her fork and hold her arm over her stomach to keep from sliding out of her chair, and Dmitri frowned. "I don't see what's so amusing."

"You, Romanov. *You* are 'amusing.'" She managed to look at him—and then promptly burst into giggles again. "Oh my God...you as a mother hen...I can't...it's too much."

He held himself with all the dignity he could manage with her laughing her ass off at him. "There's nothing wrong with being concerned with my wife's health."

"*Look* at my plate." She waved at it, still laughing, though she made a blatant effort to get her glee under control. "I'm sorry—except sort of not sorry—but you caring about what I eat or don't eat is adorable."

He didn't see what was so adorable about it, but the conversation could very easily have devolved into her furious at him for trying to meddle in her nutrition, so Dmitri considered being laughed at the lesser of two evils. "If you say so."

"I do. I do very much say so." Keira shook her head, still grinning. "Now, pick that fork back up and eat before it gets cold. I find myself eager to move on to dessert."

Eager did not begin to cover it.

CHAPTER NINETEEN

Keira barely focused on the food in front of her. It tasted good, but beyond that, nothing mattered except eating enough to satisfy Dmitri so he'd have *her* for dessert. He never took his attention off her as they ate in comfortable silence, and she couldn't help replaying his filling her plate over and over again in her mind.

He was...taking care of her.

There was no other way she could explain that action. She was functioning just fine, so there was no reason for Dmitri to be overly concerned with what she ate or her weight, but he obviously was—and not in a creepy douchey way, either. He wanted her healthy. He was offering to give her tips to help her get her muscle mass up to par, for God's sake. That was *not normal*.

Or, rather, it wasn't normal if he was thinking of her as a sexy lamp like she'd originally feared. It could be a manipulation tactic, but really, why bother to go through the trouble to lie so thoroughly? She was here, exactly where he wanted her. He didn't *have* to put forth an effort, because she wasn't going to leave as long as he kept his word and did everything in his power to maintain peace between himself and her family.

And yet he *was* making an effort.

She finished her pork chop and sat back, pleasantly full. The whole dinner had been so comfortable, she worked up the courage to ask him something she'd been wondering about since she got to New York. "What was it like growing up in this house?"

"What do you mean?"

"It's just..." She waved a hand, trying to find the words. "It's intimidating and kind of over the top. I mean, our town house in Boston is, too, but it's a totally different feel from this place." It might be the color choices—the walls and carpet skewing toward the darker end of the spectrum—or the furniture, all heavy and made of dark wood, or the striking lack of windows, but it kind of felt like she was in a modern-day gothic mansion. "You don't have your first wife locked up in the attic, do you?"

He snorted. "I'm hardly Rochester."

Of course he knows I'm referencing Jane Eyre. "I don't know. You both have the brooding loner thing going for you. Being compared to Rochester isn't a bad thing—he's sexy in that should-definitely-be-in-therapy-but-is-still-a-hot-bad-boy kind of way."

Dmitri shook his head, though his gray eyes shone with amusement. "I'll take your word for it."

"Do that. My word is excellent even if my taste in men is questionable at best." She rolled her eyes. "Anyway, back to the original question—Child Dmitri and this big, scary house."

"I never found it scary." He shrugged. "It's home. It's always been home. Though I suppose it looks that intimidating from the outside." He hesitated as if considering imparting something else, but finally nodded almost to himself. "It reminds me a bit of my father, to be perfectly honest."

A piece of personal information? Talk about striking gold! She strove to keep her tone nonchalant. "Oh?"

"He was forbidding. It's not easy to hold a territory, let alone to build one, and he wasn't interested in compartmentalizing. Everything was for the good of the family, whether it was good for the individual or no."

"I'm familiar with the sentiment." Her father had been the same, though she didn't get the same angsty feeling from Dmitri that she got from most of her siblings. Seamus O'Malley was a piece of shit, and he was more than happy to pave his way to more power on the backs of his children. Their mother wasn't much better, but she at least threw them an emotional bone every once in a while. "You loved him?"

"Love is a strange word. It calls to mind a particular feeling, which I don't associate with my father, but I suppose I did." Another shrug. "I respected him. I realized early on that his actions ensured the safety of our family and our men, and I watched closely so that I would be able to do the same when the time came."

So much responsibility to toss onto a kid. "How old were you?"

"*Ya ne znayu.* Eight. Perhaps ten."

Keira froze. "You...That's very young." At eight and ten she was still firmly a kid and enjoying something resembling an idyllic childhood as Devlin's sidekick. Her older siblings had felt the weight of their duty earlier than she had as the youngest, but even Seamus held off screwing with them until they were old enough to be useful—high school, at least.

"Don't pity me, Keira. It wasn't a bad life as such things go."

"Sure, but saying that it could be worse is silly. It could just as easily have been better." She did some quick math in her head. "Was Olivia around at that point?"

"*Da*. Though her mother was kept away for the most part, so I didn't see much of her until years later."

How incredibly lonely. At least her house had been filled with her siblings. Dmitri had only had himself. Keira gave herself a mental shake. He didn't want her pity, and whatever his childhood had been like, it was the past now. She couldn't go back and change it. She shouldn't even want to.

Dmitri swirled his sparkling water. "In a way, it's a good thing that Olivia fled to Cillian. They're bound to give Hadley more siblings to grow up with. There will be cousins as well." He met her gaze. "Your brother isn't your father."

"You don't have to tell me that." Not too long ago, she'd wondered if Aiden would follow in Seamus's footsteps—his actions had sure as fuck indicated that he'd do exactly that—but he'd shifted gears and was taking steps that she'd never expected. "It's only a matter of time before he and Charlie start popping out kids, too." Though they wouldn't start until the biggest threats to the O'Malleys were taken care of. She knew Aiden well enough to know that.

"*Da.*" He slid his plate aside. "Do you want children, Keira?"

"Do I have a choice?" she fired back—and instantly regretted it. They were actually having a nice time, and she had to fuck with it. Every single time. *I am not a possession.*

Dmitri watched her closely. "I won't force you there any more than I'd force you to have sex. It's your choice. It's always been your choice."

He might say that, but it couldn't be clearer what *his* priorities were. The dynasty. The family. Though, for the first time, Keira had to wonder if Dmitri's insistence on children was motivated—at least in part—by growing up alone in this massive house. A family would fill up the echoing space much more effectively than all his men combined.

She had to look away and then felt like the worst kind of coward for doing it. "Not yet. Not while the Eldridges are still out there and gunning for us."

"I won't let her have you."

She glanced back at him. "Which her?" Mae was scary, but she seemed to look at every problem as if it was a nail for her to hammer. One size fits all. Alethea had cunning if she was able to outsmart Dmitri for this long, and *that* was a special kind of terrifying because it meant they didn't know where she'd strike next.

The fact he thought they'd be coming for *her* spoke volumes. She frowned. "Why do you think they've focused on me?" There had been the drive-by shooting back when she was still living in Boston, but that could have just as easily been aimed at Charlie—or Carrigan for that matter.

This time, Dmitri looked away, which sent alarm bells

pealing through her head. She straightened. "Something happened that you haven't told me about."

He sighed. "Mae had a gift delivered last week."

A gift. Whatever it was, he'd gone almost pale when he mentioned it, so it had to be bad. She took half a second to consider whether she really wanted to know. *Yes, I have to know what I'm facing. If I want to be an actual partner, I have to be able to handle it.* "Tell me."

He hesitated, but almost immediately relented. "She killed a girl who looks remarkably similar to you...and sent me her head."

"Her *head*?" Her voice squeaked and she had to take a shallow breath. "That bitch cut off some poor girl's head and sent it to you." She tried to process that, tried to wrap her mind around the level of evil Mae Eldridge had to possess to think that was a legitimate step. Keira stared at the half-eaten food on her plate, feeling sick. "Have you ever done something like that?"

"Killed an innocent to threaten another? *Nyet.* Murder is a last resort—never a threat."

Which wasn't to say he *hadn't* murdered someone before. She considered that, and then compared it to what she knew of how her family operated. Keira couldn't say for sure that Aiden's hands were perfectly clean of blood, and she knew for a fact Cillian's weren't. "Would you have killed Olivia's ex if you'd gotten to him before Cillian did?"

Dmitri met her gaze steadily. "Do you want to know the truth or the pretty lie?"

"The truth."

"I would have made an example of him thoroughly enough that no one would have come near her for the rest of her life."

She should have been horrified. But all Keira could think was that maybe that would have been better than Cillian shooting the fucker. Killing him had left its mark on her brother, and she would have spared him that if she could have. He had protected Olivia and Hadley—and he would have done it all again if it came down to it—but the killing had changed him.

She set her napkin aside. "You almost killed James Halloran because my sister chose him over you."

"*Nyet*." A sharp shake of his head. "She broke her word to me, and I clearly outlined the consequences of doing so." He shrugged one shoulder. "James's brother would have struck regardless of whether he thought he had my support. If your sister hadn't broken her word, he wouldn't have had my support. It's a simple as that." His lips quirked. "I can't say I'm sorry she did, though."

If she hadn't, it would have been Carrigan sitting across from Dmitri right now instead of Keira. Maybe she should be bothered by that, but what-ifs didn't matter—only what actually happened. Dmitri and Carrigan hadn't so much as kissed, and who gave a fuck even if they had?

Me. I'd give a fuck.

She swallowed hard and stood. "Then there's—"

"*Moya koroleva*, are you going to insist on laying every one of my sins out in the open? There are many, even if you're only listing the ones associated with your family." He stood as well. "The O'Malleys were a threat and I proceeded accordingly. It became personal over time, but it didn't start that way."

She licked her lips, her gaze dragging over his suit. It fit him well, hugging his shoulders and tapering to his narrow waist. She wanted it on the floor. Keira took a deep breath and tried to focus. "If you could go back and do it again, would you?"

"I don't make a habit of second-guessing myself."

"That's not an answer." He always spoke like that when he didn't want to answer a question directly, and it made her furious. *He* made her furious, though she still wasn't sure if it was a good thing or a bad thing.

Dmitri shook his head. "I don't have an answer for you. Did I underestimate your family repeatedly? *Da*. But if you think for a second that I regret the path that brought us to this moment—with you as my wife—then you're mad." He rounded the corner of the table and took her hand, tugging her against him. "I would commit unforgivable sins as long as it ensured this same endgame. I will make no apologies for that, Keira. Not a single fucking one."

CHAPTER TWENTY

Dmitri waited for Keira's condemnation. He expected it, considering what he'd just admitted. Perhaps he should have played things smarter, should have wooed her with soft words and sincere promises, should have kissed her to distract from their conversation and let things progress physically from there.

That wasn't who he was.

He didn't hide in the shadows. He didn't flinch at what was required of him. He simply took care of business and moved on.

Still, it was a small leap of faith to lay that before her so baldly. She was right to accuse him of the shit he'd done to her family, because it was all true. He made no apologies, though. They brought him to her, and she was worth every single action. Despite everything, he'd never directly hurt a single person she cared about, and that was the only thing he couldn't come back from.

Keira ran her hands down his chest and back up again. "I don't know if I'm more disgusted with myself or with you that none of that is enough to make me turn away."

He exhaled slowly. "There is no turning away from this." It wasn't strictly true, but she fit too well into this life to do anything else. She'd had her chance to get out— several of them over the years—and she'd never taken that step. Because she didn't want to.

That, at least, he was sure of.

"Then I suppose I had better embrace it." She undid his top button slowly and dragged her fingertips down to the next to repeat the action. "I'm still not sure I like you very much."

"No lies between us." He trapped her wrists, holding her hands against him. "You like me very much."

She blinked those big hazel eyes at him. "I like parts of you, at least."

Dmitri laughed, the sound surprising him. "I suppose a man has to start somewhere."

"I know the perfect place." She extracted her hands from his grasp and undid his slacks.

Keira started to go to her knees, but he caught her elbows and kept her on her feet. "*Nyet, moya korleva.* You are a motherfucking queen, and you go to your knees for no man—not even me."

She tilted her head to the side even as she slid her hand into his slacks and grasped his cock. "You were just on your knees for me less than twenty-four hours ago."

And he'd loved every single fucking second of it. "That's different." As she was so fond of pointing out, he had all the power and she only had what he gave her. His going into a temporarily submissive position changed nothing.

Her newfound role was too fragile, and he refused to do something to create a repeat of the night before. He'd already misjudged things and spooked her—several times. He wouldn't allow it to happen again.

"Dmitri Romanov, are you trying to handle me?" She kept one hand on his cock, casually stroking, and flattened the other against his chest.

"That would be unwise of me." Even if it was exactly what he was doing.

"Yes, it would." She exerted the slightest bit of pressure, backing him up a step, and then another, until he felt the chair behind him. "Sit, boy."

"Keira—"

"Think twice before you say whatever you're about to say." She gripped his cock harder and leaned into him, the rhinestones of her dress pressing hard against his chest. "Sit down, Dmitri. Sucking your cock isn't going to magically make me something I'm not, and I'm dying for a taste of you."

His chest tightened in something he couldn't put into words. "That's not what was on the menu."

"One little blow job isn't going to ruin your ability to own my pussy for the night." She kissed his neck, speaking her next words against his skin. "But it is going to have me aching for you even more than I already am. Be good and sit down right now, and I'll hold off fingering myself while I suck you."

"You aren't a woman. You're a goddamn siren."

"*Da.*" She pushed him again, and this time he let her guide him back into the chair. Keira braced herself on the back of the chair and gave him a few more strokes. "It's really not fair that you have a perfect cock in addition to everything else. I mean, I know being a gentleman-murderer is a check in the negative column, but the balance is still in your favor." She let go of him and lifted the hem of her dress enough that she was able to go to her knees between his thighs.

With her this close, he didn't bother to resist the temptation to cup her breasts and tease her nipples with his thumbs. "My perfect cock is at your disposal."

"I know."

The words, simply stated, shot through him. Dmitri tipped her chin with two fingers. "I'm yours, Keira, and you are mine."

She gave a sexy little smirk. "I won't freak out again. Now stop stalling. Sit back and shut up while I have some fun."

He laughed again. "Do your worst."

"I intend to." She gripped his cock and licked the tip, her gaze never leaving his face. "Tell me something."

"Mmm."

"What does *moya koroleva* mean?"

She could have looked it up easily enough, but he liked that she was pushing him for the translation. He laced his fingers through her hair and pulled it back from her face so he had a clear view. "It means 'my queen.'"

Her victorious grin was reward enough. "Oh, Dmitri, I'm going to make it so good for you. You don't even know." Before he could respond, she sucked his cock into her mouth.

His thoughts shorted out. Fuck, his ability to do anything but sit there and take what she was doing to him disappeared. Keira went after his cock as if she truly needed it. She gently dragged her teeth up him and then flicked his head with her tongue. Seeing her red, red lips closed around his length was an image he'd never forget until the day he died.

She pinned him with her gaze, the defiance in her eyes telling him she knew the effect she had on him. Dmitri fought to keep his eyes open and not miss a single second of this experience. He smoothed his thumbs over her temples as he shifted his grip on her hair. "You're as beautiful like this as you are doing everything you do."

She moved off his cock just enough to say, "You're pretty beautiful like this, too, Dmitri."

"Dima."

She paused. "Dima?"

He couldn't believe he was saying this, but the words were pulled from him, as slow and sticky as taffy. "The people I care about call me Dima."

"Dima." She said it as if tasting it. Tasting him. Keira flashed him a brilliant smile. "I like it. Now stop distracting me and let me have my filthy way with you."

* * *

Keira sucked Dmitri's cock like her life depended on it. Easier to focus on the feel of his thick length in her mouth and throat than to try to unpack her feelings about his allowing her to call him Dima. *Dima.* The name didn't fit... and yet it did. Dmitri was cold and distant, the man she'd known up until moving in with him. Dima was...something else altogether. Dima was the quiet pain on his face when he caught her about to drink on the floor of her bathroom. Dima was the man who sat across the table from her and told her about his lonely childhood. Dima was his fingers in her hair and his face tense as he watched her give him the blow job of a lifetime.

She might not know how she felt about Dmitri, but she liked Dima a whole hell of a lot.

Focus on the here and now. Deal with the rest later.

Right now was about enjoying the feel and taste of him and very carefully not thinking too hard about anything else. She sucked harder, taking him deeper. *More. I need more.*

"Keira. *Moya koroleva*. I'm close."

She knew. She could tell by the way his cock swelled against her tongue and his fingers tightened in her hair as if trying to maintain control. She released him, slow and steady, and the way relief warred with need would have made her laugh under different circumstances. "Dima." Oh yes, she liked the way his name felt on her tongue.

"Da?"

He expected her to demand her orgasm before they had sex. She could tell from the hungry way his gaze fell to her breasts and then lower. He had wanted *her* for dessert, after all.

Too damn bad.

She gave his cock a slow stroke with her fist. "I want you to fuck my mouth. Come for me."

His gray eyes widened and then closed for a breath. "You will be the death of me."

"But what a way to go." She grinned because she knew she had him. He wanted her pleasure, but he enjoyed the hell out of what she was doing to him, and there was something just downright dirty about her demand that he had to love as much as she did. "Up, Dima."

She scooted back a few inches and tugged on his cock.

His brows slanted down. "You can't simply use my name to get whatever you want whenever you want it."

"Can't I?" Another tug and he pushed to his feet, his fingers still tangled in her hair. Looking up Dmitri's body while she was on her knees had her pussy tightening in anticipation. Tonight wouldn't end when he came the first time. From the forbidding expression on his face, he had all sorts of payback planned for her, and she couldn't wait to experience it.

Keira held his gaze as she took his cock back into her mouth, sucking him deep. She silently challenged him to do exactly what she'd demanded, and he cursed long and hard in Russian. Or at least she thought it was a curse. It sure as hell had the right tone for it. Abruptly, his grip tightened on her hair, forcing her still.

And then he began fucking her mouth. Shallow thrusts as first, as if testing her commitment to this. Keira practically purred and relaxed completely, taking everything he gave her, never looking away. He cursed again, this time in English, and his strokes picked up tempo. Dmitri stared down at her, his expression tight and almost pained, but there was something like wonder in his eyes.

"I'm close," he gritted out.

She ran her hands down his hips to his thighs and dug her nails in a little, a silent permission to do exactly what they both wanted. If her damn dress wasn't in the way, she would have fingered herself to the vision of his lips parted and eyes slid closed as if he couldn't hold it together for a second longer. He orgasmed, her name on his lips, and she swallowed him down.

Dmitri's grip loosened on her, but she kept sucking him, luxuriating in the feeling of his small shudders and the way his thighs shook beneath her hands.

"You will put me in an early grave." But he said it almost fondly as he hauled her up his body and kissed her soundly. "You are a gift."

"Or a curse, depending on who you ask." Instead of coming out snarky like she intended, her words were breathy. Needy.

He kissed her again, all teeth and tongue and desire. "I have one modification I'd like to make to this dress."

How the hell was he thinking about the *dress* at a time like this? She was so wet, she was pretty sure it drenched her inner thighs, and if she didn't get his hands or mouth on her, Keira might be the one expiring on the spot. She shoved his shirt off his shoulders. "Sure. Whatever you want."

She paused at the sight of him shirtless. They'd been naked together in his bed, but it was too dark to see him properly. She knew he had tattoos—of course he did—but seeing them was something else altogether. She barely got a good look at the landscape piece before Dmitri let go of her and went down on one knee. She tried not to startle at the familiar position, but at least he was distracted enough that he didn't notice her reaction. He ripped her dress with a sharp move, tearing across the tops of her thighs and across the back just under her ass. "This is the length it always should have been."

"Oh, I don't know. That might have been trashy." She snorted.

"*Nyet.*" He inched up the fabric just enough to expose her pussy. "I don't know what would be more frustrating— knowing this part of you was locked away beneath all that fabric...or knowing you were close enough to touch but being denied it until now."

When he talked like that, he made her sound like some kind of temptress. It *had* been the point of her clothing choice for tonight, but Dmitri had always looked at her the way he was now—as if he were a dog on a fraying leash, a few precious inches from the tastiest steak he'd ever seen.

He used one hand to keep her dress up and bracketed her hip with the other. He inhaled deeply. "I can smell how much you need me."

"Then what are you waiting for?" She tried and failed to keep the need out of her voice.

"Some things are worth taking your time with. Enjoying every second." He nudged her legs apart and spread her with two fingers. "I like the look of you after you've sucked me down. You loved every second of that."

"You were too gentle with me." She regretted the words as soon as they escaped, but here in this moment with him so close, her filters suffered a critical error—not that they'd been that great to begin with.

His gaze flicked up to meet hers. "Next time, I won't be."

Next time.

Oh, she knew there'd be a next time. Of course there would be. But the possessive way he said as much made every nerve in her body flare with heat. She could have Dmitri over and over again. There wasn't a limit on it.

"What's put that look on my wife's face?"

She considered commenting on his determination to name her as his wife, but decided to let it go. Tonight was a special night, for better or worse. There was no need to ruin it with petty bullshit. Keira reached down and slid her fingers through his hair. The casual touch thrilled her as much as the sexual ones did. "I was thinking that I could fuck you ten times a day if I wanted to."

Amusement flickered in his eyes and the curve of his lips. "Impossible to run an evil empire if I have my cock buried in you ten times a day." He kissed first one hip bone and then the other. "But it's a sacrifice I'm willing to make."

"Mmm." She sucked in a breath as his lips grazed her pubic bone. "Though if we let the evil empire run itself, eventually it'll fall apart."

"True." He shifted, hitching one of her legs over his shoulder and pressing her back against the table.

It was difficult to focus with his breath ghosting across her clit, but she made a valiant effort. "I think three times a day is reasonable. It's important to have balance."

Dmitri nuzzled her pussy. "Your compromise is duly noted. Now, stop talking business. My wife has needs that require attention."

"What a polite monster you are."

He growled against her skin. "Your monster, at least in this."

I am in over my head and sinking fast. She couldn't bring herself to care as he licked her like she was his favorite flavor of ice cream. Before she could really relax into it, he stood and spun her around. She caught herself on the table, knocking over his glass and sending silverware flying. Keira sucked in a breath to protest, but then Dmitri's mouth was at the small of her back.

Oh.

He pushed her dress higher as he licked his way up her spine and then finally shoved the fabric over her head. It hit the table with a heavy *thunk*, but she couldn't bring herself to care that it would be stained beyond recognition. Not with his hands cupping her breasts and plucking at her nipples. He started his way down her spine again, his palm coasting over her stomach to cup her between her thighs. He slid two fingers in her as if sure he could do anything he wanted to her and she'd welcome it with arms open wide. *He's right.*

Maybe she should be ashamed of that truth.

His other hand slid up the back of her thigh, pushing her legs wider, and squeezed her ass, spreading her cheeks. He kissed one and then the other, his tongue sliding over her skin in lazy circles as he worked her pussy with his fingers. "Tell me something, *moya koroleva*. Have you ever had a man here?" He traced a finger down the seam of her body.

She froze, trying to think past the pleasure he dealt her in waves. "That's a sexist fucking question."

His chuckle didn't do a damn thing to help her string two thoughts together. "My mistake. Have you had a man or woman here?" He exerted the slightest pressure against her ass, not quite pushing his finger inside, but definitely testing her.

She jerked forward, which only served to shove his fingers deeper inside of her. Keira gripped the table and moaned. "You're such a dick."

"*Nyet.* I'm asking a perfectly simple question." He nipped the upper curve of her ass. "Though I believe I have my answer."

She was far from a virgin, but that didn't stop a flicker of fear from starting in her chest. "Dima, I—"

"Relax." He gave her ass one last squeeze and stroked his hand down her other leg, widening her stance further. He pushed a third finger into her, never picking up his tempo, the slow stroke of ownership turning her on far more than it had a right to. "Whatever you think of me, I won't take your ass for the first time while bending you over our dinner table."

She tried to pick apart that statement. "Does that mean you fully intend on taking my ass in this position some-time in the future?"

His dark chuckle did nothing to calm her racing heart-beat. "Only if you ask me to."

Though she was tempted to tell him that would never happen, Keira wasn't anywhere near as confident of that fact as she'd like to be. She leaned over fully, bracing her forearms on the table. "I like the idea of you fucking me here, Dima. Right now."

"When I'm ready. Not before." His mouth closed around her clit and she moaned, grinding against his face. Dmitri sucked her gently, just as slowly and thoroughly as he'd been fucking her with his fingers.

She gripped the table so tightly, her knuckles went white. There would be no demands this time. She was at his mercy the same way he'd been at hers. All she could do was hang on for the ride.

Except Keira had never been that good at being passive.

She moaned, fighting to get the words out. "Dima, please. I want you inside me when I come."

CHAPTER TWENTY-ONE

Impossible for Dmitri to deny Keira when she kept requesting things he fucking *needed*. Fuck her mouth. Lick her. Kiss her. Have her coming on his cock instead of his tongue. Sheer habit had him wanting to deny her that if only to maintain control of the situation, but the truth was that he'd lost control the second her knees hit the floor.

He'd damn them both to give her whatever she asked of him, though he wasn't about to give her that ammunition on his own.

He ran his hand up her spine as he shucked off his slacks. The picture she presented, bent over the table they'd just had a meal on, her ass tipped up in offering, her pale skin flushed with desire...

"I would have this as a picture, *moya koroleva*."

She shivered beneath his palm. "Then take it."

He scooped up his phone and dropped into the chair he'd sat in while she sucked his cock. From this angle, he could just see her pussy glistening. Dmitri snapped a picture and took several precious seconds to ensure it was in a private album that couldn't be accessed without a password. She'd given him her trust in allowing this, and even if his phone rarely left his sight, he refused to betray her, even inadvertently.

As he stood, she shot him a look over her shoulder. "Dirty pictures get you off."

"*You* get me off." It was nothing more than the truth, but the way her eyes went wide made it feel like a confession. "Short of chaining you to my side, there will be times when I want you and you aren't available." He stepped behind her and bent over her body, pressing his chest to her back. "When that happens, I'll look at that picture, and I'll fuck my fist while imagining it's you."

"Mmm." She pushed her hips back against him. "If that's what does it for you, when you've been a particularly good gentleman-murderer, I'll send you something special to add to your collection."

"Cruel and unusual punishment to tease me when I can't touch you."

Another roll of her hips. "You can touch me now, Dima. Don't make me wait any more."

Dima.

He shouldn't have given her that name. It was ammunition in Keira's hands, and he had no defense against the sound of his name on her lips. None. For all his reputation and history, ironic that he'd be felled so completely by this little slip of a woman.

Dmitri fisted his cock and pushed into her, one torturous inch at a time. "This is what you need. My cock filling you."

"Yes, yes." She pushed back, sheathing him to the hilt.

Her pussy clenched around him, and he had to grab her hips to keep her from moving. His earlier orgasm should have taken the edge off, but this woman drove him wild in a way he never could have anticipated. Keira moaned. "Harder. Take me harder."

He pulled almost all the way out and thrust back into her, using his grip on her hips to do exactly as she needed. She cried out and then she was moving in counterpoint with him, slamming back to meet his strokes. The sound of flesh meeting flesh filled the room, and his world narrowed to the little sounds she made when he hit exactly the right spot, and the feel of her around him.

"*Mine*," he said in Russian. "*You're mine. You may deny it to the day you die, but it's the truth all the same.*"

"Oh *God*." She flung her head back as she came, and he bracketed her throat, holding her in position with her back bowed as he kept fucking her.

Only when her tremors stopped did he release her and allow her to slump onto the table. Keira lasted a breath, another, before she lifted her head. "You didn't come."

He kissed her shoulder, pumping gently with his hips. "I'm not done with you yet."

She shivered. "I don't think I'm complaining."

"You sound like you're not sure," he teased. Dmitri pulled out of her and turned her around to kiss him. "Come to bed with me. I'm not ready for this night to end."

Keira was already nodding. "I don't suppose you're going to fuck me all the way up the stairs to the room?"

He liked the image she created, her legs wrapped around his waist, his hands on her ass, his cock buried inside her, stopping every few steps to press her against the wall, and then again on the stairs themselves...

Dmitri inhaled sharply. "Another night when I'm sure we don't have an audience." He kissed her, quick and light. "I don't like to share."

"Pity." She slipped out of his arms and grabbed his shirt from where he'd tossed it onto the floor. She didn't bother to button the whole thing, just enough that she wasn't completely indecent.

But any of his men she encountered on the walk to their room would get an eyeful all the same.

He yanked on his pants and made it to the door just as she opened it. Dmitri didn't waste time arguing—he simply scooped her into his arms and strode for the stairs.

She smirked up at him. "Someone's feeling possessive."

"Where you're concerned? Always." He shouldn't say as much, not when she'd been so very clear about how little she liked that trait, but Dmitri was who he was. He hadn't been lying when he told her that, as her husband, he was hers, but she was still *his*. The faster she came to terms with that, the better for both of them.

They made it to the bedroom without encountering anyone, which made him suspect Pavel had cleared all but the necessary personnel for the night. Keira hadn't exactly been quiet when he was fucking her, and anyone in this part of the house would have heard and known to avoid the area until morning. Dmitri was more than capable of keeping her safe and dealing with any potential threat—and his men knew it.

He kicked the door shut behind him and let her slide down his body as he set her on her feet. Keira started to step away, but he caught her hips and kept her close. "I'm taking your ass tonight, *moya koroleva*, unless you tell me truthfully that it's something you aren't the least bit interested in trying."

She met his gaze steadily. "I want whatever you'll give me, Dima. I'm yours—at least for tonight."

* * *

Keira should have begged off. It would have been the smart thing to do. Dmitri already looked at her as if he owned her. Giving him access to a part of herself she'd never given anyone else would only confirm that he was right in that belief.

But she was so goddamn tired of the games. Tomorrow they could get back to jockeying for power and position over each other. Tonight, she only wanted him.

He led her to the bed and urged her onto it. "Trust me."

"In this? Sure."

His lips thinned, just a little. "Someday, you won't put a qualifier on that statement."

Maybe. She wasn't in the mood to deconstruct their future at this moment. Keira met his gaze and slid further onto the bed. From this angle, she got a good view of his chest piece. The landscape reminded her of the one in his office—bleak and a little sinister. She didn't think Russian criminals usually had gorgeous dark forests tattooed on their chests, but it fit Dmitri. He was king of his domain. He didn't need a throne or something gaudy and in-your-face. He owned the area depicted in his tattoo and every single thing that resided there.

Just like he did in his territory in New York.

It was something to chew on later, this strangely artistic

side of Dmitri. Right now, her only priority was driving him past the point of control. With that in mind, Keira rolled onto her stomach and spread her legs, tilting her ass up. A strained sound came from behind her, and she smiled against the sheets. Just to ensure Dmitri wasn't in the mood to talk anymore, she slid her hands down her sides and over her ass to part herself for his gaze. In her current position, he should be able to see every single inch of what he wanted. *Checkmate.*

"Do. Not. Move."

She held perfectly still as his footsteps sounded, heading for the bathroom. Dmitri didn't make her wait long, returning to join her on the bed. She heard a distinctly wet sound, and then his fingers were sliding down her ass to circle her. He dipped inside and she instinctively clenched.

"Shh, shh." Dmitri shifted to lie next to her and kiss her shoulder. "Relax. Breathe. I've got you."

"You try to relax with a finger in your ass."

He chuckled. "Perhaps next time."

That got her attention. Surely she'd heard him wrong. Dmitri Romanov did not just offer to let her return the favor. "You'd let me peg you?"

He gave a slow shake of his head. "That's not my kink, and I don't think it's yours, either."

Well, no. The idea of a strap-on left her feeling kind of queasy, if only because she didn't even know where to begin. It was the deep end and she'd barely even dipped her toe into the shallows when it came to ass play—giving or receiving. "Then what are you offering?"

"Exactly this." He slid his finger further into her. It didn't hurt in the least, but she didn't know how to even start describing the feeling. Her indecision must have shown on her face because he shifted closer and kissed her. Dmitri slid his tongue into her mouth even as he guided her closer and positioned her leg up and over his hip. It left them pressed together, and she shifted as his cock rubbed against her aching clit.

Suddenly, what he was doing to her ass wasn't the least bit uncomfortable at all.

Keira eagerly met his mouth, sucking the tip of his tongue even as she writhed to get closer. She tensed when he pushed a second finger into her, but everything else he was doing was too damn good to stop. She tore her mouth from his long enough to say, "Fuck me, Dima."

"All you have to do is ask. I crave the feel of you clenching around my cock."

She wormed her arm between them and lined him up with her entrance. He didn't hesitate to pull her closer even as he thrust, filling her completely. With his fingers inside her, her eyes flew open, startled at how fucking good it was to be filled so completely. "Oh."

" 'Oh,' she says," he murmured against her lips. "You just thought of what pleasure could be found with two cocks filling you."

There was no point in lying. He read her too damn well. "Can't blame me for that." She wiggled a little, but he had her thoroughly pinned in place with cock and fingers. "I think I'd like it."

"The filling or the two men?" His tone gave nothing away, but it was off all the same.

Damn it, why do we have to keep ruining a good thing with running our mouths? Keira kissed his jaw. "The filling. I don't figure you'd share any better than I would." She sure as fuck didn't like the idea of him with another woman...

The thought stopped her pleasure cold. She leaned back enough to meet his gaze. "No one else, Dima. If you fuck someone else after marrying me, I'll gut you."

"Vicious." He sounded almost pleased by it.

She gripped the back of his neck, forcing him to look down at her. "I'm serious." *Okay, I probably wouldn't gut him. But I would 100 percent burn this fucking house to the ground and walk away to somewhere he'd never find me.*

"I know." He sucked on her bottom lip, and her eyes damn near rolled back in her head. "There is no one but you, *moya koroleva*. After you, no one else will do." He fucked her ass with his fingers, though he kept her impaled on his cock. "And I do not share. I will fill you until you're screaming your pleasure, but there will be no other cock inside you but mine."

And, just like that, she wanted him to take her. Keira kissed him hard. "Fuck my ass, Dima."

"You keep giving orders."

"I think you like it."

She felt his grin. "Perhaps a little."

And then he released her and pulled away long enough to flip her onto her stomach. "Lift."

She obediently lifted her hips, and he slid a pillow beneath them. Keira twisted to watch him squirt some lube onto his palm. "I don't suppose you have cameras set up in this room?"

"You know I don't."

"Too bad." She eyed his cock. "I think I'd like to watch you fucking me on video." Sex tapes were so tacky, but the idea of being able to cue up one and watch his ridiculously perfect body rolling as he fucked her...Yeah, she'd make an exception to that rule.

He crawled between her legs and roughly spread them wide. "There are cameras in the dining room. I'll make you a copy."

Memories flashed before her. Her on her knees in front of him with his cock in her mouth. *His* mouth against her pussy. Dmitri bending her over the table and fucking her right there.

She gasped as he bore down and slid his cock an inch into her. Dmitri stilled. "Am I hurting you?"

"No." She wiggled, trying to take him deeper. "I'm thinking about watching that tape."

"Ah. An exhibitionist *and* a voyeur. You truly are a delight, *moya koroleva*." He slid deeper, and then deeper yet, until his pelvis pressed against her ass. He shifted her hair to the side and pressed an openmouthed kiss to the back of her neck. "And now?"

"I'm... good." It was back to being uncomfortable, but she couldn't tell if it was the intrusion or how empty her pussy felt.

As always, he seemed to know. Dmitri slid one hand between her and the pillow to stroke her clit. "And now?"

"*Oh*." She shuddered, biting her lip. "That's good. Really good."

Another kiss against the back of her neck, and she swore to God her toes curled. His rough voice vibrated against her skin. "I'm going to buy you a vibrator to fill you while I fuck you like this. Right... here." He pushed two fingers into her. "Would you like that, Keira?"

"Yes," she gasped out. She couldn't move with his weight pinning her to the bed, his cock filling her ass, and his fingers playing with her pussy. She couldn't do anything but take everything he gave her and beg for more. "I need you to move. Take me. Please. Take everything."

A slow shift of his hips and she nearly shot off the bed. It was so much better than she expected and yet totally different and...Keira didn't know. She cried out and begged and words sprang from her lips that she could barely process. Pleas and commands and begging. "Dima, please, oh my God it feels so good, don't stop, please don't stop." She orgasmed with a cry to shake the rafters, nearly throwing him off her in the process.

Dmitri thrust into her once, a second time, a third time, and then pulled out, and she felt a hot spurt on her ass. It shouldn't be this sexy. She should be pissed about... something. She couldn't work up the energy to figure out what, though. She turned her head to the side as he collapsed next to her. With sweat dampening his skin and his eyes hazy with pleasure, he looked almost...human.

Holy shit, I really do like him.

He twisted to kiss her. "Don't move."

She couldn't even if she'd wanted to. He disappeared for a minute and came back with a towel to clean her. Then he pulled the covers back and urged her beneath them. He tucked himself against her body, his breath stirring the small hairs on the back of her neck. "Sleep, *moya koroleva.*"

And she did.

CHAPTER TWENTY-TWO

Dmitri had things to do, but he couldn't quite bring himself to leave Keira in their bed alone. Last night had been a turning point for them, and he woke up wanting to ensure they didn't backslide.

With her face relaxed in sleep and her hair a tangled mess on her pillow, she didn't have her barriers in place for the first time since he'd met her. *This is what it could be like all the time if the rest of the world wasn't going to hell around us.*

The peace was a small reprieve. They had a single day until the party and a lot to accomplish in that amount of time. The danger was nowhere near past, and Dmitri should be focusing on that instead of curling Keira's hair around his finger.

Her eyes flicked open, asleep one moment and awake the next. "It's creepy to watch someone while they sleep."

"*Nyet*, we had this conversation. You're in my bed—our bed—so that gives me certain rights."

She rolled her eyes. "Always an argument with you, isn't it?"

"Can you blame me when you're so entertaining to argue with?" He kissed her shoulder. "Walk me through what you've set up for the party."

"I assumed you'd already have all the details."

Claudia *had* dropped a report on his desk, but Dmitri hadn't had the opportunity to review it yet. No, that wasn't strictly true. He'd had the chance but chose not to. This was important, and it felt almost like a breach of trust to check up on Keira after he assigned her to it. "If I did, I wouldn't ask you to fill me in."

She gave him a look that said she didn't quite believe him, but she finally rolled to face him. "Claudia had me picking menu choices—one vegan, one seafood, and one red meat. Covering all our bases. There were a lot of silly decisions to be made—reception colors, what flavor of cake, that kind of thing."

"What did you choose?"

"You really want to know?"

He wanted to know everything when it came to her. Even mundane choices offered a window into Keira. "*Da.*"

"Well then." She settled against the pillow. "Black and red for the colors. Claudia thought it'd be too gothic, but I think it fits and I like it, so I vetoed her. Cake is chocolate on chocolate." She made a face. "Damn, I probably should have asked you how you felt about chocolate, huh?"

"I adore it." He stroked his hand down her arm to her hip. "Though I don't indulge often."

"I can tell." She poked his stomach. "It would figure that you're a control freak about your body the same way you are about everything else."

It didn't exactly sound like she had an issue with it, but he still felt obliged to add, "Being in fighting shape is an asset."

"I don't doubt that." Something flickered over her face, and he could have kicked himself for missing something so obvious.

Dmitri kissed her shoulder again. "The gym I mentioned has been cleared, and you can start immediately if you want to."

She brightened and then frowned. "Part of me wants to just go for it, but we don't know how things are going to play out at the party, and I'm not going to be much use if I can't walk or move my arms because I'm so sore." She bit her bottom lip, and he had to remind himself not to soothe it with his tongue when she released it. Keira sighed. "This whole being in charge of shit has some downsides, doesn't it?"

"*Da*, though the perks are...enticing." He couldn't resist any longer. Dmitri kissed her. She tensed as if she'd pull away, but he didn't give a fuck about morning breath, or anything but doing exactly what he was doing, and Keira melted into his arms. She pushed him onto his back and straddled him, her skin sliding against his in the most intoxicating feeling he'd ever experienced. As if she couldn't get close enough, couldn't touch enough of him, couldn't think past the need for him.

Fuck, that's exactly how he felt.

He grabbed her ass and ground her clit against his cock, letting the hard ridge of him drive her wild. She tore her mouth from his with a gasp, and he growled. "I didn't intend this."

"Sounds like I did you a favor, then." She writhed, but it didn't seem to be enough for her, so Keira reached between them and squeezed his cock. "We'll make it quick.

Just a little fucking before you get back to vengeance and world domination, and I go back to that damn party." Keira didn't wait for an answer as she guided him into her in a smooth move. She braced a hand on the middle of his chest and rose to take him deeper. "Just so you know..." She rolled her hips. "I talked to Pavel about having men stationed at every exit to both the room and the house. She won't make it in, Dima. We won't let her."

It was beyond fucking sexy to hear her talking vengeance while riding him. He bent up and captured her mouth for several long seconds. "Good."

"Mmm." She clasped the back of his neck, keeping him close to her as she fucked him. She was totally and completely in control and intent on her pleasure, and she'd never been more beautiful to him. "I want Mae. I want to be the one who deals with her—for Charlie."

By all rights, he should hand Mae over to Aiden to secure what little goodwill they could scrape together, but Dmitri would deny Keira nothing. "She's yours."

She kissed him hard, her teeth scraping against his tongue, her nails pricking the nape of his neck. Her strokes hitched, and he thrust up to keep the rhythm going. She was close. He could feel it. Another stroke, a third, and then Keira orgasmed with a cry that he swallowed down.

Dmitri flipped them and drove into her, chasing his own pleasure even as he kept kissing her. *My queen. My wife. Mine.* His orgasm hit with the force of a freight train, and he sucked her bottom lip as he came. He buried his face in her neck and just let himself...be...for a moment. With Keira drawing abstract patterns on his cooling skin, his mind was blissfully blank. He dragged his mouth along her neck. "You are a gift."

"Glad you think so, but maybe wait until you see the bill for the dresses I just bought yesterday."

He chuckled. "They'll be worth every penny, I'm sure."

"They'd be a better deal if you don't make a habit of ripping them to shreds every time we have sex."

He lifted his head to find her grinning at him. He raised his eyebrows. "Worth. Every. Penny. But next time we dine alone, I want you wearing this and nothing else."

"This being...naked." She made a show of looking at the nonexistent space between their bodies. "I can get down with that."

"Much obliged." He kissed her again and slid off her. "We have work to do."

Keira stretched her arms over her head, and her entire body turned into a beautiful arch as she stretched. The move had the sheet sliding off her hips and her breasts practically begging for his mouth. He dragged his gaze away through sheer force of will, but there was no missing the laughter in her voice. "I suppose that means I shouldn't suggest showering together to save time."

I shouldn't...

The thought didn't have a chance to properly form before he rounded the bed and scooped her into his arms. "All in the name of saving time, of course."

"Of course."

* * *

The fact that Keira wasn't walking funny defied the laws of logic. They fucked again in the shower, her braced against the built-in shelf of the tiled wall while Dmitri took her from behind. Her entire body was sore in the most glorious way possible, and she still wanted to spend the next week locked in their bedroom with him. *First, vengeance, then honeymoon fucking.*

Keira took her time getting ready. Her usual outfit of jeans and a tank top didn't fit the image she wanted to project, and so she dug through the closet to find something that screamed Queen Bitch. She had to start taking this shit seriously, and as much as she liked the grunge look, maybe it was time to grow up a little. She found a color-blocked pencil skirt in black and gray, and a matching black lacy tank top. After the slightest consideration, she delved into the lingerie drawer for a garter belt and thigh-high black stockings. When Dmitri came back from wherever it was he'd gone, she'd give him a little surprise. It was silly to miss him when he'd been inside her less than an hour ago, but she swore the house felt emptier without him in it. She sighed and got dressed, throwing a slim-cut gray blazer over the top to tone down the sexiness of the lace.

One last check in the mirror gave her pause. The woman staring back at her looked only vaguely familiar. They had the same wavy hair, the same hazel eyes. But there was nothing of the self-loathing she'd borne like the weight of the world on her shoulders for years. Her hands didn't shake from needing whatever drug she could get her hands on. Her mood wasn't dark and tipping into despair.

She didn't look like a pawn.

She looked like a motherfucking queen.

She grinned at her reflection and headed downstairs to grab a quick bite to eat. Claudia wouldn't arrive for another hour or so, but Keira wanted to go over the plans with Pavel again to make sure they'd anticipated every option.

They'd need to go through it a third time with Dmitri to-morrow, but she wanted it as foolproof as it could get.

A quick bite later and she cornered Pavel in the sec-ondary office the men used throughout the day. He saw her come through the door and shot straight up. "Mrs. Romanov."

"O'Malley-Romanov."

He hesitated like he wanted to contradict her but nod-ded. "Mrs. O'Malley-Romanov."

Good boy. She noted that he very carefully kept his gaze on her face, and almost laughed. She'd obviously traumatized the poor man last night, but it was just as well. There was wisdom in not allowing any of the men to be-come too familiar with her. Right now, they weren't quite sure where she fit in with the overall hierarchy, and they weren't willing to do anything to piss her off. That suited her purposes just fine—for now. Once they were past this mess with the Eldridges, Keira had every intention of iron-ing out all sorts of shit within the household.

She gave him a tight smile. "Let's go through it once more."

"Gladly." He didn't hesitate this time, leading her to the table they'd set up with blueprints of the house. She had to wonder why Pavel didn't seem too worried that she might use the information to sneak out or maybe smuggle it to her brother, but that was something to address later.

Right now, she had a bitch to catch.

They went over the placement of the men and how they would ensure no one uninvited got past them. With Kei-ra's family attending, most of the power players in Boston would be in one place. It was practically inviting their en-emies to attack, but her siblings and their spouses couldn't skip attending any more than Keira and Dmitri could skip making the invitation in the first place. Power was a funny thing. They only had it as long as they had the perception of it. Sometimes that meant taking reckless risks instead of bunkering down to hunt their enemies to the ends of the earth.

If the people in their respective territories thought the Romanovs were afraid of the Eldridges, the people bold enough to attack would multiply.

She got it. She just thought it was silly.

Dmitri thought Alethea was going to try to leverage an invitation to the party. The more Keira thought about it, the less sense it made. Alethea might have the utmost faith in Dmitri's word—and rightfully so—but *Aiden* hadn't made any promises about her safety. If given half a chance, Keira's brother would put a bullet into both Eldridge women if only to save Charlie a future of uncertainty. Keira didn't blame him for that, and Dmitri likely wouldn't, either.

So, no, Alethea had something else up her sleeve. The question was *what*.

Keira tapped a finger to her lip. "Pavel, I have a question for you."

"*Da?*"

"Did Dmitri assign you to me because you're being punished or rewarded?" She'd seen no indication that Dmitri operated his household *that* much differently from her brother, which meant that his men shared a lot of the duties. Keira knew for a fact that they rotated through whose turn it was to leave the house for various reasons. Pavel had been designated her personal bodyguard for a reason, and she wanted to know why.

For all his talk, is he still looking at me as a possession to be protected?

She hated how the thought grated. So much so, she almost missed Pavel's hesitation. Keira zeroed in on him. "Don't even think about lying to me. It won't go over well, and I'll find out the truth regardless."

He took a slow breath. "My father was Mr. Romanov's father's second in command. I grew up in this business, and he's known me since I was a child. He trusts me."

Which meant he didn't trust someone else. *Anyone* else. She nodded, and the relief on Pavel's face would have made her laugh under other circumstances. As it was, she was too busy thinking about the implications of Dmitri not trusting his men. From what she understood, many of them had been with him for years, and he wasn't the type to keep people under his roof—and give them access to Keira—if he didn't trust them beyond a shadow of a doubt.

The only reason she could think that he *would* do that was if he didn't know *who* he could trust and who he couldn't.

Shit.

She faked a smile and put a bit of brightness into her tone. "Thanks, Pavel. We'll walk through it once more with Dmitri tomorrow and then put everything into motion."

He nodded. "It's a good plan."

This time, her smile was closer to the real thing. Their plan might be good, but it depended upon the enemy being outside the house. If one of Dmitri's men was a threat, keeping watch on the exits wouldn't do them a damn bit of good. "Thanks." She strode out of the room, already considering how best to corner Dmitri and convince him to tell her what the hell was going on. The good mood she'd captured from the superior fucking she'd experienced last night and this morning slipped through her fingers.

It's more than fucking, and no matter how many times I think of it that way, it doesn't change the truth.

She didn't know *what* the truth was, but things had changed between her and Dmitri. He'd *teased* her last night, and when she'd trusted him, he rewarded her for it. And this morning, waking up and lying there in bed talking about their plans was such a married thing to do. For the first time, she actually *felt* married—and she liked it a whole hell of a lot.

Movement at the turn in the hallway caught her eye, and she stopped short, her heart beating too hard. She'd felt safe in this house, but if there was a traitor in their midst, then anyone who wasn't Pavel or Dmitri was a potential threat.

A familiar form detached himself from the shadows—familiar and *wrong*. Keira shot a look around and hurried over. "*Mark?* What the hell are you doing here?" She grabbed his muscular arm. "Get out of here before someone sees you. And you can tell Aiden to shove his rescue mission—"

"I'm not here for you."

She froze, the pieces clicking together so quickly, it was a wonder they didn't a make an actual sound. "Aiden sent you for the Eldridges."

"For Mae," he corrected.

It was right about then that Keira realized she didn't know much about Mark at all. *Liam* was the one who had been friends with Aiden since forever. Mark was just Liam's cousin who couldn't adapt to civilian life after he got out of whatever branch of the military he'd been in and needed a job. Sure, Mark had been her babysitter more often than not for several years, but that didn't mean a damn thing. He was a shadow. He sure as hell wasn't a friend.

She removed her hand from his arm, but didn't step back. "If you're here with Dmitri's permission, that's one thing, but don't think for a second of playing the Lone Ranger and fucking up our plans."

He smirked. "You can let Romanov know that I'll play nice...for now."

Which was as good as saying he wouldn't the second it suited him. She clenched her fists at her side and strove to keep her aggravation out of her tone. "If you do something that causes the Eldridges to escape, Dmitri will be the least of your concerns."

Mark stepped close, towering over her. "Pay attention, little girl, because I'm only going to say this once—stay the fuck out of my way. You might be playing wifey to that Russian bastard, but that doesn't make you shit. You're not an O'Malley anymore, and that means I won't hesitate to put you in your place if you get between me and my mark."

If she didn't do something to regain the power of this situation, that would be the end of it. Mark had never been a particularly nice guy from what she'd seen, but he looked seriously unhinged in that moment. *Mae shot Liam.* He hadn't died, but it was a close thing. It stood to reason that Mark would want revenge.

Too fucking bad.

Keira stepped back, putting a reasonable distance between them, and raised her voice. "Pavel?"

Just as she'd suspected, he appeared from where he'd been lurking, monitoring the situation. Whether it was for her protection or because he thought she'd turn on Dmitri was irrelevant. She jerked her chin at Mark. "Remove this man from the house."

Mark froze. "What the fuck did you just say?"

But Pavel was already moving, another man appearing behind him. She made a mental note to memorize the names of all the men in the house as they took Mark to the floor and pulled zip ties from somewhere to fasten his hands behind him and bind his ankles together. It wasn't quick and it wasn't easy—Pavel was bleeding from the nose by the end of it—but they managed. They flipped Mark onto his back, and only then did she approach again.

Keira leaned over and raked a glance over him from head to toe. "My husband will hold to whatever agreement he and Aiden made. I revoke whatever permission you had to be in this house before the reception, so you'll have to find other arrangements. If you're caught trespassing, I can't be held accountable for the consequences—and you can relay *that* to my brother." She straightened and nodded at Pavel. "Please see him out."

They picked Mark up and strode away, his curses echoing the halls for several long moments after they disappeared from view. Keira turned away and picked a door at random, ending up in a small powder room. She locked the door and leaned against it. Only then did she start to shake.

Sheer bravado. That's all her act had been—an act. She hadn't known for sure that Pavel would appear and obey. He said he could be trusted, but that didn't mean a damn thing until Dmitri confirmed it. It was a gamble that Pavel would do what she commanded even if it potentially counteracted Dmitri's initial order.

Mark's words played through her head. *You aren't an O'Malley anymore.* It was nothing more than the truth, though a truth she hadn't been ready to face. She *still* wasn't ready to face it. Too bad she didn't have any choice.

To distract herself, she pulled out her phone and sent a quick text. *Kicked O'Malley man out of the house. Aiden will be pissed, but it was necessary.*

Dmitri didn't make her wait long for a reply. *Noted. I'll call shortly. Stay with Pavel.* Quickly followed by a second text. *Please.*

She let her head fall back to rest against the door. This little breakdown couldn't last long—Claudia would be waiting by now. She had to put on a smile and pretend everything was perfectly fine when all she really wanted to do was go to the nearest liquor store and buy the biggest bottle of vodka they had in stock. Her mouth actually watered as she spent several precious seconds imagining the taste of it hitting her tongue and the way it would burn her throat and warm her stomach, of the precious numbness that would spread in its wake, until she didn't care about anything but her next sip.

One breath. Two.

On the third, she forced the fantasy away. Her hands shook as she pushed her hair back and walked to the mirror to check her appearance. This time, her reflection didn't look nearly as sure of herself. *Fake it til you make it.* It was the only option she had left.

Keira threw back her shoulders and marched through the door. She had the rest of the goddamn party to get lined up, and she wasn't going to let shit get to her until she had some private time alone to deal with it—or maybe she wouldn't deal with it at all.

After all, she wasn't an O'Malley anymore. She was Keira motherfucking Romanov.

CHAPTER TWENTY-THREE

Keira didn't answer Dmitri's call. He tried once more before he stepped out of the town car currently idling at the curb. Her throwing out Aiden's man was intriguing, and he'd have to answer for it, but an explanation would have to wait until he was through with this particular meeting. Dmitri flipped his phone onto silent and strode into the hotel.

It was an old building that had missed the renovations of the surrounding area. The tired-looking man behind the counter barely glanced at him as he walked through the dim lobby and over a tile floor yellowed with age.

He took the stairs up to the second floor and let himself into the room, carefully shutting the door behind him and locking the dead bolt. The curtains were closed and the lights were off, leaving the room shrouded in darkness. He sighed. "This is rather theatrical, don't you think?"

"What I think is that I'd rather be anywhere but here,

dealing with a dirty Russian mobster." John Finch flicked on the lamp next to the desk. It was a play Dmitri had made many times in the past—sometimes theatrical was exactly what a situation called for—but he resented the fed trying to use it on him.

He crossed his arms over his chest. "You called me. I hope it wasn't to throw around insults you could have managed over the phone." He hadn't expected a call this morning, let alone a demand that he switch his schedule to accommodate the agent. "You have information for me?"

John Finch leaned back, his face in shadow. "You know we have your place under surveillance."

It wasn't a question, so Dmitri didn't bother answering. "What's your point?"

"My point is that the surveillance has been experiencing issues for several nights now. It never lasts longer than five or ten minutes, but it's consistent."

A window of opportunity. It didn't take a genius to realize *who* the opportunity was for. There were plenty of gadgets that could jam signals. Apparently the Eldridges were planning something. He'd suspected it, but the confirmation made it easier to see which direction they'd be attacking from. *My home. They're going to come to my fucking home.*

Or the mole will do something that requires leaving in a hurry. But no, that didn't make sense. He still hadn't pinned down the identity of the traitor. The cameras had been wiped for ten minutes before and after the package was delivered to his office—probably done while the fucker was *in* his office. If the man wanted to walk out, it wouldn't raise red flags because no one knew he wasn't going on some errand for Dmitri.

Unless he's going to try to take a hostage when he goes.

"Ah." Dmitri leaned a shoulder against the wall, letting none of his thoughts reflect in his expression. "That's unfortunate that your equipment is so faulty."

"Unfortunate for them. Fortunate for someone who needed that chunk of time."

John Finch had been on the scene for decades, and he was one of the best cops Dmitri had ever come across. He was also a pain in the ass, but an inconvenience Dmitri had learned to work around.

For him to offer up this information spoke volumes.

It had to be a trap. "Your warning is duly noted." He flicked a nonexistent piece of lint off his suit. "I saw your daughter earlier this week. She appears to be well on her way to making a full recovery." There would likely be scars from the time she spent as Mae's captive, but that didn't seem to bother Charlie much.

Finch's hands tensed on the arms of his chair. "That's not what this is about."

Liar. John Finch had made a shitty call when he put Mae Eldridge's arrest above his own daughter's health. Charlie had survived and would flourish in her life as Aiden O'Malley's wife, but neither of them would forget Finch's actions that night—or, rather, his lack of action. "Getting into bed with the mob is a strange way to get back into your daughter's good graces. But it's your best chance at a future relationship with her. Good luck." And on that note, he turned and walked out of the room.

It wasn't until he was secure in the back of the town car that he contemplated this strange turn of events. Though he'd poked at Finch, he knew damn well the information was being provided solely because Charlie would be in the

Romanov household in one short day. Even as shitty a parent as Finch was, he wouldn't stand by while his daughter was put in danger—again. He probably would have preferred to call her directly, but Dmitri knew for a fact that neither Aiden nor Charlie was taking Finch's calls at the moment. Which was why Finch had settled on Dmitri.

His phone buzzed, and he frowned when he recognized Pavel's number. "*Da?*"

"There was an...incident."

He checked his watch. Thirty minutes since Keira's text and Pavel's calling to report. Interesting. "I'm listening."

"The O'Malley man who arrived this morning had a run-in with Mrs. Romanov. I couldn't hear everything they said, but it was threatening on both parts. She ordered us to remove him from the house." No overexplanation. Just a report. He'd obeyed Keira despite her order counteracting Dmitri's.

It should piss him off, but a slow tether of pride uncurled inside him. *She's stepping into her role.* "Where is he now?"

The smallest hesitation and what might have been a sigh of relief. "We drove him up to Westchester and shadowed him to make sure he didn't try to come straight back. He's got a hotel room, and he hasn't left since arriving ten minutes ago. I have a man keeping an eye on him."

"You're not there yourself." If Pavel had left Keira unattended...Dmitri curled his hand into a fist, fighting for control. She was safe. Just because Finch had reported surveillance malfunctions and someone had left a fucking *head* on his desk and wiped the tapes didn't mean she was in danger right this second.

But it didn't mean she wasn't.

"No, boss. I sent Alexei and Petri."

Thank fuck. "I'll be home shortly. Don't let Keira out of your sight."

"Yes, boss."

He hung up and considered calling Keira, but he would be able to get the full details from her shortly, and she would be going over the reception plans with Claudia at the moment. If he called to check in again, she'd know something was up and it might distress her. He closed his eyes and strove for control.

The trip back to the house was uneventful, and he wasted no time tracking down Keira. Resisting calling her had taken everything he was capable of. He needed to see for himself that she was safe and unharmed.

He found her in the ballroom with Claudia as they supervised the pair of men arranging tables. He stopped short just inside the doorway, taking in the change in her. A different wardrobe shouldn't make a fundamental difference—she was beautiful no matter what she wore—but the outfit gave her a sense of command that she hadn't had in her jeans.

Then she turned to face him and he realized the clothing had nothing to do with the change. Her posture was different, from the way she held her shoulders to the casual way she extracted herself from the conversation with Claudia and crossed to him. Her smile was small but genuine. "You're back early."

"I had a change of plans."

She drew her brows together. "Pavel tattled."

"Pavel called to fill me in, yes, but my plans had changed even before that." He glanced over her shoulder at Claudia. The petite black woman nodded and turned back to bark instructions at the men, directing them to move the table two feet to the left. Dmitri took Keira's hand. "Carve out a few minutes for me."

"Sure. I actually wanted to talk to you about something." She waved at Claudia and led him out of the room. She kept going until they reached his office, and he had to wonder what she needed to say that she didn't want anyone overhearing. Keira didn't make him wait long. "Mark might be here to help, but he's here with the intention of killing Mae. He's not going to deliver her to Aiden, and he's not going to follow your men's lead. He's a liability."

Dmitri studied her expression. "If he disobeys Aiden, that's your brother's problem."

"No, shit, *really?*" She rolled her eyes. "That's not what I'm worried about. I don't want him pulling some stunt and screwing up our chance to get the Eldridges and bring Mikhail home."

If there's anything left of him to bring home. Alethea hadn't contacted him again, and she'd never sent proof of life, so Mikhail very well could have been dead this entire time. *Can't think like that. It changes nothing.*

Dmitri didn't think. He just pulled Keira into his arms and rested his chin on the top of her head. She hesitated, but it only lasted a second before she wrapped her arms around his waist. "Don't punish Pavel."

"I wasn't going to." He let himself feel her breathing and matched his own to the slow inhales and long exhales. "He made the right call." Easier to leave it at that, but in an effort to be honest, he said, "If it hadn't happened in the house, or if I was there, Pavel might have reacted differently."

"I know." She laid her head against his chest. "But if you were there, you would have given the order and I wouldn't have had to."

She had so much faith in him. More than he deserved. He hadn't done a single fucking thing to earn it other than open her eyes to something she already possessed. It was all Keira. It always had been. He sighed. "Someone—I suspect the Eldridges—has been blocking John Finch's surveillance of this house."

"What?" Keira straightened so fast, she clipped his jaw and he almost bit his tongue. "Did you just say *John Finch*?"

He released her with one arm so he could rub his jaw. "I did."

"But he hates you. Is he pissed about Charlie or about Alethea pulling strings and getting Mae released?"

"Does it matter?" The end result was the same. Mae on the streets. John Finch their unlikely ally.

Keira nodded. "It matters. No matter how pissed Charlie is at him right now, she still loves him. If he's sharing information for her, she should know." Her hazel eyes blazed. "But if he's doing this because he's pissed Mae slipped through his fingers, then he can fuck right off. We'll take his information and he's on his own otherwise."

So fierce and so fucking loyal.

He cupped her face and kissed her lightly. "I'll find out."

"Thank you," she spoke against his lips. "Pavel and I would like to go over the placement of the men with you in the morning if you can fit it into your schedule."

"I'll make it work." It was so very strange to have this conversation with her, something perfectly normal talking about schedules, when they were in the midst of such insanity. More so, when a couple days ago, they'd been at each other's throats.

"Good."

"There was something else?"

"Yeah." She raised her eyebrows. "When were you going to tell me that you might have a traitor in the house?"

He rocked back on his heels. "Pavel told you."

"Pavel told me that you trust him, which is why he's been my designated babysitter. I connected the rest of the dots myself."

"I won't let anyone hurt you." The thought of one of his men turning on him, doing something to harm Keira... He clenched his jaw. "When I find the traitor..."

"Oh yeah, I got it. Death and a painful one at that." She didn't sound too worried about it, which only made him respect her more. Keira went up on her tiptoes and pressed a quick kiss to his lips. "I just wanted you to know that I know, and I'm not going to take any risks."

"I appreciate that." He hadn't realized how worried he'd been about her doing exactly that until he heard her promise. Dmitri leaned back far enough to get another look at her, determined to lighten the mood a little. "I like this." He ran his finger down the line where her blazer met the lace shirt underneath.

"Yeah, well, you bought it." She gave him an impish grin, her seriousness gone in an instant. "Claudia and I have to deal with a couple more things, but I'll be done inside of an hour. She's more than capable of harassing the muscle into submission." Keira stepped into him. "Tomorrow we have to play politics, wrangle my family, and avoid playing into the bad guys' hands. Get done what you need to and come out with me."

"Out."

"Yes, out. Let's just pretend for a few hours that we don't have an evil empire to run and just be us. Pavel can play guard dog so no one gets any funny ideas, but I want it to just be me and you."

The concept was more attractive than he could have dreamed. Just him and Keira, sharing a meal. In public. Dmitri couldn't put his finger on why being in public made a difference, but it did. He wanted it more than he had a right to. "I'll be ready by the time you are."

"Perfect." She leaned up on her toes and kissed him again, and then slipped out of his arms. "I'll see you in a little bit."

He waited for her to close the door behind her before he circled his desk and snatched up the phone. As expected, Aiden didn't make him wait long. Dmitri barely paused for the man to answer to start in on him. "When I allowed your man into my home, I didn't expect him to verbally assault my wife."

A long pause. "You're angry."

The simmering rage that had struck the second he realized Keira could have been in danger in his own fucking home while he *wasn't there* boiled over. "You talk so strongly about family first, but that idea doesn't hold up the moment one of your siblings steps out of line. She chose, Aiden. But she is still your sister, even if she's married to me. If you can't remember and respect that—and order your people to do the same—you won't be in contact with her."

"She ordered him carried out into the street like a bag of garbage." Still Aiden kept on with that infuriating calm tone. It made Dmitri want to shred something.

"He cornered Keira in a fucking dark hallway and acted like she was shit on the bottom of his shoe. I don't know how you operate within your household, Aiden, but in mine, we take care of ours." He hung up before he could say something truly unforgivable, and sat back.

What am I doing?

He never let emotions control him, even within the relative safety of this house, let alone calling out to essentially announce that something had gotten under his skin. Never. And yet here he was, fighting the desire to drive to that piece-of-shit motel and beat some respect into Mark.

It wouldn't work. Dmitri knew the type. Ex-military. Loyal to a fault. He could beat the man within an inch of his life, and it wouldn't get through the thick barrier of training and loyalty. To try was insanity.

It didn't change his desire to do exactly that.

He ran a hand over his face. *Keira is fine. She's not hurt. She's not damaged in any way from the encounter . . . but she could have been.* If Pavel hadn't been close. If Mark was just a little more volatile. If, if, if. He could have hurt her. He could have fucking killed her.

The traitor still could.

Dmitri inhaled, held it for several seconds, and exhaled. *She is fine.* He couldn't let what-if scenarios cloud his judgment. Keira was well, and if he locked her up for her safety, she'd never forgive him. He had to remember that.

It might be worth earning her hate to know she was safe.

CHAPTER TWENTY-FOUR

Keira couldn't quite believe she'd been so brazen to demand a date with Dmitri. It seemed immature now. *Oh, please, husband, please take me on a date.* They had so much shit going on, and little of it good, and she was dragging him off-site and distracting both of them.

"Keira."

She turned to find him standing at the bottom of the stairs. He looked just as fresh and crisp as he had earlier, his suit jacket perfectly pressed, not a hair out of place. It gave her the silliest urge to rumple him a little, but she clasped her hands in front of her to keep from doing exactly that. "Hey."

He frowned. "What changed since I saw you last?" There was a dangerous edge to his tone, as if he'd go to battle on her behalf against whatever had dampened her excitement.

Which was a problem, since *she* was the issue.

She didn't bother to force a smile because he'd know she was faking it. "I'm just wondering if maybe we should save this date for when we're not on the verge of a plan that may or may not get everyone killed."

"Is there anything left you need to do to prepare for tomorrow?"

She gave the question more thought than she normally would have before shaking her head slowly. "It's all ready. Just a matter of last-minute details with the caterers and florist that we can't do until tomorrow anyway." She saw where he was going with the question before she even finished speaking. "This is a distraction." They'd done as much as they could to prepare for tomorrow. There wasn't a single reason they couldn't occupy themselves tonight— distract from the nerves fluttering in her stomach.

"Nothing so simple." He opened the front door for her. "I want to spend more time with you. You want the same. We're not neglecting any duties in the meantime. There's no reason not to go to dinner—unless you don't actually want to."

"I want to." She answered quickly—too quickly. Why pretend? Keira grabbed his hand as she moved past him, tugging Dmitri into step beside her. "You're right. Let's get out of here before something else goes wrong and ruins the night."

He squeezed her hand and kept their fingers interlaced. "Walk with me."

"Without a babysitter? Color me surprised."

"Pavel will be along shortly."

"Naturally." The walk and the almost frigid air didn't change her enjoyment of being with Dmitri and out of that damn house for a little bit. She loved the house. She did.

But going from one cage to another wasn't Keira's idea of a good time. Dmitri had said she'd be a full partner, and they hadn't had the opportunity to test that out. His bringing up the Krav Maga gym was a positive sign, but it was easy enough to say the right words without having any intention of following through with them. *Get through this crisis and deal with it after that.*

She hadn't paid much attention to the area when they arrived the first time, but now Keira looked around with curiosity. She'd been to Manhattan a few times over the years, but it felt different now that she actually *lived* here. When the current threat was dealt with, she'd take some time and walk down these streets and get to know the area better. There was plenty of foot traffic, and she and Dmitri blended into the flow of people. They could have been anyone, just a couple holding hands as they walked to dinner. She liked the feeling. A lot.

Keira stopped short when her attention caught on a brightly lit window. Three easels were set up in the display, all with varying stages of art completed in three different styles. Whoever had painted them was gifted, but that wasn't what turned her feet into cement blocks preventing her from moving further. No, that was the bits of shop she could see in the gaps between the easels. Art supplies. High-end and varied art supplies.

"Would you like to go in?" Dmitri asked it so very carefully, as if he wasn't sure which side of the coin she'd land on and wanted to prepare for either.

She did...and she didn't. Keira swallowed hard. "I want my studio. I want to create again. But it's been so long. I haven't painted since my brother died." A small part of her had decided it was a fitting penance, though what she was paying for was anyone's guess. She hadn't set Devlin on that path that night. She hadn't suspected the Hallorans would stoop to such lengths. Even if she had, at eighteen, no one would have listened to her warnings anyway.

No, the sin Keira couldn't quite let go of was that she was alive when her beloved brother was dead.

"If you aren't ready, there's nothing wrong with saying so." Dmitri moved closer, stepping behind her and wrapping his arms around her waist, letting her lean back against him. His voice was pitched low and only for her ears. "But if you want to go in—to start living again—would he truly begrudge you that?"

No. There was no question of that answer. If it had been any other of their siblings who'd died in his place, Devlin would have kicked her ass long before now. She gulped in a breath. "It shouldn't be this big of a deal to walk through that door."

"Grief does strange things to a person, *moya koroleva.* There's no shame in it."

He was so damn *understanding.* It was easier to lean on him when she didn't have to look into his face, when there were only their slightly distorted reflections in the glass of the shop. She'd thought she was ready to start painting again, had even taken steps in that direction, but this felt like standing in the sun after years pent up in a cave. "I..." It took her two tries to get the next words out. "I want to go in."

"I am here. You are not facing this alone. If you need to leave, we will leave."

Dima, I think I love you.

The feeling took residence in her chest, nestled right next to her panic and pain and the weakness she wanted so desperately to let go of. Dark, secret parts of her that she didn't share with anyone...until now.

She couldn't say the words. Dmitri had never promised her love. He'd even gone so far as to promise her that there wouldn't be anything resembling love. This wasn't a fairy tale, and she was in danger of forgetting it—again. Breaking down and telling him she loved him would only prove how weak she really was. How unfit.

She couldn't do it.

She wouldn't.

But she reclaimed his hand and held on to him like a lifeline as they walked through the door and into the art shop. A tattooed guy with dark curly hair and two rings in his bottom lip waved at them. "Let me know if there's anything I can help you with."

Keira couldn't form words, but Dmitri answered for both of them. "Thank you." He angled his body between her and the guy, his gray eyes taking in every nuance of her expression and body language. "Where to first?"

Since speaking was out of the question due to the knot forming in her throat, she turned and shuffled down the aisle with the canvases. They were standard, but she gravitated toward the stack of larger ones. If she was going to slide back into painting, there was only one size she could start with, and this fit. She had to let go of Dmitri's hand, and she cleared her throat. "Please hold this."

Next, she moved to the brushes, studying them carefully before picking three in a variety of sizes. The paints were harder. Keira closed her eyes against the array of colors and counted to ten as she focused on breathing. Color was the very essence of life, and she'd shunned it so completely for the last three years. Her art had always cut to the heart of things for Keira. If she was upset, she painted. If she was excited about something, she painted. If she had to mull through a decision, she'd paint her way out. She'd intentionally cut off that part of herself to shield from the pain of grief, and standing in this shop, it was like she'd suddenly regained feeling after years of being numb. Pins and needles and pain, all rushing through her body until she was light-headed with the sensation.

She was here. She was doing this. It didn't matter how much she wanted to flee the building and find the nearest bar, she was *doing this*. Dmitri's presence at her back calmed her nearly as much as the breathing technique did. She opened her eyes and picked six colors instinctively, doubling up on black and white. "I'm done."

"*Khorosho.* Shall we?"

She readjusted her grip on the paints and followed him back to the register. One look at his face had her quelling any mention of paying him back for the purchase, so she stood there silently while her supplies were carefully bagged up.

Keira didn't take a full breath until they were back on the street. She looked down at the bags in Dmitri's hands, and the feeling in her chest exploded. She threw herself against him and kissed him soundly. "Thank you, Dima. Just...thank you."

* * *

Dmitri picked a little restaurant whose owners knew him and were discreet. The inside was narrow and deep, so there were no windows nearby as the hostess led them to the very back of the room. Low lighting was supplemented by a candle on every table, which served the purpose of creating an intimate setting and discouraging anyone from paying too much attention to the tables around them.

He pulled a chair out for Keira, positioning her back against the wall, and then took the seat next to her. From where they sat, they could see the rest of the room, but the low light and artful shadows meant the other patrons' attention would coast right over them. Keira's eyes were a little too wide and she hadn't seemed to pay attention to the rest of their walk there, so he wanted her off the street and somewhere quiet while she had time to process.

Outwardly, it seemed such a small thing—walking into an art store and picking out a few supplies—but it was a huge step for her. What would she paint first? He'd never seen her work, but he knew she'd secured a full scholarship to one of the more prestigious art schools on the East Coast. She must be highly skilled, but art was such a strange thing. It was purely individual and offered a window into the artist's soul.

Keira's soul was stubborn and broken and unbearably beautiful, and he wanted to see it painted across those large canvases she'd picked out. After years of downward spiraling, it couldn't be comfortable, and he didn't want to push her any more tonight while she adjusted to her newfound sense of being among the living.

He couldn't stand the silence, though. Letting her thoughts twist and turn and tangle with each other, every single one so easy to read on her face, made his chest ache in sympathy. He took her hand, noting its slight tremble, and pressed her knuckles to his lips. "I'm proud of you, *moya koroleva.*"

"It's not like I just scaled a mountain." Instead of sounding sarcastic, her tone was shaky.

"Didn't you?" He kissed each knuckle and then let their hands drop to his lap as their waiter approached. Dmitri ordered them both iced tea and the special entree, and the man disappeared almost comically fast.

She sighed. "That's a horrible habit."

Even though he knew what she meant, she sounded steadier, so he poked at her a bit. "It's classically romantic."

"Romantic." She looked at him like he'd grown a second head. "Dmitri, if that's your idea of romantic, you're using a playbook that's about a hundred years out of date." Keira shook her head and muttered, "Romantic."

"Call me old fashioned."

"Start with that stunt again, and the only thing I'll be calling you is plain old *old*." Her lips twitched in a little smile, but it died almost immediately. "But it's a moot point. Your terms were pretty damn clear from the start, so don't worry about me getting any ideas."

Several beats passed while he tried to figure out what she meant. Dmitri walked back through their interchange, and his chest clenched when he realized the source of her comment. He'd told her time and again not to expect romance from him—or love, for that matter. The way she very pointedly picked up her menu and read slowly actually stung. She was giving him a chance to back off without any awkward moments. To retreat. It was the smart thing to do. He didn't know if he was capable of the kind of loving Keira deserved. He...felt things for her. Strong things. But they hadn't been together long enough to know whether his feelings were anything other than lust—or infatuation.

Surely it couldn't be love.

And yet...he wasn't willing to shut the door on that

conversation the same way he had in the past. Not completely. "Perhaps I was too hasty to take romance off the table."

Keira went so still, it was as if she'd melded with one of the shadows. "What do you mean by that?"

He wasn't a man who normally fumbled for words, but he didn't want to say something to damage the fragile moment they had growing between them. "When I first decided to marry you, I didn't quite fathom what it would be like to *be* with you. There are quite a few things I never planned on or anticipated when it comes to you, Keira. I enjoy spending time with you. I find it fascinating the way your mind works—it's as twisty as mine is." He leaned closer and lowered his voice. "And I will spend the rest of my life counting down the time until I can have you coming on my cock next."

"Okay."

He wasn't deterred by the panic blossoming in her hazel eyes. He'd just changed the game on her without warning—panic was a natural reaction. "I think we'd both enjoy adding a bit of romance to the mix."

She opened her mouth, seemed to reconsider what she'd been about to say, and closed it. Keira frowned. "Seducing me is just another game."

If he said yes, she would dismiss it out of hand—and rightfully so. What they had wasn't a goddamn game, even if neither of them had been willing to admit as much up to this point. Asking her to be the one to take that first step with no guarantee of his returning her feelings was cruel, especially after the hits she'd rolled with time and again. Dmitri squeezed her hand where it was laced with his on his thigh. "*Nyet, moya koroleva.* What I have with you isn't a game. It's as real as anything."

The hope written across her face kindled an identical feeling in him. Her smile was a little shaky, but it was genuine. "You want to date me."

"I want to romance you."

Her smile widened. "And how, exactly, does a gentleman-murderer romance his wife?"

If he could love any woman, it would be this one. Nothing seemed able to break her, and she came back swinging every time something—or someone—knocked her down. Today hadn't been easy on her, and if he hadn't had her clinging to his hand less than an hour ago in that art shop, he wouldn't know that she'd been on the verge of cracking as she stood down her demons. And still she managed to flirt with him.

Dmitri reached down and hooked the bottom of her chair with his hand and dragged it closer to him. "It begins with an intimate dinner in a small restaurant."

"Does it, now?" She made a show of looking around. "Seems like you have that box firmly checked."

"What's the point of a good plan of attack if it's not realized?"

She leaned in until her hair brushed his arm. "What's the next play?"

It was only then that he realized she'd changed something about her clothing from the last time he'd seen her. The blazer had hid it from him before, but with her current angle, he could clearly see that she'd taken off her bra, and the lace of her top did nothing to conceal her.

He went rock hard even as he narrowed his eyes. "*Moya*

koroleva, you have a habit of leaving off a necessary part of your wardrobe whenever it suits you."

"Hmm?" She ran her finger down the edge of her blazer, pulling it away from her body so her hard nipples flashed at him. "I got a little warm, so I took off my bra."

He adjusted her blazer, letting the backs of his fingers caress her through the lace. "It's November."

"Is it?" Keira fanned herself. "So hot."

"You're incorrigible."

"That right there is a ten-dollar word." She arched her back a little, pressing her breast against his touch. "I suppose now isn't the time to tell you that I'm not wearing panties, either?"

CHAPTER TWENTY-FIVE

Keira might be emotionally spinning, but the look on Dmitri's face grounded her just as effectively as his touch. He wanted her. He wanted her right there, in that chair, in the middle of the fucking restaurant. He wouldn't put her in that position, but the desire in his gray eyes had an answering tide rising in her. She recrossed her legs, letting her skirt slide up a bit. An invitation.

He saw it just like she'd hoped he would. "You've been a very bad girl, Keira."

"I don't suppose you'll put me over your knee and spank me for it?"

His lips curved. "I think you may like that too much to be an effective punishment."

Her Russian was flirting with her. Of all the sides of Dmitri, this sly, flirtatious one might have been her favorite. He seemed to save it only for her, and if it was just another part he played, she didn't want to know it. It might be a comforting lie to think he was giving her a piece of himself exclusively, but it was comforting nonetheless. "Careful there, Dima. Punishment can go both ways." She loved the way his eyes flared every time she used his pet name. Another intimacy between them. Another bridge connecting them in a way she never would have guessed was possible.

"Knowing you are sitting inches from me with nothing barring me from doing this..." He dropped his hand to her thigh and slid it beneath her skirt, the move so smooth, it would have made her laugh if he didn't choose that moment to cup her pussy. "This is punishment."

"Let's get out of here." She wanted more than his hand between her thighs, and she didn't want to wait. The only time Keira's mind truly stilled was when she was with Dmitri, screaming his name as she came. She might be trading one addiction for another, but there were worse choices to make.

"Not before dinner is served." He traced the band of her garter where it clasped the tops of her thigh highs. "How long can you last before you're begging me to let you come?"

He was evil in a way that had nothing to do with being the head of the Romanov empire and everything to do with that wandering hand beneath her skirt. Keira dragged her fingers over his forearm, pulling him closer. "Do your worst."

"Somehow, I knew you'd say exactly that." He snagged his iced tea and took a long drink, as if he wasn't tracing a circle around her clit with his other hand while he was doing it. "You are a true delight."

She leaned against him, fighting not to lift her hips to make what he was doing easier for him, enjoying the closeness they shared. It could have just been the two of them in this restaurant for all she noticed the rest of the room. *Dangerous.* But then, what *wasn't* dangerous about her life? Keira turned her head and kissed him behind his ear. "What happens after this reception is done? After you've hunted down the Eldridges? What happens with us?"

From his tension, she could tell he was considering playing the fool. Dmitri apparently knew better than that, though, because he shifted to cup her inner thigh and sighed. "I hadn't put too much thought into it."

"Liar." She'd believe that of everyone else. Not him. If anything, he had several options laid out, depending on how Keira reacted at any given time. "How many outcomes did you plan for when it came to me as your wife?"

His lips quirked. "Three."

She shifted closer and squeezed his thigh. The muscle clenched beneath his slacks, but he didn't show any other reaction as she slid her hand higher. "In one of them, I'm the pretty doll who is happy to be locked in your room and taken out to play with or display as you see fit."

"*Da*, though I think it's safe to say that option was tabled shortly after you arrived."

At least he was willing to admit it. She gripped his cock through the fabric and gave him a slow stroke. "What are the other two?" He had to know that option wasn't an option at all, but it was so very like Dmitri to keep it as a last resort despite that. She kept stroking his cock, dishing out the same medicine he had.

His hand never left her thigh, though his fingers gripped her a little tighter. "In one, you're either informant for your brother or sent to sow discontent and chaos in my household."

It was a fair thing to plan for—he couldn't have known her motivation when she met him on the street and agreed to marry him. Dmitri would guess that it was because he manipulated her into a corner, but he wouldn't be able to know for sure that Aiden hadn't outmaneuvered him. She respected that, even though part of her mourned yet another piece of evidence of the barriers between them. Sometimes, like last night and earlier today, they seemed small enough to knock over with a single touch. Other times, they might as well have been impenetrable. "Do you think that now?"

"I highly doubt it, though I'd be a fool to underestimate you. You've proven yourself more than capable of being a spy." His hips shifted and his breathing hitched. The slightest of reactions in response to what she was doing to him, but from Dmitri, he might as well have yelled to the heavens. "That said, if you're here with my destruction in mind, it's because you decided on it—not because your brother sent you." He leaned back against his chair, the tablecloth hiding what she was doing from anyone curious enough to look. The move gave her better access, and she had a truly wild moment where she considered unzipping him and freeing his cock.

The waiter approached, and she made as if to take her hand back, but Dmitri covered it with his free one in a silent command to stay. They were silent as their food was laid out before them, and he only spoke after the man had retreated. "It will take an act of God to ensure we make it home before I'm inside you."

That wicked, hopeful feeling in her chest blossomed until she was half-sure she shone with it. "I thought I was the one who's supposed to be begging."

"That was not begging, *moya koroleva*. That was a declaration of intent."

To reach for her food, she'd have to release his cock. Keira decided she wasn't that hungry, after all. She gave him another slow pump. "What's the third option?"

"Hmm?"

She squeezed him harder. "The third outcome of us marrying."

"I thought you would have figured it out by now." He turned those gray eyes on her, and she couldn't find the breath to respond. She didn't need to, because Dmitri kept speaking in that low, rough voice. "You and I as partners, creating a dynasty to outlast all others."

She wanted to believe that—she *needed* to believe that—but all she'd gotten from him was a painting with broad strokes and none of the necessary details. "What, exactly, does that look like?"

His gaze fell to her lips even as he twisted his wrist and pushed two fingers into her. "I have a number of businesses that I've been neglecting in recent years. They were all from families absorbed into the Romanov territory during my father's time, and they function more or less on their own...too much on their own if the Eldridges' actions are anything to judge by. I would have you reinstate ties and remind them who they owe everything to."

Only the slightest deepening in his voice showed that he was affected by his hand job. She had a harder time moderating her tone. "That's...a big job." She'd seen her brothers do similar things, though it was almost always Aiden who went. To have Dmitri sending *her...Holy shit, he might actually be telling the truth about what he wants from this—from us.* If she did this and fucked it up, it would have real consequences for him. The level of trust he was putting in her by offering that job was staggering on a level she wasn't prepared to deal with.

"I won't throw you to the wolves, *moya koroleva*. We'll ensure you're up to par on all the details and players before you go out, and you'll have a contingent of men with you to ensure your safety." He slid a third finger into her. "After you've brought them to heel, we can discuss expansion."

Yep, I most definitely love this evil fucker.

She should probably have a problem with the illegal aspect of his businesses, but Dmitri had never made any apologies about who he was and what he did. If she was willing to judge him for it and not her brother...No, she was raised an O'Malley, even if she was a Romanov now. They really weren't that different. *She* wasn't that different from Dmitri.

If she wanted changes, she could be the one to implement them from within.

Her body tightened in response, and she bit back a whimper. "Dmitri—Dima—I'm close."

He leaned down until his lips brushed her ear. "I know."

Just like that, she couldn't deny it any longer. Keira came, pressing her lips together so tightly, they hurt. She shuddered against him, her hand going slack on his cock. "Fuck, Dima. Just...fuck."

He slid his fingers out of her, but kept cupping her. "Eat something so we can get the fuck out of here."

Because he wants me. Dmitri's expression had taken on the wild edge that she loved so much, the monster beneath the mask of civility he wore.

The fact he was *still* trying to get her to eat—to take care of her—despite the fact that he clearly wanted to drag her out of here by her hair and fuck her behind the nearest closed door... Her heart tried to burst from her chest. She clasped his chin and tipped his head down. "Get it to go."

"Keira—"

"If you think for a second that I'm going to be able to concentrate enough to get more than a bite or two, you're not nearly as smart as we both know you are. That orgasm barely took the edge off." She lifted her hips to press herself more firmly against his hand. "I want you. I want your hands and your mouth and your cock, and I want you now. Get the food to go and you can feed it to me in bed—*after*."

For several endless moments, she thought he'd tell her no and reiterate his order for her to eat. Instead, Dmitri nodded once. "Start walking."

She blinked. "What?"

He kissed her. His tongue tangled with hers even as the feeling of him overwhelmed her. The man kissed like a homecoming warrior who considered her part of his spoils of war. He broke away, leaving both of them breathing harshly. "Better yet—run. If I catch you before you make it back to the house, I'll fuck you right there on the sidewalk."

She shivered. It could be bravado, but with the monster beneath the mask peeking out at her, she didn't think so. He was Dmitri fucking Romanov, and he could do exactly what he promised without consequence. Keira licked her lips. "My art—"

"I'll take care of it." He waited for her to meet his gaze. "Pavel will follow, and my men hold several key locations in this area. You'll be safe the entire time."

Even in the midst of his frenzy, he was still taking care of her. She took a shuddering breath. "In that case, catch me if you can."

Keira managed to keep her pace even as she wove through the tables to the front door. Pavel had taken up a spot against the wall, a cigarette dangling from his fingers. He straightened when he caught sight of her, his brows dropping in confusion. Her body hummed with the need to move, but she knew better than to bolt without saying something. She wanted Dmitri focused on *her*, not distracted because he was worried she might be snatched off the street. "Home, Pavel. Now," she ground out.

He nodded and fell into step behind her.

She ran.

* * *

Dmitri was a man possessed. He had the presence of mind to be careful with Keira's purchases, but he strode through the streets at a fast clip that dared anyone to get in his path or slow him down. The restaurant was only three blocks from the house, but it might as well have been miles. The crowd in front of him parted like the Red Sea, and he caught sight of Keira turning the corner to their home, Pavel shadowing her. She shot a look over her shoulder at Dmitri and grinned, her hand flying out in the universal *come and get it* gesture.

At that, what little part of him that cared about propriety snuffed out. He picked up his pace until he was sprinting after her. She still made it to the house before he did, but not by much.

He caught her on the stairs.

Dmitri dropped the bags on the floor and snatched her upper arm, swinging her to face him. Keira hit his chest, and he grabbed the banister to keep them from tumbling down the stairs. The sound of footsteps moving away from them assured him that Pavel was making himself scarce. *He'll need a fucking raise by the time this is all through.*

Dmitri half expected Keira to try to keep running. He should have known better. She shrugged out of her blazer and ripped his shirt from his slacks, sending buttons flying as she shoved it down his arms. "You caught me."

He shredded her shirt and yanked down her skirt. The garter belt, he left alone. Dmitri hit his knees on the bottom step and buried his face in her pussy. He craved the taste of her, needed to feel her come apart and know he was the reason behind it, needed another tether to bind her to him so she'd never try to leave.

I don't know what I'd do if she was gone.

Keira's heels slipped on the hardwood steps, and he barely caught her before she hit the stairs. As it was, they still toppled, her sprawling beneath him, his mouth never leaving her. He started to lift his head to ensure she was okay, but she threaded her fingers through his hair and kept him in place, riding his mouth as all the sexy little cries she'd kept stifled at the restaurant poured from her lips.

Her orgasm wasn't enough. He needed more. All of her. He shucked off his pants and crawled between her thighs, thrusting into her with a rough move. Dmitri tried to pull back, to regain some kind of control, to perhaps move this upstairs and away from anyone who might walk in, but Keira kissed him and wrapped her legs around his waist. "Yes, Dima. There. Fuck me like that." She slid her foot down the back of his thigh and up again. "I can't get enough of you."

"*I'll never get enough of you. You are mine and I am*

*yours, and I'm keeping you for the rest of our fucking
lives. I love you, you reckless woman, and I'm never letting you go,"* he growled in Russian. He shoved into her
harder, responding to her cries of *more, more, yes, ohmy-
god yes.* Her orgasm hit, her pussy milking him, the feeling too good to deny. He wanted his cum in her, marking
her like the fucking savage he was. Dmitri let go, burying
his face in her neck as his strokes shuddered and he came
hard enough to see stars. "God in heaven above."

Keira laughed softly. "I don't think God had anything
to do with what we just did." She shifted and winced.
"Damn."

He lifted his head. "What's wrong?"

Her smile came accompanied with another wince.
"Hardwood stairs are a bitch."

"Fuck. *Fuck.*" He pushed off her and pulled her up to sit
in a single move. Bruises already darkened her pale skin,
and there were scrapes where his thrusts had shoved her
against the edges of the steps. For the first time in his life,
he felt sick at the sight of someone else's pain. "I'm sorry."
Dmitri scooped her up and stood.

"I'm not." She let her head fall against his shoulder. Her
expression looked blissed-out, not regretful or pained at
all, but the only thing he could focus on was the damage
he'd done to her.

Dmitri did not lose control. Not ever. And yet every time
he turned around, he was doing exactly that with Keira.

He kicked the bedroom door shut behind him and bypassed the bed in favor of the tub. A hot soak wouldn't
help the scrapes, but it would ease the soreness. "Can you
stand?"

"Yes, Dima, I can stand because I'm perfectly okay. It's

going to take more than a deliciously rough fucking to screw me up."

He believed her, but that didn't mean his actions were excused. He set her carefully on her feet and got the water running. Only then did he sit on the edge of the tub and set his hands on her hips. "Turn around."

She rolled her eyes, but she obeyed. He sucked in a harsh breath. It was worse than he'd thought. "Keira—"

"No. Absolutely not." She spun back to face him, her hazel eyes furious. "Tonight was good for me—all of it. Really fucking good. I need you to not ruin it with some misplaced guilt that you should be beyond. If you didn't notice, I was screaming your name as I came for the *third* time on those stairs." She glared. "And you don't hear me losing my shit because I scratched your back to hell."

"That's different." He welcomed the marks she left, the physical representation of her abandon.

But he recognized a losing battle when he saw one. As sick as her bruises left him, if he pushed this, he'd lose all the ground they'd covered tonight—and likely more. She had him cornered and she damn well knew it. He clenched his jaw and spoke through gritted teeth. "Let me take care of you."

"You *have* been taking care of me." She stepped between his thighs and slid her fingers through his hair. "But I'll make you a deal. You can hover over and mother hen me for the duration of this bath, then you'll slap some Neosporin on my scrapes, give me a couple ibuprofen, and we'll eat leftovers in bed. Or not in bed. I don't give a fuck, but once the endorphins wear off, I'm going to be hungry."

She was handling him—offering him tasks to redirect his guilt. He almost fought her on it, but what was the point? If she said she was fine, and he didn't take her at her word, he wasn't honoring the vision he'd painted for her. She didn't believe him when he offered for her to be his queen in truth, and overriding her on something that she considered small—even if *he* didn't—would confirm her belief that he was lying about everything else.

He dropped his forehead to rest between her breasts. "You're not giving me much of a choice, *moya koroleva*."

"I know." She kept stroking her fingers through his hair. "But at least I'm giving you a choice at all."

CHAPTER TWENTY-SIX

Keira waited for Dmitri to walk out of the bathroom to climb into the tub. She was grateful he wasn't there to see her flinch as the hot water stung her scrapes. Though she'd been telling him the truth, it didn't change the fact that her back was a fucking mess. From the glimpse she'd snuck in the mirror, she'd be an ugly rainbow tomorrow, which meant she'd have to pick a different dress or she'd give her family a heart attack. Somehow, Keira didn't think they'd believe her if she told them that Dmitri hadn't been beating her—they'd just had gloriously rough sex on the stairs.

She carefully leaned against the back of the tub. Keira had never thought the day would come when Dmitri looked spooked, but he'd been a little too wide around the eyes in the last ten minutes. Giving him a task to soothe him was manipulative, but she didn't know how to help him realize that she was really okay.

He reappeared before she had a ready answer, a book

dangling from one hand. Those gray eyes studied her as if she was in danger of bleeding out the second he looked away. She bit down on the urge to tell him—again—that she was fine. The more she protested, the more convinced he'd be that she was lying to make him feel better.

So she just sat there and waited.

Finally, he crossed the tiled room and grabbed a small bench she hadn't noticed before then. Dmitri dropped it next to the tub and took a seat. "You need at least thirty minutes in the hot water."

Do not argue with the irrational man. "Okay."

He eyed her like he knew she was just humoring him. "Do you read much fantasy?"

She tilted her head, trying to see the cover of the book in his hands. "I prefer the sexy stuff."

Something in him relaxed as he chuckled. "I can see that. This is one of my favorites, and an excellent way to pass the time."

This was his rodeo—at least for the next thirty minutes until she got out of this bath—so she made a show of settling in on her side so she could face him. "I never pegged you for a fiction reader. The classics, sure, but not contemporary books."

"Oh?" His eyebrows rose. "What kind of reader did you peg me for?"

"I don't know." She swirled her hand through the water. "I just figured you read *The Art of War* over and over again until you can quote it at the drop of a hat."

" 'To fight and conquer in all our battles is not supreme excellence; supreme excellence consists in breaking the enemy's resistance without fighting.' "

Her jaw dropped. "I knew it!"

Amusement flickered to life in his eyes, chasing away some of the worry. "It's an excellent resource—one you should tap as well."

"Yeah, yeah, enough with the lessons. Read me this fantasy novel." She made a show of being the rapt pupil—which would have worked out a lot better if she wasn't naked in the tub without even a shield of bubbles and he wasn't sitting there in only a pair of lounge pants. "Is there a farm boy who needs to go on a journey to realize he's the savior of the world like every single *Lord of the Rings* rip-off ever?"

He gave her a mock severe look. "If you'll be quiet, you'll find out." He waited for her to obey, and then began to read.

Keira was instantly enraptured by his voice. Most people didn't have the cadence to read books aloud—they went too fast or too slow or didn't breathe in the right places. It stood to figure that Dmitri wasn't most people. His accent only added to the experience as he immersed her in the story. She watched his face as he spoke, loving the fact that she could do it without being caught because he was focused on the words on the page.

It didn't take long to discover why this was a favorite. The hero of the story was a bard who was smarter and wilier than everyone around him, even if those same wits got him into trouble as often as they got him out of it. No doubt Dmitri saw bits of himself in the man.

As the story played out, her bathwater cooled, but she was loath to break the moment. It was well past the thirty-minute limit when Dmitri frowned and shook his head as if shaking off a daze. "You must be starving."

She was, but this moment felt more important than a few hunger pangs. "I was enjoying myself."

"How does your back feel?"

"It hurts like a bitch, but I'm not the least bit sorry." She grinned. "Though I might need some help out of the tub."

He sighed. "There will be no reasoning with you, will there?"

"Nope." She didn't want his guilt—she just wanted him. The sex was beyond amazing, but the quiet moments that kept cropping up were just as important to Keira. She didn't want him holding back for any of it. She wanted all of him. "Now take me to bed and feed me."

Dmitri shook his head, but the guilt remained at bay. He pulled the stopper on the tub and helped her stand. Her back had tightened up from staying in one position too long, but she fought to keep her expression neutral as she stepped out of the tub and allowed him to dry her. He cursed. "You don't have to be strong for me."

"I don't know about that—you threw a hissy fit earlier."

"A hissy fit."

She glared at him, though there was no heat behind it. "Yes, Dima, a hissy fit. What else do you call that freak-out? I was lying there, trying to soak up the glory of post-orgasmic bliss, and you were going into hysterics."

His brows dropped. "Concern for you is hardly hysterics."

"I am not breakable. The sooner you learn that, the easier it will be on both of us." She strode past him and into the bedroom. The food they'd bought was set up on an honest-to-God tray designed for breakfast in bed. She shook her head, because there was no other appropriate response. Keira didn't bother with clothes as she climbed onto the mattress and picked up her fork. "This looks freaking amazing."

"*Moya koroleva*, you can't just change the subject because you're done talking about it."

She shot him a look. "Yes, actually, I can. I just did, in fact." She took a bite of her fancy-ass mac and cheese and chewed. Even cold, it was fantastic. "We're going to have to go back and eat there, but without all the finger fucking."

He gave another of those put-upon sighs and climbed onto the bed next to her. "Once you're finished eating, I'll treat your wounds."

"Scratches, not wounds." She waved her fork at him. "See what I mean? Hysterics." She let them eat for a few minutes—mostly because she really was starving—and then paused to take a drink of her water. "Do you push the visitation with Hadley because you want a hold over Olivia or because you actually care about your niece?"

"Does it matter?"

"Yes, I think it does." It was one thing that had never fit with the cold bastard he presented to the world. Her brothers and even Olivia thought it evidence that he was just that much of a bastard, but she didn't think that was it at all.

He set down his fork. "You're still trying to make me Prince Charming."

"Bullshit—though that was a nice dodge. I see you better than most, and you know it. Now, answer the question." She waited for a few seconds and then poked him in the arm with her fork. "I know you get off on being the one with all the cards, but you're going to have to open up eventually. It might as well be now."

Dmitri frowned. "My sister and niece are the last family I have left." When Keira shot him a look, he growled. "It is impossible not to love that girl, and you know it. She's sunshine and innocence and all the things that shrivel up in our world. It gives me hope that Olivia and Cillian love her so much, because they will shield her from the worst of it."

"There, that wasn't so hard." Keira smiled. "Hadley loves you, too, you know. After your visits, she prances around for days bragging about how wonderful her uncle is. It drives my brothers batty." Knowing that he loved his niece shouldn't give her hope. Just because he was capable of familial love didn't mean he'd be capable of actually falling in love, let alone with Keira.

She might as well wish on a star—it would give it the same odds of happening.

* * *

Dmitri saw the moment Keira's mood plummeted, but he couldn't begin to guess what caused it. She'd been fine, chatting and flirting and not acting at all like he'd done damage to her a short time ago. Between one breath and the other, she...wilted. She pushed her plate away. "I think the day just caught up with me."

It could be that. It could be that he was looking too deeply into things because he felt guilty.

Or it could be that she was withdrawing from him for reasons unknown.

He cleared the food and took the time to deliver it to the kitchen. The house was quiet around him as he headed back upstairs. There would be patrols at irregular intervals—both internally and externally. It wasn't something he bothered with most of the time, but he'd never had a traitor in his home before. Caught between the need to remove anyone that couldn't be trusted and the requirement of having more than just Pavel to protect the house... there weren't any good options.

When he arrived back at the room, he found Keira

brushing her teeth in the bathroom. It was such a mundane thing that something inside him clicked into place. This was right—her in his room, in his home, in his life. He'd known it before, but tonight only solidified that feeling. Where else in the world would he find a woman who was this intoxicating mix of strong and soft, harsh and flirty?

He wouldn't.

He pulled a bottle of Neosporin from the drawer. "It might be best to sleep in a shirt."

"Get me one of yours."

The sheer *rightness* of the moment staggered him. He nodded, trying to keep the revelation from his face, trying to lock down the whirlwind of emotions hitting him with the force of a hurricane. *I love her.* He found a soft T-shirt and brought it to her. "Turn around, *moya koroleva.*"

She sighed, but she did as he commanded, bracing her hands on the bathroom counter. Dmitri pressed a soft kiss to the nape of her neck. "Why did you retreat from me?"

"I don't know what you're talking about."

He raised his eyebrows at her reflection in the mirror. "Opening up goes both ways." While she chewed on that piece of information, he quickly dabbed some of the ointment onto the scrapes on her back. The bruises would be spectacular, but she was right about the scrapes being exactly that—scrapes.

"It's nothing. I'm just being unforgivably sentimental." She sighed and turned to take the T-shirt from him. "We keep going around again and again. I know what this is. I do, Dima—I swear it. But sometimes the lines get blurry and I forget for a little while, and when I remember, it's a downer." She made a visible effort to straighten her shoulders and get her smile back into place. "It's fine. I'm fine."

He had to pick through her words to understand what she was actually saying, but when he did...Dmitri found himself holding his breath. "You're falling for me." Her flinch had him correcting, "You've already fallen."

"Call it temporary insanity."

She tried to brush past him, but he stopped her with a hand on her arm. "Keira, wait."

"If you're going to give me another lecture on how this isn't a love match and I'm a fool for forgetting that, there's no need—I'm doing a damn good job of giving it to myself."

Fuck, she was killing him. He pulled her into his arms. "I love you, too." And then again in Russian. "*Ya lyublyu tebya, moya koroleva.*"

She froze. "Don't fuck with me like this. It's cruel."

"I can be cruel." He framed her face, tipping her head back so she looked into his eyes. He did his best to lower the masks he held in place through habit and let her see what she'd come to mean to him. "But I'm being honest right now. I never planned on it, but then, I never planned on you."

"You...you mean it?" she whispered.

"*Da.*" He smoothed back her hair. "How could I not?"

Her lower lip quivered, the tiniest of movements. "Take me to bed."

He let his forehead drop to rest against hers. "If I do to you what I want to, it will hurt you with your current injuries."

"Dmitri Romanov, you just told me you love me. If you don't make love to me to prove it, I'll never forgive you."

He found himself smiling, even as his concern for her back dampened his desire. "I won't hurt you."

"You're right. You won't. You'll lie on your back and let

me decide what hurts me and what doesn't." She ran her hands up his chest and kissed him. "I need you, Dima."

I need you, Dima.

The magic words of his undoing.

He could deny this woman nothing when she wielded them against him. He backed toward the bed, towing her with him. "This wasn't what I intended."

"Yeah, you couldn't be clearer about that." She shook her head and gave him a little push. He allowed himself to sprawl back on the bed, his mouth going dry as Keira climbed to straddle him. She stroked his cock, her gaze never leaving his face. "You love me."

"I love you." It got easier to say it every time.

Her brows pinched together. "You're not saying that because you think Alethea Eldridge is going to murder us all tomorrow and this is your way of getting some action before the battle, is it?"

"I believe we already established that wasn't my plan." He gave her the look that accusation deserved. "As evidenced by the marks all over your back, I don't need to lie to you to get inside you."

She gave him a squeeze. "Now, now. Those are fighting words. A girl likes to feel valued and not taken for granted."

He bent up to kiss her. "You're not taken for granted, *moya koroleva.*"

"Good." She pushed him back to a prone position and guided his cock to her entrance. "Now let *me* take advantage of you."

CHAPTER TWENTY-SEVEN

Keira spent most of the next day in a whirlwind of activity that did nothing to distract her from her tangled thoughts. *Dmitri said he loved me.* She wanted to believe it. She wanted to believe it so much, she practically vibrated from that need. If she were any other woman—if he were any other man—she *would* believe it with no qualms.

But she wasn't any other woman. She was only herself.

Dmitri wasn't any other man. He was manipulative and ambitious and surprisingly tender, all wrapped up in a complicated package.

So instead of feeling the bliss of the newly in love, she kept deconstructing every moment they'd ever spent together, trying to see it from different angles. Dmitri was so damn smart, so damn calculating, and it wasn't like he'd suddenly *stopped* being those things now that he claimed to care about her.

More than anything, she wanted to call someone to talk it out. Charlie was quickly becoming one of her best friends, but the woman didn't exactly have much in the way of relationship experience—aside from Aiden—and her loathing of Dmitri would color any advice. Keira's sister Carrigan wasn't much better, but...

No. She had to figure this one out herself.

As Mark had said when she'd ordered him out of the house—she wasn't an O'Malley anymore. *She* had made that choice.

She took an extra-long shower, wishing she could wash away her confusion as easily. Foolish of her to be so focused on it when they had all hell breaking loose in a few short hours, but she couldn't stop.

She shut off the water and closed her eyes, letting the cool air chill her. *You can do this. Shelve the feelings talk until after you figure out whether you're all going to die.*

"Keira?"

"Just thinking." *Obsessing.* She turned to find Dmitri leaning against the corner where the shower met the rest of the bathroom, well out of the way of any potential water. He wore his usual slacks and button-down, so he must have come up from the office. Now was the time to put on the brave face and pretend she wasn't hopelessly in over her head, but she just couldn't do it.

"I want a drink." Keira held up her hand. "I'm not going to have one, but I'm overwhelmed and freaked out, and part of me is so damn sure that if I just drown my sorrows a bit, it will make everything better." She could almost taste the vodka on her tongue if she concentrated.

He crossed to her, and that was when she noticed that he was barefoot. She'd never paid much attention to his feet before, but the big toe on his left foot was a bit crooked.

That slight imperfection somehow made him more

attractive, if that was at all possible. Dmitri pulled her into his arms, and hugged her tightly to him. "It will be okay."

"I'm all wet." She didn't struggle, though. Instead, she buried her face in his chest and let him comfort her. *This feels so real.*

"I'll survive." He let his chin rest on the top of her head. "Is tonight bothering you? Or what happened last night?"

"I'm just worried across the board." It was the truth, though not the complete truth.

He gave her a squeeze and released her. "After tonight, the reception will be over. We'll have made our public announcement and we can get back to us."

She tried to dredge up a smile. "Okay." There was no point in saying that the reception was the least of her worries. He knew. It was still easier to focus on the guests that were about to descend on their household than the fact that Alethea and Mae could strike at any time.

Dmitri, damn him, saw right through her. He took her hand and drew her out of the shower. She let him dry her off with one of his ridiculously luxurious towels because it felt good to have him taking care of her. But when he rose to face her, she couldn't keep it buttoned up any longer. "I don't know what's real."

He nodded as if she'd confirmed something he'd suspected. "You think I told you that I love you to keep you in line."

"It sounds extra evil when you say it like that." She hugged the towel to her chest as if she wasn't shivering and naked in front of him.

"For God's sake." He disappeared into the closet and came back with the same robe she'd co-opted that first week. He dropped it over her shoulders and watched her until she slipped her arms into it and tied it at the waist. It helped the shivers, if not her state of mind. Dmitri crossed his arms over his chest. "Explain why I would lie to you when we were finally coexisting comfortably."

He didn't have to make it sound so ridiculous. It wasn't. She lifted her chin. "You like me nice and compliant, which is a whole lot more likely if I'm all goofy over being in love with you."

"While you have a point, that's not a low I would ever hit."

She wanted to believe that, and she didn't trust him *because* she so desperately wanted to believe it. That didn't make sense, even in her own head.

Keira rubbed her eyes. "I'm scared." It felt like the words were ripped from her, but once she started, she couldn't stop. "It feels too good to be true, and that scares the shit out of me. I know you're not some Prince Charming type, and I'm sure as hell not a princess, but it doesn't seem possible that we could end up in love after everything. There has to be some plot, some manipulation, *something* going on. That's our world. It's not the one where people get happily ever afters."

He cupped her face and stroked his thumbs along her cheekbones. "What if it was?"

Her mouth went dry and her heart tried to beat its way out of her chest. "It will blow up in our faces," she whispered.

"*Mozhet byt'.*" He shrugged. "And maybe Alethea will manage to outmaneuver us and we won't survive the day, the week, the month. You can't live in fear of the bad. You have to grasp the good with both hands and fight for it." He paused. "Fight for me."

"Is that some kind of code for a game you want me to play to win your affection?"

He rolled his eyes. "*Moya koroleva*, you already possess *my affection*. I merely want you not to allow fear to get the best of you. Stand by my side. Fight with me. When we are sure of our victory, we can do whatever it takes to make you feel better about our current situation."

He was handling her, but he was also being completely transparent about it, so she couldn't be too pissed. Keira sighed. "I should have chosen a better time to freak out about it, huh?"

"I highly doubt you chose it at all." He kissed her, quick and light, a reassuring touch. "Love was unexpected for me, as well. There's nothing wrong with reacting honestly."

He didn't quite stress the word *honestly*, but she felt it all the same. Keira took a breath, and then another. "I should get dressed."

"Do you need help?"

"No, I'm fine." She would have said it even if she wasn't. He was already tweaked out about her back—he didn't need to know the bruises hurt like a motherfucker and she had a hard time twisting in some directions. It would just start another argument, and seeing as how Keira couldn't skip this party even if she wanted to, it was all a moot point.

He gave her a long look, and finally nodded. "Pavel will stick close to you." He kissed her again and released her. "We don't have much time."

A quick glance at the clock had her cursing. An hour shouldn't be the end of the world, but when it came to getting glammed up, Keira needed all the time she could get. At least if she was focusing on her lipstick, she wouldn't be focused on the fact that, in sixty minutes, she'd be face-to-face with her family and Dmitri's allies.

She wasn't sure which of them she dreaded seeing more.

* * *

Dmitri took a precious ten minutes to go over the plan with Pavel and Alexei one last time. He had no logical reason to think the attack would come tonight, but his instincts said it would. Alethea was too smart to miss the opportunity to cut him off at the knees publically. His allies and enemies knowing that he was vulnerable would do just as much damage as anything she could physically do.

They were as ready as they could be.

His men had barely closed the door when it opened again. Aiden O'Malley strode into Dmitri's office as if he owned it, but for once he was blessedly alone. He stopped too close, his green eyes furious. "Where is she?"

"Not locked in the tower, since I don't actually have a tower in this place."

His jaw tightened. "That shit is not funny, Romanov."

"On the contrary, if I didn't find your insistence on the idea of Keira as a damsel in distress amusing, it would be infuriating." For once, he found no joy in Aiden's aggravation. They didn't have time for that song and dance—not tonight. He needed Aiden O'Malley at the top of his game, and he wouldn't be if he was so distracted by his little sister. "She chose, Aiden. Respect it, or lose her."

"You mean you'll take her."

Family blurred the lines beyond recognition. Dmitri understood that, even as he wanted to shake some sense into the man. "No," he said gently. "What I mean is that Keira herself will draw the line in the sand. She's not the same baby sister you seem to be clinging to—she hasn't been for some time."

Aiden stared at him for several long moments and

finally growled. "This conversation might be put on hold until we can take care of the Eldridges, but it's not over."

Dmitri couldn't make the man see reason, but for Keira's sake, he was willing to try. A little. He and Keira had found the beginnings of a balance, but they were by no means out of the woods. She might love Dmitri, but she didn't trust him completely. That was something that could be addressed with time—actions spoke louder than words and the like. Having her family continue to insist that she didn't know what she wanted would wear on her, and it might possibly send her back to the bottle.

He couldn't risk it.

Dmitri lowered his voice so the O'Malley had to lean in to hear him. "Make no mistake, Aiden, I don't want a war with you. That was never the goal."

"Easy to say that now."

"I am not finished." He strove to keep control and not throttle this fool. "I will not take Romanov to war against O'Malley and the others in Boston, but if you harm Keira with this insistence that her choices are invalid, I will carve out your fucking heart and force you to eat it."

Aiden blinked, then blinked again. Understanding dawned across his face, and the change might have been amusing under other circumstances. "You love her."

Dmitri didn't dignify that by addressing it. "I will do what it takes to ensure she's safe and happy—and that includes removing you permanently from her life if it becomes necessary. You had her on the road to drinking herself to death and living in misery, and you never once pulled your head out of your ass to realize how close you were to losing her. I will not make the same mistake."

Aiden rocked back on his heels. "I'll take that into consideration."

He let the subject of Keira go. If her brother was willing to listen to reason long enough to put it on the back burner, Dmitri could do no less. As long as Aiden didn't fuck things up for him tonight, the rest would fall where it may. "Finding Alethea would have been more effective if we had worked together."

"You're right." Aiden scrubbed a hand over his face. "We should have been able to find her before now."

"She's being careful and not leaving a trail." Dmitri hesitated. Although he always played his cards close to his chest, there was one factor of the upcoming scenario that Aiden needed to know about. "John Finch contacted me."

"You're joking."

"Hardly." Dmitri leaned against his desk and crossed his arms over his chest. "He's been trying to get enough evidence to bring me down for years. I'm aware of it. He knows I'm aware of it. It's a game we play, because they'll never find anything incriminating, but he's too proud to admit that."

"What's that have to do with anything?"

He held on to his patience through sheer force of will. If Alethea attacked, having Aiden and the rest of the O'Malleys on his side would be invaluable. "Someone has been interfering with the cameras they have set up. It's happened several times over the last couple days, all for approximately five to ten minutes. It's not my doing, which means someone else wants access to this house without the eye of the government on them."

"Why the fuck would he tell you that..." He stilled. "Does he honestly want us to believe this is for Charlie?

He already made his priorities painfully clear when it came to her versus his job."

Dmitri crossed his arms over his chest. "Have you seen him since the events at the Eldridge warehouse?"

"No. He's called Charlie a couple times, but she's not ready to see or talk to him."

That lined up with what Charlie had told Keira—and the desperation he'd seen lurking in John Finch's eyes. "You know that saying that you don't know what you have until you lose it? Finch is old. His career has an expiration date on it, though it's not for years yet. He might have been disappointed with his so-called disgraced daughter, but she was still his daughter. And now it comes out that she was never a dirty cop and she removes herself from his life in one fell swoop?" He shrugged one shoulder. "He wasn't able to protect her—not from the dirty cops who got her kicked off the force and not from Mae Eldridge. He couldn't even ensure that Mae stayed locked up until her trial. He's a smart man. He knows Mae will want to finish what she started, and he knows that the Eldridges would see this reception as too tempting to ignore. All their enemies in one place? Even if Alethea could resist, Mae won't be able to."

Aiden's expression might as well have been stone, not a single one of his thoughts flickering through his eyes. "This is all just theory."

"It's theory grounded in fact."

Aiden finally dropped into the chair. "If I were Alethea Eldridge, I'd attack tonight. Maybe not something direct, but I'd do it to prove you aren't strong enough to protect your guests, or your people."

"That would be my play as well." He sank into the chair next to Aiden. No power plays. No trying to avoid the fact that they were equals. From the way the man's green eyes widened ever so slightly, Aiden recognized the symbolism. Dmitri leaned forward. "I'm reasonably confident I can repel whatever she throws at me, but we need to stop fucking around. I don't want Boston."

Aiden's expression gave nothing away. "I don't want New York."

"Then now's the time to decide—are we going to cling to our tangled past and bring up the bullshit moves we've made against each other every time we interact?" He sat back. "Or are we going to put it all aside and focus on the future? You've seen what can be accomplished when the three power players in Boston stopped fighting and became true allies. Be my ally in truth, Aiden. Give me your word that you'll stop the plots against me, and I'll return the favor."

The moment stretched out between them. Romanov hadn't gone into this conversation intending to shelve his history with the O'Malleys, but the more he spoke with Aiden, the clearer it became that he could never make Keira choose. As long as they fought, she would be torn between them. She loved her family. She'd never stop loving her family. He'd never ask that of her.

The only option left was the one he'd laid before Aiden.

The O'Malley stared at him a long time. "I don't trust you."

"You don't have to. Trust that I'm willing to put Keira before any blows to my pride and reputation that you've delivered."

"I'll consider it."

While he wanted an immediate agreement, Dmitri knew Aiden well enough to know it wasn't in the realm of possibility. In the other man's place, he'd do the same. He permitted himself a smile. "That's all I ask."

Aiden finally nodded. "Walk me through the plan."

CHAPTER TWENTY-EIGHT

The massive ballroom was already filled by the time Keira got downstairs. She stood just outside the door and allowed herself to take it all in. The tables were arranged to allow the different guests plenty of space to prevent potential conflicts. They'd debated whether to do a seated meal, but Keira pushed hard for a buffet style. She already felt trapped enough by the situation without forcing everyone to stay in their seats. If they *didn't*, then Dmitri and Keira would look like they couldn't control their own gathering. Better to preemptively make this call.

The centerpieces at the tables were bloodred roses in black vases, and she smiled at the sight. Maybe the color scheme *was* gothic, but she preferred to call it classic. Hell, maybe it was a little bit of both.

"Moya koroleva."

She turned to face him and tamped down the reckless urge to throw herself into Dmitri's arms. Now wasn't the time to drop the masks they both had in place—not when someone could see them. She merely slipped her hand into the crook of his elbow instead. "Hey."

"You look ravishing."

She smoothed her hands down her gray dress. The slinky fabric covered her from the hollow of her throat to the tops of her knees, but it was fitted enough that she still managed to look sexy and a little edgy. She loved it. "Thank you." Dmitri, as always, looked like he'd stepped out of some high-fashion photo shoot. "Did things go okay with my brother?" she asked.

"*Da*. We're as prepared as we can be."

It was better than she'd hoped for. Aiden could be stubborn, and he wouldn't be thinking clearly when it came to the Eldridges—not after what they did to Charlie. But those bitches hadn't made a move yet. Pavel would have warned her if they had.

She glanced over her shoulder to find him at a respectable distance, dressed in a forgettable black suit that didn't quite manage to hide the bulges of his weapons. It was a calculated detail—she was sure of it. Dmitri wasn't the type to let his men dress in ill-fitting tuxes unless he had a good reason. Intimidation came in many forms, and this one was both obvious and subtle.

Keira turned back to face the room and straightened her spine. "Then I guess we should stop lurking in the hallway and go meet our guests."

"If, at any point, you need a break, don't hesitate to ask. You're more important to me than any of these people, and I'll manage the fallout accordingly."

The fact that he offered at all had her heart taking up residence in her throat. It was considerate, though she'd grit her teeth and bear whatever she had to in order to ensure she didn't have to take him up on it. Keira had to be able to hold her own, and that started now. "I'll be okay."

Still, he didn't take that first step. "We have a full bar set up."

"I know." Keira pressed her lips together, her gaze jumping from one table to the other, and finally landing on the small bar in the back corner. Her mouth watered, and she had to swallow hard to get herself back under control. "It'll be fine. I couldn't have skipped having alcohol here without broadcasting that it's an issue for me. My family might already know that, but *yours* doesn't."

She'd actually considered skipping it altogether, but she had to be able to trust herself to be in the same room as vodka without drinking. Keira had no illusions—she was at the very beginning of a long and difficult journey that might never actually be over—but she had to take that first step at some point. It might as well be on a night when it would serve the purpose of hiding a weakness from friend and foe alike. "Let's go before they think we're scared to face them."

He leaned down and pressed a quick kiss to her temple. "*Ya lyublyu tebya.*"

"I know what that one means." She grinned. "*Ya lyublyu tebya*, too."

His answering smile was worth the hour she'd spent mangling the words this morning using her phone's translation app. Learning Russian was high on her list of things to do if they survived the coming conflict with the Eldridges, if only because she wanted to know what filthy shit he was whispering in her ear every time he was inside her. "Let's do this."

"Let's."

They stepped into the room and headed for the center table, where several Romanov cousins had already set up a space. Keira caught sight of Ivan and a tall, gorgeous blonde who must be his Natasha, as well as a group of men who were obviously their muscle.

On the other side of the room, the O'Malleys held court. Aiden and Charlie had the table in the corner, along with Olivia and Cillian. Keira paused to wonder if it was difficult for Olivia to be back in the home Dmitri's father had confined her to for several months, but it was too late to worry about it now. At the table farthest from the door were Teague and his wife, Callie Sheridan. Opposite them sat Carrigan and her husband, James Halloran.

They had all the main players in Boston's power structure here in a single place. If Alethea Eldridge didn't try something, she'd be a fool.

She leaned into Dmitri. "Are you sure everyone is safe?" They were in an interior room, so drive-bys were out of the question. The walls were reinforced, anyway, and all the windows boasted bulletproof glass—she'd asked Pavel about it a couple days ago.

"We've swept the entire residence several times—two of which were today. Nothing explosive has been smuggled in before the party, and everyone coming in now is scanned on entry for weapons."

That didn't cover their mystery traitor, and the tightening around his mouth conveyed his frustration with that. She squeezed his arm. They were as prepared as they could be. Part of her almost hoped that nothing would happen tonight and the only thing she'd have to worry about was one of her family members trying to haul her ass back to Boston for her own good.

They wouldn't get that lucky. She was sure of it. "I guess all we can do is wait, huh?"

"Wait, and deal with our guests." His gaze flicked around the room, the only sign that he wasn't comfortable with not being completely in control of the situation. "In order to avoid showing favoritism, we'll be seated at our table and let them approach."

Keira snorted. "I'm sure the power balance of acting the king and queen to their petitioners was purely coincidental."

He gave her a tight smile. "*Da.*"

"Mm-hmm."

They'd barely reached the table when Ivan and his woman met them. He looked like he wanted to sweep Dmitri into a bear hug the same way he had the first night she met him, but he restrained himself to a firm handshake. "Dima, you're looking well. Marriage agrees with you."

"I should have taken your advice years ago, *starry drug.*" He turned to the woman and took her hand, brushing her knuckles with a polite kiss. "Natasha, you're looking particularly beautiful tonight."

She gave him an arch look and focused on Keira. "So you're the woman who turned our Dima's head." Her accent was thicker than both Dmitri and Ivan's, though he'd told her that Natasha had been in the States since birth, the same as the men. Her gaze dropped to Keira's feet and coasted back up to the top of her head. "You're very beautiful." She nodded as if to herself. "You'll join us for dinner next week before we depart for Texas."

Dmitri cleared his throat. "Natasha—"

She frowned at him. "No, Dima. Do not give me these excuses about how busy you are. You are family, and you've married this woman, which makes her family. You will come to dinner. We will talk." She aimed that frown at Keira. "You will wear something more appropriate than the last time my Ivan saw you."

Her face flamed at the memory of that dress. Keira wasn't ashamed of it, exactly, but she'd been so furious at Dmitri, she hadn't bothered to think about the consequences. No, that was a lie. She'd known there would be consequences. She just hadn't cared at the time.

She cared now.

There was no time to come up with a reply—not that she had one—before they moved away and were replaced by Teague and Callie. Teague held himself tightly, as if doing everything in his power not to take a swing at Dmitri. "Romanov."

"Teague." For once, Dmitri left all mocking out of his tone. She appreciated the effort, even if it was totally lost on her middle brother.

He turned to Keira. "I'd congratulate the bride, but that hardly seems appropriate given the groom." Another glare at her husband.

Thank God for Callie. Teague's pregnant wife slipped between Teague and Dmitri, giving him her hand the same way a queen would bestow knighthood. "Dmitri, you're playing a dangerous game."

"The only kind there is." He kissed her hand and released her immediately.

She studied him for a long moment. "I see."

Keira wasn't sure exactly what her sister-in-law meant, but Callie had always been something of an enigma. Teague was savvy when he needed to be, but his emotions got the best of him sometimes. His wife rarely had that problem—except when it came to her family. They hadn't brought their daughter Moira tonight, and Keira didn't blame them. She moved forward and held out her hand over Callie's belly. "Do you mind?"

"Of course not." Callie took her hand and placed it against her baby bump. "Your newest nephew is being rambunctious tonight, so maybe he'll grace you with a kick." She lowered her voice and smiled. "Did Aiden tell you that we're naming him Devlin?"

The baby chose that moment to kick, and Keira's throat closed. It took her several tries to get a word out. "That's wonderful."

Callie didn't look away from her face. "You seem happy. Perhaps a bit more comfortable in your skin."

"I am." The baby kicked again, and she managed a smile even though the room swam around her. It was good and right that Teague would name his son Devlin, but that didn't make it easier for Keira to hold it together. "Thank you for coming tonight."

"My father was delighted for the chance to spend some time with Moira and spoil her rotten." Callie's expression was soft, but there was depth to the words.

Not *all* the power players had left Boston tonight.

"He's a fierce little thing, isn't he? Takes after his auntie."

Keira looked over as her oldest sister strolled up. Carrigan wore a short, fitted dress that would have looked downright uncomfortable on anyone else, but she managed to pull it off. She swooped in and pressed a quick kiss to Keira's cheek. "First Sloan running off with Jude MacNamara, and now you walking down the aisle with Romanov. What am I supposed to do with you two?"

That surprised a laugh out of her. She should have known Carrigan wouldn't respond the same way as the rest of her family—she never had. "You have no one to blame but yourself—*you* ran off with the enemy and made it the cool thing to do."

Her sister laughed and pulled her in for a hug that whooshed the air from her body. "God, I missed you. You really do look good, Keira. And you're—dare I say it?—*sober.*"

"I am." No reason to talk about the fact that she could tell exactly how many steps stood between her and the minibar. Keira didn't know much about addicts, other than being one, but she didn't expect that awareness would ever go away. She felt like her body was a water dowser, but for alcohol. She didn't miss weed all that much, but liquor? She could only hope that craving would get easier to bear as time went on.

"Go figure. I'm going to be in New York in a couple weeks for some business. I'm stealing you for the day." Carrigan released her and pressed both her hands to Callie's belly. "You're coming too, Callie. You've been so damn occupied with babies and business, I haven't seen you in forever."

Callie gave a small smile, her blue eyes sparkling with humor. "I suppose I could clear my schedule."

Keira eyed the careful way her sister touched her sister-in-law's stomach. "Am I sensing baby fever?" She made a show of leaning over and eyeing Carrigan's toned body. "Are you and James going to start giving me nieces and nephews?"

"Maybe." Carrigan shrugged. "Maybe not. But we're having a hell of a time practicing."

Homesickness hit Keira with the strength of a freight train. She hadn't felt it in the O'Malley house, but that building wasn't more than a physical representation of a loss she still hadn't fully dealt with. It wasn't home. *This* was. Her family.

Before she could fully process that, Carrigan turned to face Dmitri. The happiness fell from her face. "You."

"You're looking well, Carrigan."

What she was looking like was a woman willing to kill. James Halloran moved up and pressed his hand to the small of her back. He was all golden giant shadowing Keira's oldest sister Carrigan. The man was attractive in a chiseled sort of way, but he looked about as comfortable as a lion surrounded by hunters, his blue gaze flicking around the room and seeming to catalog all the threats before settling on Dmitri.

Keira tensed to move between them, but Dmitri stayed her with a slight movement of his hand. He looked into her sister's face and simply said, "I love her."

Keira froze. She couldn't believe he'd just gone and said it aloud. They might not have overt enemies in the room, but that didn't mean they were *allies*. Giving up this piece of information was as good as handing Carrigan and James the ammunition they needed to hurt him the most.

Kind of hard to doubt he loves me when he's putting it out there in public like this.

For her part, Carrigan looked at him for a long moment and then huffed out a laugh. "Dmitri Romanov, in love. That can't be a wholly comfortable feeling."

"I'm getting used to it." He shifted, letting his hand drop, and Keira slipped beneath his arm. Dmitri looked down at her and then back at Carrigan. "I understand better why you made the choice you did. If Keira was in danger, I wouldn't let anything stand in my way to save her. Not an enemy, not a friend, not even breaking my word."

It was a threat, but Carrigan laughed a little. "Yeah, I guess you do understand."

"James." Dmitri nodded at him. "Enjoy the reception."

"Oh, we intend to." Carrigan took James's hand and they walked back to their table, pausing to talk to Cillian and Olivia as they did. Charlie and Aiden lounged at the same table, their heads bowed close to each other, in deep conversation. They were all here, all except Sloan. No one was fighting. No one was posturing or yelling or threatening to kidnap her for her own good.

Teague was naming his son Devlin.

It was an honor, but it didn't change the fact that Devlin should be *there*. He should be alive and sitting in the middle of Cillian and Aiden and laughing alongside Olivia.

Pain flared, so strong it nearly took her to her knees. Keira gripped Dmitri's arm tighter. She closed her eyes and let herself envision walking to the bar, taking a bottle, and retreating upstairs until she didn't feel anything at all. She could imagine the cool glass against her palm, the bottle at her lips, the blessed numbness washing away everything.

But that was the problem. It washed away *everything*. The good. The bad. The unforgettable. The numbness didn't care that there were memories she'd carved out with Dmitri she didn't want to lose. It wouldn't matter that she'd finally made some kind of peace with the fact that she'd never quite fit in with her family, but that didn't make them love her less.

Keira opened her eyes, but the walls were still too close. Too stifling. "I need a break, Dima."

To his credit, he didn't hesitate. "Let's go." He took a step, using his body as a shield between her and the rest of the room, but his stride hitched.

She looked past him to see Aiden on his feet and starting toward them, concern lighting his green eyes. Desperation sank its claws into her. "I can't, Dima. I can't talk to him right now." It didn't matter if her brother was only going to ask her if she was okay. She had to get out of there. *Right now.*

"Go. I'll speak to him." He jerked his chin. "Pavel will stay with you."

Because she wasn't safe. Not even in their home.

Keira managed to nod, and then Pavel was there, shifting her away from Dmitri and walking her to the side door and out of the ballroom. She paused in the hallway, but her chest only tightened. "I need—"

"Outside."

She started to say that wasn't what she meant, but the thought of fresh air on her face had her hurrying to keep up with Pavel's long strides. If she could just *breathe*, then she could think straight. They walked around the long way and out through the front door. Keira let go of Pavel the second her heels hit the sidewalk. *Yes, this is what I need.* She moved a few feet away from the door and leaned against the brick building. The cold snap of the air against her face helped clear her thoughts.

It would be too much to ask that I'd be able to spend time with my family without wanting to dive into a bottle.

It would get better. She refused to allow this goddamn addiction to get the best of her. It would become easier to see her family without the glaringly obvious missing part. Eventually, time would dull the pain of losing Devlin.

But that day wasn't today.

Keira closed her eyes and concentrated on breathing slowly. She could hear Pavel shifting from foot to foot a short distance away, but she ignored him. It was cold—especially without a jacket—but she didn't mind. She spoke without opening her eyes. "Just give me a few minutes and we'll go back in." Dmitri could hold Aiden off indefinitely, but he shouldn't have to. She'd just take the time to get her barriers back in place, and then she'd walk back into that room and soldier through the rest of the night.

"Don't hurry on my account."

Keira barely had time to process the unfamiliar female voice when the icy barrel of a gun pressed against her stomach.

CHAPTER TWENTY-NINE

Dmitri kept his gaze on the door Keira had disappeared through, half listening to whatever the hell Aiden said. He finally shook his head. "Excuse me."

Aiden opened his mouth, seemed to reconsider, and nodded. "Go to her."

He didn't need the man's permission, but he recognized it for the olive branch it was. He and Aiden had managed to get through an entire conversation without threatening each other, even if Dmitri had been distracted through the entire thing. He nodded. "I'll be back shortly."

He didn't like Keira being out of his sight. The night had been going too well, and he didn't trust that. The other shoe was about to drop, and Dmitri couldn't stand the thought of Keira being caught in the crossfire.

The hallway outside the ballroom was empty.

He stopped short. It didn't mean anything. Keira would have wanted more space to get her head on straight, and the hallway was hardly offering in space. He doubted she'd go upstairs, so he turned toward the front of the house and strode in that direction. As he turned the corner, he half expected to find her in the foyer.

The foyer was empty as well.

Dmitri pulled his phone out of his pocket. He'd wanted to clear the house completely of his men, but it wasn't an option. He didn't have enough people he trusted beyond a shadow of a doubt, but he called Alexei all the same.

"Da?"

"You're manning the cameras." He didn't wait for confirmation. "Where is Keira?"

A pause, a few clicks in the background. "She and Pavel walked out the front door five minutes ago."

The front door? Why the fuck had she gone outside? If she needed air, there was the rooftop patio...Dmitri cursed. He'd never even told her about it. It was October— too cold to utilize the space—and it had slipped his mind. But Pavel knew about it. He should have known that was a safer option than standing on the street.

Alarm bells pealed through Dmitri's head. Something was wrong. Very wrong.

He raced to the front door, not caring if any of the guests saw, and wrenched it open. Pedestrians gave him a wide berth without breaking stride, but he couldn't care less about them. He looked right and then left, and Dmitri's heart stopped cold in his chest at the sight of Keira pressed against the wall, Mae Eldridge standing too close in front of her.

To the outside viewer, they might have been lovers having an intimate conversation. Mae had her strong arm braced on the brick wall over Keira's shoulder, and their faces were kissably close. It was only from his angle that he was able to see the gun in Mae's hand.

He took a step forward, but stopped short as a hand closed over his shoulder. He looked at Pavel, one of the few men he'd trusted, and he might as well have been staring into the face of a stranger. The blond's blue eyes were cold and distant. "That's close enough," Pavel ground out.

Fuck. He'd found his traitor, and far too late for the knowledge to help. One of the few men he'd considered to be trustworthy. *Not trustworthy enough*.

"Dmitri, go back inside." Keira sounded calm and reasonable, as if asking him to run down to the corner store to grab some milk.

Mae shook her head. "I don't think so. You've got a pretty mouth, but you're ultimately replaceable. *He* isn't." She gave him a snake's smile, all cold eyes and tight lips. "Isn't that right, Romanov?"

"Let her go." Despite Pavel's grip on him, Dmitri took a step closer. "Mae, point that fucking gun in a different direction."

"Or what?" She leaned harder against Keira, eliciting a flinch despite his wife's stoic expression. She had to be terrified, but none of it showed on her face. Mae laughed. "I think I'll leave this bitch bleeding in the street. How long do you think it will be until someone manages to tear their gaze away from their phones to call 911? Will she live or will she die? It's like a flip of a coin—all up to chance."

She'd do it. He didn't doubt that she'd shoot his Keira and leave her to bleed to death on the street, mere feet from everyone in the world who cared about her. Who would find her first? Aiden? Carrigan?

Dmitri couldn't think past the roaring of his thoughts.

The sound morphed into two words, repeated over and over again. *Save her.* "Let her go. I'll do anything."

Mae's eyes widened ever so slightly. "Anything."

"Yes, anything. Just let her go. Don't hurt her." Desperation made his voice rough. He could picture Keira on the sidewalk, the life bleeding out of her hazel eyes. It couldn't happen. He couldn't lose her.

"Kiss me."

"What?"

Dmitri ignored Keira's protest and shrugged off Pavel's hand on his shoulder. "Let her go first."

Mae considered him. "Pavel has his gun on her. You try anything and he'll shoot her in the stomach. You know what a stomach wound will do."

He knew. Keira's chance of survival would drop astronomically. "Let her go."

Mae released Keira and stepped back, watching him closely. Keira started for him, but he shook his head. "Go back inside, *moya koroleva.*" *Go to safety.*

Her hazel eyes shone and she started for the door, her fingers brushing his as she moved past him. She got two steps when Pavel blocked her way. "You'll watch."

"Are you fucking kidding me?" Keira glared up at him. "We trusted you, Pavel."

"You trusted wrong."

The longer they stood on the street, the greater the chance that something could go sideways. It felt like they'd been there a small eternity, but Dmitri suspected they were still well within the window of the previous tech blackouts John Finch had reported. He marched to Mae and hooked the back of her neck. She shoved her gun against his thigh, but he ignored it and kissed her. She tasted of cigarettes and rage, and he wanted nothing more in that moment than to snatch the gun from her hand and put her out of her misery.

But there was Keira to think of.

He'd kill Mae, but Pavel would kill Keira.

Unacceptable.

Once the appropriate amount of time had passed, he raised his head. "You disgust me."

The lust bled out of Mae's eyes and she sneered. "You say that now." She leaned into him, the gun never moving from where she had it pointed—right at his femoral artery. "You'll change your tune before too long."

"Dmitri, *no.*"

"Keira, get back in the house. Now." He didn't look at her, couldn't look at her. *I love you, moya koroleva.*

Seconds passed, and she finally cursed and shoved Pavel out of the way. He pinned the man with a look, daring him to make a move as she stalked down the sidewalk and into the house. *Safe.* Keira was safe. He could bear any punishment Mae would deliver because he knew she was out of that bitch's grasp.

"Let's go, Romanov." She laughed again, the sound dark. "I'm going to enjoy the hell out of playing with you."

* * *

Keira couldn't wipe the picture of Mae forcing Dmitri to kiss her out of her head. *That bitch is going to pay. And Pavel, too.* Traitor. Enemy. She'd trusted him, had worked with him to secure the reception, and he'd been planning to betray them all along.

Mae had Dmitri.

Keira bypassed the ballroom—she'd get to them in a moment—and headed straight for the lounge where the guards spent their time. She threw open the door, startling half a dozen men into reaching for their guns. A quick sweep of the room, and she found Alexei situated by a monitor. *Only get one shot at this.* If she didn't play it right, they wouldn't follow her, and Dmitri would be as good as dead. "That bitch took Dmitri." She let the pause drag out a beat. "But we're going to get him back."

She held up a hand when Alexei started to speak. "Mae took Dmitri. She took Mikhail. She will kill them all if she's given the chance, which means we can't fuck this up."

One of the men, a blond whose name she couldn't immediately place, spoke up. "Why should we take orders from you?"

Keira iced over her tone the same way she'd heard Dmitri and her brother do. "Did I fucking stutter?"

He tried to hold her gaze, but chickened out halfway through. "*Nyet.*"

"Dmitri is gone." She met each of their eyes in turn, holding their attention just long enough to make them uncomfortable. "That means I am in charge for the duration. He's my husband, and I want him back. Alethea and her bitch daughter will pay for the insult they dealt us, and they'll pay fully. I don't give a flying fuck what you think of me, but don't you forget for a second that Dmitri chose me. He married me." *He saved me.* "That's all that should fucking matter to you. Obey and you will be rewarded." She lifted her chin, focusing on ensuring her hands didn't shake and her voice never wavered. "If you can't guarantee you will obey, then get the fuck out of the way for the men who will."

Not a single one of them stepped back, but she didn't allow herself to breathe a sigh of relief. "We need to clear out our guests. I'll handle it—just follow my lead. Then we'll find Dmitri and deal with the Eldridge threat once and for all."

Keira's phone pinged, and she almost ignored it. But when she looked, she found a text from Dmitri.

I'm sorry, moya koroleva. This wasn't how it was supposed to play out.

"Dmitri," she breathed. She typed out a quick response. *Where are you going?*

We're still in the city, but I can't be sure of more than that. I'm in the back of a van with the windows painted over and they've blocked off the space to the driver's seat.

Not good.

Another text pinged through. *I love you. The various bank numbers are in the safe in our room. The code is 0693821.*

"Oh, no you don't." She strode into the ballroom as she typed her reply. *Knock that shit off. You're living through this so I can scream at you later. Hold, please.*

This situation needed to be handled as in-house as possible, but there was only one person with the skills that Keira trusted to track Dmitri's location—Cillian. The only problem being that he had no reason to do her any favors, and he *wouldn't* without Aiden's blessing. *Damn it.* With that in mind, she turned to the rest of the room. They watched her with varying degrees of concern. "Thank you all for coming. Unfortunately, something has come up that requires our attention. My men here will show you out." She motioned to Alexei and the six men who had fanned out behind her.

"Keira, what's going on?"

Right on cue. She turned to Aiden as he approached. She had to play this exactly right, or Aiden would muscle in and take control. Her men wouldn't follow him, and *his* men didn't give two fucks if Dmitri lived or died. All they cared about was killing the Eldridges. While she could get on board with Mae being removed from the face of this earth, she wouldn't risk Dmitri's life to make it happen.

She loved Aiden, but she couldn't trust him. Not in this.

His brows slammed down. "Something happened."

"I need to borrow Cillian again. Just for as long as it takes him to track a number for me." There. That was nice and neutral. She could do this. She didn't have any other choice.

If anything, he looked more forbidding. "Dmitri gave his word that he wouldn't cut me out. Is he going back on it so quickly?"

Goddamn it, this isn't a power play. She didn't say the words aloud. They weren't the truth—every single damn thing was a power play in their world, the current situation included. If it wasn't, she could have asked her big brother for help. "Dmitri isn't here right now. I am." She stared him down, refusing to let even a hint of doubt creep into her. "Are you willing to create an incident to push this?" This was it. This was the moment when he'd either call her bluff, or he'd actually believe that she was in control of herself and the situation.

He broke her gaze and swore. "Goddamn it, Keira, you know I'm not. I just want to help."

"You can help by leaving—and by lending me Cillian. Now, please."

The tension in the room was thick enough to cut with

a knife. Finally, Aiden nodded. "I'd like an explanation when this is all over."

"You'll have it." Easy enough to promise. If she succeeded tonight, there would be little enough to report. If she failed, her brother's anger would be the least of her concerns. *I can't afford to think like that. I won't fail. I haven't come this far to have happiness torn from my grasp before I have a chance to enjoy it.* "Aiden." She waited for him to look at her. "Thank you."

He nodded. "Charlie."

"I'm here." She slipped through two O'Malley men and hurried up to give Keira a quick hug. "Be safe."

"I will," she lied through her teeth. Every second she wasted here was a second she wasn't in pursuit of Mae, but she couldn't leave these people in her house—not even her family. "I'll call you tomorrow."

"Okay." Charlie let Aiden take her hand and guide her to the door, taking their people with them. The rest of the guests followed, and Keira's expression must have been forbidding, because not even Teague chose to approach and contradict Aiden's decision to let her handle it.

For that, she was grateful.

Ivan slowed in front of her and slid his arm around Natasha. "If you think it would help, I can leave a few men to pad your numbers, but it'd be best if we weren't directly involved with his rescue."

She loved him a little bit for never doubting that there *would* be a rescue. "While I appreciate the offer, we've got it covered. I'll have Dmitri contact you once he's home."

He nodded. "Tell Dima that he'll never live this down, and I expect the full story next time we have dinner."

Natasha pinned her in place with those whiskey-colored eyes. "You bring our Dima home, Keira."

"I'm going to." She wouldn't allow herself to believe anything else. "Travel safe."

"And you as well."

She glanced at Alexei. "Take your men and make sure no one wanders off on their way out the front door, and then lock this place down. Get everyone equipped and meet me in Dmitri's office when you're ready. I'll have the location by then." *I hope.*

It was a risk allowing Cillian into Dmitri's office, but it was a calculated one. Aiden had trusted her to loop him in when necessary. Dmitri's men trusted her to find him. She had to trust Cillian to do the job she asked of him. He whistled softly when he saw the computer setup. "Independent circuit?"

"I don't know what that means, so shelve the geek talk. That one has Internet." She pointed at the laptop on the corner of the desk. "I just texted you the number. Can you track it?"

"Yeah. If the phone's still turned on, it will be cake."

"Please hurry." A fine tremor worked its way through her, and she had to turn away while she fought against the urge to scream herself hoarse. *Hold on, Dima. Just... hold on.* They would get to him in time. Her standing over Cillian and demanding he hurry wouldn't make a damn bit of difference.

The door opened right as she got herself under control. Alexei poked his head in. "Mrs. Romanov, we're ready. The house is cleared except for this one." He motioned at Cillian.

"Good." When he hesitated, she raised her eyebrows. "Yes?"

He glanced at her dress, a silent inquiry. Of course. She was hardly inconspicuous at the moment. Keira cleared her throat. "Stay with Cillian." It would only take her a few minutes to change, and she wanted to be prepared for whatever situation they were about to walk into.

"Yes, ma'am."

She turned to find her brother watching her. "What?"

Cillian smiled through bloodless lips. "When did you become a leader?"

"Trial by fire." She let her hands drop to her sides. "Cillian, do you need anything else from me at this second?"

"No, but I should have a location in ten minutes or less, so whatever you need to do, do it fast." He cracked his knuckles and got to work.

Keira nodded. "I'll be right back."

CHAPTER THIRTY

I found them."

Keira didn't allow her relief to show. She rounded the desk to look over Cillian's shoulder. He'd helpfully brought up a map and dropped a pin to mark the coordinates he'd pulled from the phone. She frowned. "I don't know New York. Where is this?"

Alexei came to stand next to her. He pointed at the street running the length of the screen. "This used to be Eldridge territory before it was absorbed by Andrei Romanov." He pointed at the pin, just south of the street. "This has always been Romanov territory. Pavel's team patrolled here."

"That fucking bastard," Keira murmured. Even if they weren't traitors like Pavel was, they would have reported anything strange to him, effectively ensuring Dmitri never got word. It was brilliant, even as she clenched her fists in frustration. "What do we know about this place?"

"Those are offices slated for remodeling. They had become unsafe, and so Mr. Romanov ordered the building gutted and rebuilt. Demolition happened last month, but things have been complicated, so Mr. Romanov hasn't approved the construction schedule yet."

Complicated because Dmitri married Keira and they'd been on the verge of war ever since. "Alexei, meet me in the garage. I'll be there shortly." Without hesitation, Alexei nodded and led the way out of the office. The door shut behind them with a soft click.

Cillian turned in his chair to face her. "You're really going after him."

"Fuck yes, I am." She crossed her arms over her chest. "That bitch can't have him. He's mine."

Her brother pushed to his feet, and she tensed, half expecting him to start some bullshit, but Cillian just pulled her into his arms and hugged her tight enough that her ribs groaned in protest. "I won't tell you to be careful. But come back alive." He hesitated. "And bring that annoying-ass Russian back, too, while you're at it." He kissed her forehead. "We'll be waiting for word."

She tensed to keep her reaction in check. "I'll call as soon as I'm able to."

Cillian nodded and walked to the door. He paused and glanced back. "This might sound weird, considering the circumstances, but I'm fucking proud of you, Keira." And then he was gone, closing the door gently behind him.

Then, and only then, did Keira drop her head into her hands and exhale a long breath. That had been the *easy* part. She just had to keep moving. If she didn't stop, her mind wouldn't have time to offer up all the things that Mae and Alethea could be doing to Dmitri in the time it took them to get to that fucking building. She counted slowly to ten and then moved, pushing herself to her feet.

She took out her phone and started to type out a response to Dmitri, but stopped. He might have had it on the way there, but she had no way of telling if he *still* had it. He hadn't texted since she told him to hold on, which didn't necessarily mean anything...

But she couldn't take a chance.

The only shot they had at making this work was with the element of surprise on their side. If she texted him and one of the Eldridges saw it... "Damn it." She set her phone to silent and slipped it into her pocket.

Hold on, Dima. Stay alive until we can get there and rescue your ass.

With that, she didn't allow herself to dwell any further on all the things that could go wrong—and they were legion. Keira straightened her shoulders and headed for the garage.

She found Alexei and the rest of the men waiting. "I'm going to need a gun. Now."

He considered her. "Twenty-two?"

"Give me some credit. Nine-millimeter."

He nodded and went to a cabinet tucked against the far wall on the other side of the vehicles, returning shortly with the requested gun and two cartridges. "If you need more than this, we're dead and it won't matter."

"Noted." She tucked it into the back of her waistband. It wasn't comfortable, but it would do for the duration. "Let's go." The more time they wasted, the worse Dmitri's chances were. She couldn't think of what he might be going through right now. They'd get him out alive. End of story. To believe anything else was to court madness. *It will be okay. It has to be.*

She climbed into the front passenger seat of the SUV that Alexei was driving and took a slow and steady breath. It was time. *You made your last mistake in a long line of many, Alethea—you fucked with my man. Now I'm going to fucking bury you.*

CHAPTER THIRTY-ONE

D mitri held perfectly still as Mae cut away his shirt. The time for talking was past. Alethea had cast her lot with her daughter, knowing damn well that there was no future there.

Alethea drained her wineglass. "Kill him and be done with it, Mae."

"No." Mae shook her head slowly. "This bastard had us running around like rats scrambling for cover. He owes us, and I'm going to carve his payment out of his flesh."

"Mae," Alethea said sharply.

"I said no. Unless you want to join him in the chair?"

Alethea's face went white. "That won't be necessary."

Alethea doesn't have control of the situation. Mae does. More importantly, Alethea fears her daughter.

He could use this. He *would* use this.

He focused on Mae. She was attractive enough in a brutal sort of way...until he got to the eyes. Mae's dark eyes held madness unlike Dmitri had ever seen. She ran her knife down his bare chest, smiling at him like a lover might. "Nice ink."

He shrugged. "It goes with the territory."

"Hmm. I guess." The tip of the knife stopped above his heart, right over the darkest tree in the tattoo. "No domed building tattoos means no prison time."

He held her gaze. "If you're looking for secrets, you're wasting your time." He swept his gaze across the room and settled on Alethea. "Where is Mikhail?"

Mae sighed. "You have bigger things to worry about, Romanov." She leaned down. "He was fun to play with. Beautiful skin and unique tattoos." She sounded downright rapturous.

Still, he kept his attention on her mother. "I'm here. Let him go."

Mae lashed out, hitting him in the stomach hard enough that he lost his ability to breathe. Stars danced across Dmitri's vision, but he didn't take his gaze from Alethea. There was no air for speaking, but she flinched beneath his censure all the same. She turned to the man at her side. "Clayton, see Mikhail dropped somewhere in Romanov territory." She reached out and grabbed his wrist. "Alive, Clayton."

At least I managed that much.

Mae hit him again, and sharp pain radiated up from his left side. *Broken rib, maybe two.* A glint at her fist told him all he needed to know—she wore brass knuckles. This wouldn't be over quickly. Mae still had that look on her face that could only be described as lustful. He'd bet beating others got her off better than any sex. *All well and good to know, but that doesn't help me now.*

Did it?

His breath felt like inhaling fire. "Mae," he rasped.

"Shh." She pressed a finger to his lips. "You're prettier when you don't talk."

Alethea shoved to her feet. "Call me when you're finished."

"I always do, Mother." Mae didn't take her gaze from Dmitri, but he watched Alethea stride out of the room. She had the air of prey, and he couldn't bring himself to feel sorry for her. If she'd let her daughter stay in jail, none of this would have happened. He would have looked for her, of course, but he wouldn't have looked hard. If she'd left New York, he wouldn't have hunted her down and brought her back. With Mae destined for prison, Alethea was just an old woman without an heir or a future.

"Did you like my present?"

Dmitri dragged his attention back to the woman in front of him. "We don't kill innocents."

"Wrong. *You* don't kill innocents. Though that seems more than a little hypocritical since you seem to kill everybody else." She tucked a strand of her dark hair behind her ear. "Of the two of us, I'm just more honest about what gets me off."

"We're nothing alike."

Mae hammered another punch to his left side, and the entire room grayed out for one alarming moment. "You don't get to take that judgmental tone with *me*, Romanov. Now answer the fucking question. Did you like my present?" She grinned. "Did it send you rushing to that bitch wife of yours to make sure she was okay? I bet it did."

"If you touch Keira—"

"You'll do nothing." She dragged a finger down his chest. "You're trussed up like a pig going to slaughter. I could play with you for hours and then call your little wife and offer to trade you for her. She'll come. You know she will."

She would. He coughed. "You misunderstand the situation. I forced her to marry me. She doesn't love me. She's probably already planning on how to spend the money she'll inherit when my body is found."

Far from looking convinced, Mae actually seemed amused. "She loves you. She wouldn't have been ready to slit my throat for kissing you if she didn't." She pressed her palm hard against the spot where she'd hit him, grinding against his ribs. "She'll come."

He had to keep his jaw clenched to keep any sound of pain inside. It was only when she let off the pressure that he managed to bite out words. "She. Won't."

"Guess we'll find out, won't we?" Mae ran her hands up his thighs, expression contemplative. "Did you ever see that James Bond movie? The one with the knotted rope and him tied to the chair with a well-placed hole?"

He knew what she was talking about, and Dmitri's skin tried to crawl right off his body in revulsion. "I always liked that movie."

"Mmm. I bet you did." She sat back on her heels. "I'm not particularly interested in your cock, Romanov, but I wonder how much of a beating your balls can take before you're screaming for mercy? They're so delicate." She chuckled. "It's not like you're going to live past tonight to worry about having children."

Strange, but he hadn't put much thought into children, aside from in theory. A man in his position had certain things expected of him, and sons or daughters were one of those expectations.

That was before.

Now, he could perfectly visualize the pair of them. A boy and a girl. Dark hair and hazel eyes, and grins that promised mischief. They'd be wily and a little wild, and they'd fill the empty halls of his house with laughter.

He wouldn't give up the idea of them any more than he'd give up his future with Keira.

Dmitri shifted in his chair, judging the distance between him and Mae. "I'm remarkably attached to both my cock and balls."

"Not for—"

He kicked her in the face. She hit the ground with a muffled cry, and he shoved to his feet. Dmitri kicked her once more to ensure she stayed down, and then he walked unsteadily to the array of instruments she'd set up on the table. It took two tries to grab the knife and saw his way through the zip tie, but he managed in a short time. He cracked his neck and rubbed his wrists.

On the floor, the first flicker of fear appeared in Mae's dark eyes.

Dmitri permitted himself a smile. "Now, I think it's time you and I had a real chat."

* * *

"Drive faster." Keira stared at the GPS on her phone, as if that blinking dot was her last link to Dmitri and if she blinked, she'd lose him.

Alexei didn't tear his gaze from the road. "I drive any faster, and I'm going to draw attention. We're almost there. Hold on." He ran a yellow light and took a hard right, throwing Keira against the middle console. She steadied herself on the driver's seat and looked up.

We're here.

As much as she wanted into the building, she didn't have a death wish—for either herself or her husband. Alexei double-parked and glanced over his shoulder. "Vlad, you're on Mrs. Romanov. She comes up with so much as a scratch, you'll be the one paying the price. Sava, take the van around the block and wait for my call. Move."

They moved. Within seconds Keira was encircled by Russians, and the van had pulled back into traffic. *That's right. Nothing to see here.* She followed Alexei to the door and up the stairs. The walls were too narrow for more than walking single file, so she ended up between him and Vlad. She tried not to take it too personally that Vlad was looking at her like he expected her to be shot at any moment, his brown eyes jumping around with each step he took. *Focus, Keira.*

They stopped at the door at the top of the stairs. Alexei gave her a questioning look, and she nodded. She'd gotten them here. She wasn't trained in this kind of thing, and was more than willing to take the lead if it meant retrieving Dmitri safely. *Or as close to safely as he can be.*

Alexei held up three fingers, and dropped them one at a time.

Three. Two. One. Go!

They poured into the room. Keira couldn't see shit, and she ran into Alexei's back when he stopped short. He didn't immediately move and her heart stopped. *Oh God, Dmitri's dead.* She shoved past him, needing to see for herself, because surely the world wouldn't have kept on turning if Dmitri was no longer in it.

The sight that greeted her stopped her cold. Mae sat slumped over in a chair, her dark hair hiding her face.

And, across from her, a gun in his hands and looking a little too pale, sat Dmitri.

"How?" breathed Keira. She immediately shook her head. Mae might be secured, but that didn't mean they were out of danger. "Alexei, find Alethea and sweep the building. Vlad, with me."

He didn't so much as hesitate. He barked orders in Russian, and the men split into two groups. One went back the way they'd come, and the other headed out a door on the other side of the room. In the space of ten seconds, the room was empty but for the four of them. "Vlad, guard the door." She didn't wait to see if he'd obey.

Keira skirted around Mae and crouched next to Dmitri. The gun he held was steady, but he had a strange look in his eyes. "You came for me."

"Of course I came for you, you fool." She lowered her voice. "How hurt are you?"

"Several broken ribs. I don't believe they've punctured anything."

Even if they had, he wouldn't tell her now. She shot a glance at Vlad. "Can you stand without help?"

Dmitri gave her a severe look. "*Da.*"

He had to be more hurt than he was saying, but the hastily buttoned shirt covered up any evidence of it. Fine. If he wasn't in danger of dying right this moment, it could wait until they got back to safety. "We'll find Alethea." And then... She didn't want to think about that. Keira might want Mae dead for what she did to Charlie—what she wanted to do to Dmitri—but it was one thing to think about how much better the world would be without Mae in it. It was entirely another to shoot her in cold blood.

She eyed the woman. "What are we going to do with her?"

Mae jerked like a puppet coming to life. She lifted her head slowly, narrowing her eyes at the sight of Dmitri and Keira. "Told you so." She smiled through bloody lips.

It happened in the space of a moment. Mae shot to her feet and launched herself at them. Dmitri moved to intercept her, but he swayed, and his hold on the gun faltered. The weapon hit the floor. Keira was already in motion as she registered the flash of a blade in the woman's hand, drawing her gun and firing three shots in quick succession. Each one took Mae in the chest, stopping her forward motion.

The woman hit her knees, a look of stunned surprise on her face. "Well, fuck." She slumped over to the floor.

"I just..." *Oh God.*

"Did what was necessary." Dmitri took a gasping breath. "I might have underestimated my injuries." His eyes rolled back in his head and he went limp.

Keira barely caught him before he slid out of his chair, and even then, his weight pushed her to the floor. Vlad was there in an instant, helping her move her husband away from the dying woman. She waited to make sure he was still breathing, and then she forced herself to walk back to Mae.

This was what it meant to be Keira Romanov.

She felt sick to her stomach, but relief overpowered her nausea. This wasn't like Devlin. Mae was as far from an innocent as a person could get. If she'd played by the rules, it wouldn't have come to this. Keira crouched next to her, watching her struggle to breathe. "Charlie sends her regards."

"Bitch..." Mae took one last rattling breath and stilled, her eyes staring blankly at the ceiling.

Dead.

I just killed a woman.

No, I just killed a monster.

She pushed to her feet, and Alexei and his half of the men came back through the door. One look at his face told her all she needed to know. "You couldn't find Alethea."

"There's no trace of her."

A worry for another day. Right now, dealing with the dead body and getting Dmitri medical aid was more important than the missing woman. She waved a hand at Mae. "Get rid of her." It would have been nice to give Charlie some kind of official closure, but Mae was already a bail jumper. She would just have to be one of those unsolved cases. Charlie and Aiden would know the truth—that would have to be enough.

She turned back to find Dmitri awake. He pushed Vlad back, and Keira went to him. "On your feet, husband." She knew him well enough to know there wasn't a chance in hell of him letting his men carry him out of there. Keira helped him up, not liking the faint wheezing of his breath. "Come on, Dima. Let's go home."

CHAPTER THIRTY-TWO

The next hour passed in a blur. Dmitri was likely in shock from his wounds, but he managed to keep it together on the ride back to the house and then listened to Alexei's report. Mae's body had been disposed of, along with Keira's gun, and Alethea was missing. "Don't worry about Alethea."

"Sir?"

"We won't be seeing her again." He'd send someone after her to deliver his last message—to come back to New York was to sign her death warrant. She'd lost her heir and lost her territory. There was nothing for her in the city but a funeral. He took a shallow breath and tried to cover up how much it hurt. "They're dropping Mikhail somewhere, but they might not have left yet. Find him."

"Yes, sir." Alexei jumped to his feet and strode out of the room.

"Come on. I think that's enough for tonight." Keira

stayed under his arm and guided him to the master bed-room, and then to the stool he'd occupied just twenty-four short hours ago. She stripped him carefully out of his shirt and hissed out a breath. "Looks bad."

"Looks worse than it is."

"You'd say that even if you were bleeding internally." Keira shook her head. "Don't play the hero with me—you were unconscious an hour ago. Do you have a doctor on staff?"

"*Da.*" He didn't want to deal with that right now. He was alive and Keira was alive, and Dmitri needed a few quiet moments to process the beauty of that. "I want a real ceremony, Keira. I want to marry you again."

She crouched in front of him and began cleaning the blood from his skin. "I'd like that—but maybe we can try to get through the entire event without one of us being kidnapped?"

He laughed and winced when it pulled at something in his side. *Definitely dislocated that rib.* "I think we could manage that."

"I would have thought so, too, but with our track rec-ord, I'm not optimistic." She dabbed further up his chest. "We won today, but there was some time after she took you..." She shuddered. "I didn't know if I'd see you again. It scared the shit out of me."

"I'm sorry." He let his head rest against the cool tile of the wall. "I didn't know about Pavel. I was so sure he was trustworthy, I delivered you directly to the enemy."

"Stop that." She cupped his jaw with one hand, waiting until he met her gaze to continue. "He's dead?"

No use hiding it from her. She'd always seen the truth of him—both the light and darkness. "*Da.* I shot him, and

I expect my men will find his body stashed somewhere in that building."

"Good." Keira nodded as if to herself. "One less loose end to tie up."

"Bloodthirsty woman." He loved it. He loved *her*.

"*Da*," she mimicked, and urged him forward so she could slide his ruined shirt off his shoulders. "I don't care what his reasons were for betraying us. All the matters is that he did. He paid the price for that, and the others will remember that if they're tempted to follow in his footsteps."

"I love you."

"I know." She finally smiled, though her hazel eyes still held shadows.

"I've been thinking."

"God forbid."

Another laugh, though he regretted this one as much as the first. "You can choose Keira Romanov-O'Malley if that's what you want. I won't hold you to our earlier arrangement."

"That's sweet." Keira sat back on her heels and dropped the washcloth. "You know, I was thinking, too." She grinned, the last of the shadows fleeing her eyes. "Keira Romanov sounds pretty damn badass."

His breath stilled in his lungs. "You're sure?"

"I was an O'Malley—I'll always be one in some ways—but I'm a Romanov now, of my own choice." She ran her hands up his thighs and leaned forward to press a quick kiss to his mouth. "I choose the name. I choose *you*."

* * *

The timer went off, jarring Keira back to the present. She blinked, noting the way the light had changed in her studio, and set down her brush. A quick glance at the clock confirmed that it had, in fact, been three hours. The painting in front of her had started to take form, the curve of the grays playing against the stark white and black. Tomorrow, she'd come back in with purple to accent in a few places.

Today was the first time in a week that she'd had the opportunity to check out the room on the second floor that Dmitri had ordered converted into a studio for her to paint in, and she'd instantly fallen in love.

Too in love. She'd lost track of time.

She grabbed her phone and typed out a quick text. *Where are you?* She was going to be late for dinner, but knowing Dmitri, he'd taken the opportunity to get a bit more work done.

The reply came back almost instantly. *Office.*

She grinned and stood, stretching her arms over her head and going up on her toes. Keira turned to the camera situated in the corner and slowly unbuttoned the oversized shirt she'd thrown on before starting to paint. Her phone trilled as a text came through, but she ignored it, arching a brow at the camera. *Come and get me, Dima.* She shrugged and the shirt hit the floor.

Less than thirty seconds later, footsteps pounded down the hallway to her room.

Gotcha. She turned as Dmitri stormed into the room. He kicked it shut behind him. "What did I tell you about playing these games?"

"Not sure. Guess you'll have to refresh my memory."

His gray eyes glinted with amusement and desire. "Gladly." He stalked toward her.

She met him halfway, jumping up and wrapping her legs around his waist. It was only then that she realized she should probably be gentle with him. "Shit, I'm sorry. Your ribs."

"I can handle it." He laid her down on the couch situated under the window. The weight of his body against hers was the most intoxicating thing in the world. It buoyed her and steadied her at the same time. "I like seeing you in here," he rasped in her ear. "You look happy. At peace."

"I am." It was the truth. Some days she still craved vodka so badly her hands shook, but she no longer wanted the numbness. Keira was living her life in vivid color, and it was in large part because of the man currently looking at her like she was a priceless treasure he was about to plunder. "I love you."

"I love you, too, *moya koroleva*." He stroked a hand down her body and kissed her. "Let me show you how much. It may take a few decades, but you'll begin to get the idea."

She laughed. "I can't wait."

ABOUT THE AUTHOR

Katee Robert (she/they) is a *New York Times* and *USA Today* bestselling author of contemporary romance and romantic suspense. *Entertainment Weekly* calls their writing "unspeakably hot." Their books have sold over a million copies. They live in the Pacific Northwest with their husband, children, a cat who thinks he's a dog, and two Great Danes who think they're lapdogs.

Find out more at:
KateeRobert.com
Instagram @Katee_Robert
TikTok @AuthorKateeRobert
X @Katee_Robert
Facebook.com/AuthorKateeRobert